LORD OF BLACK CASTLE

An Irish Medieval Romance
Part of the Lords of Eire Series

By Kathryn Le Veque

ARE YOU SIGNED UP FOR KATHRYN'S BLOG?

You'll get the latest news and information on exclusive giveaways, exclusive excerpts, coming releases, sales, free books, cover reveals and more.

Kathryn's blog followers get it all first. No spam, no junk.

Get the latest info from the reigning Queen of English Medieval Romance!

Sign Up Here

kathrynleveque.com

AUTHOR'S NOTE

To be completely transparent, this novel was formerly titled *Black Sword*.

I don't want anyone to think I'm trying to pass off a book that was published a long time ago as new by slapping a different title on it, but the truth is that the book has changed significantly since the early publication. It has been updated, revised, and essentially re-written, so in that sense, it really *is* new.

There's a reason for that.

Black Sword was an Irish romance I wrote several years ago, a book that, from the moment I drew up the plot line, was always meant to be a book about conquest. The way it starts out – Irish against the English – we were bound for trouble. That's not giving anything away, but simply a statement of fact.

When the book was originally written in 2014, the opening chapters were very brutal. But the whole point was in the context of a conquest – historically speaking, conquest involves the most brutal of human acts – death, destruction, and even rape. The word itself – conquest – is not a gentle word. It does not describe something kind in the annals of history.

I was not particularly concerned about publishing the book with such a brutal opening, but as the years passed, it became less and less acceptable to publish such brutality in the context of a book labeled a 'romance'. While I am always committed to portraying historically accurate events, the truth is that no one wants to read about a romanticized rape or murder, or anything else that is so jarring and cruel. Therefore, I made the rare decision to rewrite the opening chapters in a way that is still rough and accurate, but without the brutality it once was. I believe the spirit of conquest is still there, as is the passion between the hero and heroine that starts almost as soon as they meet one another. It was lust at first sight that turned into something else quite rapidly, but they met under extremely violent circumstances. That kind of introduction is bound to be difficult.

This novel is one of only a handful that I've written that has no real ties to other series other than the fact it's set in Ireland, so it is included (peripherally) with the other Irish-themed novels I've written – High King, High Warrior, The Darkland, etc. The tale is set in Ireland, near lands owned by a family mentioned in The Darkland. One of the characters in the novel bears the name of the family from High King and High Warrior, so the novel is simply part of that Irish contingent. In revising the novel, I re-read it and remembered just how much I liked the hero. Devlin de Bermingham is quite the anti-hero at first, but he grows into the role. I believe his story tells the side of the oppressed Irish when the Normans were determined to put Ireland under Norman rule. Devlin may be the enemy at first, but his side of the story is important to note – he may be the enemy to the Normans, but to the Irish, he's a hero.

Now, a little something about Ireland herself.

The Celtic tribes of both Ireland and Scotland are closely connected, with subtle differences. In my research for this novel, I discovered that the term *clan,* used for both Irish and Scottish family groups, was actually spelled *clann* in the High Middle Ages when referring to the Irish as a plural for the collective group of families usually with a surname beginning with "Mac". After the seventeenth century, the term *clann* was changed to *sept,* which sometimes scholars still refer to them as.

As with Scotland, the term "Mac" meant "son of", and "og"

meant "of" – for example, MacKinnon (son of Kinnon) or og Michaleen (of Michaleen, usually the father). They wore tartan, too, but they had a specific tunic that was identified as strictly Irish, a long garment called a *leinte.*

I have taken liberty by placing Kiltimon Castle (an actual location) into the story about two hundred years before it was actually built. There is some speculation that there was some kind of fortification on the site prior to 1500 A.D., but not the castle we see today. Black Castle, however, is a real place with a real history. It really did belong to the family who owns it in this story, the Lords of Kildare.

And with that, I hope you enjoy the new and revised tale of the man called Black Sword in the new and improved *Lord of Black Castle.* In reworking it again, I remembered how much I loved this story. I hope you do, too!

Happy Reading!

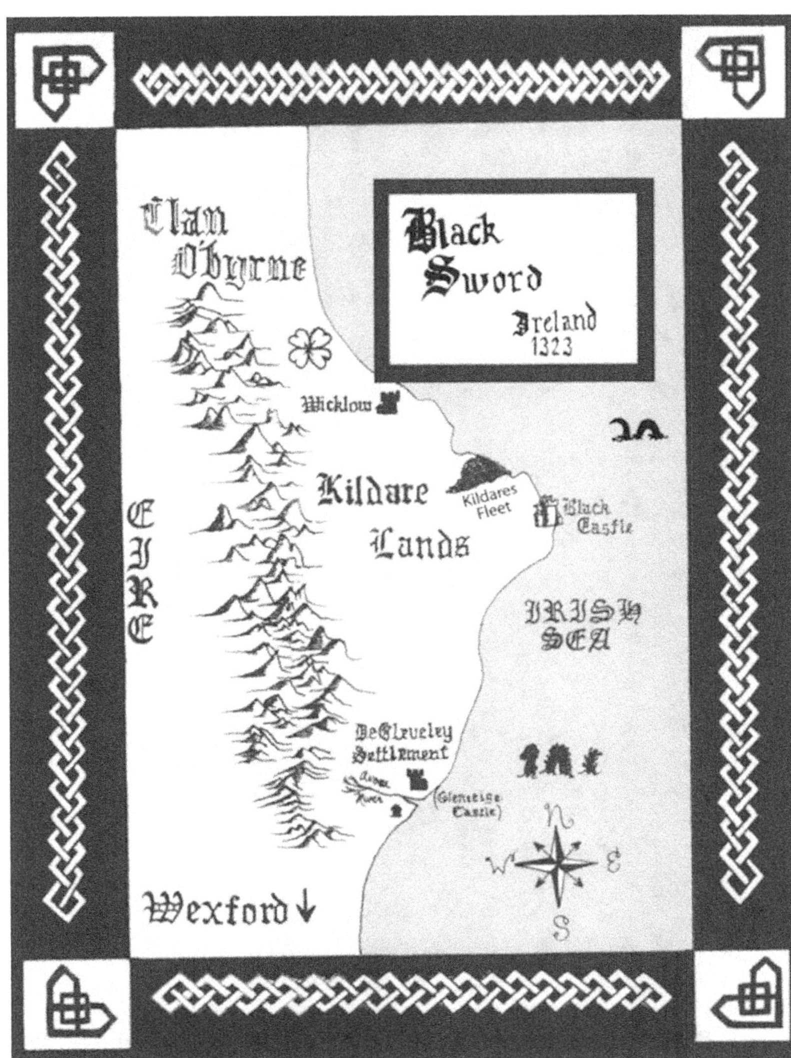

Clan O'byrne
Black Sword
Ireland
1323
Wicklow
Kildare Lands
Kildares Fleet
Black Castle
EIRE
IRISH SEA
DeGraveley Settlement
Avoca River
(Glenrise Castle)
N
W   E
S
Wexford

A brutal Irish knight conquers his hatred of the English to win the heart of the sister of his English enemy…

Welcome to the wilds of Medieval Ireland…

1323 A.D. – Devlin de Bermingham, an Irish knight to the core, is the bastard son of the Earl of Louth and the descendant of Irish kings. He is also a strong proponent that the Irish should rule Irish lands. Rebelling against his English overlord, the Earl of Kildare, he captures one of Kildare's castles south of Wicklow.

Known as Black Sword, a rebel who is both admired and feared, Devlin has set the events in motion for an enormous Irish revolt. Every Norman settlement in Ireland is at risk because of Black Sword's actions and the stage is set.

The Lady Emllyn Fitzgerald is the sister of the Earl of Kildare. When her brother sends his fleet to quell the uprising on his lands, she stows away on one of the vessels in order to follow the object of her affection, a strong young English knight sworn to her brother, into battle. It is her intention to prove to the man she is worthy and brave enough to be his wife, but she truly has no grasp of the seriousness of her folly.

As the English fleet makes landfall along the Wicklow coast, disaster strikes – Black Sword and his army of Irish rebels are waiting for them. In a devastating night of blood and mayhem, the English armada is destroyed and Lady Emllyn is taken a prize.

Join Devlin and Emllyn as they embark upon a journey of a lifetime where both will face death, defeat, and disaster, but most terrifying of all, face their growing feelings for one another in a world that would see them torn apart. How is it possible for two people from two completely different worlds to find a love so deep that it will see each of them make sacrifices for the other?

Will they be able to remain together or will politics and war keep them apart?

Join the unforgettable adventure of a lifetime and experience what lengths Devlin and Emllyn with go to in order to be with each other, lengths that will transcend their loyalty to their own people and jeopardize their very freedom.

For a love that was never meant to be, they will risk all.

CHAPTER ONE

Year of Our Lord 1323
Leinster Coast, Wicklow County
Ireland

THE INVASION HAD been a disaster from the beginning.

Waves crashed and thunder rolled. The English never stood a chance as the vicious storm bashed them against the rocky Irish coast. More than that, an entire army of five thousand angry Irishmen had been waiting for them, boarding the foundering ships and killing anything that moved. As the Irish forged deep into the belly of the rolling vessels, even the rope boys and cooks were targeted, one raggedy rope boy in particular. But this boy wasn't a boy as much as it was a young lady in a very bad way.

Slammed against the hull of the lurching ship, the sharp movement gave her enough of an edge to duck the big fist that was flying at her head. She tried not to scream, knowing that the Irish rebels would hear her woman's voice and focus on her like flies on honey. They would discover she was a woman and the moment they pulled off her disguise, they would quickly figure out that she was a very beautiful one. It would give them cause to do unspeakable things and, at this moment, she was very much coming to regret stowing away on Kildare's invasion fleet.

It had been a bad decision. But she was in the habit of making bad decisions. As the Irish warrior with the red ochre smears across his face made another swipe at her, she fell to her knees and crawled between his legs, escaping the hand that grabbed at her ankle. But she'd been forced to kick at him to keep him away and the woolen Montgomery cap on her head came loose, spilling forth long golden-red hair. When she realized that tendrils of curls were tumbling down the right side of her head, she panicked and tried to shove them back under the cap.

The woman began to run, thrusting herself between fighting Irish and English, dodging blades that were cutting through flesh and bone. She stumbled over dead bodies, becoming covered with their blood as she fell, scrambling to her feet and sprinting through the dark hold of the ship in her desperate quest to reach the upper deck. Perhaps she could throw herself overboard when she drew near the rail. She knew for a fact it was her only chance to escape this hell she had put herself in the middle of.

The ship she had stowed away upon was nearer the shore than some of the others. It had been one of the first attacked by the waves of angry Irish waiting for them. The rain was pounding when she reached the deck, gangs of men fighting on the wet wooden planks with blood running in rivers off the side of the boat. She could see the boat rail through the driving rain and she made her way towards it, terrified, slipping on the blood beneath her feet and trying not to get hit by the heavy broadswords that were swinging around her. She had no idea if the big Irish ruffian was behind her but she wasn't going to take time to look. The rail was within her grasp and she reached for it.

The wood was wet and slippery. She had a good grip on the rail but her hold was violently broken when someone grabbed her around the waist, tightly, swinging her up into the air. As she kicked and struggled, the boat lurched heavily to the starboard side and everyone seemed to roll in that direction. The woman and her attacker rolled with the ship, surrounded by the pounding rain and the sounds of battle, and both were pitched off the side of the ship and into the swirling surf.

Fortunately, the sea wasn't particularly deep. The woman struggled to find her footing and her head broke the surface as she gasped for breath. Coughing, she labored against the strong sea and wind to make her way to the rocky shore. She could see it several feet away, trying to keep away from the surging boat. It was pitching violently and she was sure she would be crushed if she drew near it. So she scrambled across the rocky sea floor, drawing on every last ounce of strength she had to reach the shore. She fell at some point, cutting her knees on the sharp rocks, and the salt water stung the open wounds. Just as she reached ankle-deep water, she was grabbed from behind.

Exhausted and terrified, she hadn't lost her fight. She began to kick ferociously, swinging her fists until her abductor managed to grab her arms and pin them. He made his way onto the shore, staggering when she kicked at his knees, but he maintained his grip. The woman was shrieking now, struggling to break his hold on her as he carried her off. She could only imagine what horrors awaited her and she was determined to fight for her life. No Irish bastard was going to rob her of her innocence, perhaps her very life, and expect an easy target. She was going to give him hell.

He trudged off the shore and into the land beyond. There was so much rain and wind from the storm that she couldn't see where he was taking her. Water was in her eyes, lashing her, and her hair was now sticking in great wet clumps across her face. She couldn't see through the soaked hair and bad weather, but she could smell the dark Irish earth and the scent of wet grass with a hint of mold. The salty smell of the sea was mingled with the storm.

The man slugged across muddy ground and eventually, they were moving up a hill; she could feel the change in elevation, in the angle of the ground as he struggled to gain traction. Although she was growing increasingly weary, she drew deep on her inherent strength and began to fight him in a new round of struggles. It was like a lamb fighting against a bull, the pathetic struggle of a weary woman against a bear of an Irishman.

The terrain leveled out. The man's grip slipped a bit and he ended up lifting her up and slinging her over his shoulder. She fought and kicked, her vigor renewed, as he carried her roughly. The woman pounded on his back and tried to kick him, but he slapped her on her arse, hard, momentarily stunning her. Although her hair was hanging in her face, she could see the rocky ground as he moved quickly. As she twisted and pounded, she began to see stone beneath his feet, then wood. Warmth hit her in the face and the smell of dirty, sweaty bodies.

Men were shouting all around her and the harsh smell of smoke filled her nostrils. There were dogs barking but she couldn't see much from the way he was holding her and the hair hanging in her face. Suddenly, the man threw her off his shoulder and she stumbled as she hit the ground, falling to her arse. Frightened, she scrambled to get away as men around her roared with laughter.

Hands were grabbing at her, yanking at the wet tunic she wore, pulling at her legs. Someone yanked a leather shoe off and she screamed, slapping at the hands that were grabbing at her. She brushed the wet hair out of her eyes, seeing that she was in a smoky and cavernous great hall, an enormous fire burning in the hearth and smoke belching into the room.

Big men with big weapons were all around her, blocking out the light from the hearth, crowded around her, laughing and grabbing at her. More men were pouring into the room, shouting about victory and glorious death. Dogs yipped. The woman screamed again as someone made another swipe for one of her legs, pulling at the woolen leggings.

She cowered against the wall, looking desperately for an exit but she couldn't see any way out. The walls were solid stone and men were everywhere. But she did spy a great and heavy banqueting table, cluttered with weapons and remnants of food. When someone else thrust another hand at her, she kicked the hand away and skittered like a spider across the floor, disappearing beneath the giant table. Hidden by table legs and benches, she huddled in fear.

The Irish barbarians thought it a great game to grab at her and try to chase her from underneath the table. She would dodge from side to side, avoiding hands and swords they were poking at her. One sword tore her hose and scratched her leg. Weeping, she kicked in terror at the men grabbing for her and promised God she would never do anything so foolish again if he would only allow her to make it out of this situation alive. She had her doubts.

Most of the Irish eventually grew tired of the game as more

men poured in from outside. A couple of the men, especially the one who had captured her, were still trying to chase her out from underneath the table but shouts eventually caught their attention. A group of heavily armed men had just entered the hall, shouting war cries of victory, and the entire room took up the cry.

As the woman huddled and softly wept, the Irish of the dank and smoky castle lauded their victory over the English invaders. On this dark and stormy night on the Ides of March, the Earl of Kildare's English forces had been defeated and their ships either burned or confiscated. It was an Irish victory in a long line of them against the English as of late.

As the men celebrated, they seemed to have forgotten about their quarry trapped beneath the table. The woman stilled her frightened tears, watching the dozens of legs moving around the table, listening to the men speak in the harsh Irish tongue. She didn't understand their language. No one seemed to be paying her any mind and her fear eased as her courage was fed. She could see the open doorway of the hall and she could smell the wet air from outside. It told her that the entry door was close. She knew she had to run or die trying.

But there were too many men surrounding the table, blocking her path. The last thing she wanted was to have obstacles in her way. Therefore, she huddled in the center of the table, listening to the men laugh and drink, eyeing the big dogs that drifted too close to her, sniffing. She was watching the entry of the hall so intently that she never noticed one of the dogs coming up behind her, sitting down politely. She was startled when she felt the heat from the dog's body, turning to see big brown doggy eyes looking back at her. She went to shove the dog away but realized he was furry and warm. She was wet and freezing. She scooted next to the dog to have some of his heat and the dog didn't seem to mind. He lay down against her.

The night wore on. The heat from the hearth was intense, even under the table. More men had entered the hall, all shouting and happy. By this time, the woman was becoming drowsy with heat and exhaustion, struggling to stay awake, fearful of what would happen if she fell asleep. But her exhausted state also lowered her guard and she was unprepared when a hand shot underneath the table again and grabbed her firmly around the ankle.

Someone pulled her free of her protective little prison. Shrieking, the woman found herself surrounded by enormous Irishmen, all leering down at her. In a panic, she scrambled to run but the man who initially captured her grabbed her around the waist and carried her over to the far end of the table where a small group of men were gathered. Roughly, he tossed her to the ground.

The men laughed when she sprawled on the floor. Terrified, the woman picked herself up and, on her knees, pushed her hair from her eyes to see what was happening. Her gaze fell on a massive man seated at the head of the table, partially illuminated by the light from the flickering hearth. She couldn't see him very well, but she could tell he was looking at her.

"What is this?" he asked, flicking a finger at the woman, his Irish brogue deep and rattling.

The man who had captured the prize beamed with satisfaction. "I am not entirely sure, m'lord," he said. "I found her on board one of the ships. I do not think she is one of the usual crew."

"So you bring her to me?"

"A gift, m'lord. A reward after your decisive victory."

The men around them cheered and the woman shuddered in fear, pulling her wet tunic more tightly about her slender body as if it could protect her from the enemy. The enormous man at the head of the table was watching her steadily and she inspected him in return; even in the dim light, she could see that he dressed in a well-made leather tunic and pieces of mail. He sat upon a very big chair, like a throne, and a dark bird of prey perched ominously on the high back of the chair. The man's hand, gripping the wooden cup, was as big as her head.

He had milky-pale skin and a big red mustache that blended into a neatly bearded chin. The rest of his pale face was shaved and smooth. He wasn't old, nor was he particularly young, but seemed to have that wise and ageless countenance. When he shifted in the firelight, she could see his chiseled and handsome face. He didn't look like the rest of the filthy barbarians around him. The eyes, glittering, stared at her.

"Who are you, lass?" he rumbled, as if he had no patience for such a thing.

The woman met his gaze nervously, defiantly. "I will not tell you."

The men snickered as the big brute who had captured her lashed out a foot and shoved her, hard. She yelped and fell over. The man was going in for another kick but the enormous man in the chair stopped him.

"Kick her again and you shall answer to me," he rumbled, watching the man back off before refocusing on the woman. "I asked you a question. Who are you?"

The woman pushed herself off the floor, meeting his gaze. Resistance was written all over her. He could see it in her expression as well as her manner. After a moment, she simply turned away and closed her eyes. A lone tear trickled down her face but she made no move to wipe it away.

The enormous man stared at her without making any move to punish her for her insolence. She was a little thing, no doubt, with ashen and creamy skin. Her features, from what he could see through the mussed hair, were fine and clear. Certainly not the features of a whore or servant.

After a moment, he set the cup down and stood up, moving to where she was huddled on the floor. He loomed over her, carefully inspecting her. He was, if nothing else, an extremely observant man and the five words out of her mouth and the accent that delivered them told him something of her background and breeding. He eventually crouched beside her, snatching one of her hands to him. As she yelped and tried to pull away, he examined her palm.

"Not a mark on her flesh," he said, looking at the very fine flesh of her tender arms. "This woman has not accomplished a day of work in her life."

By this time, the woman was shrinking from him, quivering from fear. Their eyes met and he lifted his free hand, brushing back the damp hair from her face. She tried to pull away from the hand near her cheek but he was undeterred. He seemed rather passive about the whole thing. Sapphire-blue eyes studied her fine features.

"Tell me your name," he asked quietly.

She looked at him with eyes the color of the sea. They were pure and crystal clear, an unnatural shade of bluish green under delicately arched eyebrows. Her nose was pert, straight, and her lips were lusciously full and pale. She was, upon close inspection, absolutely exquisite. He'd never seen such soft and delicate beauty. He was in the process of lingering on her flawlessly pale complexion when she shook her head.

"I will not," she whispered.

"Why not?"

She didn't like how close he was to her, the heat from his big body scorching her tender flesh. She tried to pull away.

"Because I will not tell you Irish hounds anything," she said. "You are all animals. Filthy, barbaric animals!"

The calm expression on his face faded and he stood up, yanking her off the floor and throwing her over his shoulder. As his men cheered his brutal move, he hauled his squirming, fighting quarry out of the great hall and into a very narrow stairwell near the entry. With his considerable size, it was difficult to maneuver, made even more difficult with her struggling. At one point, he turned sharply and she hit her head, causing her fighting to wane as she saw stars dance before her eyes. But the lull in her twitching allowed him to take the top of the stairs without dropping her, moving into the only chamber on the floor and slamming the rotting door behind him.

She was still dazed when he threw her down onto a mattress, stuffed stiff with old and smelly straw. Realizing he had put her on a bed, she began to scratch and kick, knowing this position only meant pain for her and she was frantic to get away from him. It was cold, wet and dark in the room, her fearful grunting mingling with the sounds of the storm outside the open lancet windows.

He easily trapped her flailing arms with one massive hand, using the other to pull at her tunic. When she violently twisted away from him in an effort to dislodge his hold, he simply threw his body down to trap her. Ensnaring her with a body that was nearly three times her size, he ripped the wet tunic down the front, exposing a soft linen sheath beneath.

He could see the shape of her figure outlined in the damp fabric.

With her body sufficiently pinned beneath his big one, the woman stopped trying to fight him. She was horrified, exposed, and frightened beyond measure. She resorted to the only tactic she had yet to employ.

She began to beg.

"Please," she pleaded. "Please… I beseech you. Do not do this. Do not…"

His eyes were on her, his face an inch or two from her own. "Do not do *what*?" he asked quietly, although he had to admit, he was not feeling as calm as his voice sounded. The little witch had his blood burning. "You will not tell me who you are. I can only assume you were on the ship to satisfy the men's needs. Now you will satisfy mine, English whore."

"I am *not* a whore," she snapped, the tears coming.

"Then who are you?"

Her jaw worked furiously as she struggled not to weep. He could tell that part of her wanted to tell him, but the defiant English part of her, the stubbornness, would not allow it. He shifted, wedging his legs between her slender white ones, pinning her wrists above her head with one hand. The other, a massive mitt, was free to roam and it moved to her hip, suggestively.

"Nay," she gasped. "Please… please…"

He fingered the flesh at her hip. "Tell me and I may show mercy."

She was weeping loudly by now, terrified. But in spite of her fear, she kept her mouth shut. He watched her face, the tightly closed eyes and rivers of tears, before moving a hand to her belly, stroking the fabric and the flesh beneath.

"Nay," she begged tearfully. "Please stop. Sweet Jesus, have you no sense of decency?"

"Nay," he said flatly. "I am an animal, remember?"

She opened her eyes, looking at him. "I… I did not mean it," she whispered urgently. "Please forgive me. I did not mean it at all."

He lifted a red eyebrow at her, now dipping his head to lick the soft skin of her cheek. "I forgive you," he said. "But you will tell me your name."

She was back to weeping again, closing her eyes tightly and turning away. His response was to suckle the flesh of her chin, feeling her squirm beneath him. She was soft and sweet, much more than any woman he had ever known. He had only started the game to coax forth her name, but now the game had overtaken him and he was lost in a haze of the most powerful lust he had ever known.

But he controlled himself.

He didn't want to be that animal she accused him of being.

"Tell me your name," he breathed, his voice quivering with desire. "I want to know who you are and why you are here. I promise I will not hurt you if you tell me the truth."

She gazed up at him, so terrified that she could hardly speak. But she could not allow her stubbornness and pride to be the cause of her downfall. It was time to push that all aside to save herself from this terrible folly.

"Do… do you swear it?" she asked.

"I swear it if you will tell me your name."

"I am Lady Emllyn Nesta Isabella Fitzgerald," she whispered after a moment's hesitation. "My brother is the Earl of Kildare and it is his fleet that the Irish destroyed this night."

He gazed down at her, believing every word. She was far too

fine and beautiful to be anything other than a noblewoman. Still, his lust had the better of him and the hand moved back to her hip moved, stroking it gently. There was something terribly personal about his touch, enough to have her quivering with terror.

Or perhaps it might even be desire.

It was difficult to know.

"Your brother is the Earl of Kildare?" he repeated in a ragged whisper.

"Aye."

"I find it difficult to believe that your brother would allow you to sail, considering this is a battle fleet."

Emllyn was terrified that hand on her hip was going to move somewhere more personal even though he'd not made the attempt.

Yet, anyway.

"He did not allow me to sail," she said. "I… I came without his permission."

His brow furrowed. "Why on earth would you want to do that?"

She hesitated and he could see the stubborn streak rear itself again. The hand on her hip moved slightly, just to remind her what could happen if she didn't cooperate.

"*Why* did you come, Emllyn?" he asked again.

She could feel his fingers brushing against the side of her buttocks now. "Nay… please..!"

"Tell me now."

She yelped as he pinched the flesh of her hip, but the message was obvious. "I wanted to come because…" She swallowed hard, struggling to keep her wits. "Because Trevor was on the ship. I… I wanted to surprise him. I wanted to be with him."

"Trevor?" he repeated. "Who is Trevor?"

"The man I love."

"Are you betrothed?"

She shook her head. "Nay," she breathed. "I was hoping… hoping to show him what a worthy wife I would be."

"And your brother has no knowledge of you coming with his fleet?"

"Nay."

"You followed a man you hoped to become betrothed to?"

"Aye."

"That was foolish. Stupid and foolish."

Her eyes lolled open, red-rimmed, to look at him. "I took the risk," she whispered, the defiance back in her tone. "I had no way of knowing that the Irish would be waiting for the fleet to destroy it."

He cocked an eyebrow. "Perhaps he should not have tried to invade," he said. "The sons of Eire are stronger than the English. 'Tis time they realized that."

"Did you have to kill them all?"

"I did."

Surprisingly, she didn't dissolve into more tears. Her gaze was steady. "I heard that man say that I was your gift for a decisive victory," she said. "You led the battle. You must be the one they call Black Sword."

"Your brother has lost two things dear to him this night," he muttered. "His sailing fleet and his sister."

She grunted as that hand on the side of her buttocks grew bolder, although she had to admit that it was not an entirely unpleasant sensation. In spite of their tense situation, it was almost… gentle.

"*Are* you Black Sword?" she asked.

His eyes glimmered in the dark room. "I am the Lord of Black Castle," he said softly. "My name is Devlin de Bermingham. If that name means nothing to you now, it soon will."

She turned away from him, feeling his hand as it began to caress her hip and buttock. It was so large that his fingers could reach down her thigh. Whatever he intended to do, she knew she couldn't stop him.

That was perhaps the most painful realization of all.

"It does not matter," she whispered, closing her eyes as the tears started to come again. "After this night, Trevor will not want me even if he has survived the battle. No one will want me. Do what you must and get on with it."

He gazed down at her, struggling against any pity he might be feeling. For the moment, all he could see was the most desirable woman he had ever known, her soft body and exquisite face the most potent aphrodisiac he had ever experienced. He was torn between finishing what he had started and walking away, although he did not know why he was so indecisive. He should not have been.

His night of dominance over the English was not finished, not in the least, and this moment would finally seal his hatred against the Earl of Kildare, the man grossly despised by his people for the inequities and injustice he had spread among them. By pure luck, he had the earl's sister and he intended to take advantage of it. His mercy, at the moment, did not include her.

At least, he hadn't thought so.

Now, he wasn't so sure.

He should have been coiling his buttocks and ramming into her tender body. Every stroke would have been for Irish freedom, something he lived and breathed every day against the hated English. It would have been better for her had she lied and told him she was Scots or French. Perhaps he would have let her go.

Perhaps not.

When there should have been anger in his movements, there was indecision. Hesitation. The hand on her hip remained there as he pondered his next move. He made no move to bruise or hurt her. She was too exquisite for that and he did not want to damage her any more than he already was, even if it was only emotional. She was frightened out of her mind. But he should have been dominating and humiliating Fitzgerald.

He should have been sending the English a message.

But he wasn't.

Eventually, he released her wrists and her little hands slapped at him, eventually falling still on the mattress as if disgusted by the very feel of him. But he remained where he was as if frozen in that position, unable to make a decision as to how to proceed. His men thought he was ravaging her and he very well should be.

Frustration swamped him.

"For years, the English have practiced the immoral act of taking Irish brides on their wedding night," he said, pushing himself off her. "English lords have demanded first right with the bride if she hails from his lands. Many English bastards have been born in Ireland and Scotland because of this deviant law. You are fortunate that tonight I did not punish you for years of English abuse. But keep in mind that I still might. Displease me and my mercy is at an end. Your brother will come to know what it is like to have someone he loves bear the bastard of the hated enemy."

Emllyn's eyes rolled open, gazing at him as tears streamed

down her temples. She lay curled up, rolled on herself as if to hide from the world.

"If that is your intention, you will be sorely disappointed," she whispered. "My brother will not care. If you believe you punish him by harming me, he will laugh at you for it."

Devlin left her lying on the mattress without another word.

CHAPTER TWO

EMLLYN AWOKE TO a surprisingly bright room. After the storm and madness of the night before, all she could feel was a sense of hollowness.

So much had happened since last night.

She lay there for quite some time before realizing she was alone. Facing the wall as she was, she hadn't been sure. Slowly, she sat up in the big rope bed with the dirty straw mattress. Inevitably, her thoughts turned to de Bermingham. He was such a big man, powerful and overwhelming, that he could have easily taken what he wanted last night. For some reason, he hadn't.

But she was certain that would not last.

Reconciling herself to her inevitable fate, the fact remained that she was here and, clearly, here to stay. It wasn't as if de Bermingham would release her. He had a prize in her and he knew it. The only thing she could do was try to survive her situation, one that she had willingly put herself in. That was the truth. De Bermingham hadn't been wrong when he said it was foolish and stupid.

It had been.

Perhaps she deserved everything that was coming to her.

Gingerly, Emllyn climbed out of bed and tried to assess the damage to the tunic she was wearing, the one de Bermingham had torn. As she struggled to pull the tear together with freezing fingers, she lifted her head to the sounds of noisy gulls, screaming outside of her window. They were riding the sea breezes outside and for a moment, she was no longer the trembling captive of a brutish Irish lord. She watched the birds and their graceful flight, taking simple pleasure in it. There was something innately soothing about their cry, comforting even. It was something familiar in this horrid alien land. But her comfort was swiftly dashed as the door to the chamber suddenly jolted open.

Emllyn shrieked with fright, arms around her body protectively as she stumbled back against the cold stone wall behind her. Her eyes widened at the sight of Devlin standing in the doorway.

He looked every inch the conquering hero; her impression of him the previous night had been that of darkness and cruelty, but even as she pondered that impression, she also remembered his warm, powerful body against hers. God, he had been so overwhelming and powerful, everything about the man filling her brittle senses.

Now, in the light of a new day, she could see just how large the man truly was; he was wearing leather breeches and a tunic that strained against his broad chest and muscled arms. His hands, those warm and rough things, were as big as her head. His red hair had brilliant golden highlights in the sunlight and the deep blue eyes regarded her carefully.

Emllyn stared back. She had no idea what to say to him but she was fearful he was going to throw her on the bed again and do more than he did to her last night. All things considered, it had been shockingly tame. But perhaps this time, he wouldn't stop at a hand on her hip. For a moment, they did nothing more than stare at each other as each one reappraised the other. There was re-evaluation in the air.

There was curiosity.

Devlin finally broke the spell.

"So you are awake," he said with his rolling Irish brogue. "I would assume you are hungry."

He started to motion to someone standing outside of the door but she stopped him. "I would rather have dry clothing," she said. "Mayhap it is much to ask, but I would be… grateful. I am cold and my clothing is still wet from last night."

He looked at her, and at her state of dress, as a big, ugly Irishman entered the room with a hunk of bread in one hand and a rough wooden cup of something in the other. Emllyn eyed the man fearfully and backed away, ending up over near the lancet window as the Irishman set the bread and cup down on the end of the bed. When the man quit the room, Devlin finally spoke.

"I will see what I can find for you," he said.

He was starting to close the door but she stopped him. "Wait," she said, coming away from the wall. Her manner was anxious, uncertain, but there was boldness there. "And… and I would like a bath if it is not too much trouble. I have sand everywhere and I would like to clean it off."

His gaze moved over her; in fact, it seemed that all he could do was stare at her as if remembering the night before and the delectable taste of her upon his tongue. Something about the woman was addicting, infiltrating his senses like a fog. Since the moment he'd touched her last night he'd not been able to shake her. This morning, the sensation had only grown worse and it threatened his control where she was concerned. He could have simply taken her and he still didn't understand why he hadn't. It unnerved and distracted him, translating into a brusque manner.

"We have no bath here," he told her, watching her face fall. He realized he didn't like that expression on her face, not one bit. "But… I will see what I can do. Mayhap there is something you can use for bathing."

"Thank you," Emllyn said. She meant it. He turned to leave but she stopped him once more with a rushed and breathless question. "What… what do you intend to do with me?"

Devlin paused at the door, his gaze penetrating. "Are you certain you want an answer to that question?"

That was a terrifying response and her fear returned. "What I mean to ask is if you intend to send me home or if you intend to keep me here… with you."

He came back into the room and shut the door. "I am *not* sending you home," he said with finality. "You stowed away on a fleet you had no business sailing upon. You knew that. You knew there were risks. Now you belong to me. You, lady, are the spoils of war."

She had to make a conscious effort not to gasp. "But I am of no real use to you," she said. "I am not a knight with money or a rich lord. I have nothing of value."

"I beg to differ."

She knew what he meant. Everything in his expression suggested it and he'd intimated the same thing last night as he'd laid on top of her and threatened her with his body. She could see, in that instance, what he intended for her.

He'd intended it all along.

God, it was horrifying.

"So you intend to damage me beyond repair," she said, her voice trembling. "I fail to see who, exactly, you are punishing by humiliating and degrading me. I have already told you that my brother does not care what you do."

Devlin had to admit that he rather liked it when she stood up to him. She had spirit for an Englishwoman, which was surprising to him. He'd always thought the English female to be a weak and foolish thing. But her spirit gave him an unintended response – it fed his lust, a flaming thing that apparently ignited at the slightest provocation where she was concerned, and he was upon her in three big strides, his big hands digging into the tender flesh of her upper arms. She gasped as he pulled her against his broad chest.

"It is not humiliation and degradation," he breathed. "It is the way of things, woman. You evidently do not understand the concept of being a captive."

Emllyn tried to push away from him, but it was difficult. She'd never been held like this in her life, or even touched like this by a man in her entire life, so the feel of his taut, warm body against hers wasn't a sensation of disgust. Not exactly. With horror, she realized that she rather liked it.

"I understand," she said, struggling. "I know you can do as you wish and you probably will."

He didn't let her go. "Mayhap I will," he said. "I've not yet decided. Shall I tell you what I should do to you?"

That frightened her and she yanked one arm away. "Tell me not," she hissed. "I do not wish to hear your vile scheme."

"It is no scheme, I assure you," he said. "What I would do to you is domination, pure and simple. It would be my punishment to your brother and to every damnable English who has ever set foot upon the green fields of Eire. I would dominate you day and night, and any other time that strikes my fancy, and I would pump you full of my seed until I beget you with child. Even then, I would continue to join my body with yours until the child is born and when I gaze upon my Irish son of an English mother, I would bed you again until you deliver unto me another son and still another. I would breed an army of sons from your body, sons that will sail upon England and wreak havoc. You, my lady, would be the mother of an army of Irish rebels that will kill your countrymen just as they have killed mine. You would be my brood mare."

Horrified, Emllyn wrenched herself from his grip and slapped him across the face, as hard as she could. But for a man that size, it hardly moved him. She would have done better striking a mountain. Realizing that her rage had no effect, she tried to bolt away, to run, but he caught her from behind and threw his arms around her so that she was facing away from him. Her sweet, soft body was pressed back against his and Devlin could feel himself growing hard for the want of her. It was purely a physical reaction from his body to hers, as a man to a woman.

And what a woman she was.

"You do not like to hear that, do you?" he whispered, his lips by her ear. "Then I will tell you more. I would kiss you so forcefully that you could barely breathe. I would strip away your clothing until your tender, white body was nude for my pleasure. I would suckle your breasts, where you would nourish our children, and your want for me would match my own. Heat would bloom between your legs as your body prepared for mine. Then, I would push your legs apart and I would join with you, my manhood finding save haven within the folds of your womanhood. And you would love me."

Enraged, but also more aroused than she was willing to admit by what she considered his filthy description, Emllyn let out a scream of pure frustration as she tried to pull away from him.

"Stop!" she demanded. "I will hear no more!"

A lick of a smile creased Devlin's lips. He was rather enjoying her anger. "You will hear all of it, my fine lady," he murmured, his hot breath in her ear causing her to shudder. "My strokes within you would be long and powerful as your body begged for my seed. Your legs would open wider to me, your body would ache for me, and I would answer the call. The warmth in you loins would become a raging fire and my mouth… you would learn to love my tongue, lass… would feast upon you. When the fire in your loins became a raging inferno, it would erupt into a burst of sparks and your entire body would convulse with pleasure along with mine. My seed would go deep into your womb to find its mark. *Here.*"

He suddenly put his hand on her lower belly, pressing hard, and she gasped and bucked at his touch. She wanted him away from her, but after what he'd just whispered into her ear, perhaps she didn't want him so far away. His words, hissed in rage and lust, had done something to her. There was a fire in her now, one that made her heart race and her palms sweat. He must have known that because he began to suckle on a tender earlobe.

"Do you feel me?" he whispered, teeth gently tugging at her ear as he gripped her belly. "Do you already feel my seed as it settles into your womb? I will be all around you, and within you, and you will belong to me. Never ask me again what I intend to do with you, lass. Now you know. And you *will* like it."

Stunned into an erotic daze as he suckled her earlobe, Emllyn heard his words but she couldn't seem to do anything about it. She should have been fighting him, biting and kicking, but she couldn't manage it. He'd used nothing more than words and his touch to convey his intentions, but he might as well have burned them into her flesh. He was stirring things within her that she'd never felt before. When he suckled on her earlobe firmly and she shuddered with delight, he laughed low in his throat.

"So you like that, you English vixen?" he murmured. "Mayhap you *are* a whore, after all."

Emllyn's eyes flew open. Quick as a flash, she balled a fist and hit him in the forehead so hard that his head snapped back. That caused him to loosen his grip and she made a break for the lancet window but Devlin was right behind her, grabbing her as she tried to throw herself from the ledge, three stories above the jagged rocks and crashing sea below. Perhaps she wasn't truly trying to kill herself more than she was simply trying to get away from him, but the result would have been the same. Now, he had her around the waist, her arms pinned, as she fought against him.

It was a vicious fight.

The mood, rather warm and sensual only moments before, was now brittle and fierce. Although Emllyn's arms were pinned, her legs were quite free and she ended up kicking him in the groin. Grunting with pain, Devlin staggered to the bed and fell upon it with Emllyn sandwiched beneath him and the mattress. He listened to her snarl and weep, so much fight in her soft little body that it surprised him. For an Englishwoman, she was tough.

And he was impressed.

"I hate you, do you hear?" she sobbed. "I will hate you until I die!"

Devlin lay atop her, his face pressed into her back between her shoulder blades. She couldn't get to him here but he knew what had triggered her rage – *whore.* He had called her the lowliest form of female life, reminding her of what her foolish actions and bad fortune had brought her. She was to be the whore for an Irish warlord who intended to use her for nothing more than breeding stock. It was a shameful and bleak existence. In that sense, he understood her reaction.

Torn between remorse and the reality of the situation, unless he wanted to physically restrain her for the rest of their lives, he had to say something to calm her. He was afraid if he left the chamber, she might try to escape in desperation and end up falling from the window. He didn't want to think of that sweet, soft body broken and bleeding on the rocks below.

It would have been a damnable waste.

"I will have a bath brought up to you," he said, his voice calm and steady. "I will send up more than bread for you to eat and clothes to wear. You will feel better after you have had a chance to eat and dress warmly."

Beneath him, Emllyn's hysteria had dissolved into tears of shame and anger. "Why?" she sobbed. "Why give me comfort? Simply kill me now and be done with it."

His cheek was against the warmth of her back. "I am not going to kill you," he said. "You are my captive and I intend to take very good care of you. You are worth something."

Emllyn's weeping lessened at his odd statement and her eyes opened. She appeared somewhat bewildered.

"I have already told you," she sniffled. "My brother will not care if you hold me captive. He will not pay your ransom demand. I am worth nothing."

Devlin could feel that her struggles had weakened. In fact, she wasn't struggling much at all. She was simply lying beneath him, trembling. Warm and soft, he resisted the urge to brush his lips on the soft skin against his cheek.

A most strange reaction to a woman who was his captive.

"I will not ransom you," he said, his voice low. "I told you – I will keep you for myself. You will bear my sons."

She didn't say anything for a moment. He felt her sigh; the tears were gone and now there was despair in the very air she breathed. It was a hollow and bitter mood, all settled in about her. He could feel it.

"I do not want to be your whore," she muttered. "Why could you not have simply killed me last night as you did all the other English? It would seem that you have shown mercy to the dead. I would like the same mercy shown to me."

Devlin lay there a moment before taking the chance and letting her go. He sat up, watching her stiffly push herself up off the mattress. She recoiled from him but she didn't try to run again. She was also quivering, with cold and emotion, and he gazed at her steadily a moment before standing up.

"If I ask you a question, will you give me the courtesy of an honest answer?" he asked.

Arms wrapped around her slender body, Emllyn turned to him. "Why?" she asked.

"Because I ask it. I would not lie to you so I do not expect you, as an honorable lady, to lie to me."

She was tired. Too tired to fight with him anymore. All of the fighting they'd done, the wrestling and struggling, had sapped her strength. She simply didn't have the will to fight in her at the moment.

"What is it, then?" she asked, averting her gaze.

"Will you answer honestly?"

"Aye."

Devlin eyed her lowered head. "When you stowed away on your brother's vessels, where did you think they were going?" he asked. "You knew his armies were sailing for Ireland. You knew it was a battle fleet. Did you not think they would find resistance the moment they arrived?"

Emllyn shrugged, her gaze still averted. "To be entirely truthful, I did not," she said. "I knew they were going to battle… that Trevor was going to battle… but I did not think it would be so immediate. I thought mayhap a battle march once they reached shore… and there would be time for me to reveal myself to him."

She was starting to tear up. He could see it. She sniffled and wiped at her eyes but he felt no pity for her.

"And then what?" he asked.

Her head came up, looking at him. "What do you mean?"

He lifted his eyebrows expectantly. "What did you intend to do once you revealed yourself to this man?" he wanted to know. "They have names for camp followers like you. They are, in fact, called whores, so mayhap I was not too far wrong when I called you one."

Her features flushed red. "I am *not* a whore," she snapped. "I love Trevor and he loves me. I want to be his wife."

"*Loved*," he emphasized, past-tense. "Your lover is dead. Did you not think that would be a possibility?"

Her tears came faster and she looked away again. She didn't reply for a moment, shaking her head and wiping at her eyes as if thinking all manner of terrible things about him. "I suppose I did not think on it," she finally murmured, her voice hoarse. Then, she turned to look at him again. "Did you *really* kill all of the English soldiers or were you simply gloating?"

He gazed steadily at her. "Those who were not put to the sword drowned in the churning waters," he said. "There are no more than twenty or thirty still alive, and those men are to be killed or sold for ransom."

She looked at him, shocked. "But…," she gasped, "but there were at least a thousand men, mayhap more. They are *all* gone?"

"I told you they are. Do you not believe me?"

Emllyn averted her eyes, unable to hold his gaze. She did indeed believe him and the knowledge sickened her. *All those men… and Trevor!*

"Trevor was a knight," she said softly. "He comes from a fine family. May I… may I see the men you have captive to see if he is still alive?"

His jaw ticked. "Nay," he said flatly, surprised at the ferocity of his reply. She belonged to him and he wasn't about to let her even think of another man. He thought it was only possessiveness but was startled to realize there was perhaps jealousy there as well. "Your lover is dead and you will put him out of your mind. He no longer exists to you."

His words had emotion to them, as if there was anger there. Emllyn's fury surged. "You cannot erase someone I love so easily," she snapped at him. "You cannot wipe a memory clear of my mind as the sea washes away the sand. I cannot forget deep and abiding memories just because you command me to."

Devlin was starting to grow angry for reasons he did not understand. All he knew was that he didn't want her thinking about another man. Even in this short time he had known her, not even a full day, something about her had infiltrated him, getting under his skin. She was English, that was true, and worse yet she was his captive… but there was something about the girl that went beyond all of that. He wasn't sure what it was yet, but until he did, she would come to understand that she belonged to him and he wouldn't tolerate her thinking of anyone else.

"I told you he is dead," he muttered. "It would therefore stand to reason that your love for him is dead, too. Why would you waste such effort on a memory?"

Emllyn stared at him, shocked by his callous words. But as she pondered them, a thought occurred to her. "Have you never been in love?" she asked, almost beseechingly. "Do you not know what it means to hold such feelings for someone that the glory of the moon and the sun pale by comparison?"

By this time, Devlin was thoroughly agitated but failed to understand why. That only made him more frustrated. He headed for the chamber door, confused and off-balance by the conversation. As his big hand held the iron latch, he turned to her one last time.

"We are three stories above the rocks and probably more than six stories above the sea," he said. "A fall from this height will not kill you but it would greatly injure you. I would suggest you consider that before throwing yourself from the window. I have no physic so the best I could do would be to stand by while your broken bones healed in terrible positions, or your useless legs caused you unimaginable agony. Mayhap we would have to cut off a mangled arm or bind up your guts and cause you such anguish that you would pray for death. If you truly wish to live out your days dying a slow and agonizing death, then that is your choice, but I strongly suggest you reconsider. It would be better for you to remain whole and sound."

Emllyn looked at him with horror, her gaze moving to the lancet window she had so recently tried to fling herself from. Well, mayhap she did not truly intend it, but in her haze of anguish she had made all indication that she was serious. Now that she was calm, the thought of broken legs or bleeding guts made her shudder with disgust.

Nay, she wasn't going to try that again so soon.

"Do not fear," she said, defeat in her tone. "I will not try and jump again. But I would like something dry to wear if you can manage it."

Devlin eyed her lowered head, thinking a great many things at that moment. Mostly, he was thinking that he had been inordinately cruel to her. But as his English captive, didn't she deserve all that and more? He refused to entertain any thoughts otherwise.

He left the chamber without another word.

THE FEASTING HALL of the castle was silent for the most part. The men who had occupied it the night before, drinking and sleeping all about the chamber, were now up and going about their duties, which left the hall vacated.

The fire in the hearth was low, a great pile of peat and wood with ashes scattered about and dog paw prints through them. It smelled of sewage and smoke, of that radiating aura of human stench that mingled with rebellion and victory. For now, the victory belonged to the Irish and the three great commanders of Devlin's army sat with him on the corner of the chipped and stained feasting table, each man contemplating the previous night's events, each man contemplating the future. There was much on their mind.

No one was contemplating more than Devlin. He sat in his customary chair, the one that had been part of the spoils of war when they had raided, and stripped, one of the English settlements to the south of Wicklow last year. It had a crest carved on it, a great preying beast attributed to the House of de Cleveley, one of the many English houses who possessed lands in Ireland. Devlin had taken great delight in scratching out most of de Cleveley's crest, slashing holes through the face of the enemy. He put his mark on it, and now the chair was his.

As he picked at the remains of his meal, a very large falcon sat on the back of the chair and every so often he would extend a piece of meat or a crust of bread to the bird, which gobbled it down. The bird was a pet, a friend, and a mascot; it was all things, the de Bermingham bird of prey that was treated better than most men. Named Neart, which meant 'strength,' the big black and gray bird hovered over his master.

"We're taking the dead to St. Mantan's church," a large man with kinky dark hair spoke. He was seated, his big leg propped upon the table. "The priests want the English brought to them but they haven't enough room in the graveyard to bury them, and we don't want them buried with good Irish folk anyway, so they're making room outside of the churchyard for the English dead."

Devlin turned to the man, a friend from childhood who had seen much life and death with him. Shain Mac Rohan was his closest, but most fiery, advisor. The man's official title was Keeper of the Blade, as Devlin's second-in-command. He would trust his blade to no other.

"I do not want my men digging graves for the English," he said flatly. "How many English prisoners do we have?"

"Thirty-three," said another man with long blond hair. Iver Blaineroe was a distant cousin, calm and wise in a land of passionate men. His official title was Master of Men because he was the man the troops were most apt to listen to. "We counted eleven hundred and seventy two dead this morning but there's more that were drown and washed away by the sea. Mayhap we'll never truly know how many Englishmen there were but for now, we have thirty-three living prisoners and piles of dead. If you want the prisoners to start burying their comrades, then we had better get started for it will take weeks to accomplish this. If we could use more manpower, however, we could finish the task in a day."

Devlin could sense a mild rebuke in the statement and he didn't like it. He didn't want his own men burying the English and would not be chided for it. Before he could speak, however, the third commander at the table spoke.

"What of the woman we captured?" Frederick óg Branach made it sound like a simple question, but it was not simple in the least. Frederick was a bloodthirsty bastard, known as the *trodaí fola*, or Blood Warrior, who had a particular hatred for the English. He had been the one who had captured Emllyn the night before and brought her to Devlin, and he had taken the greatest delight in her fear and humiliation. "What do you intend to do with her?"

Devlin was steady as he faced the man. Last night when Emllyn had been brought to him as a prize, his attitude towards her was as it should have been – she was the spoils of war and nothing more. However, after coming to know her a little, that opinion was in danger of changing. As much as he pretended that it wasn't the truth, he knew deep down that the situation was increasingly unstable. He hoped the confusion didn't reflect in his eyes.

"What would you have me do with her?" he asked.

Frederick cocked a dark eyebrow, his broad features stained with hatred. "You've already done plenty to her, so I've heard," he said, a lascivious gleam in his eye. "I approve."

"I do not care if you approve or not," Devlin said. He wouldn't warm to the man's bloodlust. "Answer my question – what would you have me do with her?"

Frederick shrugged his big shoulders and reached for a cup of stale ale with dirty, blood-stained hands. "I suppose you could give her to the rest of us when you've had your fill of her," he said, taking a long swallow of the bitter brew. "Or you could ransom her. Did you find out who she is?"

Devlin nodded, slowly reaching for his own cup of ale. "I did," he said, putting the cup to his lips. "You will never believe it."

That peaked their interest. "Who?" Shain demanded.

Devlin deliberately made them wait as he downed the contents of the cup. He set it down against the rough-hewn table.

"The Earl of Kildare's sister," he announced. "Evidently, she stowed away on one of the vessels to follow a lover. Her brother does not know we have her, as he does not know she stowed away. At least, that is what she told me. She is a foolish lass, that one. Foolish and young."

His commanders were holding various expressions of delight and surprise at the news. Iver even laughed softly.

"Kildare's sister," he repeated, incredulous. "Are you sure of this? She could be lying."

Devlin shrugged casually. "She is as fine and untouched as

any woman I have ever seen," he said. "Now she belongs to me and I am not entirely sure I want to give her up or ransom her. I will tell you what I told her – that I shall breed a host of bastard Irish sons from her, lads who will grow up and rebel against their English brethren. Mayhap I will simply keep her as a concubine and nothing more and use the woman as a personal victory against Kildare. 'Twould be humiliating for the man if his sister was the personal whore of his most hated enemy."

Even Frederick was pleased at Devlin's statement. "Grand," he agreed. "Then our victory last night will have implications long into the future. Think on the bastards you could breed with the wench; fine stock, to be sure."

Devlin agreed and went to pour himself a second cup of alcohol; it was a brew that was produced locally of barley and rye, very strong and heavy in flavor. It was easy to get drunk off of it as he had many a time. He sipped the drink as he fed the falcon another piece of old mutton.

"Indeed," he said, eyeing the men who were like brothers to him. They had all seen much life and death together, bonded by the plague of war that enveloped their land. "But I will make this clear – Kildare's sister is my prisoner and my prize. She will be untouched and unmolested by anyone. If I hear that someone has moved against her, my retribution shall be swift and deadly. Do you comprehend?"

Two out of the three men nodded seriously, but no one else seemed to be willing to agree. They seemed perplexed. But Devlin had stated his rules and didn't wish to discuss them, mostly because the little English witch had him puzzled as to what, exactly, he felt about her and her presence. He didn't want to have to explain that confusion to anyone else. Therefore, he hoped to move past the subject quickly.

"That is all I have to say about it," he said quietly. "Now, tell me of my own wounded. How many and what is the current state of my army?"

He'd hoped to shift the subject easily but Frederick wasn't so keen to let it go. He waved off Iver when the man started to speak on the status of the Irish rebels. "She is not just your personal prize, something to be hoarded and kept," he insisted. "Although I respect your plans to use her to breed fine sons, now that we know who she is, surely the terms of her captivity have changed. She belongs to us all, Dev. She is a symbol of Kildare, the man responsible for all we hate and all we have lost."

Devlin cocked a dark red eyebrow at him. "I told you that she will not be touched by anyone but me," he repeated, feeling the tension rise. "I meant it."

Frederick didn't like the response. He slammed his cup down and ale splashed from it, spotting the old wooden table. "Did you know I lost my brother last night?" he said angrily, bracing his arms on the table as he nearly yelled at his liege. When Devlin looked rather startled, Frederick simply nodded his head. "Henry was killed by the English. I found him floating in the surf early this morning. That… that *wench* you have been taking to sport is responsible for it! Is there nothing else you plan to do to make her pay?"

Devlin could see he was going to have trouble with Frederick. He remained cool as his commander postured furiously. "I am sorry to hear about Henry," he said softly. "He was a good warrior."

"Sorrow does not bring him back!"

"Nay, it does not, but I am sorry nonetheless."

Frederick wasn't satisfied. He pointed to the ceiling above, to the floor that contained the English prisoner. "Tell me what more you intend to do to make her pay."

"Pay for what? I asked you before what you wanted me to do and you gave me your answer."

"That was before I knew she was Kildare!"

"It changes nothing."

Frederick roared with anger, sweeping his arm at the cluttered table and sending food, ale, and cups flying. Iver moved out of the way so he would not be struck while Shain moved closer to Devlin in case Frederick physically attacked the man. That had been known to happen.

"My brother is dead!" Frederick bellowed. "Are you telling me that no one will pay for that?"

Devlin stood up. If Frederick charged, he didn't want to be caught sitting down. Moreover, the man was known to veer out of control and now was the time to start showing some strength or the situation could turn bad.

He fixed Frederick in the eye.

"Over a thousand English already paid last night with their lives," he said in a firm, growling tone. "There are thirty-three English prisoners in our custody. If you want to go and kill each of those prisoners, I will not stop you. Let them pay the final price. But you will not touch the lady. She belongs to me. If you touch her, I will view it as stealing my property and I will punish you accordingly. Is that clear?"

Frederick's mouth worked furiously. He was prepared to come back with a sharp retort but he had better sense than to speak without thinking. Devlin de Bermingham commanded nearly five thousand men. He had the money and power of the House of de Bermingham behind him but more than that, he was a true patriot for Ireland and men followed him for that very reason. He had fought and bled for Ireland, and his charisma and power had garnered him more followers out of respect than out of fear.

Frederick both admired and feared Devlin. He'd seen what de Bermingham was capable of and had no desire to provoke him. Therefore, he struggled to calm himself. There was more anger than grief in him at the moment, but he wasn't a fool. He wouldn't test Devlin. He took a deep breath and pushed down the rise of his rage.

"De réir do ordú, sinsear feasta," he said with forced calm. *By your command, sire.*

Devlin eyed the man, wondering if he meant it. With Frederick, one could never tell. "Téigh i síocháin," he said quietly. "Beidh mé páirt a ghlacadh leat níos déanaí."

Go in peace and I will join you later. Frederick nodded faintly and quit the room, fatigue in his movements. Devlin, Shain and Iver watched the man go before turning to one another.

"He hated his brother," Iver said in a low voice. "He is only seeking revenge for revenge's sake. It is not as if he is wallowing in sorrow. He is simply hungry for English blood and will seek any excuse to bleed it."

Devlin nodded, sighing wearily as he reclaimed his seat. "He is an excellent warrior and a trusted advisor, but sometimes he worries me," he muttered, moving to collect a piece of stale bread. "You two will watch him when I am not about. If he acts strangely or is not himself, you will tell me."

The two men nodded. Iver sat back down at the table but Shain remained on his feet. He scratched his dirty head.

"When do you plan to make the rounds, *mo tiarna*?" he asked. "We have the men breaking down the English cogs and going about their usual duties, but they will expect to see you."

Devlin nodded as he chewed his bread. "I will come short-ly," he said. "Meanwhile, send Enda to me. I have a task for her."

As Shain went to find the old serving woman who oversaw the keep, Devlin turned to Iver. His manner seemed to slow, his expression becoming pensive.

"I wonder how long it will take the English to hear of this victory and make plans to overwhelm us," he muttered.

Iver toyed with an empty wooden cup. "Not long," he said. "We destroyed a large fleet last night. Word will travel quickly. I am not as worried about Kildare as I am worried about the settlement to the south with the de Cleveley and Connaught clann. After our successful raids last year, you and I discussed plans to wipe them out entirely. Mayhap we should visit that plan again. Any English foothold on our soil can only mean danger for us; mayhap it is time to eliminate them once and for all, and send a clear message to Kildare – we do not want English on our lands. Ireland belongs to the Irish."

Devlin thought on the rather large settlement they had severely damaged last year. It had been a costly fight, but ultimately a glorious one. He drew in a long, slow breath.

"Long have we discussed their destruction," he agreed. "Mayhap you are correct; mayhap with Kildare's defeat, it is time we rid Wicklow of the English once and for all. Gather my commanders this eve and after sup, we will discuss the possibilities. We must strike while fortune continues to be in our favor."

Iver agreed. "Indeed," he replied, eyeing Devlin. "Have you thought about asking your prisoner what she knows of the English plans? As Kildare's sister, surely she was privy to her brother's intentions."

Devlin shook his head. "I have not thought to ask her," he said. "It seems to me that she was truthful when she said she stowed away on the fleet to be near her lover."

"It is possible that she was truthful, but it is also possible she knows more than what she is telling."

Devlin thought on that. "I do not believe that to be the case, but I will of course interrogate her. I would be foolish not to."

Iver nodded his head, rising to stand and clapping Devlin on the shoulder as he moved. It was a gesture of comfort, of confidence. As Devlin watched the man lumber out of the hall, he caught movement over to his left. Turning, he saw the slight figure of his chatelaine approach. When the old woman saw that he was looking at her, she bowed her head in a gesture of utter respect.

"*Mo tiarna*," she said. "How many I be of service?"

Devlin's thoughts immediately moved away from furious commanders and English settlements to the pale, lovely lady trapped in the chamber over his head. With a crooked finger, he motioned the old woman closer.

"I have a task for you, *máthair*," he said. "It would seem we have a… guest."

The old woman was frail, pale, and toothless, but she was much more robust than she looked. She was also fairly unafraid to speak to Devlin, having known him since he'd been a small lad. Old Enda, the chatelaine of Black Castle's keep, had heard the tales of the English prisoner and she had further heard what Devlin had done to her. There wasn't much she didn't know about the place, and she'd heard terrible stories. She simply nodded her head to his statement.

"I have heard, *mo tiarna*," she said evenly. "Shall I tend to her?"

Devlin nodded. "Clothing, food, and a bath," he said, rising from his chair. "Tend her well and do not let her leave that room. I shall be with the men but will return before sundown."

"Aye, *mo tiarna.*"

"She is a valuable prisoner. Treat her as such."

"Aye, *mo tiarna.*"

"And you will not let anyone in that room other than me. Make sure you bolt the door from the inside."

"Aye, *mo tiarna,*" she said obediently. "But… mightn't the vault be a better place for the prisoner than your chamber? It is better guarded."

Devlin's gaze lingered on the old woman. "Not *this* prisoner," he said after a moment. "She must be kept safe and the vault would not be a safe place for her."

Enda nodded obediently and Devlin lowered his gaze, fearful that she might read something more into his statement. It bordered on concern rather than cold indifference. He quit the room without another word but Old Enda understood, or at least she thought she did; a damaged prisoner was of no use to anyone and the way the men about Black Castle felt for the English, it wouldn't be a difficult stretch for any one of them to slip into the room and kill the wench. Sir Devlin wanted her undamaged by others so he could damage her personally. He would use her as his own personal victory over the English.

Moreover, it wasn't any of Enda's business what he did to the woman. He wanted her safe and safe she would be. She watched the massive Irish knight quit the hall before scurrying about her duties; she had a prisoner to attend to.

CHAPTER THREE

AFTER DEVLIN HAD left her that morning, Emllyn spent the rest of the day huddled in the corner of the chamber, as miserable as she could possibly be. The day that had dawned somewhat clear had turned cloudy by the nooning hour and by sunset, the rain and wind had begun.

Water lashed in through the lancet window as lightning lit up the darkening sky. Other than the bread and cup of stale ale that had been brought to her that morning, she'd had nothing else to eat. There wasn't even a fire in the dark and sooty hearth. Cold and hungry, Emllyn sat in the dark corner clad in the tatters of her sandy and damp surcoat, the remains of her shredded shift strewn about her arms and shoulders to try to give her some measure of feeble warmth.

She had dozed on and off during the day with dreams of Trevor, her tall and dark love, but then she had awoken to the reality of her situation. Worse still, she very much needed to use the chamber pot but there was none so, without any choice, she had pissed in the corner over near the window where there was a drain built into the floor. She thought it might be the garderobe but she could not be certain. Everything about the room was so old and run down and dirty.

She felt like an animal.

Emllyn was dozing once again when the door to her chamber shook. Instantly awake and instantly fearful, she remained huddled in the darkness as the panel opened. In the dim light, she could see a pair of women, entering with their arms laden with items, and behind the women came a couple of men bearing a big, dented copper pot between them.

Eye contact was made between Emllyn and the intruders. She remained coiled against the wall as the women, an older one with missing teeth and a younger one that was very pale and plain, timidly approached the bed. The men with the pot moved to the hearth and set it down, quickly vacating the room only to return with peat and kindling. The men were old, dressed in rags, and evidently servants or slaves. They deftly piled the peat and lit it before they vacated the room again and returned a third time bearing great buckets of sloshing water. The water was dumped into the pot and the pot scooted against the peat as the flame began to gain in strength.

Meanwhile, the women had been busy near the bed with its stiff and smelly straw mattress. Now, Emllyn was more curious than fearful as she watched them cover the mattress with the hides they had carried with them. Great sheep hides covered up the old mattress now as they turned to another bundle they'd brought with them and began to pull out some manner of textiles.

Several types of garments were strewn neatly across the hides. Emllyn was curious about them but didn't move from her position against the wall. She was still too afraid to. The younger woman had a hide sack with her from which she pulled out a lumpy white bar of soap and a few other things including a comb. As Emllyn focused on the soap and combs that were being brought forth, the older woman finally spoke.

"I'm Enda, m'lady," she said politely but with a very heavy Irish accent. "This is me daughter, Nessa. Sir Devlin has asked us to help ye dress."

Emllyn eyed them a moment before very slowly, and very stiffly, rising to her feet. "I am hungry," she said. "Did you bring me something to eat?"

Enda nudged Nessa and the young girl fled. "Me daughter will bring ye something," she said, indicating the now-steaming water in the pot against the fire. "Can I help ye bathe?"

Emllyn wasn't about to deny her. She was so miserable that, at the moment, she would have let the Devil himself help her if it meant warmth and cleanliness. With a short nod, she moved for the pot as Enda grabbed one of the long stretches of fabric on the bed and spread it down on the ground in front of the pot. She also brought forth a small, three-legged stool that she had brought with her and she set the stool upon the fabric on the floor. She indicated for Emllyn to sit, and sit she did.

Emllyn had no sooner sat down than the woman began to pull the dirty surcoat from her body. Emllyn felt somewhat exposed, and embarrassed, but the woman was firm yet gentle in the removal. When Emllyn was completely nude the woman began throwing bowls of steaming water on her, which splashed down onto the fabric spread on the floor. It was a mat of sorts, absorbing the water off of the stone floor. The very warm water felt wonderful and as the woman put a bowl on the floor in front of Emllyn and told her to put her feet in it, she simultaneously grabbed the lumpy white bar of soap and began to scrub Emllyn from the feet upwards.

The sand, the dirt, and the chill came off of Emllyn quickly as the skinny old woman washed her vigorously. True, she was sitting naked on a stool in the middle of the room, but the fire in the hearth was burning strongly now so she felt no chill. Enda, like any good mother, Irish or English or otherwise, used a rag and the soap to wash every nook and cranny on her body, including between her buttocks, which actually had Emllyn stifling a giggle at one point.

But the old woman took her job seriously and she cleaned the sand and dirt away. Perhaps it was the mother in her that made her sympathetic to the frightened young woman, English or no. At the moment there were no countries or enemies, simply one woman to help another.

The bar of soap smelled like grass and herbs. It was a very clean smell and one Emllyn liked very much. The old woman had lathered her up in it, rinsing as she went along, and she used the soap to lather up her hair. There was a good deal of sand in her scalp and it took several rinses to get it all out, but it eventually ran clean. When Emllyn was finally scrubbed clean, the old woman used another one of the lengths of fabric strewn across the bed and vigorously dried her off.

In the heat of the room, it didn't take long to dry her skin. Enda handed her yet another pile of fabric from the bed which turned out to be a shift made of linen that was surprisingly soft but far too large. Over that, she donned a heavy garment of green wool that was more like a giant tunic than a surcoat. It had long sleeves, a tie about the waist, and dragged along the floor when she walked, but it was very warm and that was all Emllyn truly cared about. As she sat on the stool while Enda ran a bone comb through her hair to dry it, the door to the chamber opened.

Enda's daughter appeared with a tray in hand. Upon the

tray was a bowl with something steaming in it, a big hunk of bread, a wedge of white cheese, and a warped wooden cup. There were also a pair of well-used leather slippers, which Enda promptly slipped on Emllyn's feet. They were a bit too small but still comfortable. As Emllyn slurped down a barley and bean stew, she felt better than she had in days.

As she ate her meal, Enda got down on her hands and knees and mopped the floor up with the wet mat. She swept the water in the direction of the corner drain, sweeping it out until there were no longer puddles on the floor. Nessa, meanwhile, had taken over her mother's hair-combing duty and when Emllyn's hair was nearly dry, she braided it tightly and wound the braid into a bun at the nape of Emllyn's neck. Pinning it with several big iron pins, Emllyn made quite a presentable picture.

Bathed, dressed, and combed, Emllyn swallowed down the last of her meal. She was so full she could hardly move, but still, she licked the bowl. Food had never tasted as good to her as it did at that moment. As she handed the bowl back to Nessa, hovering next to her, the rainstorm outside worsened.

It had beat steadily most of the evening but now grew stronger. Sitting near the fire on the three-legged stool, Emllyn watched the rain beat against the windowsill and splash inside onto the floor. It was near the drain in the floor and she began to see why there was a drain there; water coming in through the window flooded to the drain and was sent back outside again. As she pondered the clever Irish engineering, Enda cleared her throat and spoke.

"Will there be anything else, my lady?" she asked.

Emllyn looked over at the old woman and her daughter. After a moment, she shook her head. "Nay," she said. "You have been very kind to me. Thank you."

Enda nodded, not quite sure what to say. She had simply been doing her duty as commanded by Sir Devlin. She motioned for her daughter to begin collecting the rags and bowls they brought with them.

"I've brought hides for the bed so ye should be warm," she said. "And I've brought ye another coat and another shift to wear if the weather worsens. It can be very cold up here."

Emllyn looked at the garments the woman was indicating, strewn about at the bottom of the bed. She fingered the surcoat she wore. "Who does this belong to?" she asked.

Enda collected a wet cloth from the floor. "Sir Devlin's mother," she said. "There are several trunks with her possessions still. I will see if there are more serviceable things for ye."

Emllyn looked up from the garment she was wearing. "Is his mother here?" she asked. "At this castle?"

Enda shook her head. "She died a few years ago," she said. "Her sister is still here, a kin to Sir Devlin, but there is no more family here."

Emllyn was starting to show some interest in her surroundings as it applied to the natural flow of conversation. "What is this place called?" she asked.

"Black Castle, my lady," Enda replied, almost apologetically. "This is Black Castle."

Emllyn thought on that a moment. Devlin had told her that he was the Lord of Black Castle, so she should have supposed that was where she found herself – at Black Castle. She had heard the name from her brother, something about a rally point for the rebellion on his Irish holdings, and it began to make a good deal of sense.

Black Castle.

She was in the belly of the beast.

True, she had known that the ship she stowed away on was headed for battle but she hadn't known precisely where. That had been foolish on her part, she knew, but it didn't matter now. What was done, was done. Her idiocy had landed her in the middle of the Irish rebellion, in the very stronghold that was the heart of the resistance. Realizing that, she closed her eyes at the truth of what she had gotten herself into and she turned away.

"My thanks," she murmured.

Enda eyed the woman's lowered head. She felt some pity for the young woman but she couldn't let it interfere with her duty. Grabbing Nessa by the arm, she shooed the girl out and, collecting the rest of the things she had brought with her, quietly closed the door behind her.

Emllyn heard the door shut, turning to see that she was alone in the room once more. It was much warmer, and far better furnished, than it had been earlier, lending to a somewhat comfortable feeling, but the truth was that it was still her prison no matter how it was dressed up.

Oh, God, she thought to herself, looking around the room and feeling more despair than she ever had. The past night and day had passed in somewhat of a blur, as if she were living a nightmare, but now the nightmare had vanished and all it left in its wake was a heady sense of reality. Now, everything was real and terrible. She was in Ireland, captive in an Irish castle. She knew it was only a matter of time before Devlin did something she would sorely regret. Truth be told, the man wasn't unpleasant to look at. There was something powerful and virile about him, something that made her feel the least bit giddy along with her fear. But she would not think that way about him. She *couldn't* think that way about him. But visions of de Bermingham inevitably gave way to the very reason why she was here.

Trevor.

Dear God, what had become of him? De Bermingham said that he had been killed, but how did he know? He wouldn't let her see the prisoners for herself, so there was every chance that Trevor was alive… and every equal chance that he was dead. The thought of his demise devastated her but after all she had seen last night, the death and destruction, she realized that she was very fortunate to be alive and more inclined to think of her own safety at the moment. She couldn't spare any more tears for Trevor, not now. She had to stay alive if there was any chance of discovering his fate. And the only person who held the power to grant her request was, in fact, de Bermingham.

Deception.

If de Bermingham was the man who had the power over life and death, then perhaps she needed to give the man all of the respect he demanded in order to gain his permission to see the English captives. Perhaps if she was to be compliant and obedient, then he might grant her wish. But to be compliant and obedient with him would mean surrendering to his will. The mere thought of it made her feel hot all over, a heat that was unfamiliar and consuming. It was not as if she had any real choice in the matter, but perhaps a willing captive might make him more apt to grant her request. Perhaps she was going to have to play his game in order to gain her wants.

Compliance.

Emllyn was in the process of concocting a plan when the chamber door rattled and popped open. Startled, she looked up to see Devlin in the doorway. He was dressed in black leather breeches, a faded tunic, and a heavy black leather vest that strained against his muscular chest. He just stood there, gazing at her with that same hard and intimidating expression she had seen before, yet… there was something else there, something she couldn't quite put her finger on. His eyes, so deep and blue, seemed to have an odd glimmer to them.

It was an oddness that unnerved her and Emllyn rose slowly from the stool, facing him nervously. Her heart was beating loudly in her ears, waiting for him to reach out and grab her with those massive hands.

Compliant! Her mind screamed. *You must be compliant!*

"My lord," she greeted, her voice quivering.

He didn't reply but his gaze moved to the garments she was wearing. He seemed to focus on the clothes.

"Enda said she brought you my mother's old coats," he said, looking her up and down. "They are much too big for you."

Emllyn looked down at herself. "They will do nicely," she said. "They are warm and clean."

"And big," he said, stepping into the room and closing the door. "My mother was three times your size. She was a very big woman."

Emllyn fingered the green wool, not sure what to say to that because she was fearful of insulting his mother with anything she said.

"I find them quite suitable," she said, looking up at him. "Thank you for your generosity."

He grunted, looking around the room and noticing the hides on the bed. "So she brought you something to sleep on as well," he said, moving to the bed and flipping up the hides to inspect the quality. "These should do you nicely."

Emllyn looked at the bed and the fluffy sheep's hides. "I thank you again for your generosity," she said. "I am grateful for the consideration."

He looked at her, then. If he thought she was being too compliant, he didn't say so. He simply continued to look at her.

"Were you well fed?" he asked.

Emllyn nodded firmly. "I was, thank you."

Devlin's gaze lingered on her a moment longer before scratching his red head and easing his big body down onto the bed. The last time he was here, they'd had a rather violent encounter. But he'd also experienced attraction like he'd never known. It was an odd combination to say the least.

Emllyn hovered near the hearth, waiting for the next move, wondering if she was going to end up on the bed again with her clothes ripped off. When Devlin suddenly shifted on the bed, she jumped, but he didn't notice. He seemed distracted.

"I will ask you a question and you will answer me truthfully," he finally said, looking up at her. "Anything less than truth will be swiftly punished. Is that clear?"

Fear began to clutch at her. "It is, my lord."

He sighed heavily as he collected his thoughts. "I have spent most of the day observing the results of last night's victory," he said. "Your brother's ships are now my ships and his men are either dead or my captives. This was a resounding defeat for your brother. Do you understand that?"

"I do."

"You will tell me what you know of his further intentions to attack me," he said, his voice low. "Your brother did not send all of the men he has. Surely there are more to come."

Emllyn blinked, stumped by the statement. "I… I would not know, my lord," she said honestly. "My brother did not share his military plans with me."

Devlin cocked an eyebrow. "Yet you knew enough to stow away on a ship bound for Ireland," he said. "You knew ships were sailing and you knew where they were going. You know more than you are telling me."

Emllyn shook her head firmly. Then she gave a rather ironic chuckle. "My lord, you must understand that my brother and I were never close," she said. "He is much older than I am and we did not even grow up in the same house. He was away when I was born and when I was sent away to foster, I did not see him for almost seven years. He views me as I view him – as a distant relative. He resents me a great deal because I am twenty years of age and not yet married. He has been trying to find me a husband for years but our father left a stipulation in his will stating that I was allowed to approve or disapprove of any husband selected for me. So far, the man has selected only fools and I have not yet married. Therefore, I believe he views me as a drain on his household finances."

It was a well-spoken and frank statement. Devlin believed her. "Yet you stowed away on a ship bound for battle because you wanted to be near your lover," he pointed out. "Did your brother know you loved this man?"

Emllyn nodded. "He did," she replied, "but Trevor comes from a family that does not have a great deal of wealth. My brother wants me to have a wealthy husband so he naturally disapproves."

Devlin pondered the information but as he did so, he was coming to see one thing – when she wasn't hysterical or fighting, she was very well spoken and quite eloquent. She had a beautiful manner about her, something he found quite attractive. Dressed as she was in clean clothes and her hair pulled back in a bun at the nape of her neck, he'd never seen such a lovely woman and with that realization, he was coming to feel extremely guilty about the way he had treated her. She was elegant and intelligent; fear, battle, and the situation had turned her into something quite different, but now by the calm light of the fire and in a calm conversation, he could see what a glorious creature she was.

"Does Trevor want to marry you, then?" he asked quietly. "Surely the man would want to."

Emllyn actually smiled, but it wasn't one of joy. It was one of resignation. "I believe he is in love with the knighthood more than me," she said. "That is why I stowed away; I wanted to come with him to prove I was strong and able. I wanted to prove I was not a pampered lady, which he detests. He likes a capable woman."

Devlin's focus lingered on her a moment before he averted his gaze and resumed scratching his scalp. "Was he one of your brother's more responsible knights?"

Emllyn shook her head. "Nay," she replied softly. "He was a younger knight without command responsibilities but very skilled. Unfortunately, my attraction to him seemed to put him in a bad light in my brother's eyes. That is why he sent him to Ireland, I believe, to send him away from me."

Devlin glanced at her. "Then your brother kept men behind with him?"

Emllyn nodded. "I am not sure how many, but he kept some of his men behind in England. However, I will say with some certainty that he sent most of his men here. The castle was quite empty when we departed." She fell silent a moment, eyeing him in the firelight. "You know, of course, that my brother is the Lord Justice of Ireland. King Edward appointed him three years ago in reward for his service against Robert the Bruce. My brother can summon the king's men if he needs to."

Devlin nodded slowly, chewing pensively on his lip. "I

know," he said. "I know a good deal about your brother. What I want to know from you is what more you can tell me about his plans for Ireland."

Emllyn wasn't as terrified as she had been earlier; now, the conversation was calm, almost normal, and she was feeling moderately comfortable with it. She felt safe enough to move away from the hearth.

"Most men do not mention their battle plans to their wives, mothers, or sisters," she said softly. "Does your wife or sister know of your battle plans?"

He eyed her. "I do not have a wife or a sister," he said, although he could see her point. "But you will tell me honestly if you have ever heard your brother mention future plans for Ireland. If you don't tell me the truth, I'll turn the dogs on you."

She knew he wasn't entirely serious simply by his manner. It was surprisingly calm and almost casual. Still, she couldn't be completely sure.

Be compliant!

"I swear to you that I do not know anything of his future plans," she said, and it was the truth. "However, I do know that he has had much communication with Lord de Cleveley of Anchorsholme Castle. The man has lands south of Wicklow, I believe."

That drew Devlin's interest. "What communication?"

She shook her head. "I do not know, but I know they correspond quite frequently."

Devlin could only imagine what those missives contained. De Cleveley had a massive expanse of land to the south near what was known locally as the Vale of Clara. The de Cleveleys had been in Ireland as long as the Fitzgeralds, soaking up the good Irish soil for their greedy needs and assimilating the Irish people into their fold. If the Earl of Kildare was corresponding heavily with de Cleveley, it could not mean good things for Devlin. Perhaps Kildare's fleet was the first wave in what would be an onslaught against him. If that was the case, they met the first test of their strength well.

But more threats were coming.

He was sure of it.

As he pondered the potential implications of the communication between de Cleveley and Fitzgerald, Emllyn moved back towards the hearth and the small stool that Enda had left there. She sat upon it, averting her gaze, not knowing what more to say to de Bermingham as he sat silently upon the bed. Even though their conversation was civil, she was still on edge. All she had ever known from de Bermingham was domination and she dreaded the coming night. The man had shown surprising restraint in their violent encounters, but she suspected that wouldn't last forever.

Surely, another battle was coming.

The thought of such a struggle brought tears to her eyes. She was exhausted and afraid, and she knew she wasn't strong enough to fight him off again. *Be compliant!* Nor should she fight him off if she was to earn his trust so she could gain her wants. Still, now that things were calm between them, she thought perhaps to ask him again about the English captives. It wasn't such an unreasonable request, she thought. Moreover, she could put a spin on it that might work in her favor.

Devlin seemed concerned with future plans and attacks; perhaps she could use his paranoia to her advantage. Struggling for courage, she lifted her gaze to him.

"Even though I do not know anything about the correspondence between my brother and de Cleveley, there were many of my brother's men that were aware of it," she said, trying not to sound sly with her suggestion. "You mentioned that there were English captives. If I could see them, I could tell you who, if any, held a position of power for my brother. That man would know much more than I would."

Devlin looked at her. His first thought was that she was indeed cunning – he didn't believe for a minute that she was actually trying to help him seek answers to his questions. He knew for a fact that she wanted to see if her lover was among the captives. Still, it was a very good suggestion.

But he had a better one.

"I am sure that he would know more than you do, if such a man is still alive," he said, his eyes glittering in the firelight. "But I have a better suggestion. Does de Cleveley's commander in Ireland know you on sight?"

Emllyn had no idea what he was driving at. It seemed to her to be a swift change of subject. "I… I do not believe so," she said. "I have never had contact with any of de Cleveley's men. But I am sure he would know my name and my brother's name."

Devlin was creating a plan, one that would supersede Emllyn's. She wanted something from him; he wanted something from her as well. He stood up from the bed and made his way over to her, his massive fist resting firmly on his hips. He meant to intimidate her because he very much wanted his way in all things. He wouldn't give her a chance to refuse him.

"I will allow you to see the English captives, my lady, but first you will do something for me," he said. "I will send you south to de Cleveley's holdings and you will present yourself as my escaped captive. Surely your English comrades will take you in and protect you. While you are in their bosom, you will discover what you can about their plans against me and against Black Castle, and you will return to inform me of your discovery. I will keep the English captives alive long enough for you to return, but if you betray me or if you do not return, I will kill every one of them and put their heads on poles for all to see. Is this in any way unclear?"

By this time, Emllyn was pale with horror. "But…" she stammered, swallowing. "But how will I discover anything? They will not tell me of their battle plans."

"They will if you are clever in your inquiry," he replied, eyeing her. "You are an intelligent woman. I suspect you will be able to discover a great deal if you set your mind to it. I also suspect you will do what you are told if you know your lover might be alive. You stowed away on a ship for him. I suspect you would do anything for him."

Emllyn was verging on tears but she fought it. She found that she was very angry that he was trying to manipulate her. Still, she knew she had no choice and it was difficult for her to swallow her pride and realize he had outsmarted her.

It was a bitter pill to swallow.

"As you say, then," she whispered hoarsely. "But I want to see the prisoners before I go. I will not go unless I see all of them."

"Nay," he said flatly. "If your lover is not among them, then there will be no reason for you to infiltrate de Cleveley. 'Twill be the hope that he is among my captives that will keep you on task."

It was a rather fair deal as far as deals go, but Emllyn felt as if she were making a deal with the devil. Damnation, but the man was clever. She refused to look at him, averting her gaze and discreetly wiping at the tears in her eyes. Still, she couldn't surrender so easily. She didn't like the feeling of being bested.

"Very well," she said quietly. "I will agree to your terms. But you will agree to mine also."

She was a plucky little thing. Devlin had to give her credit. As he'd realized before, he rather liked that about her. He folded his big arms across his chest expectantly.

"What are your terms?" he asked.

She looked at him, then, and he could see a steely coldness in her pale eyes. It was a surprising show of strength. "If I discover any useful information and return to you safely, I will not tell you what the information is until you allow me to see the captives," she said. "If Trevor is among them, you must promise to let him go before I give you the information."

He cocked a thoughtful eyebrow. "How do I know you will tell me the truth? You could say that you have valuable information and after I let your lover go, you could have nothing at all. It could be a lie simply to obtain his release."

She shook her head. "I am honorable," she insisted. "I would not lie to you."

He didn't want to insult her integrity by disagreeing with her. Something about the woman made him believe completely that she would never lie to him. If he was a good judge of character, and he was, he was inclined to believe that she wasn't the type. His life often depended upon who he could and could not trust. He believed he could trust her word.

He hoped he wouldn't live to regret it.

"What if you return from de Cleveley and have no valuable information to tell me?" he wanted to know. "What then?"

She sighed faintly. "If I have no valuable information upon my return, I ask that you let me see the captives regardless," she said softly. "If Trevor is alive, then I ask that you allow me to be in captivity with him. It is a small thing to ask, I think. You would have us both remain captives."

Devlin didn't like that answer at all and immediately shook his head. "If you return to me with no valuable information, then you will not see the English captives and you will never know if your lover is among them. You will remain my prize and the English captives will be my slaves. There is no other recourse."

Emllyn was going to argue with him but thought better of it. She could agree to the terms and perhaps in time, change his mind. *Be compliant!* Perhaps someday she would see the English captives; perhaps one day they would all be freed. She would not give up hope.

"As you say," she murmured, lowering her gaze.

Devlin could hear defeat in her voice and he struggled not to react to it, one way or the other. She was very proud, he could tell. She was also stubborn. Then again, so was he. He realized he saw many of his own qualities in his captive. They were qualities to respect.

He moved to within a foot or so of her, lingering close and watching her instinctively flinch. He didn't like it when she flinched from him but he knew why – he'd only shown her aggression and dominance since they had first met. Although the man had never known a strong sense of regret, he thought he might be coming to feel something close to it. Crouching his bulk down, he met her on her own level.

"Then we have a bargain?" he asked.

Emllyn looked at him, the man's smooth skin and intelligent features. It suddenly occurred to her that he was a handsome man, although the thought just as quickly shocked her. The man was her captor, a barbarian and worse – he was an

Irish rebel, the beating heart of the resistance that had kept her brother frustrated. But he was also ruggedly and beautifully handsome, like a wild horse that refused to be tamed. The way he was looking at her made her heartbeat quicken, just a little.

"We do," she whispered. "But how will I get to de Cleveley's encampment? I do not know where to go."

Devlin was watching the way the firelight illuminated her face. "I will take you there myself," he said. "I will watch over you to make sure you make it safely to their fortress. In fact, I may send one of my men with you as an escort. He will also help you return to Black Castle when the time is right."

Emllyn's gaze lingered on him a moment longer before she averted it and looked to her hands. There was an odd pull she was beginning to feel, something unexpected and unsettling. His eyes were a vortex with which to suck her in and she averted her gaze purely out of surprise more than anything. Her heart was beating faster now and her palms were sweating, and it had nothing to do with fear or intimidation.

It had everything to do with him, as a man.

Oh, God, she was going crazy!

"When do I go?" she asked softly.

Devlin felt the pull between them, too. He also felt a jolt when she tore her gaze away, a jolt that left him with a rapidly beating heart. He almost couldn't catch his breath. He stood up and moved away from her in order to reclaim his composure.

"I am not certain," he said. "In a day or two. I must make plans and then we shall move forward with them."

Emllyn simply nodded her head, unwilling to look up at him again because she was fearful that the strange pull would start again and she might not be able to break away from it. She'd never known anything like it, not even with Trevor.

Trevor! Her thoughts drifted to him once again.

"Until such time as you move forward with your plans, where am I to be kept?" she asked.

Devlin looked around the room. "This is the most comfortable chamber in the keep, and probably the entire castle," he said. "The floor is not dirt but stone and planking. It would be better for you here."

Emllyn lifted her head, daring to look at him. "But where are the other English prisoners kept?"

His expression seemed to harden. "Deep in the ground."

"What do you mean?"

That strange pull was starting again and he struggled to ignore it, but the longer he gazed into that lovely face, the stronger the pull became.

"Trust me when I say it is not a pleasant place," he said.

"You mean the vault?"

"Aye."

"Since I am a prisoner, you should put me there."

"You are better off here."

Emllyn was feeling the pull so strongly that she almost couldn't reply. She had to think hard on forming a sentence. Tearing her eyes away from him, she looked around the chamber, seeing it as it was now, with furs and a fire. But there were things around the chamber even before those things had been brought that suggested it had not been an empty one. She'd been told it had been his mother's chamber, but there was more to it. Something told her that it had been Devlin's also and that's why she'd been brought there.

To him.

"Does this chamber not belong to someone already?" she asked.

He nodded. "It is mine."

So much for being compliant. When he admitted it was his chamber, that drew a reaction from her. "For mercy's sake," she said. "Shouldn't you move me to another chamber so I will not be caged here… with you?"

He lifted a well-defined eyebrow. "How many times must I tell you that you belong to me?" he said. "That means you will be caged here in my chamber, with me, because that act alone will preserve your personal safety. Do you realize how many men want to kill you simply for being English? You have a great many enemies in this castle, my lady. Rather than look upon me as your jailor, I would suggest you look upon me as your protector."

She was growing angry. "A protector who has intimidated me and brutalized me," she said, lowering her gaze. She spoke before she could stop herself. "A protector would keep me safe from harm, but I do not feel safe with you."

Devlin could feel himself stiffen to her accusations. Deep down, he knew she was right to a certain extent, but he didn't see it that way. He wasn't used to anyone questioning his behavior or actions, and it didn't sit well with him.

"I did not harm you," he countered. "There are no bruises upon you. You are not bleeding, nor did I break any bones. I would be careful what you accuse me of."

Her head shot up. "What I *accuse* you of?" she repeated, incredulous. "Then what you would call it?"

His eyes glittered but he held himself in check, like a coiled snake before it strikes. "I would call it victory," he said simply. "The sooner you come to terms with that, the better for us both."

Emllyn met his gaze a moment longer before looking away,

disgusted. "You are not my protector," she said. "Call me what I am – a prisoner, and you are my jailor. A protector is someone who is gallant and chivalrous, which you have not been. You did not like it when I called you an animal. Mayhap you should not act like one if you wish for me to reform my opinion."

He was rebuked. Fighting off the urge to bellow at her, Devlin stared at her a good, long moment before sighing sharply. He was resisting the strong impulse to throw her down on the bed and show her just what kind of a brute he could really be, but in that same thought, he realized it wasn't punishment as much as it was simply a very strong desire to bed her. There was so much emotion and confusion rolling around in his chest that his hands began to quiver. Why didn't he just take her and be done with it? She belonged to him, didn't she?

… didn't she?

Jesus… what was happening to him?

"For a woman who sailed to Ireland on an invasion fleet, you have little right to accuse me of being an animal," he muttered. "Your brother has slaughtered thousands of Irish and taken thousands more as slaves, and he justifies his actions because he believes Lord Justice of Ireland gives him that right. The English in general slaughter Scots and Welsh by the thousands because they covet their lands. How are the English any less animals than I am?"

Emllyn stared at the fire. "My brother does not brutalize a woman he claims to be protecting."

"So this is all about me, is it? I am the worst rebel there is and your brother is a saint?"

She shook her head. "I did not say he was a saint," he said. "But he has as much right to these lands as you do. They belonged to my grandfather and his father before him."

It was the wrong thing to say. Devlin broke from his stance near the bed and swooped in on her, grasping her by the arms and yanking her up from the stool. He had her trapped up against his massive chest, his eyes blazing at her.

"Your grandfather's father stole lands from my family," he snarled. "They do not belong to any Englishman. They belong to Ireland and if God is merciful, I will soon restore them to my people. Never again lecture me about brutality and conquest because, my lady, your people have done far worse than I could ever hope to achieve."

Gazing up into Devlin's angry blue eyes, Emllyn began to feel some fear. Not the pure, abject terror she had felt earlier, but a deeper-seated fear. She was afraid of him, but not for obvious reasons. She wasn't afraid that he was going to kill her – she knew enough about the man that she knew he would not. She was afraid of what he was going to do to her and of how she might not be willing to stop him. It began to occur to her that perhaps she was afraid of herself because she liked having him close. She liked his big, hard body against hers and his lips on her earlobe.

There was something about him that made her entire body quiver with desire.

"So you will punish them by ravaging me?" she said quietly, her voice trembling. "You have been threatening to do it since we met. You were quite clear when you told me of your plans for me. What kind of man takes out his frustrations on the weak and helpless?"

Devlin didn't answer her; he was too furious to. But he was also consumed by the feel and smell of her, something that instantly aroused him. She was provoking him; he could sense it. She was being reckless with her words, reckless to the point of punishment and as he gazed into her eyes, he could see a tumult of emotion that matched whatever he thought he was feeling, too. He didn't like it one bit. For a man perpetually in control, he didn't like the thought of being unable to control whatever it was he felt for her. If he even felt anything at all.

Perhaps all he felt was lust and nothing more.

Whatever it was, he was overwhelmed by it.

Devlin's mouth came down on Emllyn's, so hard that he drove her teeth into her soft lip. He was kissing her with something short of fury. There was passion and lust and angst there, feelings that made him pull her more tightly against him. He could taste her blood as he sucked her lips, vaguely aware that she was struggling. She was trying to pull away but she wasn't trying very hard. It was more that she knew that she should try to fight him but didn't really wanted to. As he savaged her with his lips, her struggles stopped entirely. Somehow, her body was weakening. *Relaxing.* He thought he felt her hands on his face and it threw him over the edge.

The next he realized, she was in his arms and together they fell upon the bed.

Devlin could hear Emllyn weeping softly, begging him to do... something. His mouth moved down her neck to the exposed cleavage and he grabbed the hands that were near his face, trapping them above her head. With her arms trapped, he began to fumble with his breeches, pulling them down even as he lifted her heavy skirts. Emllyn's legs were thrashing about and he wedged himself in between them so she could hardly move. His hand, now roaming free, went under her skirts and could feel the moist heat between her legs. He was no longer content with toying with her, his hands on her hips or other areas of her body that didn't bring him pleasure. Nay, he wasn't content to restrain himself any longer. Not in the least.

He wanted her.

He knew she wanted him.

Now, his hands was on her thigh. His mouth suckled her chin, her neck, and all Emllyn did was lay there and gasp in pleasure. At least, he thought it was pleasure. She wasn't fighting him any longer, soft and pliable in his arms, and he took it as an invitation.

"You are mine," he whispered, his hand hovering near the junction between her legs. "Say it, Emllyn. Say that you are mine."

Emllyn didn't have a mind of her own. Everything about him was overwhelming her and her greatest fears were realized. She couldn't resist him, nor did she want to. His touch was heated and gentle. He was being surprisingly gentle. His kisses were tender, his mouth hot, and she wasn't afraid of a touch that only last night had terrified her.

She couldn't understand it.

Perhaps she didn't want to.

"I am your prisoner," she breathed.

He lifted himself up to kiss her mouth. "Tell me that you belong to me."

"I belong to you."

"And you will give yourself over to me."

"I am your prison…"

He kissed her to silence her. "Nay," he said. "Tell me you will give yourself over to me."

Emllyn was hardly able to speak. "Give… give over…?"

A smile creased his lips. "You will like this, very much."

"Like what?"

He inserted two big fingers into her wet and glistening

woman's center, listening to her groan with surprise. She stiffened, but only momentarily, as he stroked into her with shocking gentleness.

"This," he breathed as he suckled her tender neck. "You will like *this*. Do you feel me inside of you? This is where I will take my pleasure with you and where you will bear my sons. Already, I am making way for my seed and you shall accept it, do you hear? You shall accept it and you shall bear me a son."

He thrust into her with his fingers, mimicking what he would soon be doing with his large, throbbing member. Emllyn's gasped every time he thrust his fingers into her tight, slick heat. He would have liked to have tasted her but he had her where he wanted her, and he furthermore didn't want to get kicked in the head if she started to fight again, so he settled for touching her. He liked the feel of her. It wasn't long before he could feel her body start to quiver, the beginnings of her first release of ecstasy, so he quickly removed his fingers and thrust into her as her body was overcome with a climax.

Devlin could feel her body convulsing around him as he filled her with his manhood. She was virgin, he could tell, but there hadn't been any dramatics on her part. No crying as he impaled her. He'd prepared her, and calmed her, and now she lay beneath him as he firmly thrust into her yielding form. She was hot and wet, her gasps of passion filling the air as he snaked a hand under the shift and he found her breasts, pinching the nipples and feeling her twitch. Nay, this wasn't a woman who was resisting him.

She was welcoming him.

Devlin was so highly aroused that he released himself far sooner than he had hoped, feeling his hot seed mingle with her wet heat. It was the most glorious thing he had ever known.

Exhausted, spent, he collapsed on top of her.

Truthfully, he hadn't intended to bed her, but his urges had conquered him. He was wildly attracted to her and simply couldn't deny it any longer. There had been something about her from the beginning that he'd been drawn to, something he'd never experienced before. It was true that she belonged to him, as his captive, but there was so much more to it.

He couldn't explain it.

All he could do was feel it.

The sounds of his heavy breathing filled the air as Devlin struggled to catch his breath while beneath him, Emllyn simply lay there, eyes closed and her head turned away from him. She was breathing heavily, too, lying motionless for the most part. Devlin stared at her in the firelight, thinking he'd never in his life seen anything more beautiful. He wondered what it would be like for her to respond readily to him, for her to touch him as he touched her. The mere thought was enough to harden him again and in little time, he was slowly and sensually thrusting in and out of her again. His face was buried in her neck, smelling her, as his hips moved in the ancient primal rhythm.

"Please," Emllyn gasped. "Please… I should have…"

Devlin responded by covering her mouth with his, kissing her with something just short of tenderness. It was slow and delicious, his tongue invading her mouth as he listened to her gasp. He was being very careful and deliberate, his thrusts as gentle as they could be. He was unbelievably aroused, letting go of the arms he had trapped over her head and using the free hand to burrow under her shift and fondle her breasts. That seemed to arouse Emllyn, who began lifting her pelvis to him when he thrust. It was an innate reaction, as if she'd always done it this way. Realizing she was responding to him, he moved a big hand in between them, to where their bodies joined, and began to gently stroke her.

Emllyn groaned, overwhelmed with the new sensations he was creating. Devlin was literally panting as he watched her face, seeing the pleasure upon it and knowing she was feeling what he was feeling. It was too good to be true, mating that was only dreamt of or told of in fables of lore. It was pleasure beyond pleasure, passion beyond passion, and it seemed as if their bodies were only made for each other. Devlin had bedded many women in his life, but never like this. He had never even dreamed of anything like this. When he felt Emllyn's tremors begin again, causing her to gasp frantically, he thrust into her several times before releasing in a burst of glory.

The fire in the hearth snapped softly as heavy breathing filled the room. Devlin was collapsed on top of Emllyn as she lay with her hands over her eyes. He could hardly catch his breath and neither could she, but eventually the breathing died down and the room fell silent but for the crackle of the fire. Devlin still lay atop Emllyn, his body still joined to hers, thinking a great many thoughts. Mostly, he thought he might possibly be going mad. It would seem that she was no longer the captive.

It would seem that now, somehow, he belonged to her instead.

CHAPTER FOUR

"'T IS A BOLD plan, Devlin," Shain said, his voice low. "Are you sure they will not recognize you?"

"De Cleveley has never seen me," Devlin said. "He would not know me on sight."

Devlin and Shain were standing near the stables of Black Castle's fortress complex; the keep itself was built on a promontory on the edge of the sea with a rope suspension bridge linking it to the mainland where the majority of the fortress was. It was a bridge that could be easily removed or burned to prevent access to the keep if the need arose.

Like most Irish castles, Black Castle's keep and walls were built of stone, with a muck-filled moat paralleling the outer wall. The bailey held a giant feasting hall and several outbuildings all built of wattle and daub, including sleeping quarters and a barn, while the keep itself was literally three stories and three rooms – storage on the bottom floor, a big hall on the second floor, and Devlin's massive chamber on the third floor. All of this surrounded by the vast Irish sea to the east.

Evening had fallen now as Devlin and Shain lingered near the outbuildings, and a wicked eastern wind had whipped up, battering man and structure alike. Devlin eventually pulled Shain out of the wind as they huddled inside the stables to seek shelter from the weather. It was a bitter night, made more bitter now with the conversation at hand. Devlin had just proposed a rather daring scheme to Shain and the man wasn't particularly thrilled with it. In fact, he was positively adverse.

"But you have fought de Cleveley before, many times," Shain said, motioning at Devlin's flaming red hair. "Surely someone has seen you and knows what you look like. You are rather hard to miss, you know."

Devlin shrugged. "I have always worn armor, including a helm," he said. "If they have seen me, they have never gotten a good look at me. If I thought for one moment they would recognize me, I would not have suggested my plan."

Shain's gaze lingered on him for a long, tense moment before looking away. "I understand why you would send Fitzgerald's sister into their midst," he said. "Your bargain with her is a sound one. They could very well divulge their plans to her because she is an ally. But the thought of you accompanying her… why must you do this? I still do not understand."

Devlin didn't really understand himself; all he knew was that he couldn't let her go without him. Maybe he couldn't let her out of his sight. He wasn't sure yet, but one thing was for certain – he was about to go into the belly of the beast with the woman. He would not let her go in alone.

"I will pretend to be her slave or her bodyguard," he said. "I will pretend to be mute so my brogue will not give me away. It would not be wise to let her go into the settlement without some measure of protection."

"So you would risk yourself?" Shain demanded. "'Tis madness, Dev!"

Devlin shook his head. "It is not," he replied firmly. "We have plenty of armor from the dead English. I will dress in their armor, shave my head, and generally look the part of the *Béarla* warrior. She will tell them that I am her slave and they will believe her."

Shain looked at him as if he had gone mad. "You do not look like a slave," he said. "It would be better if you were her protector, sent by her brother. You look the part of something more noble than a slave."

"Then I shall be her protector," he said, becoming irritable with Shain's resistance. "It only make sense; surely a lone woman would not be traveling alone."

"I thought you were going to tell them that she was your escaped captive?"

Devlin pondered that lie a moment and a thought occurred to him. He looked at Shain, rather slyly. "Mayhap she will tell them that I was a captive also, tortured by the Black Sword," he said, thinking aloud. "I am mute because of it. Mayhap that will create more sympathy with them towards both the lady and me."

Shain was appalled that he was starting to like the man's plan. He sighed heavily. "Is there no other way, Dev?" he asked, almost pleading. "I have no issue with the lady going into their midst, but you… if you were to be discovered, this rebellion would lose its heart. Is it worth the risk?"

Devlin nodded slowly and deliberately. "I believe it 'tis," he said. "Shain, it's my belief that the invasion fleet the other night was just the beginning. I feel that the English are planning something very big and I must find out what it is. Can you not understand that, lad?"

Shain rolled his eyes in defeat and nodded. "Of course I do," he said. "But why do you have to go with her? Why can't I go?"

Devlin was already shaking his head before Shain even finished his question. "Because this is something I must do," he said, although it wasn't the truth. There was no reason for Shain not to go; Devlin simply didn't want him to. He wanted to be the one to escort Emllyn. He wanted to be the one to be with her. "I must hear it with my own ears and see the enemy with my own eyes. I have to understand them, lad. I have to know what we are up against and if there are any weaknesses, I must know."

Shain accepted the explanation but he clearly wasn't happy. "What do we tell Iver and Freddy?" he asked. "Freddy is going to be hard to control with you away. I worry over it."

Devlin shrugged. "If it makes you feel better, lock him in the vault until I return," he said. "I know Freddy is unpredictable but he is not a fool."

"As in a fool that would try to take over your men?" Shain wanted to know. There was warning in the tone. "He loves you but he loves himself more. He believes he is in the right, always. He has the ear of the men."

"I have their ear more," Devlin fired back softly. "Shain, I appreciate your concern, but I will speak with Freddy. He will understand his place and if he does not, then you and Iver will ensure that he does not get out of control. But while I am away, you are in command. I will trust you."

Shain knew there wasn't much more he could say. After a moment, he simply nodded his head. "As you say, Dev," he said softly.

Devlin could see how unhappy he was and he clapped him gently on the head. "All will be well," he assured him. "But for now, we need to focus on today. When I came out of the keep, I noticed the men were breaking down the ships on the shore. What are you having them do with the wood and other treasures?"

Shain reluctantly shifted from Devlin's future plans to the situation at hand. "Anything salvageable, wood or rope or tools, is being brought to the fortress and stacked outside of the walls. Anything of value like personal possessions or coin is being brought inside and stored inside the barn. Would you see it now?"

"Later," Devlin replied. "Are the prisoners still in the vault?"

Shain nodded. "Still," he answered. "It is very crowded. Those chambers were made for no more than twelve men and there are thirty of them."

"Make sure they are fed and watered properly," Devlin said. "They can deal with the cramped quarters but I would make sure they are fed adequately. I've no inclination to starve men to death."

Shain cocked his head in thought. "Dev," he said casually, "do you think you should interrogate them before you depart to de Cleveley lands? It is possible that someone knows something about future attacks against us. It would be a prudent thing to at least question them."

Devlin had been thinking that very same thing. Emllyn had made mention of it last night in a roundabout way, wanting to see the prisoners to see if she knew of one of them in the commander hierarchy, but in her case it was a self-serving desire. She only wanted to see if her precious Trevor was among the captives.

In Devlin's case, he thought perhaps to interrogate them all to see if anyone knew anything valuable. Truth be told, he was more than curious to know if, indeed, Trevor was among them.

A day ago he had no interest in the man but now, he found himself more and more intrigued. Who was this man that held Emllyn's heart? Curiosity had the better of him, and another emotion he didn't recognize. He thought it might be anger or disapproval; it never occurred to him that it was jealousy. He had to see the man who had her attention.

"Aye," he said after a few moments of deliberation. "Mayhap I will visit the captives and see if I can discover anything useful. Has anyone questioned them at all?"

Shain shook his head. "Nay," he replied. "We rounded them up and threw them straightaway into the vault. With the chaos last night, there has been no time for interrogation."

"Then mayhap the time is now."

Shain agreed and they made their way out of the stables and into the brisk salty wind that blew steadily off of the sea. The bailey of the fortress was fairly empty this time of night even though his soldiers were milling about and there were men on the wall on patrol. It was a full moon over head, peeking out from between intermittent rain clouds, something that had illuminated the battle the night before much to the advantage of the Irish. Devlin glanced up at the ghostly silver moon, his gaze lingering on it. Shain caught his expression.

"What are you thinking?" he asked.

Devlin shrugged although his gaze remained on the sky. "I am thinking of Elathan, the God of the Moon," he said. "The noble and beautiful prince of darkness. My mother said he was my ancestor."

Shain's expression grew somber. "He was also a man too trusting in those around him," he muttered. "He was betrayed by a relative. Beware that you do not make the same mistake."

Devlin took his eyes off the moon, looking at his friend and seeing how serious he was. He gave him a half-grin. "That is why I have you to watch out for me."

They reached the gatehouse, wet from the rains and surrounded by mud that had spilled down into the narrow steps that led to the vault. Shain stopped and faced him before they went in.

"Tell me this," he murmured. "If Freddy goes against you, do I have your permission to deal with him?"

"How?"

"Kill him."

Devlin's warm expression faded. "Although I respect and love you, my friend, you have never particularly cared for Frederick," he said quietly. "I am not saying you have it in mind to see him dead, but you have never warmed to him. Take care that your personal prejudices against him do not cloud your judgment."

Shain grunted, lowering his gaze and fidgeting. It was clear he was uncomfortable and perhaps frustrated. "My personal feelings towards him have nothing to do with it," he said. "Freddy commands eight hundred men personally sworn to him. He is a baron's son. He is also your cousin and for that alone, he has my respect. But he loves you and he envies you, Dev. He has a devious streak in him. Take care that *you* are not blind to his true intentions."

Devlin knew that; Shain was aware that he knew it, too. It was not a new conversation with them. Giving the man another grin, perhaps one to tell him that he worried too much, Devlin descended the slippery, muddy stone steps that led down into the vault.

There were thirteen steps before they hit rock bottom into a tiny, cramped room with two small cells. The cells were separated by bands of iron, forced together with great iron bolts to create what looked like cages, all set within the stone and rock of the sandy Irish soil. A big flaming torch burned against one wall, wedged into an iron sconce and giving off heavy black smoke from the fat-soaked wick. There were two guards on this level, seated on the ground playing some manner of dice game, and they stood up when they saw Devlin enter.

Devlin didn't notice the guards; he was looking at the prisoners, literally crammed into the cages until they could barely move. Most of them were sitting but a few were standing because there was no more room to sit, and there was certainly no room to lie down. It was fairly appalling conditions. The entire room reeked of urine and feces, enough so that Devlin's eyes started to water from the pure strength of the stench. But he studied the group of men who gazed back at him with various expressions of fear and curiosity. As Devlin continued to inspect, Shain pushed in front of him.

"My name is Devlin de Bermingham," he said with authority. "My father is John de Bermingham, Earl of Louth, and I descend from the kings of Leinster. I am known as Black Sword and you are my prisoners. Who is the ranking soldier here?"

No one said anything for a moment; they simply gazed back at Shain in silence. A few lowered their gazes, unable and unwilling to speak. It was clear that the name Black Sword carried great weight with them; they all knew of the rebel leader. He was a man to be feared, the man their liege greatly hated. He was the man who had soundly defeated them. Shain grunted in mounting impatience.

"I am simply looking for one man to speak with," he said. "I am not looking to make a martyr out of anyone. Speak up, now; who is your leader?"

A rather muscular man standing in the cell on the left moved forward; he was short but clearly strong, with a bald head and trimmed mustache and beard. He had a big gash on his cheek and his tunic around his neck was stained with blood. His hazel eyes fixed on Shain.

"I am Sir Victor St. John," he said steadily. "You may speak with me."

Shain fixed on the older knight. "Are you Fitzgerald's commander?"

"One of them."

"You know that this is all that is left of your invasion force. There is no one else."

St. John drew in a long, slow breath. "I know."

Devlin could see the man had a calm and rather resigned manner about him. He stepped forward and entered the conversation. "Who remains with you?" he asked.

St. John glanced around him, at the men suffering and cold and miserable. "Infantry mostly," he said. "There are a few archers and two knights."

"How many knights did you bring with you?"

St. John turned to look at him, showing utter defeat in his eyes for the first time. "Twenty-seven."

"And there are only three left?"

"Aye."

"How many men did you have?"

St. John saw no need to keep the facts to himself; it didn't matter anymore, anyway. They had been conquered and, at the moment, there was nothing left to defend. Not even themselves. They were at the mercy of fearsome Black Sword.

"We had eleven vessels and twelve hundred and forty-three men," he said. "That is not counting the sailors or rope boys or riggers. That is simply the number of fighting men."

"I see," Devlin said, eyeing the group of very dirty captives. They were so muddied and beaten that they all seemed to be the same color in skin, hair, and clothes. "Who are your knights?"

St. John pointed towards the back of the cells. "Sir William du Reims," he said, "and Sir Trevor le Mon."

Trevor! Devlin felt a jolt as he turned in the direction that the older knight was indicating; all the men seemed to blend into each other. "Who is le Mon?" he couldn't help himself from asking.

"I am," came the reply.

A young, tall knight with piercing dark eyes stepped forward; he had been standing back against the wall, allowing one of the injured men on the floor to lean on his legs. He was very tall, in fact; so tall that he couldn't stand up straight in the cramped quarters of the cell. He was rather slender but well-built; Devlin found himself inspecting the man very closely but he didn't want to look suspicious about it so he cleared his throat.

"And who is du Reims?" he asked.

The third knight identified himself, an average-sized knight with big hands and shoulders. Devlin eyed him, not particularly interested him, and his gaze drifted back to le Mon, who was gazing at him steadily. Then, he turned and walked away, heading back up the slippery stairs. Shain was right behind him. When they were about half way up, Devlin stopped and turned to him.

"Move St. John into the guard house," he told him. "I will interrogate him there and see what he knows. Meanwhile, have someone bring hay down to those men so they at least have something dry to lie on. Bring them some blankets as well. Wet as they are, they're going to catch the damp and they'll all die from it. If I want to ransom any of them, I will not have the chance."

Shain nodded and headed back down the stairs as Devlin headed back up. He still wasn't quite over the fact that Emllyn's lover was indeed among the prisoners. He couldn't decide how he felt about it, but at least now he knew. She wouldn't, however. He didn't intend to tell her.

Shaking off thoughts of the tall, dark knight, he headed out to find Frederick and Iver to discuss his future plans with them. He also intended to impress upon Frederick that the man should behave himself in his absence. He knew Shain was right about him but Shain also tended to be an alarmist; Devlin had some trust in Frederick, otherwise he would not be one of his top commanders.

Still, Devlin didn't trust any of them completely, not even Shain. Men with complete trust tended not to live long. Unlike the moon god Elathan, the good humored and somewhat naïve Celtic deity, Devlin would do all he could to prevent being betrayed by his own people. He would take the necessary steps. But before he could worry about that, he had a bigger issue to contend with – discovering what Fitzgerald's commander knew of his liege's future plans.

And then he would decide what to do about Trevor le Mon.

CHAPTER FIVE

EMLLYN WASN'T QUITE sure what it was.

It was a person, that was for certain, but she wasn't sure if it was man or woman. Whatever it was smelled to high heaven of rot and feces, dressed in layers of raggedy clothing, and had something sticking out of its mouth that smoked up on the end of it. The smoke smelled like shite. Whatever it was had knocked on her door and when she had opened the panel, it had wandered in and taken up position on the stool near the hearth. And there it continued to sit.

Clad in the heavy shift and green coat that kept her very warm, Emllyn sat upon the bed and watched the figure curiously. She wasn't afraid of it, for it was very small and seemingly feeble. With its broad features and smoking pipe, she simply wasn't sure what to make of it. It hadn't even spoken to her. It just sat and puffed. Therefore, it was a very strange standoff.

It was the morning after the night of passion with Devlin. Emllyn had awoken alone on the big bed, bewilderment running wild in her mind. As much as she wanted to hate him, to curse him, she simply couldn't bring herself to do it. He'd done something to her, marked her somehow, and she could no longer view his actions as brutality. It was… something else. Something else that baffled her and warmed her at the same time. But one thing was certain – the girl who had stowed away on the fleet had become a woman in the bed of the enemy.

As Emllyn lay upon the bed, staring up at the ceiling and feeling more disorientation than she ever had, the door had opened and Enda had entered. The old woman had brought the morning meal of cheese and bread, and behind her came young Nessa with a bowl of warmed water and the lumpy bar of soap that smelled of grass.

After devouring the food, Emllyn had used the water and soap to clean herself, perhaps washing the smell of Devlin off of her but every time she caught a whiff of his musk, her body betrayed her by feeling warm and giddy. Furious, she had scrubbed her hands and face, and between her legs, washing all she could of the man off of her. By then, Enda and Nessa had left her, seeing that she was in no mood for their assistance.

Emllyn needed to be left alone.

But then the old creature had come, wandering in and squatting by the fire. As the day neared the nooning hour, Emllyn continued to watch the figure, wondering why it had come. It simply sat, stank, and smoked. Finally, Emllyn could stand no more. She got up off the bed and moved carefully in the creature's direction. Summoning her courage, she spoke.

"Who are you?" she asked. "What is your name?"

The old figure puffed on its pipe, filling the room with the heavy smoke of human excrement. "Each was a game, each was a jest, until Devlin spoke for naught," it said in a raspy tone. "This thing will hang over him forever. Yesterday he was larger than a mountain. Today there is nothing of him but a shadow."

Emllyn blinked, confused. "Who is shadow?" she asked. "Devlin?"

The old creature sat and puffed, puffed, puffed. Emllyn was uncertain what to do. After several long moment, she simply shrugged and turned away; the old person wasn't doing any harm, she supposed, so there was no reason to provoke it or throw it from the room. In truth, she didn't know what to do, so she wandered over to the lancet window that overlooked the sea.

The brisk breeze caressed her face and as Emllyn gazed out over the expanse of blue, she could see the gulls screaming along the shoreline. Something about the sights and smells of the ocean made her feel better, fresher and newer, and lifted her spirits. She very much wanted to walk outside, to feel the sun on her face and inhale deeply of the fresh air, but instead she was stuck in a chamber with a creature that inhaled the smoke of burning shite. It was a very strange circumstance.

From the angle of the window, she could see part of the shoreline to the north and as she strained to see what she could see, she caught glimpses of wrecked and dismantled ships. The sea was very angry, churning wildly around the doomed vessels and she could see many men swarming over the ruins. They were carrying things away; lumber or smaller objects in their quest to demolish Kildare's invasion fleet. There was a good deal of flotsam and debris still in the water and washed up on shore, and it took her some time to realize that most of the debris were human remains.

Emllyn sighed with sorrow at the sight. There were literally hundreds of bodies, going ignored by the Irish as they focused on the vessels that were of some value. She inevitably thought of Trevor and wondered if he was among the dead half-buried in the sand, washed upon by waves as if they were nothing of matter. It was sad, truly. The more she watched, the more saddened she became.

Devlin wouldn't let her see the prisoners. She accepted that for the moment because she knew at some point, she might be able to convince him otherwise. *Be compliant!* Aye, she would be compliant but just because she was compliant didn't mean she was a weak little fool. The man intended to keep her bottled up in the keep forever but she could not allow it. He wasn't here now and she seriously doubted that he had a guard posted outside the chamber. Emllyn began to feel an almost desperate measure to see if Trevor was among the dead that littered the rocky shore. At least if she found him, then she would know the truth. But if he wasn't there, then perhaps he was indeed among the captives.

Glancing over her shoulder at the tiny figure that was filling her chamber with the smell of feces, she made her way over to the bed and lifted one of the garments that were still strewn across the bottom of the mattress. She was still wearing the green coat and shift, and the heavy robe that draped over her shoulders, but she wanted more. Perhaps more would shield her from the Irish as she made her way back to the point where she had first come ashore.

A cloak of brown wool was in her grip, plain but serviceable, and she slung it over her shoulders and tied it about the neck. Quietly, she made her way to the door but as she put her hand on the latch, the tiny figure spoke.

"He showed displeasure in Finn," it said, looking at Emllyn for the first time since entering the room. The eyes were sunken and dark. "He was but distant and soon Finn would suffer."

Emllyn looked at the person, having no idea what it was

saying. Obviously, it was quite mad so she ignored it and opened the latch. The door creaked open slowly, letting forth a rush of cold air from the floor below that smelled like damp stone, but as Emllyn had surmised there was no one guarding the door. In fact, it was as dark and cold as a tomb as she slipped out onto the dim landing.

The steps leading down were narrow and well-used. Emllyn clung to the wall as she descended the spiral steps, very nervous and alert. This had all seemed like a sound and reasonable idea until she had left the chamber. Now, her heart was in her throat and her mouth was dry. Back came the memories of the night she had arrived and the terror she had felt while being manhandled up these very stairs. No matter what had happened with Devlin since then and no matter what odd emotions she had experienced, the fact remained that she was an enemy in enemy lands. There were those who would kill her as easily as look at her. She had to be vigilant.

The steps led down to the hall where she had cowered under the table the night of chaos. The table was there and she recognized it, cluttered and chipped from the Irishmen who had drunkenly supped upon the surface. Even though the hall was empty, she could still hear the cheers of the rebels and the barks of the dogs as the men hailed their mighty victory against the English. Emllyn began to feel that familiar terror again, swallowing down the bile in her throat and struggling not to panic. Men that her brother and father and grandfather had fought against had gathered in this room to declare supremacy over the English. She could feel their hatred.

But the fact remained that the room was empty except for the dogs sleeping near the hearth. As she tread carefully into the chamber, doggy heads came up and looked at her but they made no sound. There was also a very big bird near the hearth, resting on a big iron stand. The bird had a hood over its head and seemed to be sleeping. Emllyn scooted past the dogs, and the bird, and towards the great entry with light from the other side sending streams of illumination into the room. The door was big and heavy as she carefully cracked it open and peered outside.

A wide-open world rolled out before her complete with a big drawbridge that linked the keep with a massive bailey on the other side. She could hear waves crashing but she couldn't see them; it seemed that they were on an outcropping of some sort and surrounded by the sea.

In the ward beyond, she could see people moving about, strange people in strange clothing. They wore tartans, wrapping their body in dirty cloth rather than wearing the hose or breeches that the English wore. But some of the men indeed wore hose, at least that she could see, and some of them wore pieces of armor. Most of them carried a weapon of some kind. Her spirits began to sink when she realized that, given what she could see, an escape to the beach below might not be such an easy thing.

"He showed displeasure in Finn," came a voice behind her. "Finn would soon suffer."

Emllyn startled so violently that she ended up hitting her head on the door. Rubbing her bruised forehead, she turned around and saw that the mysterious little person had followed her down into the hall. It was still puffing madly on the shite-pipe, but the dark and sunken eyes were focused intently on her. Emllyn's fright turned to irritation.

"Go!" she hissed, shooing her hands at it. "Go away!"

The little person actually seemed to smile; it was hard to tell because the face was so wrinkled that one more fold didn't make a big impact. It stood there smoking and smiling before finally reaching out a hand and taking Emllyn by the wrist.

"It would soon endeavor to learn," it said as it shoved the door open wide and pulled Emllyn from the keep. "For Devlin was mountainous and gifted, but Elohr kept safe."

Emllyn wasn't sure if she should pull away from the odd little creature but the little thing seemed so very sure of itself. It pulled Emllyn out of the keep and, with determination, across the drawbridge that was more of a rope bridge that swung crazily as they crossed it. Emllyn had to hold on to the rope railing to keep her footing, looking down with some fear at the swirling sea thirty or more feet below. But the little person didn't notice the swaying of the bridge or the sea; it continued to pull Emllyn along.

As Emllyn entered the bailey, she flipped up the hood to cover her golden-red hair, trying to conceal herself from all of the Irish around her. No one seemed to be paying particular attention to her, thankfully, so she kept her head down and let the tiny figure drag her across the bailey.

The rains had cleared out from the past couple of days, leaving the air crisp and salty as a strong wind blew in off the Irish Sea. Gulls screamed above her and more than once, Emllyn looked up to see that the birds were close overhead, looking for some scrap of food. When she wasn't looking at the birds, she was looking at her surroundings and noting the enormous bailey with the wall enclosing it, a wall that was built all the way to the sea cliff. It was like a half-circle, enclosing in the ward, and a big gatehouse was built into it, facing west. The wilds of Eire were on the other side of the massive gate, a place full of rebellion and mythical creatures, or so Emllyn had been told. England wasn't nearly as frightening or mysterious as Ireland was.

Emllyn and the small figure were nearing the gatehouse and a series of outbuildings near the wall when someone grabbed her from behind. Emllyn let out a frightened yelp, terrified, until she realized she was looking into Devlin's frowning face. He had a tight grip on her arms as he clutched her against his mighty chest.

"What are you doing?" he demanded. "I told you to stay to the keep."

Startled by his appearance, Emllyn scrambled to explain. *Show the man compliance and obedience!* "I..." she stammered, pointing lamely at the tiny figure. "I... I *was* in the keep when this... this *person* came to the chamber. I do not know who it is because... well, I do not even know if it is a man or a woman because it has not spoken to me, but it...."

Devlin cut her off, looking to the tiny person that still had hold of Emllyn's wrist. His manner was stern.

"Eefha," he said, almost scolding. "You cannot remove her from the keep. For her own safety, she must stay there."

Emllyn looked between Devlin and the scruffy little figure. "Who *is* this?" she asked.

Devlin looked rather impatient. "My mother's sister," he said. "Her name is Eefha. She's quite mad."

Emllyn looked at the tiny old woman and recoiled, leaning in Devlin's direction. "Mad, you say?" she said apprehensively. "She must be to smoke that horrible pipe. What is in it?"

"What does it smell like?"

Emllyn eyed him reluctantly. "Well," she said slowly, "it smells like..."

He cut her off but not without an inkling of droll humor. "It is," he said. "She gets it from the horses, dries it out, and then smokes it. Mayhap breathing all of that foul air in contributes to her madness."

"Is… is she dangerous?"

Devlin shook his head. "Nay," he said, sounding less frustrated and more resigned. "She's harmless. She was probably taking you to add to her collection."

Emllyn looked at him. "Collection?" she repeated. "What do you mean?"

Devlin opened his mouth but the old woman interrupted. "She hath healed a monarch's eye," Eefha said, pointing at Devlin. "Many a war for she hath thou raged."

He looked at his mother's sister with a mixture of impatience and resignation. Emllyn leaned closer to him. "What does she mean?" she whispered loudly. "She was saying such strange things to me earlier. Why does she speak like that?"

Devlin glanced down at Emllyn; it took him a moment to speak because he realized, in that instance, that he had never seen the woman in the light of day. Now all he could see was creamy skin and rosebud lips. Tendrils of wavy reddish-blond hair peeked out from beneath the heavy woolen hood and for a moment he was actually speechless. Was it true there was such beauty in the world? His heart, a hardened and protected thing, began to thump strangely against his ribs in a manner he'd never before experienced.

"She always speaks like that," he told her. "It is simply her way. When I was young, she was a teacher. She would recount all of Ireland's great tales. The older she became and the more madness set in, the more she would use passages from these tales to describe what she was feeling or what she wanted to convey. For example, if she wanted to imply that danger was coming, she would say something like 'thousands rouse to battle's rage'. We knew it was from a passage of a tale of the great King Conor, a passage leading to war, so we would understand she meant danger. Unless you are Irish, however, and know the tales she is referring to, it all sounds like gibberish."

It was a vastly intriguing concept. Emllyn looked at the tiny old woman through new eyes. "So she is indeed trying to say something," she said in understanding, "but you must know what she is referring to in order to understand what she means."

"Exactly."

Emllyn gazed at the old woman a moment before looking up at Devlin. "When she led me from the keep, she said 'Devlin was mountains and gifted, but Elohr kept safe'," she told him. "I wonder what she could mean?"

He shrugged. "Elohr was my mother," he said. "It could mean anything."

Emllyn pondered that a moment, but then she thought of something else Devlin had said. "What did you mean when you said that she was probably taking me to add to her collection?"

Devlin's gaze lingered on Emllyn a moment before looking at his aunt. "She is a scavenger," he said. "She has many wonderful things among the piles of rubbish she collects."

"Can I see?"

Devlin almost denied her; he wanted to return her to the keep. She was, after all, his prisoner, and prisoners didn't usually have such freedom to roam about and visit. But the moment he looked at her and saw the curiosity and eagerness in her expression, the words of refusal died in his throat. He'd never been known to let anything sway him, but Emllyn had done it very easily. One expression from her had been the catalyst for his surrender and nothing more. Grudgingly, he gestured in the old woman's direction.

"If you must," he said reluctantly. "But know that if she tries to keep you, I may have a battle on my hands."

Emllyn grinned, a surprising gesture, and he was instantly captivated. He'd never seen her smile before; it was as if the clouds had parted, the heavens had opened up, and the brilliance of angels was now staring him in the face. It was the most beautiful thing he'd ever seen.

"A journey's long," Eefha grasped Emllyn by the arm, pulling her away from Devlin and breaking the spell between them. "And if this cometh, not to content thee."

As Emllyn was dragged along, Devlin followed. His eyes never left the small figure in his mother's old cloak as she trailed along behind old Eefha. He wasn't comfortable with her out in the open like this, certainly not after the conversation he'd had with Shain and Frederick and Iver, but he surmised that no harm could come to her as long as he was around. He would protect her to the death.

Eefha had a small hut that wasn't too far from the barn where the valuables from the wrecked ships were being kept. In fact, as they approached the rock structure that was really no more than a small room, he wondered how many times Eefha had wandered into the barn and helped herself to the booty. He wouldn't have been surprised. As they neared the lop-sided hut with the heavy sod roof, Eefha suddenly came to a halt and pointed a gnarled finger at Emllyn.

"Lady, come to that folk, to that strong folk of mine," she said as she pulled the pipe from her mouth. "And with gold on thy head, thy fair tresses shall shine."

Emllyn had no idea what the woman meant and she looked at Devlin for help. He simply lifted his eyebrows.

"Those are passages from the Romance of Etain," he said. "Mayhap she has something to make you shine, although you do not need any help where that is concerned."

Emllyn looked at him, shocked. His expression was impassive so she thought he might be mocking her. "I cannot shine in borrowed clothing that is too big for me," she said, somewhat defensively. "I left my proper clothing behind in England."

His deep blue eyes twinkled at her, amused by what she evidently thought was an insult. "You said you did not mind my mother's clothing."

She pursed her lips irritably. "I lied," she said. "Although they are comfortable and warm, it would be well and good to have a garment that actually fit me. I have tripped several times in these clothes because they are too long; it is only a matter of time before I topple and break my neck."

Devlin was fixed on her and hardly noticed when Eefha disappeared into her hut. "I will speak with Enda and see if she can find something that is more appropriate for you," he said, "but I can assure you that we have no fine silks here."

Emllyn was coming to see that he hadn't been mocking her and, with shock, realized that he may have very well been delivering a compliment. Was it actually possible?

"I… I do not need silk," she said, lowering her gaze because he was looking at her with an expression that implied warmth. "Wool or linen would do just as well as long as it fits."

Devlin studied her delicate profile as she gazed off into the ward. "I am sure we can find something suitable," he said quietly. He paused a moment before continuing. "I am sure that where you come from is quite grand and you have possessions that reflect that. We have no such grand things to provide you."

Emllyn shrugged, her attention turning to the gulls that were riding the breeze overhead. "Grand things do not matter overly," she said. "I was born at the not entirely grand Llansteffan Castle in Wales. That is where we are from, you know. You keep calling me English but the truth is that we are more Welsh than English, although my brother would beat me if he heard me say that."

He knew that about her family but he pretended to be interested simply to keep the conversation going. "Is that so?"

"It 'tis," she said as she nodded her head. "My ancestor and his brother came to England with William the Conqueror and were charged with settling Wales. My ancestor was Maurice Fitzgerald, Lord of Llansteffan, and his brother was William, Lord of Emllyn. That is where I got my name – the Lady Emllyn Nesta Isabella Fitzgerald. I am named after many people in my family, Welsh *and* Norman."

For the second time in as many days, they were having a civilized conversation. Devlin wasn't hard pressed to admit that he could have listened to her sweet and soft voice forever. He liked it very much when the mood was calm between them, now on the subject matter of her background. He was very interested in what she was saying, and in her, as if he couldn't focus on anything else.

"I see," he said. "And do you speak Welsh?"

She nodded. "I do, but make no mistake," she said as she looked up at him. "I am *not* Welsh. I am Norman. There is a distinction and my brother will make it very clear that even though our family has been in Wales for over two hundred years, and our ancestor is a Welsh princess, we are not Welsh."

He gave her a half-grin because she said it with mock-seriousness, as if she thought the whole idea of living in Wales for two hundred years but not being Welsh ridiculous. "Then I will make sure not to call you Welsh," he said.

Emllyn fought off a grin and lowered her gaze again, feeling a distinct charm from the man and having no idea how to handle it. He was making her a bit giddy. "Have you never been out of Ireland?"

Devlin shook his head, folding his massive arms over his chest as he thought on his reply. "Never," he said. "There was never any reason to go anywhere else. I fostered here on Kildare lands and I was trained by Norman knights to serve Kildare. I am a knight sworn to your brother, you know. Or, at least I was. Now I am sworn to myself and to my father."

She dared look up at him, the giddy feeling in chest growing worse as she gazed upon him. "Who is your father?"

Devlin's warm expression faded somewhat. "John de Bermingham, Earl of Louth," he said. "I am his eldest son. Even though I am a bastard, he has acknowledged me. Black Castle is his holding, at least it is now that we have taken it from Kildare, and I lead his rebellion. Ireland will belong to the Irish once again and it is my honor to fight for my kinsmen."

Emllyn was gazing up at him quite steadily. The giddy feeling in her chest was very strong but she found she did not want to turn away from him. Something about the man, in spite of everything he'd put her through, kept her interest. The confusion she had felt that morning, the bewilderment and guilt, was turning into something else. She wasn't sure what it was yet; all she knew was that, at the moment, she had no desire to fight it.

"When we first met, you introduced yourself as the Lord of Black Castle," she asked softly. "But I'd only heard of Black

Sword. Why do they call you that?"

He could hear the nearly-gentle quality in her voice and it captured his full attention. He'd never heard that tone come from her before and he rather thought he liked it. It made him strongly inclined to answer whatever question she had for him, speaking in such a tone. He grinned modestly as he answered.

"Because when I was newly knighted, I fought a very nasty battle against the Normans," he said quietly. "It was against the Earl of Ormond's armies, in fact, and it was for your father at a time when I still served Kildare. I had killed many men that day, so many that I was covered in blood and so was my broadsword. When I returned to camp after the battle, the blood had dried to a sticky black. It covered my blade and the older knights began calling me Black Sword. It was a sign of respect. It implies fierceness in battle."

Emllyn nodded thoughtfully, imagining the man in the heat of battle. As big as he was, and he was enormous, she could only imagine that his formidable skills matched his reputation. She'd been hearing the name Black Sword for many years. Now, not only was she coming to understand the legend, she was coming to understand the man behind it.

Before they could continue their conversation, Eefha emerged from her hut with her arms full of items. Puffing furiously on her shite pipe, she approached Emllyn and began extending things to her; scarves of glorious colors, a belt or two, a pair of beautiful shoes, a fine white garment that might have been a shift, and at least two surcoats or other manner of dress. It was difficult to tell. Emllyn ended up with a big pile in her arms, looking rather stunned at all of the items.

"What is all of this?" she asked Devlin. "Where did she get this?"

Devlin picked up the garment on the top of the pile, a yellow linen that was embroidered with fine silver thread. "As I said, she is a scavenger," he said. "There is no telling where she found this."

Emllyn could tell that it was very fine; she'd seen enough finery to know. "This is something a great noblewoman would wear," she told him. "She did not… did she steal it somehow?"

Devlin began taking the pile from her. "I doubt it," he said. "She barters for things, as well."

"With the way she speaks?" Emllyn said, dubious. "How would anyone know what she wanted?"

Devlin took the remaining items from her and shifted them to one big arm. "She will find a way," he said, reaching out to grasp Emllyn by the arm. "Let us return to the keep now. You can try on your finery and see what fits."

He had her by the elbow as he turned around but the moment he did, something in his line of sight had his full attention and he handed the garments back over to Emllyn, piling them on so she could barely see over the top. He had to clear his arms quickly because he didn't want to be caught in a compromising position. He needed to be free to move and to protect both himself and Emllyn if necessary.

Approaching rather swiftly from the northeast corner of the bailey were Frederick and several of his men.

CHAPTER SIX

"I HAD HEARD you let her out of her cage," Frederick said, nearly yelling because he was still several feet away as he drew near. "I hope I didn't miss anything."

He meant something undoubtedly humiliating or painful. Devlin tightened up one of his leather gloves, trying to remain casual about the entire thing. However, whenever Frederick was involved, the situation was anything but casual. The mood of the conversation could go from light to deadly in a fraction of a second. Devlin wondered if the man was going to bring up the subject of Emllyn paying for his brother's death again; he hoped not. Still, he was tightening up his gloves in case he had to throw a punch if the man made a swipe for her.

"You did not miss anything," he said evenly. "We were just returning to the keep."

"Why?" Frederick put out his hands to stop them, his gaze riveted to Emlyn as she was nearly buried with the garments in her arms. "She looks better than she did the night I captured her. In fact, she looks rather pleasing. I had no idea English women were anything other than slovenly hags."

The men who had accompanied Frederick tittered rudely.

Devlin's expression was impassive. "We came to find some clothing that would fit her," he said evenly. "Eefha has all manner of goods."

Frederick didn't take his eyes from her as he moved towards her, inspecting her as one would inspect a prized mare. He walked a slow circle around her, scrutinizing her from the front and from the rear.

"Eefha has everything one could possibly want and a few things one does not," he said, a leering glint in his tone. "I would say that Kildare's sister doesn't want for anything. She is quite fine."

Throughout the exchange, Emllyn stood stock still, terrified by the big Irish warrior's attention. All of the fear and terror she had felt the night she had been captured came roaring back, causing her knees to weaken and her palms to sweat. *She looks better than she did the night I captured her.* So it was this big, beefy knight who had chased her down and carried her off like so much baggage. He had been very rough and very rude.

She was absolutely terrified.

"Shain has an English knight in the gatehouse for questioning," Devlin said, trying to distract Frederick. "You will go and help him. Do not lay a hand on the prisoner, however, at least not until I get there. I do not want him beaten and dazed when I arrive, so much so that I will not be able to get anything intelligent out of him. We need answers, Freddy. See to it."

Frederick nodded lazily, still inspecting Emllyn. In fact, he was standing directly behind her, looking at her backside. The man was oozing lust; it was evident in everything about him and Devlin struggled to keep a rein on his anger. If Frederick sensed anything other than indifference in his attitude towards Emllyn, there would be trouble. Frederick would make it so.

"Aye," he said, his focus on her bum. "She will breed you a host of strong Irish rebels and mayhap a daughter or two for the rest of us. I should have kept her for myself, Dev. Had I gotten a better look at her that night, I would have."

"Go, now," Devlin told him, ignoring his statement.

Frederick looked up at him, his eyes twinkling. "Can I have a go at *her*?"

Devlin simply pointed to the gatehouse as Frederick's men laughed lewdly. Emllyn lowered her head and struggled not to cry. Devlin didn't say a word as the men wandered away. He watched them as they moved towards the gate house and saw clearly when Eefha moved towards the group; the old woman had her hands up at them, claws bared, as the shite pipe smoked furiously in her mouth. Frederick's men instinctively shied away from the woman as she began to hiss.

"The blood in thy breast, it boils," she said. "Oft didst thou wrest Victory's spoils."

Frederick recoiled, too, when he heard the breathy words. "Dev!" he said, backing away in the direction of the gatehouse. "You said you would not let the old witch curse me! She is doing it, do you hear?"

Devlin held a straight face even though he wanted to laugh; it was always hilarious to him to see big, powerful knights turn into frightened children at the first sign of a curse or witchcraft. Eefha had that effect on all of them with her odd speech and garbled appearance. It was humorous how one tiny little woman could put the fear of the devil into men three times her size. Devlin waved the man off.

"She is simply telling you not to be so greedy," he said. "Go, now, to the gatehouse. I will be there shortly."

Eefha threw up her hands and growled at Frederick and his

men, sending them scampering away. Devlin did grin, then, as he turned back for the keep and grasped Emllyn by the elbow. They were moving across the muddy bailey when he heard her soft voice.

"You… you have an English knight in the gatehouse?" she asked timidly. "Is… is he a young knight?"

Devlin was seized with a fit of jealousy before he even looked at her. Once he saw the eager expression on her face, he was positively enraged with it.

"Nay," he said, looking away and struggling with the alien emotions that were running unbridled through his veins. "He is an older knight, and I told you to forget about your lover. He no longer exists."

Emllyn lowered her gaze, thinking on all of her brother's knights, or at least the ones she knew of. She'd never been around them much but she did know a few. They were a strong and loyal group.

"Do you know his name?" she asked. "I may be able to tell you how high he was in the chain of command."

It was a suggestion he hadn't thought of and he was embarrassed by it. What was this wild sense of possessiveness towards her that seemed to get stronger with every pull? Was it truly jealousy? He tried not to sound too interested or grateful in his reply.

"St. John," he said, eyeing her as casually as he could manage. "Do you know him?"

Emllyn immediately nodded. "His daughter is my friend," she said, looking at him with that beseeching expression he seemed unable to resist. "He served my grandfather, too. Is he well? Oh, please do not hurt him. He is a good man. His wife is very kind and they have five daughters. As I said, his oldest daughter is my best friend in the entire world and her father… well, he means a great deal to her. I will gladly take whatever punishment you intend for him."

His expression was serious as he gazed down upon her. "Don't you think you have taken enough punishment on behalf of Kildare?" he asked softly.

Emllyn looked as if she had been struck. The comment was blunt but the tone nearly regretful. It made her feel sickened. She had no response for him as the great keep of Black Castle swallowed them up into its cool, dark innards.

Escorting her in silence to the chamber at the top of the keep, he left her there alone while he went about his business.

He had a knight to interrogate.

"'Tis as we feared," Shain told Devlin in a low voice. "De Cleveley and his allies are planning something big."

Devlin, Shain, Frederick, and Iver were huddled in the guard room of Black Castle's big gatehouse. It was a very cramped room with a small hearth that gave off as much smoke as it did heat. Even now, the air was filled with a thin blue fog of smoke. The guards had taken Sir Victor back to the vault, leaving the knights in private conference. Three hours of interrogation had given them some answers but not all. There was still much more they should know.

"Aye," Devlin agreed, running a hand through his short red hair. "He has told us that the missives between Kildare and de Cleveley had to do with quelling the rebellion and regaining Black Castle for the English, but no more than that. We still do not know how or when."

"You should have let me have a go at him," Frederick grumbled. The man was standing in the shadows, his big arms folded across his chest. "Mayhap he knows more than what he was willing to tell."

Devlin glanced over his shoulder at him. "Do not let your desire to damage more English flesh be your excuse to interrogate the man for additional information," he said. "St. John is a seasoned knight and, like the rest of us, no amount of interrogation in the world is going to loosen his tongue if he does not wish to speak. We had a civil conversation and I am convinced he told us what he knew. Beating the man into giving us false information simply to be done with the pain does not help is in any manner."

Frederick wasn't convinced but he didn't argue. "So what do we do?" he asked.

Devlin cast a long glance at Shain before continuing. "It is my intention to use our lady captive to our advantage," he said. "As I told you, the lady was following a lover who was part of the invasion force. She knows that we have several prisoners and she wishes to see if her lover is among them. I have told her that she may see the prisoners if she completes a task for me, and that is to go south to de Cleveley's settlement and tell them that she has escaped from me. She will then make her way into their confidence to see if she can find out when, and how, they plan to attack us. When she completes her task to my satisfaction, I will let her see the prisoners so she may discover if her lover is among them. For that reason alone, the prisoners must be kept alive until she returns."

He was looking at Frederick as he spoke the last sentence. Frederick was looking rather serious about it, as was Iver. "You intend to send her in to the English settlement?" Frederick said, rather surprised. "Once she's in their bosom, she'll surely remain. They will not let her leave!"

Devlin held up a quelling hand. "They will indeed," he insisted, "because I intend to go with her. I would not send her in there alone. I will pose as a fellow prisoner who escaped Black Sword's dungeons along with the lady. I will pretend to be mute so that nothing about my speech will give me away. Shain has expressed concern that I will be recognized but to that I say this: I have fought de Cleveley many times but I have usually worn a helm. But to alleviate the possibility of recognizing this shock of red hair, I will shave my head. I will pose as a beaten and tortured companion to the lady, a protector of sorts, and surely draw their sympathy. But make no mistake; I will be there to protect the lady and when our task is through, I will find a way to flee the settlement and return here."

Shain had already heard all of this so he wasn't overly emotional about it, but Frederick and Iver had different reactions; Iver appeared uneasy but Frederick was positively livid. His dark eyebrows shot up as the scheme settled into his psyche.

"Are you *mad*?" he demanded. "Going into de Cleveley's settlement is… is suicide! They will kill you!"

Devlin shook his head calmly. "Not if they do not know who I am. The lady will verify that I am a prisoner, too."

That didn't ease Frederick at all; he threw up his hands. "And what if she betrays you?" he wanted to know. "She could easily turn you over to them."

"Then she will never know if her lover is among our captives," Devlin said coolly. "I suppose it will come down to who, and what, is more important to her – her lover, or turning me over to the English."

Frederick didn't know what else to say; he was flabbergast-ed. True, it seemed like a sound plan but it was still extremely risky. He looked at Iver, hoping the man would support his outrage.

"Have you nothing to say about this?" he asked him. "Tell him how foolish it is!"

Iver was characteristically calm. He glanced at Frederick although his focus was mostly on Devlin. He didn't seem to be particular adverse to the scheme but he wasn't obviously open to it, either.

"And the lady is agreeable to all of this?" he asked.

Devlin nodded. "She is."

"Do you know if her lover is among our captives?"

Again, Devlin nodded. "He is."

Iver showed a measure of surprise. "You know this for certain?"

"I do indeed."

"Will you tell her?"

"Not until our task is complete. That is the bargain."

The commanders looked at each other, silent words of concern and approval passing between them with a myriad of glances. No one was quite sure what more to say considering Devlin seemed very determined and, ostensibly, had a solid plan. They had all known Devlin de Bermingham long enough to know that once his mind was set, there was no changing it. He was as willful and stubborn as they come. Therefore, there wasn't much more they could do than support him. There was no other choice.

"Very well," Iver said with a heavy sigh. "If you feel you must do this, then I will not protest. But I fear what Freddy fears; what if she betrays you?"

"I have mentioned that to him also," Shain said before Devlin could reply. He looked seriously at his leader. "Dev, if she betrays you, we will not be able to help you."

Devlin knew that. He wasn't entire sure that Emllyn would not betray him but he was fairly certain given the fact that she very much wanted to know if her lover was among the English captives. Still, there had to be more assurance. He would not wager on the scheme with the intention of losing.

"Then I will make certain that the lady understands that if I do not return with her to Black Castle, you will be under orders to kill all of the English captives," he said, adding with emphasis: "Right in front of her."

Frederick liked that suggestion very much. He nodded firmly, smacking a balled fist into his palm enthusiastically. As he was mentally gearing up for the delight of killing thirty-three English prisoners, Iver was more serious.

"What about *her*?" he asked. "If she returns here without you, what do we do with her?"

Devlin looked pointedly at him. "You will assume that she has betrayed me," he said. "Traitors are put to the blade and their flesh fed to the dogs."

Frederick seemed to be the only one excited about that directive, too. Iver and Shain passed disquieted glances.

"And you?" Shain asked softly. "Who will assume your command?"

Devlin glanced at the man who had been his best friend since childhood. "You will," he said, making sure Iver and Frederick heard him. "If I do not return, my command goes to you. I will depend on you to carry on my cause. But know this; there will be no reason to announce that Black Sword has been killed. You will maintain the illusion that I am still alive as long as you can. It will be important for morale. As you once said, I am the heart of the rebellion and the men cannot know that the heart is gone."

There was nothing more to say to all of that. The proposal had been laid out and all contingencies planned for. Now, all they could do was let Devlin execute his scheme and pray for the best. As Devlin and Shain and Iver began to engage in lighter conversation that didn't involve betrayal and death, Frederick's overactive mind began to wander.

Devlin's presence in the English fold would be a very big secret, indeed. The man, if captured, would be the ultimate prize. Perhaps the lady wouldn't betray him; perhaps she would. As Devlin said, it all depended on what meant more to her – her lover or betraying Devlin to the English. The woman would indeed hold the key to Devlin's survival or lack thereof.

With Devlin captured or dead, the command would fall to Shain, but Shain was a man who was too timid sometimes. He was an excellent warrior but was often too cautious for Frederick's taste. Then, there was Iver… a very wise warrior but he was better when someone else was telling him what to do. And then there was himself… Freddy, as they called him. He thought he was the best warrior of the bunch but he'd been under Devlin's command most of his life. He'd never truly had a chance to show is mettle. If Devlin was gone, then he might have a chance. But unless the man was betrayed or eliminated somehow, there would never be an opportunity.

So perhaps the lady wouldn't betray Devlin… but what if someone else *did*?

As Devlin and the other commanders continued to chat, he slipped from the room.

CHAPTER SEVEN

S HE WAS BACK.

It was nearing the evening hours as Emllyn sat upon the chair that had been brought to her chamber that afternoon by one of the raggedy male servants, along with a table to go with it. It seemed that, bit by bit, the room was becoming more furnished and Nessa, Enda's silent daughter, had even brought an armful of willow branches and tossed them onto the floor around the bed. The smell of fresh cut branches filled the room. But then, Eefha returned and the entire room smelled like her shite pipe again.

So she was back.

After a morning of reflecting on the fact that she'd lost her innocence to the Irish rebel and had actually enjoyed it, Emllyn had mercifully been alone to ponder that very fact. Hours of sitting and dwelling on a situation that had quickly veered out of control and how she'd done nothing to stop it. Her body had betrayed her and her mind had gone along with it, but it left her in a peculiar situation. Devlin was her captor. He was her enemy.

But he was also something else.

She wasn't sure what that was… *yet.*

Before she'd had time to really think about it, the furniture had started coming. Food came. Eefha appeared and after that, she thought of Devlin no more. She decided to go about her business, which happened to be trying on the garments Eefha had given her. In fact, she was rather excited to try on the new clothing.

Her first order of business was to sort all of the items out and she took to the task eagerly. When all was said and done, with everything, including the garments Enda had brought her the day before, she had two shifts, three surcoats, a red silk robe that had beautiful gold stitching around the edges, a cloak, three belts that were made from various metal links or fabric, two pairs of leather slippers, and a leather sack that contained a bone comb, fine strips of cloth that were meant to tie off hair with, some kind of pomade in a small, heavy clay pot that smelled of rosemary and mint, and a very lumpy white hunk of what she assumed to be soap that smelled of pine, she thought. There were even flecks of green in it.

In all, it was an interesting horde, and Emllyn was quite pleased with all of it. Enda had left her a pitcher of water and a bowl earlier; she used the water to work the soap bar up into a reasonable paste just to make sure that it was, indeed, soap. The pomade in the pot that smelled of rosemary and mint seemed to be something to soften the skin because she rubbed it on her chapped hands and it soothed them nicely.

Next, she tried on the fine white shift and pulled another surcoat of white wool over it. It was very warm and fit her rather well. A belt of green silk with tassels draped around her waist. Thrilled that she finally had clothes that fit, and decent clothes at that, she proceeded to comb her hair with the bone comb and braid it. A heavy, silky reddish-blond braid draped elegantly over her right shoulder.

One of the belts seemed to have an issue with the weave so she sat in the chair again and tried to fix the problem. All the while, she kept glancing over at the stool next to the hearth where old Eefha sat. The woman was staring into the flames, puffing away on that stinky pipe. Emllyn found her attention increasingly on the silent old woman and she eventually lowered the belt to her lap.

"I am not entirely sure if you can understand me," she said politely, "but I want to thank you for what you have given me. You are very kind. I realize I am the enemy and you could have very well disregarded me, but I am grateful that you did not."

The old woman puffed and puffed, seemingly ignoring her. Emllyn wasn't sure what more to say because the woman clearly didn't understand her. Maybe she'd lost the ability to communicate normally long ago, speaking strangely as she did. With a sigh, perhaps of some regret that the woman didn't understand her gratitude, she returned to the belt repair and murmured a song from her childhood simply to pass the time.

> *"'Though oft of Fairy Land they spoke,*
> *No eerie beings dwelled therein,*
> *'Twas filled throughout with joyous folk*
> *Like men, though freed from death and sin.'"*

She continued to hum the tune and muttered a word now and again as she worked on the belt. She was about to start on the next verse when, from across the room, she heard another voice.

> *"'And sure those bards were truest knights*

Whose thoughts of women high were set,
   Nor deemed them prizes, won in fights,
But minds like men's, and women yet."

Emllyn's head popped up after the first few words were sung, realizing the old woman was doing the singing in her raspy, ancient voice. It was a common enough song but somehow, in those verses, meant they were speaking the same language. They both knew the same song. When Eefha finished the last word, she continued to stare at the fire and puff on her smelly pipe. Emllyn watched her closely for some kind of additional response but there was none. Then, she ventured softly with the last verse to see if she could elicit the same reaction as before.

"'In forms like those men loved of old,
Naught added, nothing torn away...."'

Emllyn trailed off, waiting to see if old Eefha picked up the queue. It took several long moments but, eventually, the old woman finished the song.

"'… The ancient tales again are told,
Can none their own true magic sway?"

When she finished the song she paused and puffed her pipe before very slowly turning to Emllyn. Their eyes met and, for a moment, they simply stared at one another. There was something warm in the air, perhaps a measure of understanding. Then, Emllyn broke out into a timid smile. This time, she was sure the old woman smiled back. And then she went back to smoking her pipe.

Emllyn laughed softly and returned to finish her belt but she felt, in that moment, as if she had accomplished something. Somehow, in the verses of that old song, she and old Eefha had communicated. It was progress. As she worked with the knots on the belt that needed mending, the chamber door rattled violently.

Startled by the loud burst, Emllyn nearly dropped the belt. Heart pounding in her throat, she didn't move; she sat and waited for something else to happen. It wasn't long in coming.

"Open the door, wench!" came a booming bellow. "Open it up or I'll break it down."

Emllyn was terrified. She sat, rooted to the spot, too frightened to even open her mouth. She simply sat there, hoping whoever was demanding entry would go away. But he banged on the door again, louder than before.

"Open this door, I say!" he yelled. "Open it or I shall beat you severely when I get into the room, and trust me when I tell you that I *shall* get into the room."

Jolted out of inaction, Emllyn began looking around frantically for a weapon of some kind. She wasn't entirely sure the old bolt would hold and wanted to make sure she could protect herself. As she bolted from the chair and began searching the room for something, anything, to protect herself with, Eefha quite calmly stood up from her stool by the hearth.

Emllyn was in the process of inspecting the chair she had been sitting on, undoubtedly to use it like a club, as the old woman headed for the door. Emllyn had her back to Eefha, unaware that the old woman was calmly moving for the bolted panel, and she was further unaware that the woman had unsheathed a sharp dagger buried in the folds of her robes. Emllyn only realized the old woman had moved when she heard the bolt unlatch. As she turned in horror, convinced she had just been betrayed, the old woman pulled open the door and plunged the dagger into the man standing on the landing outside. As quickly as she had buried the blade in his flesh, it was with equal swiftness that she removed it.

Frederick looked with shock at the wound in his gut. He stumbled back, howling, as he slapped a hand over the bleeding puncture. Seeing that it was Eefha who had stabbed him, his features contorted with pain and surprise. But the old woman simply lifted a clawed hand in his direction.

"Of great woe, for that cry is of thy own foolish mistake," she said ominously. "Beware the protection dear of the fairest lady. In the next, thy life is forfeit."

Frederick sagged against the corridor wall, his expression wrought with disbelief and agony. She had plunged the blade into the curve of his torso and he was bleeding fairly profusely, but he knew from experience that it more than likely wasn't a mortal wound. Still, it hurt a great deal and needed to be tended immediately. More than his shock, he was bloody well furious.

"Why did you do that, you foolish sow?" he demanded.

Eefha didn't say another word. She shut the door in his face and threw the bolt. Then, quite calmly, she returned to her stool and sat. All the while, she had been puffing steadily on the shite pipe. She never missed a puff.

Emllyn was stunned. She could hear Frederick on the opposite side of the door, cursing and grumbling, and she kept waiting for him to kick the door in and kill both her and Eefha. But he never touched the door; he cursed steadily and loudly and eventually his voice faded away. That was how Emllyn knew he was leaving; eventually, he simply faded into silence.

It was quiet again but for the popping of the fire. Emllyn

looked at the smelly old woman through new eyes. The woman had clearly protected her from the enraged Irish warrior and Emllyn was shocked, appreciative, and touched. She was trying to figure out what to say to the old woman, conveying words of gratitude that she might hopefully understand, when the door jolted again with a series of heavy blows.

"Open the door!"

It was Devlin. Emllyn jumped up and raced to the door, throwing the bolt and pulling open the heavy panel. Before he could say a word, Emllyn pointed at Eefha.

"Your aunt stabbed a man who appeared at the door and demanded entry," she said, breathless. "He came to the door and demanded I open it but I did not, so he said he was going to break into the room and punish me. Your aunt went to the door and stabbed him!"

She was pale-faced and excited. Devlin's gaze lingered on her a moment before passing an amused glance at his aunt.

"Why do you think she has been coming to this chamber to sit with you?" he asked, pushing into the room and closing the door behind him. "She is a better protector than any seasoned warrior."

Emllyn looked at the old woman with her mouth agape. "She is here to *protect* me?"

"Of course," he replied as if an old lady with a knife was the most natural thing in the world. Then he began looking around the room and noted the table and new furnishings. "I see the accommodations are better today. Have you eaten yet?"

Emllyn shook her head. "I have not."

Devlin ran his hand over the old table, warped and leaning. "We shall remedy that," he replied. "Do you recognize this table?"

"Should I?"

"It came from one of your English ships."

Emllyn looked at the table, the chair, pondering his statement, but she just as quickly pushed it aside. She wasn't yet finished with the discussion of Eefha's shocking offensive.

"Wait," she demanded, throwing out her hands as to stop all chatter and action. "I care not where you got the table and chair at the moment. I want to know how you can so easily brush off what your aunt did. She *stabbed* a man!"

"I know. I saw him downstairs in the hall."

Emllyn stared at him, aghast. "Is he dead?"

"Nay, but she sufficiently wounded him."

"But you said she was not dangerous!"

"She is not dangerous to *you*," he said, amused with her bewilderment. "Lady, Eefha is here to protect you. She did what she is supposed to do. Freddy will think twice before coming back up here and trying to molest you. In fact, I would wager to say he will not try it again, at least not with Eefha around."

Emllyn let it all sink in. So she was being protected by an old mad woman who was fearless with a dagger. It was unconventional to say the least but in the same thought, it was quite pleasing. She felt strangely comfortable with the old woman's protection. Still, one more thought crossed her mind as she gazed at Devlin. It was a serious thought and her expression reflected it as such.

"Will she protect me from you?" she asked.

Devlin's humor faded. "She will not need to protect you from me," he said. "I will not harm you."

She lowered her gaze. Technically, that was true. He'd never harmed her. But he had given her the most glorious experience of her life, wicked as it had been. *Be compliant,* her mind screamed because, so far, being compliant had worked wonders. The mighty beast of de Bermingham had softened to her. But the last shards of stubbornness flared in her at his softly uttered statement. She found she could not keep silent on the subject.

But, God's Bones, the man's mere presence was making her heart race.

"That is a matter of opinion," she said. "It is true you've not drawn blood or physically caused me great pain, but you have… that is to say, you *have* touched me."

Devlin didn't disregard her remark as he would normally have done. He didn't posture angrily and point out that she belonged to him again because she already knew that. So he met her head–on.

"And you have hated every minute of it, have you?" he asked in a mocking tone. "I know for a fact that you have not. You have derived as much pleasure out of it as I have. Your consent was in your actions, lass. I heard you loud and clear."

The conversation was turning serious and uneasy, mostly because he wasn't wrong and she knew it. Emllyn kept her gaze averted, her cheeks flushing a dull red as she moved towards the lancet window. She was trying to put distance between their conversation and Eefha. Although she wasn't entirely sure the old woman could understand what they were saying, still, it was a private and embarrassing subject, one she did not wish to discuss in front of a third party.

"I wish you would stop," she finally whispered. "I do not want you to do that to me anymore. Please, for mercy's sake, I beg you."

Devlin's eyebrows lifted. "I have every right," he said. "By the laws of my people, you are my property now. I have marked you and no other man will touch you."

"What do you mean you have every right?"

"You are my concubine."

Emllyn's mouth popped open in outrage. "Your *concubine*?" she repeated, appalled. All thoughts of being compliant fled and she was no longer willing to bow down to the man, not now. Not with that foolishly uttered statement. *Damn her pride!* "I am no such thing!"

Devlin nodded patiently. "The first time I touched you as a man touches a woman, you became my concubine," he said. "Men in the Bible had concubines. I will have one also. In fact, there is a story I once heard about a man named Jacob who had a wife *and* a concubine. There is no shame in such a status."

Emllyn gazed at him in utter horror. He was absolutely serious and after a moment, she plopped down onto the chair behind her. Then she burst into tears.

Devlin frowned, watching her weep. He went to her. "Why do you weep?" he asked, his tone considerably softer than it had been moments before. "You do not like the term 'whore'. I thought 'concubine' would be better."

Emllyn howled angrily. "I do not want to be a concubine," she sobbed. "It is as bad as being a whore and you cannot make either term sound remotely acceptable. I am the sister of an earl, descended from Welsh royalty, and I fostered in one of the finest houses in all of England. A proper and advantageous marriage was always planned for me. Now I find myself the whore of an Irish rebel and you tell me there is no shame in that?"

She was so angry that she was off the chair, wagging a finger at him. Devlin had never seen her truly furious and he had to admit that she was rather intimidating. He realized that he wanted to appease her. Seeing her so upset made him uncertain and frustrated.

"Then what do you want?" he asked. "Do you want me to marry you? Would it be better to be the wife of a rebel than the whore of one?"

Emllyn froze in the midst of her tears, her eyes wide with astonishment at his suggestion. After a pause of epic proportions, she squealed with fury and was off on another crying jag, this one louder than before. She was so angry that she stamped her feet as she turned her back to him, evidently having a full-fledged tantrum right before his eyes.

Devlin wasn't sure what more to say. Anything he said seemed to make it worse. Uneasily, he sat down on the bed, far away from Emllyn and her fit, and pondered his next move. She didn't want to be a whore, a concubine, or a wife. But what she wanted was of little matter; he would do what he had to do. He would not apologize for anything he had said or done, but it was becoming increasingly difficult to hold his tongue. He didn't like upsetting her, although it truthfully shouldn't matter to him if she was upset or not. But it did. In confused silence, he left the chamber.

With the object of her frustration gone, Emllyn eventually calmed her weeping and stamping. Exhausted both emotionally and physically, she sat morosely, cursing the day she decided that stowing away on a ship bound for battle had been a wise decision. She had placed herself in this predicament and now there was no escape. She would have to face her mistakes and live with the consequences. Perhaps the reality was that being a concubine now was the best she could hope for. It was a sickening realization.

Depressed over a future filled with nothing she had imagined for herself, Emllyn eyed the old woman sitting by the fire, puffing on his shite pipe that now seemed to be running out of fuel. Was this to be the rest of her life now, being protected by a crazy old woman and bearing children for a man who viewed her as his whore? A day ago, the situation did not seem real, but as of this evening, circumstances were beginning to settle. Reality was upon her.

Aye, *now* this was her future. Even if she discovered that Trevor was still alive in Black Sword's dungeons, he certainly would not want her now. She was destined to stay with de Bermingham forever because the man had indeed marked her. She belonged to him and no other. Sadly, she sighed.

"I do not want to be here, Eefha," she muttered. "Can you not understand? I want to know if Trevor is alive and then I want to go home. I do not want to be a concubine of an Irish rebel."

The old woman continued to puff and Emllyn knew her words were falling on deaf ears. Pulling the robe she wore more tightly around her to ward off the cold evening temperature, she gazed out of the lancet window and up to the stars on a surprisingly clear night. It was beautiful outside, crisp now that the storms had blown away. As she sat and gazed into the blanket of stars, the door to the chamber lurched open.

Devlin entered with Enda and Nessa behind him. The women were bearing great trays of food and Devlin was carrying a clay pitcher and a pair of pewter cups. He directed the women to set the food over on the table and they did, with Nessa giving Emllyn a shy smile. Emllyn smiled back, somewhat startled when the girl pressed something cold into her hand before fleeing the room. Emllyn kept her hand in her lap, glancing down to see what Nessa had given her, as Devlin pulled up the second chair up to the table.

"I thought you might feel better if you ate," he said as he began pulling apart of big, thick-crusted loaf of bread. "We have bread, cheese, boiled onions with mustard, roast fowl, figs, and walnuts. Help yourself, my lady."

Emllyn was looking at the trinket that Nessa had slipped into her hand; it was a hair comb made of nickel or tin; it was hard to tell. Someone had rather skillfully worked it into the shape of a butterfly, and it was evidently well-used as it was bent a bit, but it was a very sweet little comb.

Emllyn fought off a smile as she gazed down at the gift from an Irish lass she'd never said more than two words to. It was a very nice gesture, surprising since she thought all of the Irish in this Godforsaken castle hated her. She would make sure to thank her next time she saw her.

But the smell of the food on the table was distracting her. The scent was divine and Emllyn's dark mood began to lift as she tore off a leg of the roast bird and began to eat. The meat was succulent and juicy and in little time, she was competing with Devlin for who could eat the most and not vomit it all up. The feast had her attention at the moment and for a few minutes she could actually forget about everything. At the moment, there was no captivity or concubine; it was simply the food and that was all she focused on.

It was a rather oddly silent meal, Devlin was thinking as he watched Emllyn stuff food in her mouth. He knew she was distracted, and saddened, but at least she wasn't hysterical any longer. He was grateful for that. After taking Eefha a bird leg, he returned to the table and sat heavily as he collected his cup of wine.

"We shall be leaving for de Cleveley's settlement on the morrow," he told her as he poured more wine. "We will have to travel lightly; practically nothing at all since we are supposed to be prisoners escaped from Black Sword's dungeon. Think carefully about what you will take with you because even then, it may be too much. You must think of what only a prisoner would be allowed to possess or would be able to steal."

Emllyn looked at him in mid-chew. "I *am* a prisoner," she said flatly. "I will take the clothes on my back and nothing else. What more do I have? And what do you mean by *we* are supposed to be prisoners?"

He took a long drink of wine before looking at her. "I am going with you."

She cocked her head curiously. "To escort me as you said you would?"

He drained his cup. "I am going with you into the belly of the beast," he said, realizing she had no knowledge of the plans he'd discussed with Shain and the others. "You see, lady, I do not want you going in there alone. I fear that they will never let you go if you do. Therefore, I will go with you. We are to pose as two escaped prisoners from Black Sword's dungeons, you being Fitzgerald's fine sister and me being a warrior from an enemy clann. We will tell them I am mute because in that respect, they may trust me more and of course you will validate my presence. You will tell them that I helped you escape and that I have been your mute protector ever since. If you trust me, they will trust me. Then we shall discover what we can and flee. Is this in any way unclear?"

Emllyn was looking at him with wide, astonished eyes. "Are you serious?"

"Of course," he said. Then, he reached out and grabbed her wrist, his iron grip conveying a thousand silent words of intimidation and foreboding. "If you do not do everything in your power to convince them I am no threat to them, or if you betray me, know that I have given orders to have every one of the English captives killed. Their lives depend upon your behavior."

By this time, she was pale with apprehension and fury. "Why do you threaten me?" she asked hoarsely.

Devlin's jaw ticked. "I tell you the truth. Betray me and everyone dies. Obey me and mayhap you shall discover that your lover is indeed still alive. Are we agreed?"

Emllyn thought about yanking her hand free from his grasp but stopped short. He was holding her so tightly that she would probably snap her wrist in the attempt. His grip was heated, too, and her mind inadvertently turned to those very big hands and how they had touched her body. His big fingers had penetrated her, making her experience things she had never known to exist. Shuddering, she forced away those thoughts and lowered her head. Back came thoughts of Trevor, of the English captives, and of the Irish rebels to whom she was at the mercy of. *For God's sake, now is the time to be totally compliant!*

"I will not betray you," she muttered.

"Swear it on the Blessed Virgin."

"I swear."

"Then I believe you."

"Let go of me now."

A flicker of humor crossed Devlin's expression. "Why?"

"Because I have asked you to."

"And if I do not?"

Emllyn turned her head away. "It would be nothing new."

"What do you mean?"

She tried to pull away. "When have you ever done anything I asked?"

Devlin was feeling his alcohol. He'd had most of the pitcher and could feel the warmth in his veins. *When have you ever done anything I asked*? He had never done anything she'd asked. But, then again, it wasn't her place to ask anything of him. She was the captive and he was her conqueror. The sooner her proud English soul recognized that, the better for them all. God, he could feel his lust for her flushing his veins like a wildfire as he watched her squirm. He wanted her more than he'd ever wanted a woman in his life.

Swiftly, he stood up and yanked her to her feet. Emllyn let out a startled cry as he scooped her into his arms and, in three long strides, tossed her onto the bed. Emllyn barely had time to scream before he was on her, his soft lips and bristly beard covering her mouth. His enormous arms wrapped around her body as his mouth suckled her with all shades of lust and glory.

Emllyn tried to avoid his seeking lips, to turn her head, but he would have no part of it. She pushed on his shoulders as he kissed her lustily, sucking the air right out of her.

"Nay," she breathed when she managed to pull away. "Not when you have been drinking!"

He ignored her as his hands began to roam, tugging at belts and tossing them aside. But Emllyn wasn't fully compliant yet.

"Your aunt is in the room," she hissed. "Please, for the love of God, not in front of *her*!"

His mouth was forging a blazing trail across her jaw. "She is asleep," he said breathlessly. "Can't you hear her snoring?"

Emllyn had no idea if she could hear the woman snoring or not. All she knew was that Devlin intended to take her in front of an audience. She was horrified. As she opened her mouth to protest, he clamped his lips down over hers and kissed her so hard that she nearly lost consciousness.

She couldn't breathe. She could hardly think. Devlin's mouth finally released her and she twisted away from him, weakly trying to climb off the bed. Collecting the belt he'd pulled off her waist, the one she had repaired that afternoon, he managed to capture both flailing hands and using the belt, he tied them together snuggly. Then he took the tail end of the belt and lashed it to the head of the bed.

Emllyn's arms were effectively trapped but she didn't give up the fight. She tried to kick him in the groin when he shifted and she barely missed. Devlin pushed himself off of her, rolling over to sit at the edge of the bed. He put out a hand and shook Eefha gently.

"*Aintín*?" he said gently, waking her. "Go to bed, now. I will see you on the morrow."

Eefha snorted and shifted on the stool, puffing furiously on the now-cold pipe as a reflexive action of being awoken out of a stone-cold sleep. She grunted and waved Devlin off, standing up wearily and making her way to the door. She never once looked at the bed or noticed Emllyn. The old woman shut the door behind her and Devlin bolted it.

When the door was secured, he turned to his captive on the bed. She was in a perfect position for him to have his way with her but he didn't; something was holding him back although he wasn't sure what. Perhaps it was the fact that she'd asked him not to brutalize her anymore. As much as he hated to admit it, perhaps he was actually bending to her request. She was very compliant when he coaxed her enough. That was the Emllyn he wanted. But she gazed back at him with an expression between fear and outrage.

"Untie my hands," she demanded.

He put his hands on his hips. "I will not because you will

only try to kick me again."

"I kick you to defend myself," she fired back.

He continued to face her, fists on his hips, and an odd expression on his face. Emllyn kept waiting for him to pounce on her but he remained standing. She watched him warily because he seemed rather pensive. After several long moments, he broke his stance and shifted towards the bed.

"Tomorrow we embark on a journey that, in order to be successful, must see some measure of trust between us," he said quietly. "You and I are not comrades. We are not family nor are we even remotely kin. You are the sister of my enemy, a man I am rebelling against because he claims my lands as his own and holds my people as slaves. Did it ever occur to you that I am treating you the way your brother treats my people?"

He was being somewhat deliberate and calm in his delivery, a far cry from the lustful man from moments before. It was difficult not to take him seriously because his expression and words were sincere. Emllyn gazed back at him as she pondered the different responses she could give him. She settled on one.

"My brother does not force himself upon women as you do," she said, trying not to sound angry or accusing. "I fail to see the similarities."

Devlin cocked his head thoughtfully. "Your family has raped Irish lands for decades," he said. "Our women have been taken back to England as concubines or worse. You know this to be true because you have Irish women working for you at Llansteffan."

"How would you know that?"

"There is a great deal I know."

He was, in fact, correct. Emllyn watched him a moment, studying his handsome face, before relaxing somewhat. The conversation was strangely civil and her terror from moments earlier was gone. "I asked you this once before," she said. "Are you to punish me for the sins of my brother and father, and all of my male relatives before them that have staked a claim in Ireland?"

Devlin shook his head. "Punish you?" he said. "Nay, not punish. But I have made it clear that you belong to me. I will never, ever return you to your brother and it is my intention to breed strong sons from you. If this is distasteful, then I am sorry for you. But it is the way of things."

Emllyn could feel the familiar sting of tears but she resisted. It would do no good to cry, anyway. She had learned that much about him.

"What would you have me say to all of that?" she whispered. "There is nothing I can say and nothing I can do. But you and I have a bargain and I will hold you to it; you want to discover what de Cleveley's plans are for you. I want to know if Trevor is among the captured. I told you that I would discover what I can and I have no intention of going back on my word. You have mentioned that there must be some trust between us – my word is my bond and I would assume the same with you, as a knight. You told me I could see the English captives once our task is finished. I am trusting your word just as you are trusting mine. What more do you want?"

Devlin listened to her reasonable words. She made sense. After a moment, he shook his head. "I told you I believed you when you swore not to betray me," he said. "I still believe you. That has not changed. But… but I do not want to be fighting with you the entire time. We must have some level of cooperation or I fear we will fail, and that will mean death for us both."

Emllyn tried not to give him an expression of total disbelief.

"It is a simple thing to gain cooperation if that is what you truly want," she said. "Untie my hands. Treat me with respect and you shall gain mine in return. Mayhap it is foolish to tell the man who took my innocence that I will show him a measure of respect, but I sense in you a man of honor, Devlin de Bermingham. I am not sure how or why, but I can see it in you. You are indeed a paradox; brutal and barbaric one moment and then civil and intelligent the next. I should hate you with every drop of my blood but I cannot seem to manage it because if I admit it to myself, you indeed have a grievance. I cannot say I would not behave the same way if a family that had no right to my lands or property claimed it for their own. But what you've done to me… I had nothing to do with my brother or father or grandfather's claim in Ireland, yet you have indeed punished me for their sins. The barbarian in you ruined me but the warrior in you… he is a different man, one who is trying to save his people. I can understand that. But the barbarian… I hate him as much as he hates me."

Devlin was stunned by her words. But along with that sensation came a sense of regret and guilt so powerful that he actually had to lower his gaze. He couldn't look her in the eye. He had sworn all along that he would not be sorry for how he had treated her but at this moment, he was. Odd how this one moment in time and the lady's gentle statement had turned the tides in his heart. His remorse was overwhelming, but not enough to let her go completely. She was still his and he intended to keep her, but not simply because she was his captive. There was something about her, as a woman of spirit, that he didn't want to be without.

Silently, he went to the bed and untied the belt, letting her hands go free.

Emllyn sat up, rubbing her wrists and watching him as he

went to the hearth and stoked the fire, throwing a few chunks of peat on it. He seemed very subdued and she wondered if her words had any impact on him. With de Bermingham, it was difficult to tell. She couldn't read the man's moods by any means.

"We will leave early on the morrow so I would suggest you pull together what possessions you plan to bring," he said, giving the fire a final poke before rising. "When I leave this chamber, bolt the door behind me but know I will return."

Emllyn simply nodded, watching the man make his way to the door, catching a glimpse of his big hands as he moved past her and thinking those same heated thoughts she'd had before – hands that had made her feel things she had never felt in her life, sensations of such pleasure that even the mere thought of them was enough to cause her breathing to quicken. She was almost sorry that he was leaving. Part of her wanted him to stay, part of her wanted him to go.

It was a very strange conflict.

Devlin quit the room and Emllyn got up out of the bed to throw the bolt behind him. There was such an odd mood between them, something she pondered deeply as she went in search of her meager possessions as Devlin had instructed. Even as she packed, she thought of him, of their conversation, and how he had seemed rather vulnerable at times.

She knew there was a sensitive man beneath the warrior façade. She could sense it. A barbarian with a poet's soul, a brute with a soft heart he kept hidden. She didn't know how she knew, but she did. As she finished tying off her possessions that she had wrapped up in one of the hides, she lifted her hands to smell them. She could smell Devlin's scent upon them from where she had fought with him.

The scent made her heart flutter.

CHAPTER EIGHT

"**I** THOUGHT YOU said we were going alone," Emllyn said, looking at the escort around them. "Don't you think an escort of this size will attract attention?"

The voyage into enemy territory had begun. It was just past sunrise on a misty spring morning and they were still within sight of Black Castle as they moved south. Wrapped up in the heavy brown cloak that had belonged to Devlin's mother and seated behind him on a fat brown courser, Emllyn was referring to the other horses surrounding them. For a mission that would depend upon secrecy and a tentative lie at best, they were starting out rather boldly about it. There was a whole gang of escorts for allegedly escaped prisoners.

A knight who had been introduced to her as Sir Iver rode point on his shaggy white courser while to their right was another knight known as Sir Shain. They were dressed in traditional Irish *leintes*, or long padded tunics, not armor as English knights would have been. They had shown Emllyn complete indifference, to which she was grateful. Big Irish knights frightened her. There were also several men on foot, blending in with the foggy landscape. They were the eyes and ears of the escort party, protecting them from danger. But most of all, there was a smelly old woman smoking an equally smelly pipe plodding along behind them.

Eefha had been waiting for them before dawn as they went to gather up their horses. She never said a word about riding escort, or about her intentions; she had simply been waiting for them astride a small and worn-looking palfrey near the stables where the other horses were tethered. Devlin didn't say a word to the woman, as if her presence had been expected. Even now, he was fairly dismissive of Emllyn's concerns.

"They will ride with us only a short way," he told her. "When we get within range of de Cleveley's scouts, they will return to Black Castle."

"But what of Eefha?" Emllyn wanted to know. "Will she turn back as well?"

Devlin glance over his shoulder at the old woman, muttering to herself as she plodded along on the palfrey. "I am not sure," he said. "She may choose to go with us. She will be a good set of eyes for us if she does. People often ignore a mad old woman, not realizing that she is indeed taking notice of what goes on around her."

Emllyn looked over her shoulder at the old woman, too. "God's Blood," she muttered. "Even if she does hear something that will be of help, how is she going to tell you? Is she going to tell you a tale of a great battle and hope you understand what she means?"

Devlin fought off a grin. "That has been known to happen."

Emllyn was cut off from replying when Devlin suddenly lifted his right arm, a heavily gloved appendage, and a falcon of magnificent breeding swooped in and landed on it. Startled, Emllyn cowered behind him as the bird fluffed its features and stretched out its wings, settling in on Devlin's arm. He lifted a hand, still holding the reins of the horse, and stroked the bird on its chest with a big finger.

"Where did he come from?" Emllyn asked, eyeing the enormous talons that were cutting into Devlin's leather glove.

Devlin smiled faintly at the bird. "From the gods," he said affectionately. "Have you not yet met Neart?"

Emllyn thought a moment, a flash of a memory from the night she was captured popping into her head. She remembered a big, dark bird hanging over Devlin's head the first time she ever saw him and now the animal's presence was starting to make some sense.

"I think I may have noticed him on the night you and I were introduced," she said somewhat wryly, watching the bird as its head swiveled around, searching for predators or prey. "Is he your pet?"

Devlin nodded. "Pet and protector," he said. "He has been with me for many years. Much like Eefha is an unconventional protector, Neart is much the same. I raised him from a very young bird and he is quite attentive to me."

Emllyn watched the bird as he ruffled his fathers and preened. "He is a beautiful creature," she said. "Do you plan to bring him with us, then? I am not sure an escaped prisoner would have a falcon of this magnificence."

Devlin's focus was still on the bird. "You worry much," he said. Then, he murmured swift words to the bird. "Neart, *cuardach*."

He lifted his arm and the bird took off, sailing into the air like a great preying beast and disappearing into the mist. Emllyn was fixed on the spot where he had vanished, trying to see if she could spot him in the fog.

"Where is he going?" she asked.

Devlin glanced up at the heavy white mist surrounding them. "His eyes are far better than ours at seeking out danger," he said. "If he sees something, he will call out to me."

"Like what?"

"The enemy."

"Patrols from de Cleveley?"

"Aye."

"How far is their settlement from Black Castle?"

"Twenty miles," he replied. "Tonight, our escort will turn back and on the morrow we shall see the English settlement by mid-day."

"Is it possible that de Cleveley has sent patrols this far north?"

Devlin lifted a dark red eyebrow. "After Kildare's defeat three days ago, anything is possible. News of my victory will travel fast and we must be vigilant."

Emllyn fell silent after that, mostly because she wasn't sure what more to say. Three days ago she was on a ship foundering on the Irish coast; now, she was in the midst of a fog in enemy lands, heading for her brother's allied encampment. There was a sense of adventure to it all, of disbelief in the situation in general, but in truth all she could manage to feel was apprehension. This was dangerous, and unfamiliar, ground.

But the course was set and there was no turning back. The party from Black Castle traveled into the mid-morning, avoiding the main road and plodding through fields and copses. Eventually, the mist lifted, revealing the brilliant green landscape of Wicklow.

As they moved inland from the coast, it became dotted with green hills and overgrown vales, and there were patches of heavily forested areas. The grass was very thick and about knee-high on the horses, and they trudged silently through the growth as they made their way over hills and down into ravines. It was long and slow going in the cold and brisk air, but Emllyn remained huddled up against Devlin's back, covered by her borrowed cloak, and it wasn't so bad. As the morning passed into afternoon and they rounded a particularly tall hill and headed down to a vale with a swiftly running stream, Devlin called halt to their travel.

"We will stop here and water the horses," he said. "Take what rest you can. We will not stop again until after dark."

The two knights accompanying them climbed off their coursers and moved the animals to the water to drink. Devlin also dismounted, glancing at their surroundings before turning to help Emllyn from the horse. She was fast, however, and had slid down before he had the chance to assist her. She was already looking around, evidently searching urgently for something.

"I have… business to attend to," she said. "I need some privacy."

He knew what she meant. Overhead, they could hear Neart screeching and Devlin let out a piercing whistle between his teeth, lifting his arm for the bird to zero in on. Only when he was sure the bird was heading in his direction did he turn to Emllyn.

"There is a copse of trees over to the east," he pointed to a group of saplings sprouting from the side of a rocky hill. "Go there but no further."

Emllyn looked at the rather sparse trees. "There is not much privacy there."

"That is your only choice. Take care of your business and be done with it. We must continue on."

Giving him an expression of extremely disapproval, she nonetheless dutifully trudged off in the direction of the trees. Devlin's gaze lingered on her as she moved, distracted only when the bird settled on his arm. Still, his gaze returned to Emllyn as she slugged up the hill towards the trees. Having ridden all morning with her pressed against his back, he was not hard pressed to admit he had liked it. He felt oddly settled and content with her against him, like he'd never felt in his life.

Since he had met her, each hour of the day was bringing him feelings and thoughts he had never believed himself capable of. Each minute was a new discovery and it had occurred to him sometime during the morning that he had ceased to view her as a prisoner and now viewed her as something else. He wasn't entirely sure what; a possession perhaps or something more, something companionable. All he knew was that she didn't seem like his prisoner any longer.

She was something else.

As Emllyn reached the group of trees and faded into them, he returned his attention to Neart. The heavy bird on Devlin's arm began to fuss and he began to dig around in his saddle bags for some jerky for the animal. Neart ate rodents and other small creatures but he was particularly fond of jerky. Just as Devlin laid his hands on a bit of food, the bird suddenly screeched and took off, launching itself into the sky and screaming as it usually did when danger was sighted.

In fact, Devlin's men froze at the sound and looked to the sky. It was an instinct with them; Devlin always took the bird into battle and for very good reason – Neart's bird of prey intuitions were never wrong. They had depended upon the animal's cries at the start of their rebellion and even on the stormy night when Kildare's fleet had come ashore, the bird had alerted them. He had eyes and ears and senses that no human being possessed, so as the bird cried overhead against the cloudy sky, the men instinctively went for their swords. Their first hint at danger wasn't long in coming.

Oblivious to the screaming bird, Emllyn had just finished relieving herself in the grove of trees. As she lowered her skirts and came out of the foliage, she heard a noise behind her. Turning to see a group of men dressed in tartans approaching through the leaves, she let out a yelp of fear and bolted in Devlin's direction. In her haste, however, she slipped on the muddy slope and fell flat on her face. Before she could get to her feet, someone grabbed her by the ankle and she screamed as loud as she could.

"Devlin!"

Devlin and his men saw her near the copse of trees, on her belly as men swarmed around her. Seized with fury and panic, Devlin leapt onto his horse, as did Iver and Shain, and made haste in Emllyn's direction. His foot soldiers, thirty of them clad in stolen tartan from various clanns so de Bermingham men could not be identified to outside observers, ran after the knights on horseback. The scent of battle filled the air and the Irish breathed heavily of it; battles were commonplace and they were prepared. They fed on the rush and were prepared to kill.

Devlin reached Emllyn quickly, just as men were trying to drag her away by her feet. She was fighting them furiously, kicking heads and slapping hands as she was able. Devlin charged his horse right up to her and swung his sword at the nearest man, cleaving his head cleanly off at the shoulders. His head hit the ground right next to Emllyn; in fact, she looked over and next to her shoulder were a pair of sightless eyes gazing back at her. Screaming hysterically, she kicked a man holding her left foot right in the face and bolted to her feet.

A nasty fight was going on around her but the only thing she could see was Devlin's hand reaching for her. Once, she would have recoiled from it but at the moment, it was safety. She grabbed hold of the extended hand and Devlin yanked her up onto his horse. Emllyn settled in behind him, threw her arms around his waist, and held on with a death grip.

With Emllyn safe, Devlin was better able to function. Odd how the moment he saw her being dragged away, his mind had clouded over and all he could see, think, or feel was Emllyn's predicament. Nothing else at that moment mattered. Until she was safe, he could think of nothing else so now that she was tucked in behind him, he was capable of functioning.

Rage overtook him now. These men had tried to abduct Emllyn when she quite clearly belonged to him, so he reckoned to punish them just as he would have punished anyone else who had tried to take what belonged to him. Swords were swinging, as were clubs, and he buried his sword in two of the men who had tried to take Emllyn from him. He had seen them; he never forgot a face and he had singled these men out to pay for their sins. They were all going to pay. Already, it was a bloodbath as Black Sword's fury was unleashed. There were more than one headless body lying about.

Devlin's first thought upon reclaiming Emllyn should have been to remove her from the fighting, but it was not. He felt that she was safe enough on the back of his horse that no one would try for her again, but he was wrong. As he sliced through one man's shoulder, he felt Emllyn lurch behind him. Screaming, she began to slide away but he grabbed her hands, still wrapped around his waist, and realized at that moment that he should probably remove her. As long as she remained with him in battle, she was a target. Spurring his courser forward, he plowed through a gang of fighting men in order to flee to safety.

The horse thundered across the wet grass and towards the area where they had originally paused to rest. Eefha was still there, still sitting on her palfrey and puffing on her shite pipe. As Devlin pulled up beside her on his sweaty, bloodied horse, he was rather surprised when the old woman reached up to pull Emllyn off the steed. Usually she wouldn't have bothered. But as Emllyn slid off the animal, Devlin could see why.

Emllyn had been wounded.

Her left leg and the bottom portion of her surcoat was stained with blood and she winced as Eefha helped her to the ground. Devlin forgot all about the battle going on several dozen yards away; he bailed off his horse and was at her side in a moment.

"Let me see how badly you're wounded," he said calmly, although his heart was racing with fear and adrenalin. "What happened?"

Both Eefha and Devlin lowered Emllyn to the ground. As she sat upon the wet grass, Devlin lifted her surcoat to get a look at the injury.

"Someone with a blade cut me," she said, pain in her voice. "One of those men who tried to carry me away. I think they were aiming for you but when you turned the horse, they cut me instead."

He looked at her as her words sank in. *They were aiming for you.* God, he had been so foolish not to have removed her from the battle immediately. Arrogance had kept him fighting, thinking of himself before he thought of her. Feeling horribly guilty, he returned his focus to her leg to see that she had been sliced cleanly just below the knee, a cut a couple of inches long. It wasn't terribly bad but it was still bleeding a great deal.

"Eefha," he said. "In my saddle bags there are medicaments and boiled linen. Will you please get it?"

Puffing on the pipe and creating a smelly cloud above Emllyn's head, Eefha stood up and went to Devlin's bags. Sticking her hands in, she began pulling forth bandages and other items. Handing them off to Devlin, she then went to her own bags and began rummaging around. Emllyn's attention moved between the old woman's busy movements and Devlin's careful touch on her wound.

"She understood you," she murmured. "I did not think she understood normal language."

Devlin grinned weakly. "She understands more than she lets on," he said. Then, he glanced at her, almost apologetically. "I must put a few stitches in this. It is fairly deep."

Emllyn struggled against her fear; she wasn't very good with pain and didn't relish a needle to her flesh. But she swallowed bravely.

"It will look better to de Cleveley if I have an injury as a result of my escape from Black Sword's dungeon," she said with forced confidence. "How fortunate this occurred."

Devlin didn't believe her for a moment but he admired her courage. "I shall be quick," he said softly.

For the first time since their rough introduction, there was trust in her eyes as she looked at him. Perhaps there was some appreciation, too, for the fact that he had saved her from cutthroats. Whatever the case, there was something different in her expression that he had never before witnessed. Her lips curled into a faint smile.

"Thank you," she murmured.

Devlin smiled in return and then went to work. There was all manner of warmth between them, of gentleness in his touch that Emllyn had never experienced. *It is so odd*, she thought to herself as she watched him tend her wound. *'Tis almost as if he... cares.* But that wasn't possible. She was a concubine and nothing more, as he had reminded her many times. He was simply protecting his property.

As the battle raged on the hillside, Devlin put five small stitches in Emllyn's leg with slippery but thick cat gut and Eefha bandaged it tightly. It had been painful but Emllyn had never uttered a sound. As Eefha mixed powdered willow bark with some water from the stream and had Emllyn drink it, Devlin stood off to the side and watched the battle in the distance dwindle. He would not return to it and leave an old woman and an injured lady unprotected, so he remained where he was and watched as Iver and Shain chased off the remaining bandits.

As Devlin urged Eefha to hurry and finish tending Emllyn, Neart returned from his aerial reconnaissance and Devlin perched the bird on his saddle with a bit of jerky as a reward. When the tide of dirty men finally seemed to be moving well off into the distance, Shain gave a sharp whistle and Devlin's men began to retreat. As Devlin watched, the familiar throng moved back in his direction. It was over, for now.

Fortunately, Devlin hadn't lost any men in the skirmish but he had six wounded, one of them fairly seriously. It was an older soldier who had been cut in the face, slicing through an eye. Shain and a few other men tried very hard to staunch the blood flow and get the man's eye wrapped so they could move out, but it was a bad wound indeed. It took more time than Devlin would have liked to get him stable. They did what they could and then assigned four men to escort all of the wounded back to Black Castle. When Devlin lifted Emllyn onto his courser and ordered his group to move out, ten men headed back for Black Castle while the remaining twenty five continued south towards de Cleveley territory.

"De Cleveley's men?" Devlin asked as they resumed their pace.

Both Shain and Iver were riding to his right; the question was directed at them. They were a bit dirty from the muddy battle but none the worse for wear. Shain was the first to reply.

"Nay," he said. "They were Irish; no English mixed among them, which is usual for de Cleveley. Plus, their weapons were crude and de Cleveley's men are always well armed. They were also wearing O'Byrne tartan. Didn't you notice?"

Devlin thought on that information. His heart sank at the thought of his hated enemy, the clann O'Byrne, a large faction that lived to the north of Black Castle and were the traditional enemy of de Bermingham and their allies, the O'Connor. Devlin hadn't had any trouble from them lately but they were always lurking, waiting to strike. They envied what de Bermingham had.

Devlin fought off a sense of frustration; he had enough trouble with the English. He didn't need the O'Byrnes resuming their raids on top of everything.

"Truthfully, I was so busy trying to assist the lady that I did not have time to notice everything," he admitted. "How many did we kill?"

No one said anything about the fact that Devlin had just called Emllyn the "lady" rather than the "prisoner", or the fact that he had taken her out of the battle and not returned. He had chosen to stay with her, all extremely unusual actions for the usually hands-on commander. If they were confused by it, they kept silent. They focused on his question instead.

"I counted eleven," Iver said. "They had at least thirty or more men. When they retreated, they left the dead."

Devlin glanced over his shoulder at the battle site that was now in the distance. "They will be back for them," he muttered. "We must make sure we are well away by nightfall. I do not wish to remain awake all night waiting for retaliation from O'Byrne."

Shain glanced over his shoulder, scanning the landscape for more threats. "Do you think they followed us out of Black Castle?"

"It is possible," Devlin said. "Those bastards are never far off from us. 'Tis better we get clear of this and settle down for the night."

Everyone seemed to agree on that point and the pace for the group picked up as they moved through a wide brook and into a field full of blooming flowers. Overhead, the overcast sky was beginning to darken and they could smell rain, which would make for unpleasant travel. As Shain and Iver spread out to more vigilantly scan the area, Devlin's attention turned to Emllyn.

She was unusually quiet and rather limp. He gave Neart a soft command and sent the bird up again to scout the area before looking over his shoulder and trying to get a look at Emllyn.

"Does the wound pain you?" he asked.

He heard her sigh heavily. "A little," she said. She sounded groggy. "Whatever Eefha gave me to drink has made me very sleepy. Will it be long before we stop for the night?"

Devlin looked up to the sky, noting that it was growing increasingly dark and that fat, angry black clouds were now blowing in off of the sea.

"A few hours," he said.

She sighed again and he could feel her leaning heavily on his back. "I look forward to it."

Devlin went a few more feet before abruptly bringing the horse to a halt. He dismounted so swiftly that Emllyn nearly fell off because she had been resting against him. But she steadied herself and watched him curiously as he moved her forward in the saddle so that she was nearly sitting on the horse's neck, and then mounted the animal again, only this time he was sitting behind her.

He didn't say a word as he shifted her to a more comfortable position in such a way that she was leaning back against him and her left leg was propped up on the horse's withers. Wrapping his mother's old cloak tightly around her, he pulled her back against his chest and cradled her with his right arm. Then he spurred the horse forward.

"You may sleep now," he told her. "I will steady you so that you will not fall."

He said it emotionlessly but the truth was he went through some trouble to move her around, and him around, so she could be more comfortable. Emllyn was grateful that he had made the effort to ease her.

"I am rather tired," she admitted. "What did Eefha give me?"

Devlin moved her so that she was cradled in his right arm, held against his chest to keep her steady. He glanced at her pale, weary face.

"Poison," he said.

Emllyn's eyebrows shot up. "She did *what*?"

He broke down into snorts, grinning at her reaction. "A

jest," he assured her although her expression remained fearful. "I promise it was not poison. Mayhap it was a potion that will make you sympathetic to the Irish."

Emllyn sighed with relief to realize he was only teasing. It *was* rather devilish and his attempt at humor surprised her. She hadn't seen it in him up until now. But there was nothing humorous about the subject matter of the latter part of his statement.

"What makes you think I am not?" she asked. "I am coming to understand what it is to be held as a slave, robbed of freedom. I believe that qualifies me to understand the oppression you have suffered."

Devlin's humor vanished as he looked down at her, knowing there was unhappy accusation in her tone. He wasn't willing to be reprimanded by her. "The difference is that you did something foolish to end up as you have," he said. "My people have done nothing. We were quite happy ruling our island until the Normans came."

Emllyn looked away. She didn't want to engage him in another conversation of his repressed people so she let the statement fade. She let him get in the last word, at least this time. *I am being compliant,* she reminded herself. Compliance would get her everywhere, she knew. Amidst thoughts of submission and her reward once they were finished with this foolish mission, her eyelids grew droopy again and she faded off into a heavy sleep. In her dreams, a man was there but this time it wasn't Trevor. He had red hair and a red beard, and he used his hands and mouth in ways that made her quiver.

Devlin felt her tremble in her sleep, watching as she twitched and sighed. He tried not to watch her because her subtle movements were arousing him, so he spent most of his time pretending to find interest elsewhere. But his gaze always moved back to Emllyn.

He watched her sleep for the rest of the afternoon.

CHAPTER NINE

Devlin's group had stopped well after dark in a wooded area between two small hills that sheltered them from the surrounding countryside. It was a safe spot and one they could easily protect. A small brook ran to the south and as Iver immediately set sentry posts, the rest of them settled in for the night.

Eefha refused to camp near the men, however. She set up station on the crest of one of the small hills and smoked her pipe, filling the area with the smell of burning shite. She ate from whatever stores she had brought with her and made no move to share anything, so the men went about their business down in the vale below, all but ignoring the strange old woman.

Devlin ignored her for the most part, too, mostly because that was what she wanted. If Eefha wanted to be part of the group, then she would make it so. Otherwise, it was best to let her do what she wanted to do. Devlin was pretty sure she had accompanied them as a chaperone and protector for Emllyn but he wasn't entirely sure. She could be coming along because she knew he was going to the English settlement where she might be able to obtain more things for her collection. With Eefha, it was often difficult to know what her true intentions were.

Devlin had Shain lay down some hides almost the moment they arrived, whereupon he immediately deposited Emllyn. She was still sleeping heavily from Eefha's potion and she remained sleeping as the men set up camp for the night. Devlin allowed them to make a couple of small fires, deep in the shield of the vale, for both warmth and cooking, and they had brought a fair amount of food with them to eat. Rabbit was the main course and it was into the night that the smells of succulent roasting rabbit lifted.

But the smell didn't wake Emllyn, nor did the commotion, for she remained sleeping where Devlin had put her. Several feet away from the group and away from the fire, she slept soundlessly as Devlin, Shain, and Iver sat around one fire while the rest of the men huddled around the other. Both Shain and Iver noticed that Devlin kept glancing over to the sleeping lady as he sucked down his roast rabbit. In fact, he seemed more interested in her than in the rabbit.

Clues were starting to come together that neither Shain nor Iver wanted to believe. They had seen evidence of them earlier when their commander had tended to a wounded woman rather than leave her to someone else. Anytime Devlin de Bermingham voluntary left a battle, there was something odd afoot. More than that, it was in the way he spoke of her or looked at her. Something was in his expression when he spoke of the lady, something both confusing and strange, and his men were starting to figure it out. What their sharp minds told them was something both incredulous and distasteful.

"We will head back before dawn," Shain said as he tossed aside the bones he had been sucking on. "I would head back tonight but with what happened this afternoon, I think it would be safer for all of us if we camped here for the night and got a fresh start in the morning."

Devlin extended a piece of meat to Neart, who was perched on a rock beside him. "Agreed," he said. "De Cleveley's settlement is about a half day's travel from here. I think we can make it there without further incident."

"Unless you run into a patrol from de Cleveley," Iver said. He was well into his bladder of ale, looking drunk and sleepy. "Have you schooled the woman well on how she is to behave and what she is to say? I will admit that I worry, Dev. This entire undertaking has my stomach in knots."

Devlin eyed his friend, feeding the bird more meat. "I told you," he replied calmly, "that she understands any betrayal will result in the death of thirty-three English prisoners. It is enough to motivate her."

"Did you tell her that her lover is alive and among them?" Iver asked.

Devlin shook his head. "Why would I?" he replied. "If I did, I would lose my leverage."

He glanced over his shoulder again as he said it. As he was looking at Emllyn, Iver and Shain exchanged knowing glances. It was Shain who finally spoke.

"Dev," he began slowly. "The woman… is there something else we should know about her?"

Devlin looked at him. "Like what?"

Shain cocked an eyebrow, pointing in Emllyn's direction. "Like you cannot take your eyes off of her?" he said. "We have been watching you all day with her and I can say without a doubt that I have never seen you treat any prisoner the way you are treating her."

Devlin cooled; he didn't like his motives or actions questioned. More than that, the confusion and attraction he had been feeling towards Emllyn was something that evidently he'd been indiscreet about. He immediately went on the defensive.

"Mayhap that is because she is unlike any prisoner we have ever had," he said with an expression on his face that dared them to contradict him. "She is the most valuable prisoner we have ever had the fortune to come across and, quite literally, our entire rebellion can hinge on her because of who she is and what she can do for our cause. Can you not see that?"

Shain and Iver could see he was defensive, but he was also making sense. Perhaps there wasn't more to the man's attitude towards the prisoner than simple and uncomplicated concern; still, he was being extraordinarily attentive to the point of suspicion. After a moment of reflection, Shain nodded.

"I do," he replied. "But I will say this, Dev, because you are my friend and I know you understand that my motives are true. Do not let yourself become emotionally involved with her; mayhap she is using her feminine wiles on you and you have been blinded by her charm. Mayhap she is well-spoken and intelligent, enough so that she is able to manipulate you. Whatever the case, do not let her sway you from your mission, my friend. It will be the death of you."

Devlin didn't become enraged as he might have if someone else had been truthful with him. After a moment of staring into Shain's eyes, he simply hung his head and put the rest of his rabbit bones in front of Neart, who picked at them eagerly. Devlin found that, for some reason, he couldn't look the man in the eye. He was afraid he would see emotion there that didn't belong.

"She will not sway me," he said quietly. "But it is important to keep her safe and close to me if we are to achieve the goals I have set. I want to know what de Cleveley and Kildare are planning and that woman over there is the only way I can find out."

Shain watched Devlin as the man wiped his fingers off on his breeches. He noticed that he was having difficulty meeting his eye, which only served to fuel his suspicions that Devlin was feeling something for the English prisoner. Still, the man had denied it. It was possible that he didn't even realize it.

"I hope so," Shain finally said after a lengthy pause, one that was filled with unvoiced doubt. "I sincerely hope so. In any case, when do you think we can expect to see your return? Do you have a timeline planned?"

Devlin inhaled thoughtfully, glad to be off the uneasy subject of Emllyn. "It is difficult to know," he said. "The lady will need to gain the confidence of de Cleveley's people first and that will take time. It will be weeks, at least. Try to hold off Freddy and his hunger for power for at least that long. I will return as soon as I can but I would say that if I have not returned within two months, then you will assume something has happened to me. If you can send scouts in to infiltrate the settlement and find me, it might be a good idea. If the lady betrays me and I end up in the stocks, I will need help."

It was the first time he admitted that such a thing might be possible. Shain simply nodded while Iver finished drinking his entire bladder. He didn't like any of this and worry of this magnitude was often drowned in drink. He simply couldn't help himself. The entire situation had him on edge.

Shain, Iver, Neart, and the rest of Devlin's men were gone well before sunrise, back to Black Castle to await the fate of their leader and his English captive. Would Devlin's scheme work? Would the lady betray him?

Only time would tell.

THE SMELL OF smoke was heavy.

As Emllyn emerged from a deep and heavy sleep, the first thing she became aware of was the acrid smell of smoke as it filled her nostrils. It seemed difficult to breathe so she tried to move her head, away from the smoke, but it seemed to be everywhere. Coughing, she opened her eyes.

It was a cold and dreary morning, just before sunrise. She knew that because she could see a faint gray glow through the clouds to the east and the birds were starting to rouse for the day. There was quite a bit of bird chatter. As she looked around, she noticed that the smoke was coming from a smoldering fire a few feet away. The misty morning was causing the smoke to lay close to the ground, which was why the smell was so heavy. She also noticed that there was no one else around; Devlin's men had evidently already left for home. Rolling onto her back, she found herself looking up at Devlin.

He was leaning over his satchel, dressed in clothing she'd never seen before; usually, the man was impeccably attired in a leather vest, leather breeches, and a long Irish tunic that always seemed to be remarkably clean. But at the moment he was dressed in what amounted to little more than rags. He was a very big man all wrapped up in a ratty tunic, rough hose, and a big cloak that had holes in it. But that wasn't the worst of it; he had shaved off all of his beautiful red hair and was as bald as a stone.

Startled, Emllyn sat up, her eyes wide on his appearance.

She hardly recognized him. Somewhere between last night and this morning, he had shaved all of the hair off of his head but had left his beard intact. Rubbing her eyes as if to clarify the shocking vision, she peered at him more closely.

"God's Blood," she muttered. "What have you done to yourself?"

Devlin looked up from where he was stuffing the remainder of his possessions into his satchel. The look on her face somewhat amused him. "So you are awake? You slept the sleep of the dead."

Emllyn didn't want to talk about that. She wanted to talk about his drastic appearance and she pointed a finger at him. "You are bald!"

His eyes widened and his hand flew up to his head. Letting out a short, high-pitched scream that would have made a woman proud, he ran his hand over his shiny scalp. "What happened to me hair?" He embellished the words greatly and Emllyn retracted the pointing finger, puzzled by his reaction for a moment before realizing he was jesting with her. Rather than giggle at him or ignore it altogether, she decided to play along.

"Mayhap the fairies took it," she said. "I hear they are all over these lands. Mayhap they shaved you bald in the night. Did you not notice?"

His brow furrowed thoughtfully as he rubbed his scalp. "Am I still beauteous?"

She turned her nose up at him. "I would not know," she said stiffly as she rose to her knees. "I have never noticed that about you one way or the other."

He could sense a game afoot, one that bordered on gentle flirtation. "Be truthful," he prodded. "You have noticed that about me and more."

She snorted as she stood wearily, wincing when her injured leg pained her. It was swollen and achy this morning. "What more is there?" she wanted to know. "You have your adoring Irish throng to tell you how beauteous you are. You do not need me."

He fought off a grin. "Aye, I do," he replied. "I need the rumors of my comeliness to be spread all over England and Wales. Will you start these stories?"

Emllyn looked at him, an expression of utter disinterested on her face. "I would spread stories of your arrogance," she said, noticing that he was fighting off a grin. It made her want to grin, too. "But if you allow me to return home when I have served my purpose with de Cleveley, mayhap I will consider telling everyone that you are generous and pleasant-looking."

He lifted a red eyebrow. "That is the best you can do? That I am pleasant-looking?"

"I would not consider my captor any better than pleasant-looking. I should not even contemplate that."

The banter faded as the Emllyn brought about the reality of the situation between them. He was so willing to overlook it, to morph it into something more than it was, but Emllyn was unwilling to entertain the thought. She was a prisoner, a concubine as he once put it. But she had to admit he could be charming when the mood struck him. She'd seen glimpses if it before. He had a very infectious charm that was difficult to resist.

He was also quite smart and able to read the situation for what it was. Devlin sensed that perhaps she was softening to him somewhat. It was in her manner, the way she looked at him. There were moments when she let her guard down and he could see that intelligent, warm woman that he wanted to see more of.

"At the moment, I am not your captor," he said quietly. "I am a fellow prisoner. We are equals. We will enter de Cleveley's settlement as equals and we will leave as equals. You want something from me, I want something from you, and we will combine our forces to ensure each of us gets what we want. That makes us equal."

He was correct in a sense. But it was a technicality. "Then if I wanted to go home now, you would let me, as an equal, of course."

"If you go home, you will never find out if your lover is in my vault."

Stymied, Emllyn thought a moment before regrouping. "It has not occurred to me until now," she said, "but you could be lying for all I know. I never actually saw any prisoners at all. Who is to say that you have any? This could be an overt fabrication."

"If it is, then you fell for it," Devlin said, cutting her down. "Who would be the bigger fool? Me for fabricating it or you for falling for it?"

He had her. Emllyn sighed heavily before averting her gaze. "I am the biggest fool of all for stowing away on my brother's warships to begin with," she muttered with regret. "But you and I have a bargain and I will not go back on my word. Before we enter de Cleveley's settlement, mayhap you should tell me what it is I am supposed to say so that we have our stories straight."

Feeling victorious in their battle of words, Devlin finished cinching up his satchel. "I touched on it before but to be clear, you will indeed tell them the truth – you are Kildare's sister and you stowed away on your brother's war fleet," he said as he finished with his bag and moved for the hides that had constituted her bed. "You will tell them that Black Sword captured you and threw you in the vault, where you were stored with other prisoners, of which I was one. We were able to escape when I overpowered a guard and stole his keys, and we escaped in the middle of the night through a postern gate near the kitchens. I have accompanied you because I am a mute and have nowhere else to go. You will stress that I am to be kept with you because you feel safe with me; otherwise, they could throw me in the vault again."

Emllyn watched him as he rolled up the hides and basically cleaned up their camp. All of it seemed like a very daunting task. "I will admit that I am apprehensive," she said. "I have never done anything like this before. I am not sure if I can be convincing."

"If you are not convincing, you will never see your lover again."

"And they will kill you."

"I would prefer that not happen."

It was a wry statement, a bit of levity to break the tension. With a heavy sigh, Emllyn nodded. "Very well, then," she said, pulling the cloak more tightly about her against the early morning dew. "Let us get started. Where is Eefha?"

She was looking around, trying to see through the mist. Devlin took the hides and his satchel and began heading up one of the small hills that surrounded the vale.

"I do not know," he said. "She was gone this morning before my men pulled out."

"Do you think she went back to Black Castle?"

"It is hard to say with her."

Emllyn began looking around as if she could somehow spot the small old woman in all of this fog. She felt a strange sense of loss with Eefha gone because she had established something of an attachment to the woman who had saved her from the frightening Irish knight who had come pounding on her door. She was so involved in scanning the mist that it took her a moment to notice that Devlin had all but disappeared. Curious, she made her way towards the hill where she last saw him when she suddenly saw the tree on top of the mound rattle. Peering closer, she could see Devlin up in the branches of the big, old oak.

"What are you doing?" she called up to him.

The branches rattled and one of them, a rather large branch, crashed to the ground. "Hiding my possessions," he said. "We may need them when we escape and head back to Black Castle. I want to try to keep them safe."

"In a tree?"

"In a tree. No one ever thinks to look up in a tree."

Emllyn watched the man fumble around in the branches before eventually lowering himself to the ground. For such a big man, he climbed rather agilely. He brushed the prickly oak leaves off of his ragged clothing as he approached.

"There, now," he said. "All finished. How is your leg, by the way?"

Emllyn instinctively put her hand down to the painful, swollen spot. "It hurts."

"We have quite a bit of walking to do. Can you make it?"

"I will have to."

"If it becomes too painful, I will carry you."

She looked at him as if disgusted by the suggestion. "You will do no such thing," she said primly. "I will walk."

She was being stubborn about it. As she tried to walk away from him, he grabbed her by the arm.

"Wait," he commanded softly. "Sit down."

Emllyn frowned. "Why?"

His reply was to direct her to a rock that was jutting out of the side of the hill and pushed her down on it. As she fussed at him, he lifted her skirt to reveal the wrap that Eefha had put on it. He went to unwrap it but Emllyn tried to stop him. Pushing her hands away, he unwrapped the wound.

An angry, oozing injury faced him and his heart sank. He could see that it was becoming poisonous and he touched it, feeling that it was very hot. Emllyn winced in pain at his touch and pushed his hand away, but he ended up cupping her face with both hands to feel that she was with fever. It wasn't bad but he knew it soon would be. He tried not to feel an inordinate amount of panic.

"Your wound is developing poison," he told her as he took his hands from her face. "You have a fever."

Startled, Emllyn put her hands to her face as if to confirm his diagnosis. "I do?" she felt her cheeks. "But I do not feel terrible, simply tired."

Devlin's gaze lingered on her face a moment before returning his attention to her leg. He sighed heavily. "This changes things," he muttered. "I cannot take you back to Black Castle because it is too far away on foot. De Cleveley's settlement is closer."

Emllyn was puzzled by the comment. "We are going there anyway, are we not?" she said. "I fail to see why anything has changed."

She wasn't feeling his apprehension; Devlin could see that. Either she was too foolish or too naïve to realize the danger she was in, but he brushed it all aside. He had to get her to help no matter how unconcerned she was. But he would try to do what he could before they set out on foot, at least enough to keep the poison from growing rapidly. They had so very few possessions with them, and certainly nothing that could ease poison from the body. They were supposed to be escaped prisoners, and escapees didn't usually travel well-stocked. Thinking quickly, he stood up and pointed a finger at her.

"Remain here," he instructed. "Don't move."

He moved away from her before she could answer and headed to the small steam that flowed near the base of one of the hills that surrounded the vale. Emllyn's attention was divided between her swollen, oozing injury and Devlin's movements. He crouched down beside the stream and she could see that he was doing something although she couldn't see exactly what. It looked to her as if he was playing in the mud along the banks of the idyllic water. He was rubbing and kneading very seriously. Eventually, he stood up with his hands cupped together and headed back in her direction.

Emllyn watched curiously as he knelt beside her and began packing mud against her wound. But there was something else in the mud because she could see white and green flecks. He packed the mud tightly and she winced.

Devlin noticed that she was flinching with every poke and every press, but she didn't utter a sound. She seemed more interested in watching him work.

"What are you doing?" she finally asked.

Devlin wiped his muddy hands off on his hose and picked up the bandage that had been wrapped around her wound. He began to re-wrap it.

"The mud will help draw out any poison," he said. "I found some snowdrops and clover by the stream which helps with healing. I'm afraid it is the best I can do for now. I don't have anything else with me to tend the wound so we will have to make haste to de Cleveley's village and depend on their mercy."

Emllyn watched him as he tightened the bandage. "I truly do not feel that bad," she assured him softly because he seemed to be worrying a great deal. "I am tired, but other than that I feel well enough."

Devlin didn't say anything. He didn't want to frighten her. Truthfully, her wound could go either way; it could clear up on its own or it could get very, very bad. He hoped it wasn't the latter. When he was finished tightening the bandage he scooped her up into his big arms and stood up.

"You will not be walking," he informed her in a tone that suggested the subject was not up for debate. "I will carry you the rest of the way."

Emllyn wrapped her arms around his neck purely to steady herself, realizing almost instantaneously that the last time she was this close to him, he was doing unspeakable things to her. She could smell his skin and feel his warmth all around her, and her heart began to thump against her ribs. Perhaps it was fear, but it didn't feel like it. It felt more like excitement.

The man was big, strong, and passionate about everything he did. During the times he'd taken her, it had been with such passion that, although rightly terrified and embarrassed, it was something that had ultimately not left an unpleasant taste in her mouth. He hadn't hurt her in any way; all he'd done is give her pleasure like she had never known to exist. More and more, she realized she couldn't bring herself to hate him for it. It was a ridiculous realization, but one she couldn't deny.

Cradled in Devlin's arms as he began their trek south towards de Cleveley lands, Emllyn tried not to look at him more than necessary and she definitely tried not to make eye contact with him. Her thoughts were running from silly, foolish thoughts of the man's powerful arms to the reflection of the past three days with him. She was more concerned than she dared to admit about the man placing himself in danger simply to gain information that might save his people and, consequently, his rebellion.

Emllyn was very concerned that she might say or do the wrong thing that might jeopardize her chances of keeping her end of the bargain, but more than that, she was concerned that something terrible might befall Devlin. He was a rebel, a thief, and in many eyes a murderer as well, but he was also someone who was trying to do something noble for his people and doing it any way he could. Her opinion, and her defiance against him, was starting to waver.

After an hour or so of such thoughts, her mind began to grow muddled and weary. It wasn't long before her head was against his shoulder and her eyes were drooping. She was so very, very tired, and she soon fell into a deep and dreamless sleep.

Emllyn was passed out cold with a raging fever by the time the old wooden and stone walls of de Cleveley's settlement came into view shortly after mid-day.

CHAPTER TEN

T HE GREAT SETTLEMENT of the House of de Cleveley, heirs to the barony of Bowland, was one of the largest Norman settlements in Ireland. An early Lord de Cleveley had come to Ireland a few years after William the Conqueror had started his systematic takeover of England and had staked out rich and prosperous lands in Wicklow with the help of a few thousand Norman soldiers. He used local and conquered tribes to build him a castle in the village of Wicklow proper and also one to the south near the small village of Glenteige.

Wicklow Castle had been captured by the O'Byrnes about five years earlier. On the coattails of the O'Byrnes, Devlin and his father had managed to clear the de Cleveleys out of a major portion of Wicklow and subsequently chase the Fitzgeralds out of neighboring lands, resulting in the capture of Black Castle. While Devlin had an organized rebellion against Kildare with the purpose of regaining a massive portion of Wicklow for the de Berminghams, the O'Byrnes ran wild in Ulster, burning and looting and killing, which had reduced the de Cleveley holdings to the southern portion of the county.

It was a bit of a complex situation and one that was extraordinarily volatile. It was for that reason that the de Cleveley settlement was surrounded by an enormous wall built from wood and stone, and surrounded by a ditch that was several miles in length. The ditch was filled with seawater which washed in with the tides because some Norman engineer had designed an ingenious system. It was a fairly impregnable compound.

Devlin had never been inside the complex but he had seen it, many times, and he had even helped the O'Connors lay siege to it twice. He knew that the wall surrounded a settlement that housed several thousand people and he also knew there was a central castle and keep buried deep in the complex. Being that it was a village, a living and breathing entity, the gatehouse remained open during the day for trade and commerce to commence. There were always dozens of guards near the gates and the gatehouse itself were heavily manned by English soldiers who hated the sound or sight of anything Irish.

It was going to be a problem for Devlin considering the plans he had forged at Black Castle, the scheme he and Emllyn had rehearsed over and over, was now nil. Emllyn had been unconscious for a few hours at least and would be unable to tell anyone who, or what, she was. Worse, Devlin's plans of pretending to be a mute were now dissolved. He had to speak because Emllyn couldn't, so he had spent the past two hours desperately trying to concoct a believable story. He'd come up with two or three versions but wasn't entirely comfortable with any of them. Still, he had little choice; Emllyn needed a surgeon. With each step he took, he was growing increasingly worried over her condition.

He found himself wishing Eefha had not deserted them because he knew the old woman would know what to do. Eefha had a way of healing. He also began to wonder if it wouldn't have been better for him to return to Black Castle, but that would have taken at least two days on foot. It was no option at all. As he drew closer to the gatehouse of the de Cleveley settlement, he braced himself for what was to come and prayed he could come across convincingly in this new plan he was forced to perpetuate. Their lives depended on it.

Being that it was after midday, most of the farmers and other vendors that usually did business in the morning hours were gone and there wasn't a great deal of traffic at the gates. Sentries were checking everyone who entered the complex and as Devlin drew close, he took a deep breath for courage and moved towards two English soldiers who were watching the activity of the gates.

"M'lords," he said, trying to sound timid and polite. "I have come from the north. There was a great sea battle there four nights ago at Black Castle. Have ye heard?"

The soldiers, dressed in well-worn mail and de Cleveley tunics, looked at him with both curiosity and suspicion.

"What sea battle?" an older soldier asked.

"Kildare," Devlin said, struggling not to react to these English soldiers who represented everything he hated. He'd probably fought them on many occasions, and even killed some of their kin, but he couldn't think of that now. "Kildare came ashore at Black Castle and was destroyed by Black Sword. Have you not heard the news?"

The soldiers looked at him with shock. One even called his superior officer and relayed the news. The superior officer was an older knight, short and bald, with dark eyes and a growth of beard. He eyed Devlin a moment, his focus shifting between Emlyn's limp form and the very big Irishman in rags.

"What's this you say about a battle at Black Castle?" he asked. "Where did you come from?"

Devlin increasingly struggled with his attitude towards the haughty English. He wanted very much to reach out a massive fist and smash the swagger right out of the knight's face. Instead, he clutched Emllyn tighter, finding a strange and calming comfort in her. She soothed him in ways he couldn't begin to understand.

"To the north about ten miles, m'lord," he said. "I have a farm to the south of Black Castle. There was a great sea battle four nights ago and the English were defeated. I have come because this woman washed upon the shore and I found her. Before she went unconscious, she told me that her name was Emllyn Fitzgerald, sister to the Earl of Kildare. She's very sick, m'lord. She needs help. I tried to tend her but she is so much worse."

The bald knight's gaze lingered on Devlin a moment before focusing on Emllyn. He went to her, peering down at her unconscious face curiously. He eyed the clothing she wore, as it was Irish in design and fabric. He didn't look particularly sympathetic.

"What would Kildare's sister be doing on a battle armada?" he asked dubiously.

Devlin didn't hesitate. "She said something about witnessing the victory for her brother," he replied. "Will you please help her?"

The knight eyed Devlin for a long moment before turning and walking back into the gatehouse. Devlin could see him in the shadows of the gate, speaking with another man dressed in expensive mail. The second man was tall, with gray hair, and he kept looking at Devlin as the bald knight spoke to him. Finally, he emerged from the gatehouse and approached Devlin with the bald knight following close behind.

"Who are you?" the gray-haired knight demanded. "No lies, now. Who has sent you?"

Devlin didn't like the man in the least; he had a very clipped and unsympathetic manner about him. Rather than react with hostility, he fought down his instincts and labored for control.

"As I told these other knights, m'lord, there was a great battle at Black Castle four nights ago," he said. "Kildare's fleet was destroyed and this woman washed upon the shore. She says she is Kildare's sister. She is very ill so I brought her here."

The gray-haired knight did the same thing the others did; his gaze lingered on Devlin with suspicion before turning his attention to Emllyn. He leaned over to peer at her but didn't touch her. After a few moments of inspection, he lifted his eyebrows.

"Hmmm," he said. "I was not aware that Kildare had a sister. Even if he did, what on earth would she be doing on a ship bound for battle?"

Devlin repeated what he'd told the bald knight. "She said that she was there to see victory on behalf of her brother," he replied. "She has a bad wound on her leg. Will you please help her?"

The gray-haired knight pondered the question. He stepped back from Devlin, sizing him up. "What do you do?" he demanded. "Are you a warrior? A soldier? Answer me."

"I am a farmer," Devlin replied quickly. "I tend the soil. I grow vegetables and sell them at market."

"Where at market?"

Devlin had already told them his farm was south of Black Castle so there was no alternative but to tell him the closest marketplace which, in fact, was Black Castle. He had absolutely no choice and prayed his answer wouldn't cost him.

"At Black Castle," he replied steadily. "It is the nearest marketplace."

The gray-haired knight's manner turned to one of marginal interest. "You have been inside the castle?"

Devlin nodded. "I have."

"Do you know Black Sword?"

"Do *you*?"

The gray-haired knight wriggled his eyebrows and glanced at the soldiers around him. "Nay," he admitted reluctantly. "But you did not answer my question. Do you know him?"

Devlin replied carefully. "I have seen men I was told were his generals but Black Sword keeps himself hidden," he said. "I was told the man is eight feet tall and breathes fire."

That brought a grin from the gray-haired knight. "Ah, the ignorance of the Irish, and this one as big as a bull."

The men around him laughed at Devlin's expense. After that, they all seemed to loosen up a great deal as they came to realize that Devlin wasn't there to do them any harm. Devlin was trying to come across as an ignorant peasant and evidently doing a good job of it from the reaction of the English. The gray-haired knight nodded his head in Emllyn's direction.

"One of my men will take her," he said. "As for you, I am interested in speaking with you further to discover what more you know about Black Castle."

Devlin didn't like that at all. He shook his head. "I will not leave the lady, m'lord," he said as respectfully as he could. "I found her and I am responsible for her. I'll not leave her alone with a host of English soldiers to molest her."

The smile faded from the gray-haired knight's lips and his

eyes turned hard. "Turn her over," he commanded. "You will come with me."

Devlin refused and took a step back, away from a soldier who was coming for Emllyn. But the man came too close and Devlin threw out a big elbow, catching the man in the face. Blood spurted and as he fell back, a gang of soldiers rushed forward with the intention of separating him from Emllyn. As Devlin held Emllyn tightly and prepared to fight for his life, a shout from the gatehouse brought the mounting skirmish to a dead-halt.

"Cease!" a man roared. "De Ferrer, what goes on there?"

Sir George de Ferrer, the gray-haired knight, turned swiftly in the direction of the command, as did Devlin and the other soldiers. Standing just inside the gatehouse was a tall, well-dressed knight with a very finely clad woman on his arm. The gray-haired knight immediately broke away from the group and headed towards the pair.

"My lord," he greeted politely, then bowed respectfully to the woman. "Lady Elyse. You are looking very well this day."

The well-dressed knight spoke before the woman on his arm could respond. "What is going on?" he asked. "Who is that man? And what happened to the woman he is carrying?"

De Ferrer looked over his shoulder at Devlin, now surrounded by a host of hostile English soldiers.

"That man claims he is a farmer from the Black Castle area," he said. "He told us that four nights ago, there was a great and terrible sea battle in which the forces of the Earl of Kildare were defeated by Black Sword. The man says that the woman in his arms washed up on shore after the battle and that she is badly injured. He also told us that she is the sister of the Earl of Kildare."

Before the well-dressed knight could reply, the woman on his arm, the Lady Elyse, let go of his arm and swiftly made her way over to Devlin. The English soldiers gave her a wide berth, making way for her, as she came to within a few feet of Devlin. She came to a halt, then, and looked timidly at Devlin.

"I am the Lady Elyse," she introduced herself politely. Then she gestured at Emllyn. "May I see her, please? I only wish to help."

Devlin gazed steadily at the Englishwoman; she was short, with very blond hair and big blue eyes. She had a very polite and practiced way about her, refined and elegant, and Devlin was put at ease. He couldn't sense anything hostile from her in the least. After a moment, he nodded stiffly, and Lady Elyse advanced.

With small, white hands, she carefully touched Emllyn's face and lifted up an eyelid, peering at a sightless eye. Then she felt the pulse on her neck. When she was done with that, she looked up at Devlin.

"What happened to her?" she asked. "Where is she injured?"

"Her leg," Devlin replied. "She has a wound that is poisonous. She needs help or she will die."

Lady Elyse nodded fervently. "I will help her, have no fear," she said, her gaze lingering on Devlin. "What is your relationship to her?"

Devlin was moderately honest, at least as much as he intended to be. "I found her," he said. "I am responsible for her. I will not leave her alone with men I do not know or trust."

Lady Elyse smiled faintly. "I do not blame you," she said. "Will you trust her with me?"

"I will."

Lady Elyse turned to the men behind her. "I will take the lady to my chamber," she announced. "Send the surgeon to me immediately."

At her command, men began to move. It was as if God himself had issued the order. As a soldier ran off to fetch the surgeon, the well-dressed knight who had been Lady Elyse's escort was evidently uncomfortable with what she was suggesting. He sought to plead with her.

"Your chamber?" he repeated. "We could put her in the servant's quarters just as well. She does not need to be in your chamber."

Lady Elyse turned to him. "She is very ill," she said, seriously but sweetly. "I must tend her and you would not want me spending an inordinate amount of time in the servant's quarters, would you?"

The man was trapped. He cleared his throat unhappily. "Of course not," he said. "But *your* chamber?"

Lady Elyse waved him off as she walked past him, turning to motion Devlin to follow. "Bring her along," she told him. "Hurry, now. There is no time to waste."

Devlin didn't argue; he found himself thanking God for the appearance of this small woman who could move men to do her bidding better than any battle commander. Swiftly, he moved after her, not daring to look at the English warriors he was leaving behind in his wake.

Lady Elyse was fast as she led him through the gatehouse and out into the complex beyond. Devlin glanced at his surroundings as he followed her; it was as if an entirely new world opened up before him, one of neat dirt avenues and huts made from wattle and daub, with thatched roofs. People were everywhere, children and men and women, going about their daily lives. Lady Elyse led him through a town square of sorts, small in size, but with a central well and businesses and trades surrounding it. He could smell the acrid smoke from the smithy shacks. Everything was surprisingly well organized and more populated than he would have imagined. It was an interesting bit of knowledge on a well-protected settlement. This was some of the intelligence he was hoping to obtain.

But he didn't have much time to inspect his surroundings as Lady Elyse swiftly took him down a larger avenue which opened up at the end. Spread before him in all of its glory was another wall, this one of big gray stone, with a moat around it. The moat was as a moat should be; filled with muck and sewage, smelling up the area horrifically. The site was heavily guarded and Lady Elyse waved off the soldiers who stepped forward to inspect Devlin. The men backed away, eyeing Devlin with hostility and suspicion, as the Lady Elyse brought him into the guarded complex.

Inside the inner compound, the layout was simple; there was a block of stables to the left, another wattle and daub building to the right that was big enough for a substantial great hall, and the keep directly in front of him.

It was the keep that had his attention as Lady Elyse led him towards it. It was at least three stories, built of the same gray stone that the wall was built from. It was sunk deep into the side of a small hill, as the entire complex was on a slight slope, and the entry door that opened wide to them was a massive thing built of iron and wood. The keep was also built in an odd shape; it seemed to have what looked like small wings off to the east and the west. He didn't have time to study it, however, as Lady Elyse brought him swiftly into the dark depths of the donjon.

Once inside, Devlin struggled to adjust his eyes to the darkness. The massive door had been deceiving, for the entry it opened into was very small and box-shaped. There were also holes in the walls on either side of the room and he realized they were archer holes; should the door be breached, archers would be positioned to shoot down anyone foolish enough to enter. It was rather clever.

Lady Elyse directed them down the narrow corridor leading from the entry, which opened up into a large room that stretched for the length of the keep. It was a feasting hall because it had several well-worn tables arranged in it and a massive hearth that was spitting ribbons of gray smoke into the air. Dogs were wandering the room, scavenging for scraps, and Lady Elyse rushed past them. At the far end of the chamber was a spiral staircase, built into the thickness of the wall, and she encouraged Devlin to follow her.

He did, struggling with his bulk to make it up the stairs and not smack Emllyn's head into the wall into the process. It was then that he realized several men were following them including Lady Elyse's escort. Devlin wasn't surprised but he knew he might be in for great difficulty once he turned Emllyn over to Lady Elyse's care. He was fairly certain the English were going to try and separate him from Emllyn. He had to be prepared.

The third floor was arranged exactly like the second floor which, he discovered, was fairly complex in design. This was a Norman castle and reflected the engineering skills of that race. The third floor also had the big room that stretched the length of the keep, this one with big wooden dividers in it that separated bed chambers, but next of this room was a second room that also stretched the length of the keep. It was into this chamber that Lady Elyse took him.

"There," she pointed at an enormous canopied bed over

near the equally enormous hearth. "Please put her there."

Devlin did as he was told, making his way through the sumptuous and well-appointed chamber to lay Emllyn gently on the bed that was surely covered in feathers. He'd never seen anything so light or soft. He stood there a moment, gazing apprehensively at Emllyn, as Lady Elyse came up beside him.

"Where is her wound?" she asked.

Devlin lifted Emllyn's skirts to reveal the bandaged left leg. "Here," he said. "It looks like a battle wound, evidence that she was indeed in some sort of battle. That is why I believed what she said, that she was on Kildare's armada. And she… she is very fine. Her hands are fine and her skin is fine. She is a woman of great breeding."

He didn't realize that his voice had softened dramatically as he spoke of Emllyn, but Lady Elyse was very aware. In fact, she actually came to a halt in her inspection of the unconscious lady, staring at the massive farmer who spoke of the woman with such tenderness. It was a surprising show of emotion.

"I promise I will take great care of her," she assured Devlin softly. "Now, let me take a look at her wound."

Devlin was very aware of the English knights standing back by the door to the chamber. He could feel their stares upon his back. He knew they wanted to speak with him but he remained next to the bed, vigilant, as Lady Elyse carefully unwrapped Emllyn's leg. As she pulled the last of the wrappings off, she saw the mud poultice and stopped any further unwrapping.

"Sir," she said to Devlin as she gestured over near the hearth. "There is a bell for the servant. Will you please ring it?"

Devlin looked over his shoulder. He saw no bell at first glance but he saw a silken cord that was strung up along the top of the wall. Following the silk cord until it ended, he could see a big silver bell at the end of it. He tugged on the end of the cord so hard that it pulled right off and rang the bell crazily. He turned to Lady Elyse apologetically with the cord still in his hand.

"I am sorry," he told her, laying the cord down at the end of the bed. "I suppose I shouldn't have pulled so hard."

Lady Elyse was grinning. "You must be careful with your strength," she agreed, eyeing the pure size of the man. He was quite handsome in her opinion, and she thought the fact that he seemed so protective over the lady to be very sweet. "What is your name?"

Devlin hesitated slightly; it was the only part of his plan he hadn't covered because up until a few hours ago, he was to be a mute. He wouldn't have to tell anyone his name and he figured that Emllyn would call him something and he would just accept it. But now, he had been asked, so he said the first thing that came to mind.

"John, m'lady," he said. "It was my father's name."

It wasn't a lie; indeed, it was his father's name. Lady Elyse smiled politely. "You are a farmer?" she said, repeating what she had heard the soldiers say. "That is a difficult profession. No wonder you are so strong. You must work very hard."

Devlin could see that Lady Elyse was a genuinely kind woman and he was surprised; all he'd ever heard of English women was that they were frail and silly. But Emllyn had changed his opinion and now Lady Elyse was coming to change it as well. He nodded at her statement.

"Aye, m'lady."

Lady Elyse maintained her polite smile and was preparing to say something more when she caught sight of a servant out of the corner of her eye. Excusing herself, she went to speak to the servant, leaving Devlin standing alone with Emllyn. His focus returned to Emllyn, lying so pale against the fine coverlet. As he stood gazing down at her, his chest tight with apprehension, Emllyn suddenly stirred. Then she stirred again and groaned when she moved her leg. Devlin bent over her about the time her eyes fluttered open.

"Shhhh," he whispered to her. "You are safe. Speak quietly, Emllyn. There are many ears around us."

All Emllyn could see was Devlin's big face filling her field of vision. She blinked her hot, crusty eyes. "Dev… Devlin?" she breathed. "What has happened?"

He shushed her again, his gaze soft upon her. "You must not call me by my name," he whispered. "I am John. You must remember that – John."

Emllyn was disoriented. "John?"

Devlin nodded faintly, a quick bob of the head because he knew the English soldiers were watching him. He was terrified that one of them was going to walk up and pull him away, so he spoke quickly. "Can you listen to me?" he breathed. "It is important."

Emllyn blinked her eyes again, becoming more lucid. She could see that they were in a room, somewhere, and there were things about her that she did not recognize. Frightened, she fixed on Devlin.

"Where are we?" she murmured.

"De Cleveley's settlement," he whispered. "You must know me only as John. I am a farmer who found you after Kildare's defeat. Do you understand me?"

Emllyn could only slowly comprehend. After a moment, she nodded. "Aye."

Devlin's eyes twinkled warmly at her. "Good lass," he murmured. "The poison in your leg is raging so I brought you here. A very nice lady is willing to tend you, so I don't want you to worry. All will be well."

Emllyn only moderately understood what she was told. Her mind was very muddled. As she lay there, gazing up at Devlin and struggling to digest what was happening, she caught a glimpse of a small, elegant lady with blond hair. Startled and apprehensive, she grabbed hold of Devlin's hand as Lady Elyse drew near.

Lady Elyse was surprised to find her patient awake. She smiled kindly at Emllyn. "Greetings, my lady," she said in her soft, sweet voice. "I am the Lady Elyse de Noble. You have been brought to me because you are very ill. I would like to help you if you will allow it."

Emllyn was frightened and bewildered, and tears popped to her eyes. "Aye… aye, I would be grateful," she murmured as a tear trickled down her temple. "Where am I?"

Elyse had a bowl of warmed water a servant had brought her and sat on a stool that another servant had pulled up to the bed for her. "You are at Glenteige Castle," she said. "My father is Sir Raymond de Noble, commander of Lord de Cleveley's garrison. You are safe, I assure you."

Emllyn was still holding on very tightly to Devlin's hand; he ended up taking a knee beside the bed, holding her small hand between his two big mitts. Emllyn's attention moved back and forth between Elyse and Devlin before finally settling on Elyse.

"I am the Lady Emllyn Fitzgerald, sister of the Earl of Kildare," she said softly. "He is allied with de Cleveley."

Elyse nodded as she and another servant began to bathe the mud off of Emllyn's wound. "I know," she said. "We are most honored to have Kildare's sister as our favored guest."

Emllyn seemed to relax somewhat although she maintained a tight hold on Devlin. "Thank you," she murmured. "I... I do not even know how I came here, to tell you the truth. I do not remember much, but please know that I am very grateful for your hospitality."

Devlin thought he should probably say something to address her complete bewilderment in the situation. She was waking up to a strange place and strange people. He didn't want her to inadvertently contest his story because, at the moment, they were scrutinizing everything about him. One wrong word might see him living the rest of his days out in the vault.

"I found you washed ashore on the beach after Kildare's defeat at Black Castle, m'lady," he said. "You told me that you were aboard the armada to witness your brother's victory over Black Sword. You also had a very bad wound on your leg. Do you not remember any of this?"

He lifted his eyebrows at Emllyn as he spoke. *Please understand what I am telling you; this has become our story now!* Emllyn gazed back at him intently as her mind churned over information that, in a better frame of mind, she would have caught on to quickly. It took her several long moments but eventually he could see the glimmer of understanding in her eye. Yes, it was all coming clearer now. A brief nod of her head told him that.

"Aye," she finally said. "I... I believe I do. I was on my brother's flagship and we sailed to Ireland to meet the rebels who had taken over his lands. The ships... they crashed against each other when they made shore because the weather was so bad. I... I truly do not know how I made it out alive."

Devlin breathed a long sigh of relief. "I found you on the beach," he repeated. "You must have swam away from the destruction.”

Emllyn blinked, struggling to think clearly. “Mayhap,” she said softly. “I do not remember clearly.”

There wasn’t much more to say; she had played into his plans perfectly and Devlin could not have been more pleased or more at ease. He squeezed her hand and resisted the urge to kiss it as well; instead, he turned his focus to Elyse as the woman began to gingerly bathe away the mud from Emllyn’s leg.

“It was very swollen and painful,” he told Elyse, trying to be helpful. “I had nothing to give her for the pain.”

Elyse was focused on her work, eventually washing away the mud to see the angry red cut beneath. She visibly cringed when she saw how bad it was.

“We will remedy that,” she assured him as she looked up at Emllyn. “I will try to be very gentle, my lady. If it hurts, you will tell me and I will stop.”

Emllyn gazed back at the woman with a mixture of fear and trust. “I will,” she said. “I am very thirsty. Could I please have something to drink?”

The words had barely left her mouth before Elyse was in motion, whipping her servants into a frenzy as they disappeared out of the service doors and went scurrying around the room. As a pale young servant girl brought Emllyn a cup of whatever was in the pitcher by Elyse’s bed, they heard commotion at the chamber door.

“Cattle!” came the screech. “All of you crowded around this door like cattle! One would think you have never seen a lady’s chamber before and judging by the lot of you, that’s probably close to the truth!”

Devlin, Emllyn, and Elyse looked over to the chamber entry to see a small man with a worn leather satchel push his way through the knights that were clustered there. He was round and pale, with sparse graying hair and clad in dirty brown robes. He looked like a monk. He waddled his way over to the bed where Emllyn lay, eyeing the wound on her leg before he ever looked his patient in the eye.

"Barbarians," he hissed. "Who sewed this wound? My dog could have done a better job of it."

Elyse vacated her stool for the man. "This is the Lady Emllyn Fitzgerald, sister of the Earl of Kildare," she said, eyeing Emllyn and hoping she wasn't frightened by the man's curt manner. "My lady, this is Merradoc, our physic."

The old physic barely flicked an eye in Emllyn's direction; his focus was entirely on the wound. He set his satchel on the floor next to him and began pulling out pouches and phials.

"I need vinegar and the strongest ale you can find," he snapped at Elyse. "You will also bring me silk thread. I must re-sew this. And put the powder in that brown pouch into a half-cup of wine and bring it to me. Do this now before I grow old from sheer boredom and the lady dies from a raging infection."

He was dramatic and snappy in a hilarious sort of manner. Had Devlin not been so taken aback at the man's horrendous bedside manner, he would have laughed at his brusque impatience. Elyse, however, was on the move, handing off the pouches to her servants as more of them rushed through the servant door with boiled linens in their arms. Everyone was running around doing Merradoc's bidding and soon enough, there was a half-cup of wine being handed to Elyse. She brought it over to Emllyn's bedside.

"You must drink this," she said softly. "It will make you sleep while he tends your leg."

Emllyn wasn't so sure about being put into a drugged sleep;

she was still holding Devlin's hand tightly, eyeing him anxiously as she spoke to Elyse.

"What will the physic do?" she asked.

Elyse glanced over her shoulder at the old physic, who was pulling out a razor-sharp knife from his satchel.

"Clean your wound and fix it," she replied gently. "You do not want to be awake for that, my lady. Please drink this."

Emllyn knew the woman was trying to help her but she was still frightened. Devlin squeezed her hand reassuringly and she looked up at him, perhaps more fearful for him at the moment than she was for herself. She could see the English knights clustered back by the door. She had a feeling they were not there for her.

"He stays," she said to Elyse. "I do not want him going any-where. Even if I fall asleep, I do not want him removed. Please make it so."

Elyse nodded firmly. "I will not allow him to go anywhere, I promise," she said. "Will you drink this now?"

Reluctantly, Emllyn complied, and within fifteen minutes she was snoring upon the linens. She seemed to be very sensitive to sleeping potions, as she had been sensitive to the draught Eefha had given her as well. Once she was fully asleep, evidenced when the physic pinched her toe, the old man finally went to work.

As promised, Devlin remained at Emllyn's bedside. He sat on the floor by Emllyn's head as the physic removed the cat gut sutures he had put in her leg and replaced them with boiled silk thread. He put in fine, neat stitches. The physic also cleaned the poison out of the wound and doused it repeatedly in vinegar and ale. When he was finished with that, he bound her leg up tightly and left her to sleep. The entire procedure took less than fifteen minutes, a swift and confident undertaking by the snappy physic. When he was satisfied with his work, he began packing his items away.

"I am going to bring her some rotten tea," he told Elyse. "I will return later tonight with it. It will help her fever."

Elyse listened to him intently. "What should I do for her in the meanwhile?"

The physic glanced over his shoulder at the sleeping patient. "Keep her warm and watch her closely," he said as he collected his satchel and moved for the door. "If she begins to sweat or becomes delirious, send for me. Otherwise, I will return tonight."

Elyse thanked the man and ushered him to the door. The physic beat back the three remaining knights who were still standing in the entry, as the rest of the crowd had returned to their duties. De Ferrer remained, as did Elyse's escort and another man, an older one who had made an appearance only a few minutes earlier. He had seen the old physic as the man finished stitching up the leg of the strange woman lying on his daughter's bed, but nothing more than that. He stopped the physic before the man left the room completely.

"How is the lady?" he asked.

Merradoc glanced back into the room again, at the big bed where an enormous man sat on the floor next to it and an injured lady slept peacefully. He shrugged his shoulders.

"We shall see," he said. "The cut is deep. It looks like a sword wound to me. I shall see what I can do for her but no promises."

The older man nodded and let the physic continue out of the room. Then, he stepped into the chamber and headed for Elyse.

"I hear we have had a visitor," he said, eyeing Devlin seated on the floor. "De Ferrer told me about the lady and her savior. I have come to see for myself."

Elyse smiled at the man. "Greetings, Father," she said as she gestured to Emllyn, fast asleep. "This is the sister of the Earl of Kildare, the Lady Emllyn Fitzgerald. She had sailed on her brother's war fleet but was injured in a battle at Black Castle. She washed ashore and this farmer found her and helped her. We owe him a great deal of gratitude for saving her."

Sir Raymond de Noble was fixated on Devlin. A tall man with a full head of gray hair, de Noble seemed rather calm and wise, giving Devlin a good going-over as he stood there. De Noble's dark eyes missed nothing as he studied him. Devlin stared back at de Cleveley's brilliant commander. He'd fought the man before; now, he was seeing him face-to-face. It was an odd realization.

"Indeed we do," de Noble finally said, but it was clear he wasn't finished scrutinizing Devlin. "What is your name?"

"John, m'lord," Devlin replied.

De Noble acknowledged him with a bob of the head. "John," he repeated. "I was told you have a farm south of Black Castle."

"Aye, m'lord."

"I am also told you have been inside of Black Castle."

"Aye, m'lord."

"Where do your sympathies lie, John?"

It was an interesting question, now with the other knights listening in. Devlin wasn't a fool; he knew he had to play the game, but it was harder than he thought. He wanted to jump up and roar for the victory of the Irish, but he kept still. He had been fighting men like de Noble for years and had served under them for longer still. The English had always given him commands or oppressed him one way or the other, and his natural urge to rebel was strong. But his sense of self-preservation, and of the preservation of Emllyn, was stronger.

"I have never had a quarrel with the English," he said. "In fact, my fellow Irishmen seem to give me more trouble."

"How is that?"

Devlin shrugged, thinking now would be a very good time to start gaining English sympathy and trust. "Men from Black Castle raid my fields and steal my vegetables," he said. "The O'Connors have been known to steal my stock. When the English want something from me, at least they pay me for it."

That brought a thin smile from de Noble. Looking Devlin over, he could see that the man appeared very exhausted. The dark blue eyes were dull. But as he gazed at him, he also found the man strangely familiar. He couldn't put his finger on it, because all Irishmen looked alike to him, but there was something vaguely recognizable. Ah, perhaps it would come to him at some point. For now, he was intent to glean what information he could out of the man about Black Castle, only his tactics were far more subtle than his lesser officers. He was a man who knew how to get what he wanted.

"That sounds typical," he replied after a moment. "When was the last time you ate, John?"

Devlin thought about it. "Yesterday, m'lord."

"You must be starving," de Noble said. "Would you join me for a meal? I have not yet eaten myself and I would like to hear more about this defeat of Kildare's armada."

Careful, Devlin told himself. He knew it was more than an invitation; it was a directive because they wanted to probe him. He was on to their game. "I am not sure what I can tell you, m'lord," he said. "I only heard about it from others."

"But you found a woman who said she was with Kildare's fleet."

"Aye, I did, but she didn't tell me more than that."

De Noble didn't push. He would get the information he wanted, eventually. "Will you come and eat with me, John?"

Devlin hesitated; he didn't want to walk into a trap, lured by a smooth-tongued Englishman, but he knew he could not refuse. "Can I return when we are finished?"

"Of course."

Elyse, who had been listening to the conversation, went to Devlin and put her hand on his arm. "Go now and eat with my father," she said encouragingly. "He will bring you back here when you are finished."

Devlin didn't want to be rude and refuse, not when he was trying to establish some trust, but he was very hesitant to leave Emllyn. Still, he had little choice. Stiffly, he climbed to his feet.

"Will you send word to me if something changes with her?" he asked Elyse.

The woman nodded patiently. "Of course," she said, giving him a little push in her father's direction. "Go and eat now. We will be here when you return."

Genuinely exhausted, Devlin allowed himself to be led out of the chamber by de Noble and wasn't surprised when the knights who had been lingering by the door closed ranks behind him, effectively escorting him out of the room. Together, the small group made their way back down the stairs to the feasting hall below.

De Noble called for food and soon, they were swarmed with more food and drink than Devlin had seen in a very long time. He was starving, shoving the succulent beef into his mouth and downing very good English wine. De Noble ate along with him and gave him plenty of time to drink more wine before commencing with the questions.

It was then that Devlin realized he shouldn't have drunk so much wine. The clear-headed English commander had plenty of questions for him.

CHAPTER ELEVEN

"**B**LACK CASTLE," DE Noble said slowly as he poured Devlin more drink. "I was there once, several years ago during the peace. Before the rebellions, when it was still Kildare's holding. It is a big place."

Devlin was minimally drunk and he could clearly see that de Noble was trying to get him drunker. He was fairly certain that the man didn't suspect his true identity but he knew the man was trying to press him for information. If Devlin had been in de Noble's position, he would have done the same thing. Sometimes the peasants heard and saw things that were valuable during a time of crisis. With that in mind, Devlin put the ale to his lips but he didn't drink; he just pretended to. He wasn't going to allow himself to become more addled than he already was.

"Me da used to take me there," Devlin said, playing the part of the ignorant peasant. "Me da was a farmer, too, and we would take our produce to Black Castle when I was young, when Kildare was still in possession. I still remember the big English knights and their big swords. As a boy, that was exciting."

De Noble smiled faintly. "And now?" he asked. "Do you still find big English knights with their big swords exciting?"

Devlin shook his head and pretended to take another drink, spilling some of it clumsily as he set the cup down. That would throw de Noble off somewhat on exactly how much he had imbibed.

"Nay, m'lord," he said, wiping his mouth with the back of his hand. "I don't find it exciting. I find it a burden."

"Why?"

"Because I take me produce to market at Black Castle but the peasants are so a-feared of Black Sword that there is hardly any commerce there anymore," he said, pretending to be upset by it. "Black Sword keeps the castle fairly bottled up. Not many pass between the gates these days. But… well, I shouldn't be telling you this, but I was there about a month ago. I had gotten to the castle before sunrise and sold some of me goods to the castle cook. As I was leaving, many men entered the castle, men in blue tartan that someone said were O'Connor men. There must have been hundreds of them. It looked as if Black Sword was planning a meeting with them."

De Noble was listening intently. "What kind of a meeting?"

Devlin shook his head and took another pretend drink of the ale, spilling it on his chin to disguise the fact that he'd swallowed nothing. He was starting to see that de Noble was willingly listening to anything he said so he thought it would be a great opportunity to feed the man false information. His clever mind was working quickly; if de Noble was foolish enough to try and play him for an idiot, then Devlin would comply – and he would turn the tables on him.

"I don't know," Devlin said, pretending to be very dumb about the entire thing. "But there were a lot. Do you think they were the same men who destroyed Kildare's fleet? It could have been. I heard that the Irish banded together for that battle, uniting under Black Sword. They say they are remaining united, for something very big. At least, that's what I've heard."

By this time, de Ferrer and the Lady Elyse's escort, a tall and handsome man introduced as Sir Christopher Connaught, were leaning in to listen. They were all evidently very interested in what the enormous, and rather dumb, Irishman had to say.

"*What* is very big?" Connaught asked; he had a slight Irish accent mixed in with his Norman speech pattern. "What have you heard about Black Sword's future plans?"

Devlin looked at the man with feigned reluctance, as if he had already said too much. "I shouldn't have said that," he said, looking uncomfortable. "I'm just a farmer and that is all I want to be. I don't like war and I don't like the Irish who wreak havoc for havoc's sake. I don't like the English who rape our women and steal our lands. I just want to be left alone."

De Noble silently waved Connaught off. "You know," he said casually, "you speak very well for a farmer."

Devlin looked at the man. "What do you mean?"

"I mean that you speak like an educated man."

Devlin just stared at him. Then, he smiled weakly and averted his gaze. "Me mother could read," he said. "She taught me what I know. I can read and I can write a little."

De Noble nodded faintly, although he was staring at Devlin with more than an intense stare; there was something glittering in the depths of the man's dark eyes, something knowing. Devlin didn't want to stare at him too much to try and figure it out; all he knew was that it made him uncomfortable. He didn't like the way the man looked at him. It was more than scrutiny; it was calculating. De Noble was being very calculating.

"So you do not like the Irish yet you do not particularly like the English," de Noble ventured after a moment. "In truth, I do not blame you. For a peaceful and simple man, these are difficult times."

"Aye, m'lord."

"When were you last at Black Castle?"

Devlin pretended to think. "Over a week ago, I think," he said. "It was the last of my winter produce and my spring crops are just little seedlings now."

"I see," de Noble said thoughtfully. "And when you were last there, what was it like? Were there still O'Connor troops there?"

Devlin's brow furrowed in thought. "If they were, they must have been hiding, for I don't remember seeing a lot of men," he replied. Then he reached for his drink and knocked it completely off of the table, spilling it. He grinned apologetically. "I fear I've had too much to drink, m'lord."

De Ferrer picked the cup off the floor and handed it to de Noble, who picked up the ale pitcher and refilled it. "Nonsense," he said. "For aiding the Lady Emllyn, you deserve a rest and good food and good drink. You will be our guest for the night."

Devlin nodded gratefully. "Thank you, m'lord," he said. After a moment's hesitation, he continued. "I would like to know how the lady is faring, if I can."

De Noble was looking at him with his razor-sharp stare. "She is no longer your concern, John," he said steadily. "We will take care of her now."

Devlin could feel his heart begin to race, just a little. "But… but I told you I would not leave her with people I did not know or trust," he said, suddenly sounding not quite so drunk. "You promised the lady that I could stay."

De Noble shook his head. "My *daughter* promised that you could remain," he clarified. "I said nothing of the kind. A lady of that high ranking wants nothing to do with a dirt farmer. Surely you know that."

Devlin didn't react for a moment because he could feel rage building in his chest and he knew that it would do him no good. Therefore, he could do one of two things – he could protest vigorously, which would only get him thrown out, or he could try another avenue, one of sympathy and pain. Swallowing his pride and his natural urge to battle the English, he lowered his gaze and stared at his lap.

"I do," he muttered. "'Tis just… well, I have protected her since I found her. I hid her from a patrol of Black Sword's men after Kildare's armada was destroyed and I've kept watchful eye on her. You see, I lost… I lost me own wife and daughter not too long ago and the lady reminds me a good deal of me wife. If… if I could just see the lady for tonight, to see how she is feeling, I would be grateful. I know the English are more generous than me own people, so I would hope for your permission."

He kept his gaze lowered, hoping his lie would garner some sympathy. If it didn't, he wasn't quite sure what more he was going to do except lay siege single-handedly to the keep, which would not produce good results.

As Devlin hoped, de Noble relented somewhat. It wasn't an unreasonable request so he truly had no reason to deny it. The older knight took a drink from his cup, his gaze shifting from Devlin and taking on a far-away look. He was reflecting on something.

"I know what it means to lose a wife," he said finally. "My

wife died a few years ago but I think I lost her even longer before that. She did not like Ireland. She wanted to remain in England, so I permitted it."

Devlin could see that he'd hit a nerve with his talk of a dead wife. He took advantage of it. "Me wife was a good woman," he said. "We had grown up together so we had been together a very long time. But she got sick, as did my child, and I lost them both."

De Noble wallowed in his own reflection a moment longer before looking at Devlin. His expression went from wistful to controlled in a split second; he didn't like to think about his dead wife and he certainly didn't want to discuss her with this peasant. He was an intensely private man.

"Then I am sorry for you," he said. "I will permit you to know how the lady is faring, then. But after you stay here tonight, you will return home. There is no longer any need for your presence."

That wasn't a directive that Devlin wanted to hear. He decided to swallow his pride completely and open himself up, hoping they'd let him stay. He didn't want to leave Emllyn and the very thought was causing him tremendous grief.

"But… I can be of help to you here," he said eagerly. "I am strong; I can shoe horses or help in the kitchens. I can butcher animals or tend the horses. As I told you, my crops are seedlings and I have no more income for a while. With the Irish raiding my fields, I have almost nothing left. I would be a good worker, m'lord, I swear it."

De Noble's gaze lingered on him a moment before he turned his attention to de Ferrer and Connaught. He smiled faintly as he toyed with his cup.

"He *is* a big one," he said. "I wouldn't mind using him as a body guard. I would imagine he'd be fairly formidable in a fight."

De Ferrer and Connaught looked at Devlin from across the table, each man studying him. Devlin could feel their stares, the hostility, perhaps the jealousy or curiosity. It was difficult to get a read. He was trying to look hopeful and not look intimidating, which was a difficult stretch. He hated being at the mercy of the damnable English, begging them for a job. It was to gain information, that was true, but more than that, he realized he didn't want to be separated from Emllyn, not even for an hour. Already, it was killing him and it hadn't even been that long. All he wanted to do was go back and sit by her bed just to be near her. It was a stunning realization but a powerful one nonetheless.

He simply didn't want to be without her.

"Can you fight?" de Ferrer asked, breaking into his thoughts.

Devlin pushed aside images of Emllyn and focused on the older knight. "I can use me fists and feet," he said. "I've been known to brawl."

"Have you ever fought for the rebellion?" Connaught fired at him. "Have you ever joined your kinsmen in taking up arms against the English?"

Devlin looked at the man, studying him a moment. There was something brash and fiery about him. "I have never fought for the rebellion," he said. It was the truth; he had *led* the rebellion. "And who are you to ask me? I detect Irish in you, lad. So you take up arms for the English and fight against your countrymen?"

Those were hostile words as far as Connaught was concerned. He bolted to his feet, hand on the hilt of his sword in threat. "You will not question my loyalty, you lowly whore-skin," he snarled. "I am an English knight and you are shite beneath my feet."

"Sit down, Chris," de Noble held out a hand to him, easing the young man back into his seat. "He didn't mean it as an accusation. It was merely a question."

Connaught wasn't happy in the least. He hissed his displeasure and plopped down in his seat, unwilling to participate in the conversation any longer. De Noble's attention dwelt on the man for a moment to make sure he wasn't going to rise up and charge their guest before returning his focus to Devlin. His expression seemed to harden.

"Connaught is a legacy knight for de Cleveley," he said. "He was born in Ireland and his heritage is Irish, but his family is sworn to de Cleveley. His father and father before him served as ambassadors for de Cleveley here in Ireland."

The worst kind of Irishman as far as Devlin was concerned. Traitors to their own country. Devlin couldn't help the look of contempt he gave Connaught, who fortunately wasn't looking at him. If he had, there might have been punches thrown at the very least. Devlin eventually returned his focus to de Noble.

"You have many Irish here that serve you," he said. "Allow me to serve you as well. You have been helpful and kind in assisting the injured lady and I owe you me gratitude. At least let me repay you your kindness."

De Noble sat there a moment and gazed at him. It was clear he was contemplating something. With a long sigh, he moved to pour himself more wine. He also poured more in Devlin's cup even though Devlin hadn't touched it since the last time he'd filled it. Now, they were getting down to business.

"If you want to show your gratitude, then I have a proposition for you," de Noble said. "You claim you have been to Black Castle and, presumably, the people at Black Castle know you as a farmer. You can move easily in and out of Black Castle and no one would question or suspect you. John, we have been at war against Black Sword for quite some time. He is a great battle commander and men naturally follow him. However, it has been our suspicion for some time that Devlin de Bermingham is gathering the clanns to launch a massive attack against Glenteige. When you told us that you had seen O'Connor troops there, that only confirmed our suspicions. My proposition to you is this – if you return to Black Castle and gather information about what Black Sword is planning against us, I will let you return to see your lady friend. I will even let you spend time with her. But you would be far more help to us inside of Black Castle, seeing what Black Sword is up to, than you would be here shoeing horses or butchering pigs. Will you do this for us, John? Will you do this for your lady friend who will undoubtedly be in danger should Black Sword lay siege to our settlement? There is information I must know and I think you are the perfect man to get it."

Devlin was stunned by the proposal. His first reaction was to laugh at the suggestion but he wisely kept his reaction suppressed; of all of the tasks or questions or proposals, he had been asked to spy on himself!

It was nearly too much for him to bear but in the same breath, he realized that he could beautifully manipulate the situation if he had de Noble's trust. But he would very carefully have to temper what information he gave the man because if they discovered who he was and of his treachery, then they would logically suspect that Emllyn was a part of it. It would reflect horribly on her.

Nay; that couldn't happen. In order to keep Emllyn safe, Devlin would have to be extraordinarily careful. He could hardly believe how twisted and complex the situation had become. He had set out to make Emllyn as spy on his behalf and now, he was to become a spy for the English.

The tides had turned on him and it would take a calm and intelligent man not to be caught in a trap of his own making. This was a chance of a lifetime and he truthfully had no other recourse than to take it. He was in deep and it would only get deeper.

"Aye," he said after a moment, with a hint of reluctance. "I will do it. To keep the lady safe, I would do anything."

De Noble's expression was as close to triumphant as the emotionless man could get. "Excellent," he said. "Then let us eat and drink to celebrate our new association. I will send a servant up to see how the lady fares but on the morrow, you will set out for Black Castle."

Devlin didn't feel much like talking after that and he pushed the alcohol away so he wouldn't drink anymore. He tended to get moody when he'd had too much to drink and he didn't want to do or say anything that might jeopardize everything. The English knights, however, were quite willing to drink to excess and eat. Devlin simply sat in silence and watched them.

A servant was sent to see to Emllyn's welfare and returned some time later to say that the lady was asleep and that Lady Elyse was watching over her. It was the only bit of news Devlin received and it did not make him happy. As the evening wore on, he became increasingly unhappy and morose as the feasting English continued into the night.

By midnight, he had shifted to a seat by the massive hearth, surrounded by farting and snoring English dogs, wondering what in the hell he had gotten himself in to.

WHEN EMLLYN OPENED her eyes, it was dark in the chamber except for the glow of the firelight.

She lay there a moment, studying her surroundings without moving her head, unable to see much in the dark reaches of the room. It took her several moments to orient herself and remember where she was, and then it all came back to her. *De Cleveley's holding,* Devlin had told her. They had gained entrance according to plan. She didn't know if she felt better or worse to know that.

They were in.

But what wasn't according to plan was her wound. That had nearly destroyed everything. Shifting slightly, she had barely moved when there was a face in her field of vision. She recognized the gentle and lovely features as the Lady Elyse.

"My lady?" Elyse said, a warm smile on her face. "How are you feeling?"

Emllyn wasn't entirely sure; she blinked as she pondered the question. Her thinking and reasoning seemed to be clearer, at any rate.

"My head aches a great deal," she said, her voice hoarse and scratchy. She moved her body a little, including her leg. "My leg hurts also, which is of no great surprise."

Elyse smiled sympathetically. "I know," she said, putting a gentle hand on her forehead to feel for fever. "Your fever seems to have eased."

"Is it still there?"

"Still, but it seems much less."

Emllyn was grateful for the improvement. She began to look around the room, noting that other than Elyse and a serving woman who was over near the hearth, they were alone. Devlin wasn't in the room. Seized with anxiety, Emllyn tried to sit up.

"Where is D… John?" she stumbled as she tried to climb off the bed. "Where did he go?"

Elyse rushed to her side, putting her hands on the woman to try and keep her in bed. "He is supping with my father," she assured her quickly. "He is well, my lady. Do not fear."

Emllyn wasn't eased in the least. Her eyes welled with fat tears. "Bring him here," she begged tightly. "Please bring him here."

Elyse was trying her best to soothe her. "My lady, I swear he is unharmed," she said. "As soon as he finished eating, he will return."

Emllyn struggled with her fear, wiping away the tears that fell. Elyse was so soothing and kind that she couldn't help but be eased. Still, she was very worried.

"I am afraid the knights will try to harm him because he is Irish," she said. "He… he saved my life. I owe him much. I do not want him out of my sight."

Elyse nodded soothingly, gently forcing her back on the bed. "I will go myself and bring him here," she said. "He seems to be very attached to you as well. I suspect we could not keep him from you if we tried."

Emllyn's anxiety eased as a concern of another sort took hold at Elyse's statement. *He is very attached to you.* There was something about the way she said it, as if Devlin's attention was more than just simple camaraderie. She said it as if it was meant to be something sweet, and the statement unnerved her. It also excited her.

"Why would you say that?" she asked.

Since her patient was now awake and fairly mobile, Elyse began to remove Emllyn from the heavy cloak she was wearing. It was filthy and torn.

"Because he is very protective of you," she said, gently pulling at the cloak and removing Emllyn's arms from it. "It is apparent that he feels responsible for you."

Emllyn fell silent, pondering the woman's observations, as Elyse proceeded to remove her from the cloak and surcoat. When she was down to the shift, she called for a bath and in little time, a small army of servants brought forth a big copper tub, lined with linen, and began filling it with warm water.

Meanwhile, Elyse had gone to her wardrobe, overflowing with goods, and brought forth a beautiful silk robe that she put around Emllyn's shoulders as the servants filled the tub. She also brought forth things for the bath; soaps, scrapers, oils, and a giant sponge.

Emllyn watched the activity and felt tears sting her eyes again; God, it would be so good to be clean and warm again. She felt as if she hadn't been clean or warm, in pleasant company or in a well-furnished room, for years. The past few days of her life had made such an imprint on her that it was difficult to think past them. She was to be treated with kindness and civility again, and not surrounded by people that hated her. The tears were those of joy.

When the tub was nearly full, Elyse put her hand in it and tested the water. Satisfied, she poured a measure of oil in the water that made the room smell like roses. Then she went to Emllyn where she sat upon the bed.

"I realize that you have an injury and that you still are with fever, and mayhap it is very foolish to put you in water under those conditions, but mayhap a bath will make you feel better," she said. "Let's try, shall we?"

Emllyn nodded as she went to stand gingerly on her sore leg. Elyse grabbed hold of her and steadied her as she walked to the bath.

"Thank you, my lady," Emllyn said. "Your thoughtfulness is appreciated."

Elyse simply smiled as she helped remove Emllyn from her shift, exposing her naked body to the glow of the firelight. Elyse tried not to stare but she had to admit that Lady Emllyn had a delicious figure, ripe and round in all of the right places. Elyse was rather slender, everywhere. She wished for such full breasts as Emllyn had. As Emllyn carefully lowered herself into the bath, Elyse helped her keep her leg out of the water by propping it up on the edge of the tub.

"I am sorry the water is not terribly hot," Elyse said. "I did not want to aggravate your fever. But we shall get you warm and clean, my lady, have no fear. Water will wash away all of the sins of the world, I say."

Emllyn closed her eyes as Elyse and a servant went to work, pouring water over her head and setting about scrubbing and oiling every inch of her body. The water smelled like an entire field of roses and Emllyn settled back, letting Elyse take charge. Already, she was feeling better.

"May I beg you to tell me a little about yourself, my lady?" Elyse asked as she worked. "Living here at Glenteige with only my father and a few others for company, I very much miss the companionship of ladies such as yourself. It is a rather lonely life here at times."

Emllyn had been laying against the back of the tub, eyes

closed but she opened her eyes and looked at Elyse when the woman spoke.

"Well," she said thoughtfully, "I am afraid I am not very exciting. I went to foster at Kenilworth Castle when I was very young. In fact, Kenilworth feels more like my home than my brother's castle ever did. I had many friends there. I was sad to leave when I had to return home."

Elyse was busy scrubbing the toes of her left foot. "Tell me of your friends at Kenilworth," she said. "Were they handsome and dashing knights or fine and fair ladies?"

Emllyn smiled at the memories the question was provoking. "Both," she said. "I had friends that were male, of course. Two that come to mind are Kenneth St. Héver and Stephen of Pembury. They would try to play jokes on me but I was smarter than they were; I would turn the tables on them. Oh, they were good times."

Elyse smiled because Emllyn was. "Young knights?"

Emllyn nodded. "Very young," she said. "We were about the same age and they always thought they could tease me. Well, at least Stephen did. He was a terrible jokester. Somehow Kenneth always got into trouble, too, because the two of them were inseparable. I can still see the earl berating the pair for having played a joke on me which I turned around on them. It was great fun."

Elyse was still smiling as she rinsed off the left foot and moved onto the right. "I have fond memories of fostering, too," she said. "I fostered at Winchester Castle."

Emllyn watched the woman wash her foot. "When did you come to Ireland?"

Elyse's smile seemed to fade. "Two years ago," she said. "It was after my mother died and my father did not wish me to stay in England alone, so he sent for me. I have no other family, you see. Just my father. I had a brother but he was killed by Black Sword in the wars a few years ago."

Killed by Black Sword. Emllyn's smile faded and her nerves began to make a return, for Devlin's sake. To be truthful, she'd only heard two sides of Black Sword's legend – her brother's version and Devlin's version. She was curious about Elyse's version but she was also curious to know if the woman had any insight into her father's activities against Devlin. Devlin wanted to know if de Cleveley intended to launch an attack against him; perhaps this was a place to start. Women often heard things they weren't supposed to.

"I am sorry for your brother," she said softly. "Black Sword destroyed my brother's entire fleet. It seems to me that he is very powerful."

Elyse shrugged as she finished with her right foot and put it back into the water. "He is very much hated," she said. "Everyone in the settlement both hates the man and fears him. I do believe some of the knights even admire him. They say he is very clever."

Emllyn simply nodded her head to the statement as she deliberated what direction to take the conversation in. She'd never been particularly manipulative so this was new territory for her. Worse, she was actually coming to like Elyse. The woman was very kind and seemingly genuine. She didn't want to use that kindness in a self-serving way but she had little choice. She was here on a mission and would do what she had to in order to achieve her goal.

"He must be if he defeated my brother's armada as thoroughly as he did," she said. "Has no one even tried to meet with the man and see what his demands are? I realize I am not a warrior, and I'm not even particularly clever, but it seems to me if there is a problem that men should discuss it. What good is it to go around killing each other if no one really knows what it's all about?"

"They know what it is all about," Elyse corrected her. "It is about the Irish wanting to rule their own lands when everyone knows they are too stupid to do so. Except for Black Sword; I have heard my father say he has the makings of a great ruler."

"Why?"

"I do not know. I believe it has something to do with the way he plans his battles." She paused and appeared thoughtful. "He is the bastard son of the Earl of Louth, you know. He served with his father in the Irish Bruce Wars a few years ago and it was said he was instrumental in a very big victory. His father's family has been in Ireland for centuries and even though they are descended from Normans, they are still considered Irish. And Black Sword's mother is the daughter of kings, so I suppose that makes him royalty."

Emllyn tried not to show much interest in what she was saying, although it was more than she'd ever heard about Devlin. "How would you know all of this?"

Elyse grinned. "My father told me," she said. "He says that Black Sword has all of the cunning and savagery of the Irish gods. He says that Black Sword always has great plans."

Emllyn shrugged as she began splashing water on her face. "Then mayhap your father should meet with the man and discuss a plan that will not see so many men die."

Elyse grinned at the frank assessment of a complex situation. "My father *has* met him, once," she said. "It was a long time ago but he said even then, in his youth, there was something about Black Sword that spoke of greatness."

Emllyn's blood ran cold. *My father has met him.* God's Blood, was it possible the man had recognized him? Was that why he invited Devlin to sup with him? Emllyn began to feel very, very nervous.

As Elyse washed her hair with soap and rinsed it with flat ale, all Emllyn could think of was Devlin sitting in the midst of English knights, men who would gladly run him through if they knew who he was. She was wrought with worry over Devlin's current status, so much so that she had ceased to enjoy her bath and now saw it as an obstacle that stood in the way of having Devlin returned to her room. She had to tell Devlin that de Noble had seen him once and quite possibly might recognize him. It was a terrifying thought.

When the bath was over, Elyse and the serving woman helped Emllyn from the tub and dried her off with a soft linen towel. Standing in front of the fire where it was nice and warm, the servant rubbed rose-scented oil all over her skin as Elyse began to comb through her hair to dry it. When the oil was absorbed into her skin, the servant put the beautiful silk robe back on her and Elyse had her sit down in front of the fire so that the heat could better dry her hair.

As the red-gold hair dried into fine, soft curls, Emllyn could wait no longer. She had to see Devlin. When the serving woman brought her mulled wine to drink, she turned to catch a glimpse of Elyse as the woman worked steadily over her hair.

"Will you please return John now?" she asked. "I would like to see him."

Elyse nodded, immediately switching places with the serving woman and removing the apron she had donned to help Emllyn bathe. She was quick and efficient in her movements, exuding the image of the perfect chatelaine.

"I will go and find him," she said. Then, her gaze lingered on Emllyn hesitantly. "Of course, it is not my place to say so, but it is my sense that it would not be entirely… proper for the man to stay here with you. In fact, I will be sleeping in this chamber and although I know John makes you feel safe, to have him sleeping here is rather… discomforting to me. Moreover, my father would never allow it."

Emllyn thought on that a moment. "I have no desire to make you uncomfortable, of course," she said. "But… you were right when you said I feel very comfortable with John. I am sorry if that seems strange, being as I hardly know the man and he is not my husband, but I would prefer to stay with him. He makes me feel very safe. If you must move us out of your chamber in order to accomplish that, I would be very grateful."

Elyse appeared rather distressed. "But," she said hesitantly, "my lady… he is…."

"He is the man who saved my life and took great care of me until now," Emllyn said, interrupting her hostess. She wasn't trying to be rude but she truly didn't want Devlin out of her sight, fearful of what would happen if they were separated. "I find myself in a strange castle with people I do not know and even though you have been sweet and gracious, I am not trying to be cruel when I say that I would feel much more comfortable with a man I have established some trust with rather than a lady I have only known a few hours. Please do not think me unkind; it is simply the way I feel at this moment."

Elyse sighed and forced a smile; she would not argue with her guest. "If that is your wish, then of course I shall comply," she said. "There is a small chamber on this floor where I can put you. It is rather cramped, but I will make it comfortable for you."

Emllyn nearly collapsed with relief. "Thank you, my lady," she said sincerely. "And I will put your mind at ease that nothing inappropriate or unseemly shall occur. I look at John as my watchdog, and so should you. He gives me comfort and that is all."

Elyse merely smiled without answering and Emllyn suspected it was because she didn't believe her but was too polite to say so. Putting her apron down, she scooted out of the chamber and shut the door softly behind her. Emllyn had a feeling that she had offended the woman with her requests but it couldn't be helped; her concern was for Devlin.

While Elyse went in search of Devlin, the serving woman helped Emllyn change into a lovely soft shift and heavy sleeping robe that was lined in rabbit fur and had long, belled sleeves. It was a gorgeous piece of blue brocaded silk. The serving wench also put warm doeskin slippers on Emllyn's feet that were a bit too small but nonetheless comfortable. Then, she braided her nearly dry hair into a thick braid and wrapped it around her head in an attractive style, securing it firmly with iron pins.

Feeling warm, clean, and tended, Emllyn sat down on the bed with her leg elevated and indulged in more mulled wine, cheese, bread, and dried apricots. She was full of food and good wine when the door opened but instead of Elyse returning, it was Merradoc.

The old physic barged into the room with his satchel clutched under his arm, immediately waving a careless hand at the serving girl.

"Wine!" he snapped. "Enough for two. Bring it now, you silly wench, before I grow moss on my north side from having been kept waiting too long."

The serving girl fled and Emllyn sat up straight on the bed

as the man approached. Merradoc went right up to her and put a fat hand on her forehead, paused, then felt the pulse of her wrist. After a moment of feeling the strength of her heart, he peeled back her right eyelid and looked into her eye. Satisfied, he set his bag down on the bed next to her and began rummaging around. The first thing he pulled out was a long, black strip that looked like leather. Then he pulled out a second one. He handed her one of the strips.

"Chew it!" he barked.

Emllyn immediately put it in her mouth, fearful of what would happen if she didn't. Merradoc began chewing on the second strip and within the first few chews, Emllyn made a horrible face.

"What *is* this?" she asked.

"Licorice root," the old physic told her. "Children and imbeciles like it."

Emllyn didn't like it at all but she continued chewing it. "It's terrible," she said. "What is it good for?"

"Nothing," Merradoc said. "I just thought I'd give it to you. Now, tell me how you feel and no lies. I will know."

Emllyn took the licorice root out of her mouth because it was truly foul. She made a face and stuck out her black tongue.

"I felt better until you gave me that odious root," she said, licking her lips of the disgusting taste. "But I suppose I do feel much better. My leg aches but I am sure that is a normal occurrence."

With the root sticking out of his mouth, Merradoc lifted up the edge of her robe and began unwrapping the wound. Emllyn watched apprehensively as he unwrapped it completely and then eyed the wound intently. She strained to catch a glimpse of the cut, now sutured up with fine white silk thread. It was still red, but the swelling had gone down considerably. The physic eyed it for a few more moments before returning his attention to his satchel and digging around again.

Emllyn watched him curiously as he rummaged about. The serving girl returned with a crystal decanter of wine and two fine cups, and she set it upon the table next to the bed. Merradoc downed two cups in swift succession before removing a bladder from his satchel, popping open the plugged top, and pouring the dark contents into an empty glass. He filled it about half full before sealing up the bladder and lifting the cup to Emllyn.

"You will drink this," he said.

Emllyn wasn't so apt to take it after he'd tricked her with the licorice root. "What is it?"

"Rotten tea," the physic replied. "You must drink it three times a day for the next five days. It will cure the poison in your leg and heal you completely."

Dubious, Emllyn peered at the dark liquid but when she went to smell it, the stench nearly knocked her over.

"God's Blood," she hissed, pinching her nose. "What *is* this terrible stuff?"

Merradoc had no time for her foolishness. "I told you, silly goat," he said brusquely. "Rotten tea. It will cure you. Do you want to live?"

"Of course, I do, but…."

"*Drink it!*"

He nearly roared at her and, fearful, Emllyn instinctively downed the tea in one big gulp. It was horrible and she nearly vomited it up back up again but the physic handed her a glass of the fine wine, ordering her to drink it immediately, and she did. It killed most of the terrible taste, but not completely. She burped and the taste came up again. She almost gagged.

"Oh, my," she breathed, hand at her throat and an awful expression on her face. "What is that made from?"

Merradoc shrugged as if it was the simplest thing in the world. "Bread is rotted until it grows green fuzz, and then the bread is put into water and kept warm for days on end. It creates a liquid that cures almost anything."

Emllyn exposed her tongue as if the air would dry away the awful taste. "If that potion does not kill me, I will surely be surprised."

Merradoc set the bladder with the rotten tea in it on the table next to the bed. "I would not worry over the taste," he said. "If we do not cure the poison in your leg, you could lose it. Is that what you want? To be a one-legged maiden? No man will want you then because you will be both freakish and revolting."

Emllyn looked at the man, horrified and disgusted. "By God, man, you surely speak your mind in crude and ghastly ways," she said. "Have you never been told this?"

Merradoc fought off a grin. "All of the time," he said. "But they need me around here so I can say what I please. If you do not like it, then do not drink my potion and I shall have to cut your leg off. I shall make it extra painful, too, to teach you a lesson."

Emllyn could see he was trying to get a rise out of her and she refused to give it to him. He was, in truth, rather humorous; or at least he would have been had he not been saying those hateful things to her. To another, it would have been great fun.

"I will not give you the satisfaction," she declared. "I will heal and you'll not take a knife to me, you bloodsucker. Leave this room before I slap your face."

Merradoc let out a crow of laughter. "My lady, I retreat in

terror," he said, throwing up his hands. Then he poured himself another cup of wine and downed it in one swallow before collecting his satchel. "Mayhap you will overcome your violent tendencies by the time I return later tonight to see how you are faring. It will be another opportunity for me to shove more of that terrible brew down your throat."

She scowled at him. "And I'll not give you the satisfaction for that, either," she said. "I will drink the potion before you come so you shall not see me suffer. You shall get no more gratification out of me, wicked man."

Merradoc laughed all of the way to the door. He put his hand on the latch. "I do hope you survive this, my lady," he said. "I rather like you."

"Well, I don't like *you*!"

He howled with laughter as he quit the room. Emllyn could hear him laughing as he descended the stairs and it made her grin. She had to admit that she was looking forward to his return, if only for the entertainment it brought. Now that she understood him a little, it would make conversations with him much more interesting.

Once the laughter was gone, she sat upon the bed and finished off what was left of the wine. The serving wench remained crouched by the hearth, keeping the fire stoked and boiling water in a small iron pot over the fire. She was also doing something else, which actually looked like baking, but Emllyn couldn't tell. In truth, she wasn't much interested because it occurred to her that Elyse had not yet arrived with Devlin. His retrieval was taking some time.

As the night deepened and still no Devlin, Emllyn began to seriously worry. She had no idea what would be keeping both Elyse and Devlin unless something terrible had happened. Not knowing the layout of the castle or even the town, it wasn't as if she could go out looking for them. She would have no idea where to look. Furthermore, she suspected she wouldn't get very far on her bad leg. Therefore, there was nothing left to do but wait.

… and wait….

CHAPTER TWELVE

I N THE WEE hours of the morning, de Noble and his men retired to sleep, leaving Devlin seated by the fire with about ten dogs surrounding him. He even had one on his lap. De Noble had told Devlin to find a place to sleep in the hall and that he would see him in the morning, so Devlin bid the man a polite good sleep and watched him trudge up the spiral stairs that led to the upper floors where Emllyn was.

The hall was cold now, with phantoms lurking in the corners and odd shadows dancing on the wall as the firelight reflected on the stone. It was a fearsome and evil place, this English nest in Irish lands. Devlin sat and debated about going upstairs to where Emllyn was, but he wasn't sure where de Noble's chamber was and he didn't want to risk running into the man, so he continued to sit by the fire and brood about the twist the situation had taken.

He was to spy on Black Sword. It wasn't the intelligence gathering for the English that concerned him, for he knew that he could concoct a great bit of gossip that would see de Noble play right into his hands. It was the sheer fact that any such betrayal would harm Emllyn should she remain here. Already they had their claws in her and didn't want to let her go. It was a fearsome scenario he kept rolling over and over in his mind, keeping Emllyn safe while destroying the English. He wasn't sure how it could be done but he would have to figure it out.

As Devlin stared into the snapping flames and pondered the situation, he heard footsteps coming from the stairs. Glancing over his shoulder, he could see a small woman appearing in the shadows of the hall. As she drew closer, he could see that it was the Lady Elyse. Shoving the dog off his lap, Devlin bolted up from his chair and went to her.

"My lady," he greeted with eagerness in his voice. "How does Lady Emllyn fare?"

Elyse smiled up at the very big and very handsome Irishman. She thought it was very sweet the way he worried about Emllyn, and she knew the feeling was very mutual. Lady Emllyn was just as concerned for her protector. It had the stirrings of a tender romance that touched her young and idealistic heart.

"She is much better," she assured him. "I have promised her that I would bring you to her, but you must listen to me carefully – my father would never allow you to be alone with an unchaperoned lady, so you must be very quiet. I am going to take you to another chamber where you and Lady Emllyn may stay. But you must be completely silent and remain in the chamber no matter what. If you leave, you risk running into my father and that would not do. Is this clear?"

"Aye, m'lady."

With a faint smile, she collected her skirts and beckoned for him to follow. Devlin was as quiet as a ghost as he followed her up the stairs. His big feet, clad in peasant boots of rough leather and bindings, made soft footfalls against the stone. Up they went on the narrow spiral staircase to the third floor where the

Lady Elyse's chamber was. Exiting the stairwell, Devlin could immediately see the partitioned chambers to his left, rooms that had been fashioned with partial wooden walls. He could hear snoring.

Elyse took him past those rooms and past the door to her chamber where Devlin last saw Emllyn. Devlin eyed the closed chamber door curiously, wondering if Emllyn was behind the panel, but Elyse took him behind a massive supporting pillar to a door on the other side. Quietly, and in the darkness, she pushed it open.

There was a small chamber beyond, tucked into the corner of the keep where the main portion of the building and one of the oddly designed wings joined. The room had one big window that had oiled cloth curtains covering it, a built-in window seat that made the entire window design look like a modified oriel window, and pillows strewn across the window seat. On either side of the window were two large iron wall sconces that contained an earthenware jar filled with oil and a burning wick. Thin trails of black smoke drifted up to the ceiling, and the room was well lit.

Over in the corner of the chamber was a large and very well furnished mattress but no bed frame; the mattress sat on the ground but was covered in a great feathery coverlet, fine linens, and mounds of pillows. To the right of the bed was a small table and two chairs, containing a pitcher and cups and a bowl of small red apples, and then behind the door where they were standing was a smaller mattress that was less luxurious but nonetheless well furnished. In all, it was a very well appointed chamber and very comfortable. Devlin looked around the room before turning to the woman with some confusion.

Elyse was gazing back at him with an expression filled with

hesitation. She was staring at him as if trying to decide if her actions were of the correct course. Honestly, she didn't know, but she would not go back on her word to Emllyn. She finally sighed heavily.

"I should not be doing this," she said with disapproval in her tone, "but Lady Emllyn has been nearly frantic to see you and I promised her that I would let the two of you remain in the same room. She has assured me that you are her watchdog and nothing more."

Devlin nodded. "That would be a fair statement, m'lady."

Elyse cocked a dubious eyebrow. "And you swear you will not molest her?"

"I swear."

She sighed heavily again. "If my father finds out, I will be in for a row."

"He will not find out. And I am grateful for the kindness, for I am leaving tomorrow and it may be some time before I see the lady again, if ever." He paused, his dark blue eyes glimmering with worry. "You… you will take care of Lady Emllyn, won't you? Since I will be leaving and unable to watch over her, you will do it, won't you?"

Elyse cocked her head with concern. "Where are you going?"

Devlin didn't want to tell her what he had discussed with her father so he skirted the truth. "Your father has asked me to leave and I must comply," he said. "I worry over the lady's safety while I am gone."

Elyse shook her head, putting a gentle hand on his wrist to comfort him. "Do not worry," she said. "I will take care of her. She is in good hands."

Devlin nodded, feeling depressed and resigned. "You have

my thanks."

Elyse remove her hand from his wrist. "It is my pleasure," she said. "Lady Emllyn seems like a kind and lovely woman."

"She is, m'lady."

Elyse smiled at him, sensing his morose mood, and moved for the chamber door. "I will go and get her now," she said softly. Then, she glanced around the room. "This is usually an alcove for the servants but I made it as comfortable as I could in what short time I had. I hope it is enough."

"It is finer and lovelier than anything I have ever seen."

Elyse smiled demurely, a practiced gesture. "Thank you," she said, lifting the latch on the door. "You will stay here and I will return shortly with Lady Emllyn."

She left Devlin standing in the middle of the lush chamber, surrounded by stone walls, fine silks, and softly glowing lamps. A gentle breeze blew at the curtains, lifting them slightly and sending wisps of cold air into the room. He noticed there was an elaborate brazier near the smaller of the mattresses and it was giving off a fair amount of heat. It made the small chamber rather cozy.

As he faced the larger bed, inspecting the myriad of lush silk pillows thrown about it, he heard the door latch lift. By the time he turned around, Emllyn was moving stiffly but quickly into the chamber. He could see Elyse outside as she guided the woman in and then shut the door silently behind her. The moment the door was shut, his attention riveted to Emllyn.

Clad in the blue brocaded robe and with her hair artfully arranged, she looked beautiful and ethereal. It was as Emllyn was always meant to be, a glorious angel in the midst of a colorless world. Devlin just stood there and stared at her, a million words running through his head. He could hardly grasp just one. But when she smiled timidly at him, everything came crashing down around him and his heart leapt into his throat. He'd never been so glad to see anyone in his entire life.

"Are you well, Emllyn?" he asked softly.

She nodded. "Much better," she said. "My fever is nearly gone and my leg is doing very well, thank you."

He smiled faintly at her, his heart beating so loudly that he could hear it in his ears. His chest was tight and his arms tingled. He was all shades of giddy at the sight and sound of her.

"De Noble, the commander of Glenteige, has ordered me to leave on the morrow," he said, his voice strangely tight. "Somehow, our great plans are not happening as they should."

The smile vanished from Emllyn's face. "You are *leaving*?" she gasped. "Why? What has happened?"

Devlin could see how the idea crushed her so. It crushed him as well. The more he stared at her, fumbling for an answer, the more everything crushed down upon him until he could hardly breathe.

In two giant strides he was upon her, his big hands cupping her face and his lips slanting hungrily over hers. It seemed the most natural of things to do, a kiss that was the best and purest kiss he had ever given, meant only for her. There was no lust in it, no selfishness. It was honest and true, an expression of his feelings for her, feelings he hadn't fully realized until this very moment.

Once his captive, she was now much more. She was all. Everything came spilling out before he could stop it.

"Forgive me," he breathed. "You were right, Emllyn; you were so right. I was brutal and barbaric when we first met. I took a possession, a prize, an object and nothing more. In the heat of battle you represented everything I hated and everything

I was fighting against, but now… God forgive me for the way I treated you. I am so very sorry. I tell you this because… because I have missed you so terribly. I thought never to see you again with all that has happened and now that you are here, all I can feel is utter happiness. Please… for what I have done to you in the past, I beg your forgiveness."

Emllyn's hands were on his wrists; they had been since the moment his lips had claimed hers, clinging to him as he held her head and kissed her. There was joy and relief in her heart that she couldn't begin to describe, a euphoria that was enveloping her in a warm and liquid embrace until she could hardly stand. In fact, her knees gave out and Devlin picked her up, holding her against him as his mouth ravaged her. Emllyn wrapped her arms around his neck as if to never let go, tears of joy and adoration falling from her eyes.

"You are forgiven," she whispered. "I know it was war that drove you to do what you did. That barbarian is not the Devlin I have come to know."

He pulled his mouth away from her, nearly ripping himself free, and his dark blue eyes bore into her as if to reach in and clamp onto her very soul.

"I love you," he whispered, his mouth quivering with emotion. "I think I have known it from the start but I did not want to admit it. I did not want to admit that I could love you, a Fitzgerald, but when I look at you I do not see Irish or English. I only see joy and comfort as I have never known."

Emllyn's eyes were wide with shock at his admission and, after a moment, the tears of joy fell faster. She put her hands on his face, touching the red stubble, before kissing both cheeks in a manner so tender that Devlin audibly gasped. Each kiss was like an arrow through his heart, drawing him to her even more closely until all he could think or feel was Emllyn. She kissed his nose, and finally his soft lips. They were kisses of pure and unadulterated worship.

"I did not want to admit I could love a man such as you, either," she whispered, her eyes glimmering with happy tears. "You were right when you said that I belonged to you, Devlin. I have always belonged to you. I love your strength, your humor, and your sense of justice. You are noble and wise. I know that you are a hated rebel, a warrior to be feared, but I do not see those things in you any longer. I only see the man that you are and I love him so very much."

Devlin's emotion was written all over his face. It was greater than he had hoped for and more than he could bear. He stumbled over his words. "My God," he breathed. "But… but what of Trevor? You followed the man into battle because you loved him and…"

Emllyn put her fingers over his lips to stop him. "I was a fool," she murmured. "I know he does not love me and in hindsight, I did not love him, really. Mayhap it was my pride that made me follow him, the desperation of a woman who was terrified she would be an old spinster if she did not coerce a man into marrying her."

"You will *not* be an old spinster."

"I realize that now," she said softly. "Oh… my sweetest darling, I realize that now."

Devlin emitted a noise that sounded strangely like a giggle. Coming from a man of his nature, a serious and intense warrior, it was an odd sound. But Emllyn giggled, too, and soon they were giggling together between heated and joyful kisses. Devlin carried her over to the big bed, ended up tripping on a pillow on the floor, and fell down upon the mattress with

Emllyn in his arms.

Their kisses were passionate, fueled by emotion and fed by dreams, and Devlin knew that he very much wanted to take her. He wanted to feel her body against his, feel her respond to his touch as he had once dreamed of, but he didn't want to make a move against her because she was no longer an object of lust or revenge. She was the woman he loved and a lady to be respected. He was about to tell her so when she suddenly began unfastening her robe.

"Give me your son, Devlin," she murmured as she pulled off the beautiful brocade robe and began untying the neckline of her shift. "Tell me how much you love me and give me your son. I would be filled by you and only you. Touch me as you did before only this time, I will touch you in return."

He wanted to so badly but he hesitated. "Are you sure?" he whispered, concerned. "I do not want you to think I am that barbarian, Emllyn. I only want to show you the greatest esteem."

She smiled, running a finger over his wet, red lips. "I no longer think of you as that barbarian," she murmured. "I want you to touch me, Devlin. Show me the man I have come to love."

Of course he couldn't refuse. Her heated words had his resistance shattering and he yanked the shift over her head, his hungry gaze on her shapely body and his nostrils filled with the rose scent of her skin. Quickly, he removed his raggedy tunic and hose, tossing them aside, his big and naked body swiftly covering her softness. He lay atop of her, rubbing himself against her, as a big arm cradled her neck while he kissed her.

His hand, so big and rough, fondled her breasts gently before his mouth moved from her lips to claim a rosy nipple.

Emllyn groaned, her hands on his stubbled head, as he nursed furiously at one breast and then the other. His fingers moved to her thighs, stroking them, before moving to the junction between her legs. Like a flower unfurling its petals, he stroked her gently, feeling her quiver, opening her to his attentions, and then inserted two big fingers into her already-wet body.

Emllyn groaned and brought her knees up, her legs opening wide in preparation for welcoming him inside her. Devlin didn't wait; he mounted her swiftly, driving his massive erection deep into her body and listening to her gasp. Her hands caressed his arms, his shoulders, until he took one and put it on his buttocks. She was timid at first but as he thrust into her, she gained in confidence and tenderly caressed his buttocks as well. In fact, she got a good grip on him and pulled her to him as he thrust, as if urging him onward.

Her hands on his buttocks were driving him mad with lust. He bit gently on her upper arm and shoulder, suckling her nipples as he drove into her sweet and yielding body, being very careful of her bandaged left leg as he moved. Emllyn seemed to be very interested in touching him everywhere, even his heated phallus as it plunged into her body, but the moment she touched him there, he erupted in a powerful climax.

Feeling his manhood twitching and pulsing inside of her caused Emllyn to explode in a euphoric release. She began to gasp loudly and Devlin covered her mouth with his, kissing her passionately to drown out her cries of passion. After all, he had promised Lady Elyse he wouldn't molest Emllyn. He didn't want the woman to hear evidence that he'd broken his promise.

"I love you," he whispered against her lips. "With all that I am, I am yours, Lady Emllyn Fitzgerald. Never forget that."

Emllyn snaked her arms around his neck, feeling him as he

continued to thrust into her, gently now after their passion had peaked. His massive member was still hard, still stroking her sensitive core, and she trembled again as a weaker climax rolled over her. It was an overwhelming sensation, so raw and delightful. As the ripples died away, she kissed his mouth tenderly.

"Everything I am belongs to you," she murmured. "I will love you until I die."

Exhausted, emotional, Devlin lay on top of her, struggling to catch his breath and feeling her body heave breathlessly underneath him. It was an experience liked he'd never imagined, something beyond the lust or need he'd experienced in the past. Nay; this was something far different.

This was joy.

Devlin kissed her hair, the side of her face, eventually shifting himself off of her and holding her tightly. There was a warm and gentle silence between them as they held each other close, lost to their own thoughts. Devlin thought she might have actually fallen asleep because she was so still and silent. However, the moment he closed his eyes, she stirred.

"Why is de Noble sending you away?" she whispered. "Where are you going to go?"

Devlin's eyes opened. "I told him that I was a farmer who sold my wares at Black Castle," he murmured. "We discussed a great many things, including you. He was clear in his opinion that I am no longer responsible for you now that you are under his roof, but I resisted him. I asked to see you and to inquire on your health. De Noble is a clever man, however. He knows how to get what he wants. Since I am able to move in and out of Black Castle freely, as a farmer selling wares, he intends to use that to his advantage. He told me that if I return to Black Castle to gather information on Black Sword, then he would let me see you again and even speak with you. Somehow, I have agreed to spy on myself."

Emllyn didn't react for a moment. Finally, she shifted enough so that she was gazing up at him, her face very close to his. He smoothed her lovely mussed hairstyle with a big hand as he gazed back.

"You agreed to do this because of me?" she asked, incredulously.

"You have a great deal to do with it," he said softly, smiling at her to let her know that he wasn't upset by it. "I am afraid de Noble intends to separate us and this I will not tolerate. In order to remain in his good graces, while you remain here and hopefully are able to discern elements of his plan against me, I have agreed to supply him with information from Black Castle."

She was still amazed. "So you are returning to Black Castle to spy for the English?" she clarified, an expression of increasing disbelief on her face. "I still do not understand why he has ask you to do that. Does he fear an attack from you now that my brother's fleet has been destroyed?"

Devlin nodded. "He has heard rumor that Black Sword has called the clanns together to launch an attack against Glenteige Castle."

"And you have heard that the English are banding together to attack Black Castle."

"Odd how rumors twist and turn until they become one and the same."

Her mouth popped open in surprise. "What will you do?" she asked. "Are you indeed gathering the clanns to launch an attack on Glenteige?"

He shrugged vaguely. "There is always that possibility, but I have no immediate plans. My priority is banishing Kildare from Wicklow completely. After that, I will think about de Cleveley lands."

"What will you tell him, then?"

Devlin sighed faintly, reaching up to toy with a stray tendril of hair around her ear. "I am not certain yet," he murmured. "But one thing is for sure; de Noble believes me to be a farmer and he believes that I will return to Black Castle and gather information for him. That is all you must know and all you must ever speak of. If they find out who I am, it could reflect very badly on you because you have known my identity all along. They will think you a traitor."

Emllyn gazed at him a moment before averting her gaze, thoughtfully. "I am," she murmured. "If I had to make the choice between you and Glenteige, my brother's ally, I would choose you. I am indeed a traitor to my own people."

He kissed her forehead tenderly, not knowing what to say to that, mostly because she was correct. Lacking a comforting response, he changed the subject.

"I am not certain how long I will be gone, but it will not be too long," he said softly. "I cannot stomach the thought of being away from you, not even for an hour. My one and only thought will be of returning to you."

Emllyn smiled faintly, reaching up soft, white fingers and running them over his perfect lips. "And my thoughts will only be of you," she whispered. "But there is something else you should know – Elyse said that her father met you once when you were young. It must have been some time ago if he did not recognized you immediately. Still, you must be cautious. It may suddenly occur to him one day where he has seen you."

Devlin cocked a thoughtful eyebrow. "Now it makes some

sense as to why the man stares at me so intently," he said. "He recognizes me but does not know from where. I will have to be very careful, indeed."

It was a fearful thought. Emllyn fell silent, snuggling up to Devlin and burying her face against his shoulder. His skin was so pale, so warm, and immensely comforting. She would relish this memory of her body against his, his heart beating in rhythm with hers, for the rest of her life.

It was a tender and wonderful moment, one that she never wished to end. Her hands moved up his arms, to his broad shoulders, acquainting herself with the feel of him against her palms. She never knew she was capable of emotions such as this, emotions that had been developing quite steadily over the past two days. When they erupted, it was with the unbridled restraint of an exploding star and now the only thought that occupied her mind was Devlin. Her captor had managed to capture not only her body, but her heart as well, and she did not regret it.

Devlin could feel her hands moving over his skin, touching him, and it was wildly arousing. He put a finger under her chin, tipping her head up and kissing her sweetly until a knock on the door startled them both. Devlin was already out of the bed, gathering his ratty hose and tunic, heading for the mattress that was near the door. Emllyn grabbed her shift from where Devlin had tossed it, pulling it swiftly over her head.

"Who comes?" she asked, hoping she didn't sound as breathless as she felt.

"Merradoc!" Came the boom. "Open the door before I am set upon by cutthroats out in this corridor. It is dark and terrifying out here!"

Shift over her head, Emllyn pulled on the lovely brocade

robe as she made her way to the door. "A moment, please," she said, swiftly fastening the robe.

A glance at Devlin showed that he was fully dressed as he sat upon the mattress. He winked at her and she grinned. Taking a deep, steadying breath, she opened the door.

Merradoc barged in without a word, practically shoving her aside. When he was about half-way into the room, he sniffed the air suspiciously.

"It smells as if animals have been mating in here," he said. "What have you..?"

He turned and caught sight of Devlin sitting on the mattress near the door. Gazing down at the big, bald man with the enormous arms, he wriggled his eyebrows. "That explains quite a bit," he muttered, turning away from Devlin and moving for the table. Setting his satchel down, he began to rifle through it. "I do not suppose you would take my advice if I told you to refrain from, shall we say, physical activities until you are completely well?"

Emllyn couldn't help it; she flushed a dull shade of red. She didn't dare look at Devlin. "I do not know what you mean," she said primly. "John is my watchdog and nothing more. He protects me from spikey old men who come banging at my door at all hours."

Merradoc sniffled loudly, wiping at his nose to hide his grin. "Mayhap," he conceded, "but do not let de Noble find him here."

Emllyn didn't have a witty response for him. She ended up looking over at Devlin, who by now had stood up and was hovering in the shadows. Their eyes met, expressions of apprehension passing between them, before Emllyn returned her attention to the old physic.

"It is none of de Noble's business what I do," she said. "I am not under his command."

Merradoc was pouring a measure of the rotten tea into a cup. He handed it to her. "Drink this," he ordered. As Emllyn made a face and downed the entire thing in one swallow, he took the cup away from her and set it aside. "Nay, it is not the man's business, but he is no fool. He is a man of decorum and propriety. If he discovers what you and your lover have been doing, he will more than likely have something to say about it."

Emllyn had her hand to her throat, her face twisted with disgust as the remains of the rotten tea slid down her gullet.

"You are not to worry over that," she said, raspy from the terrible medicine. "And you will not say anything to him, do you hear?"

Merradoc snorted. "I see nothing and I hear nothing," he said. "I am a physic, not a gossipmonger. Oh, and beware of Connaught, too. He is the suspicious type."

Emllyn licked her lips, still overcoming the taste of the medicine. "Of me?"

Merradoc shook his head, pointing at Devlin. "Of him," he replied. "I may not be a gossip, but I hear things. I'm not particularly fond of Connaught because the man it too self-righteous. He is also arrogant, thinking that he is with surety to be pledged to the Lady Elyse. Mayhap he will, mayhap he won't; in any case, he believes he will be the commander of Glenteige someday. If that is the case, God help us. He does not have the patience and cunning that de Noble does."

Devlin didn't say a word but he was listening carefully; he often found the best intelligence came from outside observers. He was curious to know in what direction Emllyn would take the conversation.

"It matters not to me," she finally said, turning for the table where a pitcher of wine and two cups sat. She poured herself some wine to get rid of the rotten taste. "I will be leaving soon and returning home. I am not concerned for the politics at Glenteige."

Merradoc watched her drink. "I heard de Noble say that you would be a fine companion for his daughter," he said quietly. "This is not gossip, mind you, for I heard him say this to the Lady Elyse. His daughter is lonely here and she has taken a liking to you. I believe that de Noble will write to your brother and ask that you remain here."

Emllyn looked at the man. She wasn't particularly surprised to hear that but she didn't protest it. She was coming to think that perhaps Merradoc wasn't as tight-lipped as he said he was, which concerned her. What she said might make it to other ears. Therefore, she didn't react one way or the other.

"Lady Elyse is a very sweet woman," she said neutrally, sipping at her wine. "I like her a great deal."

Merradoc's gaze lingered on her a moment before returning his focus to his satchel. He began packing items away. "I will return in the morning," he said. "In the meanwhile, stay off of that leg and limit your nocturnal activities. You need your rest."

He was looking at Devlin as he said it. But Devlin didn't react and the old man collected his bag, pushing past the two of them on his way to the door. Hand on the big iron latch, he paused before leaving.

"I would not sleep in the same bed if I were you," he said quietly, looking between the two of them. "Lady Elyse is an early riser and unless you want her to find you together, I would suggest you sleep in separate beds."

Emllyn gave one last stab at maintaining a proper illusion

between her and Devlin. "We most certainly will not sleep in the same bed," she said firmly. "You are a nosy old man with unclean thoughts."

Merradoc's lips tugged with the beginnings of a smile. "And you, lady, smell like a man has been all over you."

Emllyn's eyes narrowed. "How would you know what such a thing smells like? I would wager it has been centuries since you last saw companionship."

Merradoc snorted as he opened the door. "Mayhap, Lady Emllyn," he said, shaking a finger at her. "Mayhap indeed. But you must be careful nonetheless."

He shut the door softly behind him and Devlin moved over to throw the bolt, locking the door. He turned to look at Emllyn, who was still standing by the bed with a cup of wine in her hand. They stood there a moment, looking at each other, each feeling a certain measure of apprehension.

"You will not trust anyone here," Devlin finally said, his voice soft and firm. "Especially not him."

Emllyn nodded, downing the rest of the wine in the cup. "It is strange," she said quietly as she set the cup down. "When I was at Black Castle, I could not trust anyone," she said. "I was surrounded by people who considered me the enemy. Now, at Glenteige, I still cannot trust anyone even though we are allies. It is a difficult world I live in."

Devlin could see her perspective. In many ways, her world was more difficult than his; at least he had people he could depend on. She had no one. But she had him.

Silently, he made his way over to her and wrapped her up in his big, strong arms. Emllyn collapsed against him, her arms around his waist and her head against his chest. It was the most wonderful feeling in the world. There was so much warmth and comfort between them, so much power and emotion, that it brought tears to her eyes.

"Promise me that you will not leave me here long," she whispered. "Promise me that you will return for me very soon."

Devlin kissed the top of her head. "I swear I will not leave you here any longer than necessary," he said. "I want you with me and not imprisoned in this English hell. My greatest thought will be of taking you back with me to Black Castle where we both belong."

Emllyn looked up at him, her eyes moist with unshed tears. "I told you once I did not want to be your concubine," she murmured. "I have changed my mind. It would be an honor."

He smiled faintly. "I would rather have you as my wife," he said. "Would that not be a greater honor?"

"The greatest."

He grinned and kissed her, tasting her sweetness as if he had been longing for it all of his life. To feel such a connection with someone, to feel physical pain at the thought of separation or physical excitement when their bodies touched, was an entirely new experience for him. Even now, the thought of leaving her tomorrow made him feel ill. He was dreading it.

"Then I will marry you the day we return to Black Castle," he said. "I will cherish the day when I can call you Lady de Bermingham."

Emllyn grinned, touching his face and watching him kiss her palms. "It will give my brother fits."

"Does this concern you?"

"Not in the least. You are the most important thing in the world to me." Her smile faded as her thoughts turned to the bargain they had struck back at Black Castle. It seemed so long ago now. "Dev, what of the English prisoners you still hold?

Will you still kill them? Or will you let them go?"

He sobered, thinking of Trevor, the man who had literally brought them together, moldering down in his vault. "Do you still want to see if Trevor is among them?" he asked even though he already knew the answer. "I will allow you to check if you wish."

"It hardly matters now."

"Then what do you want me to do with them?"

Emllyn pondered his question seriously. "It was our bargain that you let me see the English prisoners if I came to Glenteige to discover de Cleveley's plans against you."

"I know."

"I will discover what I can without need to see the prisoners. I simply do not care any longer if Trevor is with them or not."

He debated whether or not he should tell her what he knew, but he opted not to mention that Trevor was indeed among his captives because he didn't want anything to cloud their joy. He was selfish, he knew it, but he didn't care. He didn't want her to think thoughts of Trevor when she should only be thinking of him.

"Then I will put them on a boat and send them back to England," he said quietly. "I have no more use for them. If you wish for me to spare them, then I will."

She smiled at him; it was surely a generous offer coming from Black Sword and the importance of it was not lost on her. "You are very generous," she said. "I am grateful."

His smile broadened and he gazed at her steadily for several long moments. It was evident that he was pondering something. After a moment, he reached out to tenderly touch her cheek.

"My mother used to say something to me when I was young, something that I never fully understood until this moment," he said softly. "She used to say to me, 'Everything leads me to thee'. I was her only child and she was very attached to me, and every time she left me, even if it was just for a short while, she used to say that. 'Everything leads me to thee.' Now that I look at you, I understand what she meant. There isn't a move I will make or a thought I will think that will not cause me to think of you. Everything, ultimately, will lead me to thee so when I leave on the morrow, I want you to remember that. Everything leads me to thee, and I will return for you."

It was such a sweet sentiment. Emllyn smiled sweetly at him. "That is the most wonderful thing I have ever heard."

"Say it for me."

She did. "Everything leads me to thee," she murmured.

Hearing it in her voice made him believe the words as if God himself had spoken it. Devlin kissed her forehead and her cheeks before lifting her up and carrying her over to the big, luxurious bed. He carefully laid her down and then lay down beside her. They faced each other, their first moment together on a bed when they weren't fighting with one another or experiencing untold passion. It was just the two of them, a man and a woman, embarking on a remarkable voyage of discovery.

They talked of all things, both serious and trivial, for most of the night.

CHAPTER THIRTEEN

Two weeks later
Glenteige Castle

IT HAD BEEN thirteen days since Devlin's return to Black Castle, but to Emllyn, it felt like a lifetime.

Seated in Elyse's fine solar, so fine and fancy that it looked as if a queen lived there, Emllyn sat before an embroidery frame, working on a piece she had started a few days before. It was of an angel in the Garden of Eden, an ambitious piece with flowers and birds. Emllyn was very good at sewing, so she took delight in a challenge.

Emllyn had been sewing on the piece steadily since she had started it, putting angels and animals to needle when her thoughts were far away with Devlin. At the top of the piece were the five little words Devlin had said to her, words she would never forget. They were the most important words she had ever heard.

Everything leads me to thee.

This day in March was cool and dreary, as a storm had blown in off the Irish Sea and continued to drench the country-side with a heavy downpour. A fire burned brightly in the hearth as a cool and damp breeze blew in through the thin lancet windows. Emllyn sat, wrapped up in a fur-lined robe and warm slippers, as Elyse chattered continuously as she sat at her beautifully carved drawing table and sketched with charcoal. These days with Elyse were comfortable and companionable, and Emllyn had come to like her a great deal.

Elyse was quite an artist, the result of many hours of spending time alone. She had to fill the time somehow, so she had practiced her drawing and had become very proficient at it. At this moment, she was working very hard on something that Emllyn had yet to see, but she knew the woman had been working on it for a couple of days. Charcoal on parchment made for the most beautiful and emotive art. But the woman was talking so much that Emllyn was surprised she was able to get anything accomplished at all.

"… and then he told me that he did not even like for me to look at another man," she was saying as she sketched. "Of course, I told him he was ridiculous. We are not even pledged, after all."

Emllyn smiled weakly, glancing up from her sewing. "Has he spoken to your father yet?"

Elyse shook her head. "Not yet," she said. "I believe he feels as if it is a mere formality. After all, he is the most eligible candidate at Glenteige so I do believe he feels as if it's understood by all that he will someday be my husband."

Emllyn wriggled her eyebrows as she focused on her needle. "Very presumptive," she said. "I do not like any man who assumes things before he has been given permission."

Elyse stopped drawing and looked at her. "Nor do I," she declared. "In fact, I have been thinking of ignoring him for a time to teach him a lesson. I'll not come so easily to him, you know. I am not a prize to be won or a commodity to be bartered for."

Emllyn grinned. "Are there no other eligible bachelors here other than Connaught?"

Elyse cocked her head thoughtfully as she went back to work. "Christopher has a younger brother, Drew," she said. "He is quite handsome. But he is also quite young and quite frisky with women, if you get my meaning. I have heard he has at least two bastards."

Emllyn giggled. "You do *not* want a man with bastards," she said. "Who else?"

Elyse was carefully shading something. "There are a couple of lesser knights," she said. "My father has an entire stable of knights, but only a few I would even look at more than once. I suppose the reality is that Christopher is the only true marital candidate for me."

Emllyn looked up at her. "And this displeases you?"

Elyse shrugged. "It would be nice to have more of a selec- tion," she said. As they giggled, her focus on Emllyn grew more intense. "And what of you? Do you have any prospects for marriage?"

Emllyn was careful in her answer. "Nay," she said softly. "I have told you of the man I thought to marry, but he was killed."

Elyse had heard the story of Sir Trevor, Emllyn's one and true love, and how the man had been killed in the battle at Black Castle those weeks ago. She had tried to get more of the story out of her but Emllyn didn't seem to want to talk about it. Although Elyse was trying to be tactful when discussing Emllyn's recently lost love, it frustrated her to no end that the woman wouldn't elaborate. She was very curious.

"I am sorry for you, of course," Elyse said quietly. "But

shouldn't you think of your future, or do you plan to pine away for a dead man? You are young and beautiful, but you will not be that way forever. You must marry while you are still attractive."

It was a harsh way of putting it but she wasn't far wrong. Still, Emllyn shook her head. "Mayhap," she said. "But I am not thinking of marriage now."

"But you will someday?"

"Of course I will."

Elyse sighed dreamily, thinking on Emllyn's future lover. "Will you at least invite me to your wedding when you do marry? I should like to see the husband you finally choose."

Emllyn had a mental picture of Elyse at her wedding to Devlin and it almost made her laugh. "If you will come, of course I will invite you."

Elyse was thrilled. She went back to her drawing. "My father would chastise me if he heard me say this," she said, "but I have seen many handsome Irishmen since I have been in Ireland. I swear that the country is overrun with handsome men. It is unfortunate that I cannot marry an Irishman, for I would dearly love to have a handsome Irish husband."

Emllyn grinned at her. "Connaught is not handsome or Irish enough?"

Elyse waved her off. "He is very handsome," she said. "But he is so… *English*. To hear a man say my name in an Irish accent… 'tis heavenly!"

Emllyn giggled at the woman's silly romantic notions. They were sweet. As she focused on her work again and took another stitch, she heard Elyse's soft voice upon the air.

"John is a very handsome man," she ventured. "He told my father that his wife and daughter died. Do… do you know much about him?"

Emllyn's good humor fled and jealousy filled her veins. She could tell just by the woman's tone that she was interested in Devlin and it was an effort not to fly over the table and wrap her hands around Elyse's neck. But she remained calm and cool, reminding herself that Elyse had no true knowledge of who Devlin was or of his relationship to Emllyn. Moreover, she couldn't fault the woman for her excellent taste; he most definitely *was* a big, handsome man.

"He is a farmer," she said, avoiding the question. "Your father would never allow you to marry an Irish farmer."

Elyse sighed. "I know," she said. "But he is still devilishly handsome. What do you know of him?"

It was the same question; Emllyn realized that the woman wasn't going to let it go. She had insatiable curiosity, more than likely because she really hadn't had any female companionship to talk to before Emllyn had come along. It was as if she was making up for all of those lonely days with no one to pass the time with.

"Not too terribly much," Emllyn replied, focused on her needlework. "He was very kind to me and helped me a great deal."

"He cares for you."

Emllyn shrugged. "It is only normal concern, I am sure."

Elyse had stopped drawing; she was gazing intently at Emllyn. "To dream of a man like that with his arms around me, in my bed," she murmured. "It makes me warm all over."

Emllyn's head shot up, looking at Elyse with a mixture of curiosity and shock. "God's Blood, Elyse," she said; she had long since stopped addressing her formally as "lady" since they had become fast friends. "What a deviant mind you have."

Elyse cocked an eyebrow at her before breaking down into giggles. "I have a healthy curiosity for men in general," she admitted. "Christopher may be handsome but he is a boring lover. I've had better."

Emllyn nearly choked. "Better *lovers*?" she repeated. "Surely you do not mean…?"

Elyse nodded swiftly, cutting her off as she returned to her drawing. "The young, strong ones are usually more exciting in bed, but often with them it is over too soon," she said. "Older men can control themselves better but they are usually so unimaginative."

Emllyn's eyes widened. "Elyse!" she gasped. "You are shameless!"

Elyse giggled. "Do not play coy with me," she said, a knowing twinkle in her eye. "Merradoc told me what you and John did. He said the entire chamber smelled like rough and sweaty mating. Tell me – was his manhood big and full? Did he use it wisely?"

Emllyn almost fell out of her chair. She could hardly believe the twist the conversation had taken, shocked to the point of giggling uncontrollably. Elyse giggled right along with her. Emllyn covered her mouth, giggling so hard that she could barely breathe.

"But… but your father," she gasped. "He is a very proper and moralistic man. How do you… what if he…?"

"I am very careful," Elyse said. "But the truth is that my father does not come near my chamber. His chamber is on the second floor and he leaves me well enough alone."

Emllyn was still struggling with the thought of a reckless and sexually active Elyse; she'd never heard anything more astonishing because the woman, for all appearances, seemed like a properly prudish lady. After having sat with the woman for hours each day for the past two weeks discussing all manner of subjects, this was the first Elyse had mentioned her carnal pleasures. The realization was therefore a shock.

"God's Blood," Emllyn finally hissed. "You are full of surprises, my lady."

Elyse nodded as she continued to titter in a maidenly manner. "Let us speak of John again," she said. "Was he wonderful? He is such a big and strong man, I imagine it would rather be like mating with a bull."

Emllyn's giggles diminished as she considered Elyse's question. She certainly didn't want to discuss it but she had a feeling Elyse wouldn't understand that. The seemingly pure and pristine English lady evidently had a nasty streak. So she tried to form an answer that would satisfy her.

"Merradoc has a wild imagination," she said. "John is a complete and utter gentleman and we enjoy a fine friendship."

Elyse looked confused. "Then... then he did not bed you?"

"I have already told you my heart lies with another," she said. "To take another man to my bed would be wrong at best. How much plainer can I be?"

Even though Emllyn's fine English knight was dead at Black Sword's hand, in Elyse's mind, there was no reason why the woman couldn't immediately focus her attention on another man, especially one as big and handsome as John. Elyse cocked her head curiously.

"Then mayhap I can find out what John is like, then," she said. "My father said he should be returning soon. Mayhap I can coerce him into my bed. I will let you know what you have missed."

Emllyn clamped her lips together, wanting very much to tell

the woman that Devlin was her property and to leave him alone, but she had a feeling that Elyse already suspected that and was simply trying to get a reaction from her. So she shrugged her shoulders.

"I wish you luck," she said, returning to her sewing. "It may be quite a task. Mayhap he doesn't even like women."

Elyse grinned slyly. "I will find out."

Emllyn didn't like that reply at all. She stabbed at her sewing with increasing frustration, irritated at Elyse and her wanton ways. But any word out of her mouth would find its way into the rumor mill; she knew that now. Between Elyse and Merradoc, all of Glenteige seemed to be full of gossips. She'd certainly come to discover that, too, in the past two weeks. As she sat and fumed in silence, Elyse began to speak of a stable boy she once shared her bed with. It was rather ribald talk that was fortunately interrupted by a knock on the solar door.

Elyse rose to answer the door, permitting a few serving women entrance. Their arms were laden with trays and pitchers.

"It must be time for the nooning meal," Elyse commented as the servants moved to put the items on a pretty carved table. "I had completely lost track of time."

Emllyn was grateful for the distraction. "It is easy to lose track of time when you are focused on your task," she said, gesturing towards Elyse's drawing table. "What marvelous thing are you working on? May I see it?"

Elyse grinned and went over to her drawing table as the servants spread out a beautiful meal on the other table. Picking up the rather large piece of yellowed parchment, she blew any remaining grains of loose charcoal off of it as she brought it over and presented it to Emllyn.

"There," she said. "What do you think?"

Emllyn found herself looking at a perfect likeness of herself, skillfully sketched in charcoal. Elyse had drawn her looking over her right shoulder with her hair flowing and curled, and flowers woven into it. It was astonishing and life-like, and so very beautiful. Emllyn's jaw dropped.

"Oh… my," she breathed. "Elyse, you drew an image of *me*. I have never seen anything so remarkable. It's magnificent!"

Elyse beamed. "I am not done with it but it is a good start, don't you think?" she inspected her drawing carefully. "You are an excellent subject because your features are so fine. Do you like it?"

"I love it," Emllyn exclaimed. "I have never seen myself like that before, ever. May… may I have it when you are finished?"

Elyse nodded. "Of course," she said as she headed back over to her drawing table and deposited the parchment. "I made it for you."

"You are incredibly generous," Emllyn said sincerely. "I am very touched."

Elyse continued to grin, pleased by her friend's reaction, when another maid servant entered the room and headed directly for her. The girl in rough linen clothing and a torn apron curtsied quickly as she extended what looked like a piece of parchment to Elyse.

"M'lady," the servant said. "I have a message for the Lady Emllyn."

Elyse eyed the girl. "Who is it from?"

"I have been sworn not to tell, m'lady."

Elyse took the parchment from her and dismissed her. She promptly went to Emllyn, extending the parchment to her.

"Another note," she said knowingly. "That makes three

notes in the past five days. Who are they from, Emllyn?"

Emllyn could sense curiosity and jealousy from Elyse. It wasn't surprisingly considering Elyse had been the only fine lady in the castle until thirteen days ago. Now, others were noticing Emllyn. Although Elyse pretended to be excited and thrilled for her, there was something in her tone that suggested otherwise.

Reluctantly, Emllyn took the note and popped open the wax seal. There was no signet ring in the wax, nothing to indicate who had sent it, but the note itself was short and brief. It was the third note asking for Emllyn to meet her secret admirer in the ward of Glenteige near the well at sunset. There was no signature other than: "Your Devoted Servant". With disinterest, she passed the note to Elyse.

"See for yourself," she said. "Whoever it is never signs it."

Elyse read the note with great relish. "How romantic!" she exclaimed softly. "You should meet him, Emllyn, by all means. Mayhap you shall fall madly in love with him!"

Emllyn shook her head. "God's Blood, Elyse, I am surely not interested," she said with some exasperation. "I told you once that my only true love was a knight who was killed when Black Sword destroyed my brother's war armada. I have no interest in another, not a man who writes me notes or a farmer named John. Why can you not accept that?"

Emllyn had told the story about Trevor to throw Elyse off when the woman began prying into her personal life at the beginning of their acquaintance. Certainly, the conversation had never reached the bawdy levels that it had reached this day because the day's conversation had indeed been enlightening. Elyse had let her prim façade down to reveal the tigress beneath. And the gossip. Emllyn was very glad she'd never confided in her about anything critical or personal, and she knew now that she never would.

Elyse, however, did not share her friend's sense of reserve. She pressed the note against her breast in an amorous gesture.

"You must meet the man and put him out of his misery," she said, still holding the note as she went to the table where a fair amount of food was laid out. "It has taken much courage for him to write to you, Emllyn. It would be polite to meet him for his troubles."

Emllyn eyed her, cocking an eyebrow. "And thank him by bedding him?"

"If he is handsome enough."

Elyse burst out laughing and Emllyn grinned, shaking her head reproachfully. Elyse began eating the fruits that were upon the table and Emllyn was just finishing up her final stitch when a serving woman approached her from behind, a pewter plate of apricots and apples in her hand. She extended the plate to Emllyn, nearly blocking her vision of her loom.

"Food, m'lady?" the woman rasped.

Annoyed, Emllyn's head came up with the intention of chasing the woman away when her gaze fell on a set of familiar features. It took Emllyn a moment to realize that she was looking at Eefha. Startled, she dropped her needle but recovered quickly, stabbing herself in the process. All the while, her gaze barely left the gnarled old woman. She could hardly believe her eyes.

When her mouth popped open, a sure sign of realization, Eefha shook her head faintly as if to admonish her to be silent. Emllyn remained silent but she had never been so astonished, by anything, in her entire life.

"Emllyn?" Elyse called to her, mouth full. "Will you come

and eat with me?"

Emllyn stood up on shaking legs. "Of course," she said, trying not to stare at Eefha as she moved past the woman. She desperately wanted to say something to her but wisely kept silent. She forced herself to focus on Elyse. "What delicious dishes do we have today?"

Elyse had her mouth full. "My favorites," she said. "Brined beef with cabbage and carrots, and duck with honey sauce."

Emllyn pretended to be very interested in the dishes but the truth was that her mind was still on the shock of seeing Eefha. She didn't want to lose sight of the woman, not for a moment, so she popped a piece of cheese into her mouth and turned around to see if the old woman was still in the room. She, lingering by the chamber door. Emllyn called out to her.

"You, there," she said, pointing. "Can you please go to my chamber and bring me my wrap?" she asked. "My chamber is on the top floor at the end of the corridor behind the pillar. There is a red shawl on my bed."

Eefha didn't say a word; she simply disappeared from the door. Given the woman's speech habits and patterns, Emllyn wasn't even sure if Eefha understood her but she couldn't have very well sung the request or delivered it via an anecdote about ancient Irish myths. Her entire purpose of sending Eefha to her chamber was so the old woman would know where she slept and, hopefully, would return to her at some point. But, then again, as Devlin once said, Eefha did what she wanted to do, when she wanted to do it. Who knew why the old woman was here or what she was doing? Emllyn pondered the mystery as she returned to the lovely meal.

"Emllyn," Elyse said thoughtfully after Eefha had fled the chamber, "do you not think that you should at least meet the man who has been writing you such notes if only to tell him that you are not interested?"

Emllyn sighed with frustration as Elyse went back to the subject of her secret admirer. She was getting rather tired with the woman's pestering and it was a struggle not to become short with her.

"I do not plan to meet him," she said as she put food on her plate.

Elyse wasn't happy with the answer. "But why?" she pressed. "Surely you should tell the man that he is wasting his time."

Emllyn stopped what she was doing and faced the woman. "Elyse, if you are so concerned, then *you* meet him by the well tonight," she said with strained patience. "Tell him that I am not interested in his notes. Mayhap he will start writing them to you instead."

Rather than refuse, Elyse saw it as an opportunity. Her face lit up. "May I meet him?" she asked happily.

Emllyn waved her off and returned to her food. "You have my permission," she said, disinterested. "Tell him I have no time to spare his nonsense."

Perhaps she didn't, but Elyse certainly did. She was very much looking forward to meeting Emllyn's lover by the well, if only to see who it was and, if he was acceptable enough, to make another conquest. Emllyn might not have been interested in men but Elyse certainly was. As they sat down to the feast before them, the solar door opened again and Merradoc appeared.

He had been a fixture in Emllyn's life, sitting with her when Elyse wasn't, telling his frank and brutal and terribly funny stories to keep her entertained. Even after her leg healed completely, he still kept coming back because he enjoyed her company so much. When he marched into the solar and saw what the women were doing, he threw up his hands.

"Excellent!" he exclaimed. "Let us do what the Romans did; let us become ragingly drunk and then tell our fortunes from our own vomit."

Emllyn burst out laughing. "God's Blood," she said. "You certainly know how to have a good time."

Merradoc nodded vigorously as he poured himself a large cup of wine and went to sit next to Emllyn.

"I do, indeed," he said, eyeing her and slapping her lightly on the thigh. "Let me see your leg, you little goat." When Emllyn began to lift her leg to show him the nearly-healed wound, he slapped her leg again and pushed it down. "Never you mind. I don't care in the least."

He was quick-witted and hilarious. With a shrug, Emllyn lowered her leg, returning to her food as Merradoc drank deeply of his wine.

"I have heard something very interesting," he said, smacking his lips. "It would seem that someone in this room is receiving letters from an admirer."

As Elyse tittered, Emllyn stopped eating and looked at Merradoc with outrage. "God's Blood!" she exclaimed. "How would you know that? This entire castle is maelstrom of rumors and lies!"

Merradoc put his hand affectionately on her arm. "Everyone is concerned for everyone, little chick," he said. "Of course we talk about one another. We have nothing better to do."

Emllyn made a face at him. "Everyone is in everyone else's lives and business," she countered. "Never have I seen such nosy gossips!"

Merradoc was grinning at her. "Nosy or not, tell me of your notes and spare me nothing," he said. "Have you decided who is sending them?"

Emllyn gave him a look of utter exasperation before motioning to Elyse, who was still holding on to the parchment. Elyse handed it to Merradoc, who studied the handwriting carefully. After a moment, he crowed.

"Of course I know who this is!" he announced.

Both Emllyn and Elyse perked up. "Who?" Elyse demanded.

Merradoc began laughing. He read the carefully scribed note twice before holding it up in the air and howling with laughter. "Remarkable, I say!" he cried.

Emllyn and Elyse were nearly crazed with the need to know. "Tell me who it is!" Emllyn demanded. "Stop cackling and tell me, do you hear?"

Merradoc jumped up from his chair. "You will guess," he told them. "I will give you clues and you will guess."

Emllyn and Elyse were eager for the game. They put the food and drink aside, hanging on Merradoc's every movement. At first, he stood up very tall and put his hand at his hip as if holding onto the hilt of a sword. Then, he beat at his chest and pretended to lower the visor of a helm. Emllyn leapt to her feet.

"A knight!" she exclaimed.

Merradoc nodded vigorously and moved over to Elyse, whom he began to pat on the head. Then, he put his hand to his heart as if to signify that he loved her. He did this several times until Emllyn spoke again.

"A love?" she said, thinking aloud. "Someone who loves Elyse? Is it Connaught?"

Merradoc shook his head, scowling at her incorrect answer. Then, he took an apple from the table and held it next to his groin. He pointed at the apple, and then his groin, repeatedly in that order. Then he pointed at Elyse. Emllyn and Elyse looked at each other in total, utter confusion.

"An apple and… and a man's member?" Elyse ventured.

Emllyn wasn't much clearer but she began to think aloud. "An apple and… wait… no, is it fruit?" she said, watching Merradoc nod firmly. "Then it is fruit and… and a groin? Fruit and… and… no, not groin. Is it loins? Fruit and loins? Fruit *of* loins and…?"

She gasped, looking directly at Elyse as realization dawned. "Fruit of his loins?" she said, pointing at Elyse. "He means your father! You are the fruit of his loins!"

Elyse's eyes widened with shock. "My *father* has been sending you notes?" she gasped. "Sweet Jesus, Joseph, and Mary!"

With his job finished, Merradoc sat back down at the table and collected his cup of wine as he tossed the note back onto the tabletop. He was quite smug about it all.

"That is de Noble's writing," he said, taking a big gulp of wine. "It would seem that he has affections for our lovely Lady Emllyn."

Emllyn didn't know what to say; she looked at Elyse in shock, unsure how her friend was going to handle the news. She couldn't tell from the woman's expression.

"Are you still going to meet him by the well?" she finally asked. "You cannot do that now that you know it 'tis him."

Elyse appeared concerned but not distressed. "Mayhap… mayhap you should just continue to ignore the notes," she said. "Although I do not want to see my father disappointed, mayhap it would be best if you did not respond."

Emllyn agreed. "I will not," she said, eyeing Elyse. "I am sorry if this makes you uncomfortable."

Elyse shook her head. "It does not," she said. "I simply cannot believe my father is showing interest in a woman. It is shocking."

Merradoc entered the conversation, sitting forward to look Elyse in the eye. "By God's Holy Rood, Elyse," he exclaimed softly. "Your father is not dead. He saw an attractive woman and reacted naturally. There is nothing mysterious or shameful about that."

Elyse thought on that a moment before nodding her head. "I suppose not," she said, regaining some of her humor. "It is a bit strange, though."

Emllyn agreed, sipping her wine but refraining from saying anything more. She was already uncomfortable enough as it was.

The three of them continued to drink and tell stories for the rest of the afternoon until the storm outside passed and shades of a lovely sunset were visible to the east. At that point, the ladies excused themselves to prepare for the evening meal while Merradoc, with de Noble's note still in his hand, wandered out to the well at sunset just to see what he could see. The note had said the well, after all.

De Noble was indeed waiting. Merradoc was initially going to have some fun with him but when he saw how disappointed the man became when Emllyn didn't appear, he decided against it. After some general chatter and nonsensical conversation, none of which had anything to do with the subject of Emllyn, Merradoc escorted the man into the feasting hall of Glenteige and sat with him while he became drunk and depressed.

It would seem that prim and proper men had deep and fragile hearts.

CHAPTER FOURTEEN

Black Castle

THE WIND WAS whipping and the rain lashing as a violent storm battered the coast. Black Castle, caught in the storm's path, took the brunt of it. The wind howled and the seas swelled as inside the keep, the smaller feasting hall was stuffed with men, smelling of vomit and unwashed bodies.

It was much like the night when Kildare's fleet ran aground; men were high on glory and bellowing stories of victory, but these were not of victories over the English. They were victories over the Irish. Devlin sat in the chair he had stolen from de Cleveley with Neart perched over his left shoulder, watching Shain and Iver and Frederick tell grand stories of battle. Even though Devlin's mind should have rightly been on the stories being told, all he could see to think about was the fact he had met Emllyn on a night not dissimilar to this one.

Everything leads me to thee.

God, she was all he could think of. It had been two weeks since he had left Emllyn at Glenteige and traveled back to Black Castle; initially, he thought to stay away only a week, enough time to pretend he'd been doing what he'd agreed to do, but on the eve of the sixth day, they'd had an unexpected rush from the north.

The Clann O'Byrne, the hated enemies of de Bermingham, had made an unexpected push against Black Castle because of all of the booty they had collected from Kildare's fleet. Rumors, of course, had spread about Devlin's victory against the armada and his men had been pulling apart the ships for weeks, storing the treasures.

The O'Byrnes, a greedy and barbaric clann, had decided that they wanted some of the English treasures and had laid an unorganized but somewhat intense siege to Black Castle, an event that lasted for four days and nights until Devlin and his men launched a counter-attack that had seen brutal combat for nearly two days. It was combat that had seen Devlin lose more than two dozen men, but the O'Byrne losses had been even greater.

The O'Byrnes had retreated and Devlin's men had set about congratulating each other on their victory. Even now, they had been feasting for two solid days, celebrating victory and planning their next battle. De Cleveley's settlement had come up several times as a target. Devlin knew his men were charged up on the smell of blood so he simply let them vent. But all he could think about was how the O'Byrne's unexpected siege had delayed his return to Glenteige, and to Emllyn.

Frederick was the worst of the revelers. He was absolutely electrified with the scent of battle, feeding off of the excitement of the men, and he had been telling great and bloody tales of victory against O'Byrne. As this evening dragged on and the storm outside intensified, Frederick became more and more drunk. He soon ran out of tales about O'Byrne and moved back to the destruction of Kildare's fleet, which got the men riled up again. Not only did Devlin have to worry about the English planning an attack against him, but now he had a resurgence of violence from the O'Byrnes, and Frederick was more than happy to work the troops up into a frenzy about it. It was coming at Devlin from all sides but he was able to keep a cool and calculated head about it. He would have to or all would be lost.

"I say we take the English prisoners in our vault and make an example out of them," Frederick was saying; he was drunk, which always gave him an overflowing mouth. "Why are we keeping them locked up if we do not intend to do anything about them?"

The men roared in agreement, banging their tankards against the heavy feasting table. They were banging so hard that chips of wood were spitting all over the floor, sending the dogs scurrying with fright. All attention inevitably turned to Devlin, who was sitting quite calmly with one big leg thrown up over the arm of the chair. He was watching everything with calculating eyes and when he saw that he had the attention of his men, he knew he had to speak or Frederick might cause him some serious problems.

"Those men are mine to do with as I please," he said loudly, turning a baleful eye to Frederick. "I will decide what's to be done with them."

"But *what* will you do?" Frederick demanded. "We have a right to know what's to be done! We should have the right to *say* what's to be done!"

Devlin could feel his patience waning. "You have no rights. I will tell you what your rights are."

Frederick's dark eyes bulged and he jabbed a finger in the direction of the gatehouse and subsequently the vault. "Those

English belong to all of us, not just you!"

Devlin was finished humoring the man. If he didn't make a show of strength now, in front of everyone, it was possible that the situation might turn even more volatile. Men were on edge, fed by blood. Quick as a flash, Devlin launched himself out of his chair and, in the same motion, clobbered Frederick in the jaw with a crushing blow.

Frederick was a big man but he wasn't nearly as big or as powerful as Devlin, which made withstanding a blow such as the one Devlin delivered an impossible feat. Frederick tumbled backwards, falling over the feasting table and several men in the process. Devlin went after him, kicking men aside as he reached down and grabbed Frederick by the neck, throwing another punch into his face that knocked the man out completely. Picking Frederick up, he turned to the room full of stunned and confused men.

"Is this who you listen to?" he bellowed. "A fool of a man who uses drink to bolster his courage? Freddy is a good warrior and he is my kin, but I swear by God I will kill him and every man who listens to him if he goes against my directive. There can only be one leader and that is *me*!"

With that, he tossed Frederick into a group of men seated several feet away, and the entire collection crashed to the floor with Frederick on top of them. Devlin leapt onto the feasting table and beat at his chest.

"I am Devlin Mac Niall de Bermingham," he roared. "I am Black Sword and any man under my command will follow with complete and utter obedience, or I will destroy him. Is this in any way unclear?"

The men roared in return, approval and support shouted back to Devlin, who was showing distinct signs of fury at this point. "I fight for Ireland and for you and your families," he shouted. "I fight for freedom for our people. Do you fight with me?"

"Aye!" they cried.

"*Do you fight with me?*"

"*Aye!*

Devlin had managed to work the men up more than Frederick ever could; he was a great leader, a man of tremendous charisma, and his men loved him for it. Frederick had the ability to interest men but it was Devlin who had the ability to capture their minds and hearts. As Devlin jumped off the table, he moved back to his chair and collected his falcon. Then he turned to Iver and Shain, standing nearby.

"Put a few men on watching this group to see that they don't get out of hand," he said. "Freddy has them so worked up that I am concerned they will form a mob and kill the English prisoners when my back is turned."

Iver nodded, snapping his fingers at a couple of men standing a few feet away and motioning them over. Meanwhile, Shain moved closer to Devlin.

"What about Freddy?" he asked, his tone low. "What do we do with him?"

Devlin looked at him. "Do you really want to know?"

"Indeed I do."

Devlin lowered his voice; his dark blue eyes were deadly. "I have had enough of him," he muttered. "I grow weary of him questioning my command and I fear we are on a path for Freddy's personal rebellion. He is increasingly vocal against me and that makes the men uncertain. This I can no longer tolerate. Put him on the back of your horse and take him someplace far and dump him."

Shain liked that idea a great deal. "Finally, Devlin," he hissed. "You give the command I have been waiting for. But if you do not kill him, he will come back for you. You cannot leave him alive."

Devlin knew that. Although he was reluctant to order the man's death, he knew that Shain had a point. Frederick was a good enough warrior that he could very well come back to try and kill him. If it was a choice between ordering the man's death or looking over his shoulder for the rest of his life, he knew what he had to do.

"Then make it quick and dump his body in the sea," he whispered. "Do it now while he is still unconscious and cannot fight back."

Shain was gone, commandeering a few men to carry Frederick's still-unconscious form out of the hall. Devlin watched them go, not feeling the least bit remorseful for the brutal command. This was survival, in his opinion, and he would do all he could in order to survive.

As Shain quit the hall with Frederick's limp body, Iver came to stand next to Devlin. "Where are they going?" he asked.

Devlin glanced at Iver before motioning the man to follow. "Come with me."

He did. The pair of them headed up to Devlin's chamber above the feasting hall, the chamber that Emllyn had stayed in during her days at Black Castle. It still looked as if a woman lived there with hides on the bed, the table and chairs in the corner, and other items that had been brought in to make her more comfortable.

Once they entered the room, Devlin shut the door behind them and perched the falcon on the back of one of the chairs. With a heavy sigh, he pulled off the black glove he always wore to battle, the one that Neart perched on, and tossed it onto the table. Outside, the thunder rolled and the waves crashed. It was a night of evil tidings.

"Where did Shain take Freddy?" Iver asked again, watching Devlin pour a measure of wine from an old earthenware container.

Devlin handed him the wine. "I can no longer tolerate the man's attitude," he said, watching Iver drink deeply from the cup. "Freddy borders on rebellion more and more every day. I am afraid that one of these days, he will turn my own men against me with his lies. He has the ability to manipulate and most of these men are fairly simple minded. They love me, that is true, but if Freddy works them into madness, they will follow the crowd. They will not think for themselves. I have therefore ordered Shain to kill him."

Iver sighed faintly and drained the rest of his cup. "We have been telling you that for quite some time, Dev," he said. "Freddy is no longer content to follow. He wants to lead."

"I know," Devlin sighed, pouring himself some wine as well. "He has good ideas and he is ambitious, but I am finally forced to agree that his ambition is to replace me. He is a cousin on my father's side, after all, and I did not want to believe a relative could be out to destroy me. But…."

He was interrupted by a loud thump. Turning around, he saw Iver on the ground. Rushing to the man's side, he watched in shock as a white foam spilled out of Iver's lips. The man twitched and twitched some more, and then he fell still. Devlin searched frantically for a pulse but there was none. Iver was dead.

Seized with shock, with disbelief, Devlin shook Iver as if to bring the man back from the dead. He began to look for a puncture wound or some other kind of injury that would kill him but as he did so, his gaze came to rest on the empty cup of wine the man had just finished. It was still sitting on the table where Iver had put it. Devlin's astonished gaze returned to Iver and the white froth coming out of his mouth and nose. And then, it began to occur to him.

Poison.

Filled with grief, Devlin stood up unsteadily, his gaze still on Iver. Someone had meant that poison for Devlin, someone who was clever and bold. It had to be someone the servants trusted because he knew for a fact Enda or Nessa would not have done it. They had served Devlin for years and Enda had helped raise him. Nay, it wasn't them; but in order to put poison in his room, it had to be someone the servants trusted. No one else would have been able to gain access.

His commanders.

Nausea joined his sense of grief now as he realized that Iver, Shain, and Frederick would have been allowed access to the chamber. The servants wouldn't have questioned them. It wouldn't have been Iver, for the man wouldn't have knowingly drank wine that he had poisoned. And Shain was as loyal as a dog; nay, it could not have been him. That left Frederick.

Devlin bolted out of the room faster than he had ever moved in his life.

Glenteige Castle

"HE KEEPS STARING at me," Emllyn said. Then she grunted in

frustration and turned her attention to the oriel window that overlooked the east portion of Glenteige's complex. "I know you do not understand a word I am saying, but I do not want to complain of this to Elyse. It is her father, after all. I just wish he would not stare at me. I cannot even eat my meal at sup because the man watches every chew I make!"

In her quiet, comfortable, and cramped chamber, Emllyn was spending a rare afternoon by herself. Elyse was off somewhere with Connaught and, whenever that happened, Emllyn would shut herself up in her chamber because she wanted to stay away from de Noble. So far, he'd been completely polite and considerate, but she didn't want to give the man the opportunity to talk to her alone.

But she wasn't exactly alone. Eefha was with her, seated over at the small table near the bed, working with some kind of mortar and pestle, grinding and grinding something that Emllyn couldn't really see and couldn't really ask about because Eefha had no way of answering her. It was just like old times back at Black Castle, frustrating as those times were. But it also brought her some comfort.

The old woman spent most of her time in Emllyn's chamber, sleeping in the corner and leaving only in the morning to wander the keep and sometimes work in the kitchens. Oddly enough, no one ever stopped her or questioned her. They assumed she was a servant and that's exactly what she was posing as. As Devlin once said, no one gave notice to a mad old woman, and he had been right. Eefha was able to move freely anywhere in the keep.

With a heavy sigh, Emllyn peeled back the curtains that were blowing softly in the wind. It was a wet day, as a violent storm had passed over the night before, leaving the landscaped whipped. She could see more angry dark clouds in the distance, hovering over the sea. As she leaned against the windowsill and inspected the wet grounds below, she began to smell something awful.

Scrunching up her nose, she looked around to see where the smell might be coming from but she saw no smoke or hint of stench. It smelled heavily of shite. Her eyes widened as a thought occurred to her and she turned in time to see Eefha puffing great clouds of smoke into the air. Emllyn pinched her nose.

"Eefha!" she exclaimed softly. "What in heaven's name are you smoking?"

The old woman didn't say a word; she simply continued to puff on that awful pipe. Emllyn couldn't stand it; she climbed off the window and went to the old woman.

"Please, Eefha," she begged. "Do not smoke that pipe in my chamber. It is too small and the room fills up with that terrible smell. Please?"

Eefha puffed a few more times defiantly before easing up considerably. It was the first time that Emllyn could remember that Eefha actually understood what she had said. Emllyn put her hand on the woman's shoulder.

"Thank you," she said sincerely, eyeing the mortar and pestle still spread around the table. "Is… is that what you were making? Something to smoke in your pipe?"

Eefha's reply was to shake off the mortar and pestle until a small pile of pulverized material lay upon the table. Then, the old woman took her small bone pipe and began shoving the pile into the end of her pipe. It was enough of an explanation for Emllyn and she patted the old woman's shoulder again before turning away and heading over to the window seat where her embroidery loom was lodged against the window.

In reality, she had two looms; one in Elyse's fine solar and one in her room. It was too bulky and complicated to carry the big looms up and down the spiral stairs, depending on what room she was in, so she had two projects in the works. Elyse had been kind enough to loan her two looms. This particularly project was of ships and battle. It was from the night she had met Devlin.

Everything leads me to thee.

Emllyn sighed as she sat down on the window seat, remembering Devlin's words as she arranged a few pillows comfortably, and sat forward against the loom. His words were all she thought of, day and night, and she tried not to grow concerned that it had been over two weeks since he had left her. She missed him terribly. She never knew her heart could ache so much. With another sigh, she picked up her needle and continued on the mast of one of the ships. It was a small distraction to take her mind off Devlin but it never worked. He weighed more heavily on her mind now than he ever had.

"Where do you suppose he is?" she murmured, both a rhetorical question and also a question for Eefha. "I do hope nothing terrible has happened. He said he would return and I must trust him."

Eefha didn't reply for a moment. When she did, it was in a low and hoarse voice. "I am a spear that roars for blood," she murmured. "I am a tide that drags to the death."

Emllyn stopped sewing and looked at her, surprised that the old woman should even answer her but frightened by the words. "What does that mean?"

Eefha was staring off into the dimness of the room, her gaze fixed on nothing in particular. She simply sat, cloaked in her raggedly gray cloak, the bone pipe protruding from her olds lips. She was as still as stone but there was something ominous there. Emllyn felt it.

"What is it, Eefha?" she hissed at the old woman. "Are you trying to tell me something? You know I do not know the cycles of Irish stories that you tell, so if you could…."

She was interrupted by knock on the door. Emllyn turned her attention to the door, frustrated by the interruption and unwilling to greet the caller. It would be better if people thought she wasn't here; the door was bolted so they could not arbitrarily enter, but she still didn't want any company, especially now that Eefha was muttering words of death and blood. It concerned her. But several seconds after the first knock came a second knock, louder than the first. Emllyn sighed sharply, hoping she could easily send them away.

"Who is it?" she called.

There was a brief pause. "Sir Raymond, my lady," he said. "May I have a brief word with you?"

Emllyn's eyes widened; it was de Noble! Of course she didn't want to have a private word with the man; she'd spend weeks avoiding him and ignoring his notes. He was the last person she wanted to speak with.

"I….," she swallowed and started again. "I am afraid I am not feeling entirely well, my lord. Mayhap we can speak at another time."

De Noble wouldn't give up. "Just a brief moment of your time, my lady. I promise I will not take long."

Emllyn still refused. "Later, my lord, I beg you."

"Please, my lady," de Noble implored politely. "A brief word and I shall leave you to rest, I swear it."

Unless she wanted to be rude and tell him to go jump in the

well and drown, she had a feeling the man would beg until she opened the door. Peeved, she jabbed her needed into the fabric with the intention of answering the door when Eefha suddenly stood up and moved very quickly to the panel. Emllyn didn't even have the opportunity to call her off because the woman had moved rather swiftly. She opened the panel, hiding behind it, as de Noble stood in the doorway.

He was tall and very distinguished in his clean tunic and clean boots. He had even combed his graying hair and greased it down. He looked very much like a man who had carefully prepared himself to call upon a woman. When his gaze fell upon Emllyn still seated behind her loom, he turned in her direction and bowed gallantly.

"My lady," he said in his deep, authoritative voice. "You are looking very well today. Very well, indeed."

Reluctantly, Emllyn stood up and curtsied before sitting back down again. "My lord," she greeted with a hint of disappointment. "What did you wish to speak to me about?"

De Noble took a few steps into the room, heading in her direction. He was seemingly very nervous, for his hands were clasped together and he was fidgeting with his fingers. Emllyn would have felt some pity for the man had she not been so adverse to his overtures. She didn't want to give him any false hope.

If de Noble sensed her resistance to him, he didn't let on. He smiled politely and bowed again. "Are you comfortable enough in this chamber, my lady?" he asked kindly. "If not, we could move you to the larger chamber on the floor below. I realize that it is right off the feasting hall, but the door is good and solid, and I am sure no one would bother you."

Emllyn shook her head. "I like this room quite sufficiently, my lord," she replied rather stiffly. "Was that all you wanted to speak with me about?"

She was polite but she wasn't warm. De Noble could see that and it was difficult not to let her attitude deter him. As he fumbled for more words, Emllyn could see Eefha moving from behind the door, emerging from the shadows. She had something in her hand and Emllyn could see it reflect in the weak light. A bright, silver, and sinister flash. It took her a moment to realize that it was a dagger, and the old woman was sneaking up behind de Noble with the intention of using it. Startled, Emllyn bolted to her feet and bumped into the loom, sending it crashing to the floor.

De Noble instinctively bent over to pick up the fallen loom. As he did so, Emllyn frantically waved off Eefha, who was just preparing to lift the dirk and stab the man in his back. But Emllyn's desperate gesture had the old woman sheathing the dirk and fleeing from the chamber just as de Noble was righting the loom.

"Here you are, my lady," he said, righting one of the legs. "No harm done."

Heart pounding in her chest with the sheer fright she had just experienced, Emllyn forced a smile from what must have surely been a grimace of terror on her lips as she repositioned her loom.

"How clumsy of me," she said. "Thank you."

De Noble smiled in return; he was a genuinely handsome man and would have been an excellent prospect had Emllyn's heart not already been spoken for. As it was, he simply made her cringe with his eager attitude.

"My pleasure, my lady," he said, but he could see she was expecting him to come to the point of his visit. "I… well, I have come to see if you would honor me by allowing me to escort you on a walk into the village. You see, they are having a sort of farmer's faire there today and there will be many things to see and to purchase. I have even been told there will be entertainment in the form of a puppet show. I thought mayhap that you would like to escape this dreary keep and take in some fresh air."

He said it so courteously; in fact, Emllyn realized that she was very tempted simply at the prospect of getting out of her room and seeing something new, but she was terrified that it would give the man encouragement. She forced a cough and delicately covered her mouth.

"It sounds very lovely, but as I mentioned, I have not been feeling well," she said. "I would prefer to stay to my room today."

De Noble's hopeful expression fell somewhat. "Elyse is in town with Connaught so I thought that you might be lonely for companionship," he said. "I am not as witty or as pretty as my daughter, but I would be deeply honored if you would allow me to stay a few minutes and make conversation."

It was another polite request and Emllyn was coming to feel sorry for the man that she was repeatedly rebuffing him. But it could not be helped.

"Mayhap another time, my lord," she said, forcing another cough. "I am simply not up to it today. If you would please leave me in peace, I would be grateful."

De Noble's face fell completely and his smile faded. Stung, he nonetheless nodded politely and headed for the chamber door. She had told him to leave and he would. But he paused a moment before leaving completely, his expression somewhat dull as he turned to her.

"Mayhap there is one more thing you would care to know before I leave you to your illness," he said, defeat and depression in his tone. "I have received word that Black Castle was besieged a week ago. It would seem that there is a good deal of warfare going on south of Wicklow. Clearly, your brother could not have summoned more men this quickly and my men tell me that other Irish clanns have converged upon the castle. I have sent your brother word of this latest attack, and I have also sent him a request that you should be aware of. I hope you are agreeable to it."

By this time, Emllyn was looking at him with a great deal of fear as a result of the information on Black Castle. But his last few words had her confused attention.

"What request?" she wanted to know.

De Noble bowed to her again, this time with less fanfare and more emotion. There was a warm glimmer in his eye, a light of hope everlasting in the face of the unwilling object of his affection. The man was an optimist.

"I have asked your brother for permission to court you," he said. "You see, I have admired you from afar since nearly the moment we met. I believe you have been aware of it by several notes I have sent you, notes that have gone unanswered, I might add. You are a kind and witty woman, and you have made Elyse very happy. She speaks quite highly of you and I would like to know such happiness again, too. I have decided to no longer hide my interest in you behind anonymous notes. Now you know it is I who have sent them. I would hope that, in time, you are agreeable to my suit."

Emllyn wasn't particularly shocked by the request, but she was stunned by the entire situation.

"Sir," she gasped. "I have never given you any indication

that I would be willing to accept such a suit."

He nodded. "I realize that," he said. "I have been rather ambiguous about my interest so I assumed that you, as a proper maiden, would not have rightly responded to something as bold and coy as anonymous notes. I commend you for your behavior and apologize for mine. It was forward of me."

Incensed, Emllyn's mouth popped open. "Sir, you misunderstand," she said firmly. "I am not interested in your suit. I wish you well in finding affection, but it will not be with me."

De Noble tried not to appear too defeated. "I understand the past few weeks have been very disorienting for you," he said. "Mayhap with time, you will reconsider. I am a patient man."

Emllyn had no idea how to respond so for lack of any response at all, she simply turned away from him. She didn't see de Noble's expression of disappointment. All she heard was the door as he quietly shut it. With a grunt of frustration, she ran to the door and bolted it. She didn't want the man coming back in again.

Standing at the door, leaning against it, all she could feel was utter bewilderment. There were so many thoughts rolling around in her head that it was difficult to single out just one. *Damn de Noble for pressing his suit,* she though angrily. A note to Kildare would only result in a confusing reply which would completely disrupt her story about sailing on the fleet to oversee the victory for her brother. In fact, it very well might destroy everything.

Yet, she couldn't think about that now. She would deal with it when and if the time came, because even more pressing than that was the news of Black Castle's siege. The very thought had her wracked with distress. It explained why Devlin hadn't returned to her yet; he was caught up in something terrible.

Mayhap he had even been injured in the siege, or worse. She couldn't imagine why he hadn't come for her if he remained healthy and whole.

Emllyn put her hands to her head at that thought, horrified. *God's Blood, it can't be! Devlin can't be injured or dead!* He had promised to return for her.

Everything leads me to thee.

He had promised!

Eefha. She had to find Eefha. Putting her ear against the door, she waited a nominal amount of time for de Noble to leave the area before quietly opening the door and peering outside. It was dark in the corridor beyond, with Elyse's empty chamber off to the right and the partitioned chambers for female servants directly in front of her.

Quietly, Emllyn slipped out and shut the door behind her. She had to find the old woman. Perhaps the woman, for once, might actually be able to communicate with her. The rumors surrounding Black Castle were indeed serious. She had to figure out what to do. If Devlin couldn't come to her, then she would have to go to Devlin.

No matter what the cost.

CHAPTER FIFTEEN

FREDERICK HAD PUT up a fight, one that had almost cost Shain his life. He had awoken from his drunken stupor as Shain and two other men had carried him out of Black Castle on that dark and rainy night and just about the time they reached the suspension footbridge that linked the keep with the rest of the fortress, Frederick had come alive.

The two men carrying him had caught the brunt of his panic and fury. He managed to stab one man with his dirk and the second man had been tossed over the bridge, forty feet down into the rocks and roiling sea below. Shain, who was already across the bridge at that point, unsheathed his broadsword and raced back onto the bridge to engage Frederick in a fight for his life. Frederick was without his broadsword but he had his dirk, a long and wicked looking thing, and he had charged Shain with it, who had easily knocked it out of his hand.

But Frederick wasn't finished. He kicked at Shain, driving the man off of the bridge so that he could come off of it, too. Once on solid land, he reached down and grabbed a great handful of dirt and rocks and threw them right at Shain's face.

Shain had been hit in the nose by a fairly large rock and had been momentarily stunned from the blow. It had been enough of a pause for Frederick to gain the upper hand; the man then slugged Shain in the face, sending him to the ground. Then he stole Shain's sword and gored him in the shoulder. It would have been the chest but Shain had turned just in time and took the blade in his upper arm. With Shain's sword, Frederick had fled.

Devlin had come barreling out of the keep in time to see Frederick steal a horse and ride from the gates, just as Shain was struggling to pick himself up off the ground. As he helped Shain, the sentries shouted to him and told him what had happened. Devlin didn't order anyone to follow Frederick; it was too dark and the weather was too threatening. Frederick would be lucky if he survived such conditions, so Devlin wasn't going to be foolish enough to send anyone after him. He was more concerned with the one remaining commander he had left.

He let Frederick go.

Now, on the morning following Iver's death and Shain's injury, Devlin sat in the hall of the keep, his feet propped up on the table as he pondered the smoking, glowing hearth of the now-quiet chamber. Shain had been put on a pallet next to the fire and had been sleeping heavily since Enda had given him a sleep potion the night before. Both Enda and Nessa had tended Shain in the absence of Eefha, who normally did most of the tending of the ill, and the pair had done an excellent job. Shain's injury wasn't serious but he had lost a fair amount of blood. He was weak. Devlin had stayed with the man the entire time, and sat with him even now. Exhausted and on edge, he hadn't slept at all.

Neart sat over on another chair, pulling apart a small rodent he had captured. The bird had been kept inside during the siege by the O'Byrnes, mostly because everyone knew about Black Sword's falcon and there would be many archers poised to take the bird down. Devlin, exhausted and pensive, eyed the animal affectionately. The bird was the one thing in his world that had always remained constant, so much so that it was like a family member. Its mere presence gave him comfort in a world that had little.

"Have you slept, Dev?"

Devlin turned away from the falcon pulling at the flesh of the rat to see Shain looking up at him. The man was pale but he was smiling. Devlin gave him a half-grin.

"I do not need to sleep," he told him, eyeing him with concern. "How are you feeling?"

Shain took a deep breath, wincing when his shoulder hurt. "Well, considering," he said. "I have been worse off many times. This is nothing but a scratch."

Devlin pulled his legs from the table and sat forward so he could see Shain better. "I agree," he said. "But it is best if you rest for today."

Shain nodded faintly. "I suppose," he said, his smile fading. "I am sorry about Freddy, Dev. I should have been more vigilant. I have no excuse."

Devlin waved him off. "It is not your fault," he said. "Freddy was out to kill us all, I think. He poisoned my wine. Iver drank it before I did and it killed him."

Shain's eyes widened. "Iver is dead?"

Devlin nodded, struggling against the sadness. "It was a swift death," he said, although it didn't make him feel any better to say it. "Then Freddy tried to kill you."

"I was going to kill *him*," Shain said softly.

"That is true, but there is no way Freddy could have known that," he said. "He was unconscious when you took him out of the hall. For all he knew, you were taking him back to his bed to sleep off too much drink. The sentries who saw what happened said he attacked you."

Shain nodded faintly, recollecting the events from the previous night. "It happened very fast," he muttered. "I should have been prepared."

Devlin reached down and put a hand on the man's arm. "I am simply thankful you are alive," he insisted quietly. "But now we have a bigger problem; Freddy has fled. If he survived the initial flight into the darkness and in the bad weather, then the question needs to be asked – *where* would he go? Freddy is half mad with ambition and anger, so I am sure he was not thinking too clearly when he left here. He has no close relatives; his brother Henry was killed during the destruction of Kildare's armada, although I do believe he has an aunt on his father's side who lives in Dublin. Would he go there, I wonder?"

Shain was silent for a moment, eyeing a big dog who wandered past him, searching for scraps.

"Think about it," he said. "If you had tried to murder your liege, and then tried to kill another knight, and you were furious and hurt that your grab for power had failed, where would *you* go?"

Devlin thought about that for a moment, pondering what his reaction might have been under such circumstances. "I would want revenge, I suppose," he said. "If it were me, I would want to gain revenge on those who humiliated me."

"And if you wanted to destroy them, where would you go? Think, Dev; *think*."

The line of reasoning was beginning to become clearer. Devlin could see what Shain was driving at.

"My enemy's enemy is my friend," he said softly, the light of understanding coming to his eyes. "I could go to O'Byrne and pledge loyalty, or I could go to de Cleveley and ask for amnesty in exchange for what I know about Black Sword."

Shain turned to look at him, nodding his head. "If Freddy goes to de Cleveley, Lady Emllyn is there," he reminded the man of what he already knew. "You told me and Iver and Freddy of your plans with de Cleveley, and you further told us that you had posed as a farmer and that de Cleveley's commander had asked you to return to Black Castle to spy on Black Sword. You agreed to do so to get into the man's good graces in order to find out if he was planning an attack against you. You wanted to earn his trust."

By this time, Devlin was on his feet, seized with the idea that Frederick might be heading to Glenteige Castle to betray both him and Emllyn. It was as good a possibility as any.

"He will tell de Noble that I am Black Sword and that Emllyn was in on the deception all along," he said, feeling his heart race and his palms sweat with panic. "Sweet Jesus, if he does that, de Noble… de Noble could very well put Emllyn in the vault or, worse yet, execute her for treachery."

"Frederick could have the last word in all of this," Shain said softly. "He could ruin everything you've worked for."

Devlin stared at him and Shain could see the emotion in the man's face. It brought back the memory from their trip south, when Devlin had been so protective over Lady Emllyn and had shown her such consideration. Shain had asked him then if there was something between them but Devlin had skirted the subject. But now, looking at Devlin's face, he could see that there was indeed something between them. Devlin must have sensed his thoughts because he lowered his gaze.

"Shain," he said hesitantly, "I must tell you something, something I've not told anyone."

"What is that?"

Devlin drew in a deep breath. "The night that Freddy brought Emllyn to me, I abused her," he said quietly. "I abused her badly. I told her I wanted to fill her full of Irish sons to rebel against the English. But she was strong, Shain; she was so very strong against me. She was wise and she was reasonable. I have never met a woman like her."

"I see."

Devlin shook his head. "That isn't what I wanted to tell you," he went on. "She intrigued me more than I wanted to admit. And she is so incredibly beautiful. She is also witty and intelligent. She's the most marvelous woman I have ever met."

"Is that so?"

Shain was remaining very neutral about the whole thing and Devlin suddenly looked at him. "I love her," he blurted, then winced because he had spilled it out without tact. He struggled to recover. "I love her and I do not regret it. She is the most miraculous thing that has ever happened to me, Shain. She has made me feel things I never thought I would feel. She is my sun and the stars. If she wanted the moon, I would give it to her."

Shain had guessed as much. Although he didn't exactly approve, he couldn't fault the man his happiness. Still, it might come at a price.

"If Freddy has headed for Glenteige, then he will be there before you," he said. "When you return there, and I know you will, you must be prepared for the damage he has done."

Devlin thought on that long and hard. "It will all depend on if he can convince de Noble of the fact that the farmer he knew as John is actually Black Sword," he said. "If he is able to do that, then they will know Emllyn was in on the treachery."

"Not necessarily," Shain said. "Didn't you tell me that your story to de Noble was that you were a farmer who found the lady upon the shore? It would be possible that she really didn't know you were Black Sword and only a man who found her and saved her after she washed ashore."

Devlin shook his head. "I am not entirely certain she will deny knowing my true identity," he said. "She is a righteous woman and not given to lies. If confronted, she could very well confess."

Shain pondered that. "Then if that is the case, you will need to go to Glenteige and be prepared to bargain for her release," he said. "You have thirty-three English prisoners in the vault. Mayhap they will exchange one small lady for thirty-three English soldiers."

It was as logical a solution as any, at least initially. But Devlin knew it wouldn't end there. "I have a feeling they will overlook the soldiers in favor of me," he said softly. "They will want *me* in exchange for Emllyn's freedom. Black Sword, after all, would outweigh the import of thirty-three Englishmen."

Shain couldn't disagree. He watched Devlin carefully, waiting to see how the man was going to react to all of this. But Devlin seemed to be oddly calm although it was evident that there was much on his mind. So much had happened, and so much was looming, that it was difficult to consider it all without emotion. Devlin was having to face a situation he'd never before faced; the peril of someone he loved.

"Mayhap I should go and see the English prisoners," he

finally said, rising wearily from his chair. "Mayhap they can give me insight as to how de Noble will deal with Emllyn if Freddy manages to destroy all I have worked for."

He turned for the door but Shain stopped him. "Dev?" he called softly.

Devlin paused and turned. "Aye?"

"What will you do?" Shain asked. "If they want you in exchange for the lady, what will you do?"

Devlin sighed heavily and averted his gaze. "I will not let her suffer," he muttered. "I could not live knowing she was imprisoned, or worse."

Shain felt genuine apprehension at Devlin's apparent intentions. "Don't do it," he begged quietly. "There can be another way, but if they get their hands on you… everything will be lost. We have told you that before, Devlin. You are the heart of this rebellion and if you are removed, then everything dies. *Ireland dies.*"

Devlin lifted his head and looked at him. "Ireland will not die," he said. "There will be others to take my place. As for me… mayhap I have done all I can do. Mayhap it is time for this rebellion, and for me, to evolve."

He left the hall after that, lumbering out into the early morning. He was a man of deep feeling, of deep intelligence, and now of deep pain. So much had changed. It would probably never be the same again.

Shain lay there with tears in his eyes.

THE VAULT SMELLED worse than Devlin had remembered. As he

headed down the dark, narrow stairs that led to the pit of despair, the pure stench from the urine nearly burned holes through his eyes. They were watering profusely by the time he hit the bottom and he nearly tripped because he was rubbing at them.

There were no longer any guards at this level because of the stench. A single torch burned, barely illuminating the darkness, but it was enough light for Devlin to see many weary and distraught faces. They were all gazing back at him as he stepped from the stairs and headed towards the iron cages. The first face he came to was Sir Victor's.

The man had a growth of beard and the hazel eyes were dull with defeat and disillusionment. Devlin looked around at the others, seeing Trevor buried back in the group. The young knight looked haggard. Dirty, feces-covered straw covered the cells but men were sitting on it, anyway. They had no choice. It was a horrific sight and the longer Devlin gazed at it, the more disgusted he became. Turning around, he hunted for the key that was always kept on a peg upon the wall. They often kept it there to completely discourage the prisoners, who had no way of retrieving the key that would see them to freedom. Collecting the old iron key, he turned to Sir Victor on the other side of the iron grate.

"This is no way for men to live," he said quietly. "I will release your men and they will follow me to the next destination without resistance. They will obey me implicitly, for the first man that tries to run or refuses my orders will be killed on the spot. Is that clear?"

Sir Victor drew in a long, deep breath and looked around to the men, all of whom were slowly dying. He was willing to agree to anything at that point and the prospect of being released, by

Black Sword no less, was almost more than he could bear. Up until a few moments ago, he surely thought they were all going to die here, alone and forgotten. Hearing Black Sword's proposal was a distinct shock. After a moment, he nodded.

"Aye," he said, his voice hoarse and raspy. "I understand. No one will run or disobey."

Devlin nodded shortly. "Then I will trust you."

With that, he unlocked the first cell, Sir Victor's cell, and swung open the door. Then he unlocked the second door and forced that one open as well. Men began to move slowly, groaning, as some held on to others for support. As the men were rousing, Devlin went to the stairwell and whistled sharply, producing several of his men who gathered at the top of the steps. No one dared come down into that stench. Devlin called up orders and a couple of the men began to move while the others remained in order to both assist the prisoners and guard them. Slowly, very slowly, men began to come out of the cells. Devlin directed them up the stairs.

It was a slow and laborious process, moving injured and weak men up that skinny flight of stairs. It was like moving a herd of animals. Devlin remained at the bottom, directing men up and steadying a few that wobbled as they moved. But gradually, they all moved up except for three of them who were directing the others. They had remained down in that horrific vault alongside Devlin, allowing the others to go first.

Devlin realized that Sir Victor along with Sir Trevor and another man were still with him, the remaining three knights from Kildare's stable of twenty-seven that had come over on the battle armada. Even in defeat, they were still following protocol, still thinking of their men first. Their attitude impressed Devlin. He finally directed them up the stairs and followed on their rear.

Once up in the bright morning, Devlin could see that his men had held the prisoners at the mouth of the gatehouse until further orders. The entire group was sagging, dragging, and otherwise shielding themselves from the muted sunlight. To men who hadn't seen the sun in weeks, it would take some time for their eyes to adjust. Devlin intended to take them all over to the great hall where they would be fed a decent meal and be tended to, but he soon realized that the stench from the vault had followed them into the daylight. The entire group smelled like hell. He wasn't about to bring that kind of smell into the great hall.

So he set about cleaning them off. In the bright morning, oddly void of the clouds that were so prevalent this time of year, he had his men heat up vast iron kettles of water, and in the stable yards, they forced the English prisoners to wash themselves down. Clothes were taken from them and boiled, laid out in the sun to dry, and the English used lumpy bars of white soap to wash weeks of filth and despair from their bodies. Moods and manners soon perked up as the English scrubbed away.

But they were heavily guarded by Devlin's men. The Irish lined the stable yard, armed with spears and swords, as the English washed themselves and each other. Razors were produced, only a pair of them so they could not be used as weapons, and the English were permitted to shave their faces. Since the sun was out, and vaguely warm at that, hair and bodies and clothes dried quickly. It was a perfect day for it.

Devlin stood and watched everything with a critical eye. He was mostly watching Sir Trevor as the man washed his tall, sinewy body and his dark hair. He was rather handsome, as Devlin was coming to discover, and he could feel the pangs of jealousy clutch at him. It was little wonder that Emllyn had fallen for the man. But as he continued to watch, he noticed that Sir Trevor and another man seemed particularly close, washing each other, laughing together, or passing what could have been interpreted as rather meaningful glances. It was rather odd. As Devlin pondered the behavior, he was approached by Sir Victor.

Shaven and clean, Sir Victor remained in his damp breeches and bare feet as he respectfully acknowledged Devlin. Massive arms folded across his chest in a somewhat intimidating stance, Devlin bobbed his head slightly.

"St. John," he said. "I must say that you look rather different."

Sir Victor smiled weakly. "I suppose that I do," he acknowledged. Then, his smile faded. "I wanted to thank you, de Bermingham. What you are doing for us… you did not have to do this. I have never heard of any man treating prisoners this way and I am genuinely humbled. On behalf of my men, I thank you deeply."

Devlin eyed the man. "I am not the beast that everyone thinks I am," he muttered, looking out over the gang of washing men. "And your men are not animals. The vault you were in was not meant to hold so many men. It is only humane that I remove you and tend you. But know this; I have done this for a purpose. If I did not have a purpose, I could have very well left you down in that hole to rot."

Sir Victor held an expression between curiosity and wariness. "What purpose would that be, my lord?"

Devlin looked at him, sizing him up. "I will tell you when you've had food in your belly, but for now, I must ask you something."

He motioned the man over and Sir Victor went willingly.

When he drew close to the big Irishman, Devlin spoke.

"That young knight," he said, pointing over at Sir Trevor as he spilled water over his head. "That is Trevor le Mon?"

Sir Victor nodded. "He is," he replied. "Why? Do you know of him or his family?"

Devlin shook his head. "Who is his family?"

"The le Mons of Chateroy Castle, descended from the kings of Anglecynn," he replied. "He comes from a fairly important family. I am sure they would pay a hefty ransom for his return."

Devlin cocked an eyebrow at him. "And you would willingly divulge this information to me?"

Sir Victor shrugged. "You will want to know it eventually, and we wish to return to our families. I see no reason to withhold truths if it will get us home faster."

It was the logical thought process from a seasoned veteran. "I take it that you have been ransomed before, then?" Devlin asked.

Sir Victor smiled ironically. "Twice," he said. "My family is fairly wealthy as well. Name your price and I am sure they will pay it. I have a wife and five daughters waiting for me at home."

Devlin grunted his disapproval. "Then I must send you home if for no other reason than to give your wife a son," he said. "No man should be publicly thrilled with five daughters."

Sir Victor laughed softly, surprised by Black Sword's sense of humor. Or, at least de Bermingham's sense of humor. Somehow, the two entities were becoming separate as a result of de Bermingham's humane treatment. There was the legend… and then there was the man.

"They are good girls," he said. "But I must find husbands for them eventually, so do not ransom me for too much. I will need that money for dowries."

Devlin's lips twitched with a smile. "You will need to kidnap men in your own right to hold them for ransom so that you may pay for that brood," he said, but le Mon caught his attention again. "Le Mon… he and that man he is with seem like good friends. Is it his brother?"

Sir Victor glanced over at the pair as le Mon ran his fingers over his companion's wet hair. He shook his head. "Nay," he replied, the humor gone from his tone. "That is his lover."

Devlin tried not to look too shocked. "*Lover*?" he repeated. "He is not… that is to say, he prefers men?"

Sir Victor nodded and looked away from the affectionate pair, rolling his eyes. "Pity," he said. "The man is a fine knight, a good commander, and comes from an excellent family. He could command a very fine wife, but he has no interest in women. In fact, my eldest daughter has made no secret of her interest in him but he repeatedly rebuffed her."

Devlin had to make a conscious effort to hide his shock. "*Your* daughter?" he said, confused and astonished. "Your daughter is interested in him?"

"Aye."

"But… what of the Lady Emllyn?"

Sir Victor looked at him. "So you have heard of her?" he asked. Then he shook his head. "As far as I know, the Lady Emllyn showed no such interest in him. She and my daughter are great friends, you know, or at least they were until the Lady Emllyn died of a fever last winter. Cate still has not recovered. She and Emllyn were friends since birth, practically. They grew up together, fostered together. They had all of the same friends and essentially the same life experiences. It was a terrible blow to her to lose her very best friend."

Devlin was reeling. In fact, the world was rocking unsteadily and he struggled to gain control over his equilibrium. "Cate? She is your daughter?"

Sir Victor nodded. "Her name is Catherine but we call her Cate," he said. "She is my eldest. You've never seen a more beautiful woman; refined, talented, intelligent. She is a good girl with excellent common sense except when it comes to Trevor le Mon. She is mad over him and I do believe she would do anything for him."

Devlin felt sick; literally sick. He couldn't seem to wrap his mind around the fact that from what St. John was describing, it was his daughter who had been in love with le Mon and not Emllyn. *Emllyn Fitzgerald was dead.* Was it possible, then, that his beloved Emllyn wasn't Emllyn at all? Was it possible that she was, in truth, someone else?

It didn't make any sense. The sickness swept him and he began to sweat profusely. He remembered back to when he had told Emllyn that Sir Victor had been in the vault and how she had begged for the knight's life. *Of course she would have! He is her father!* There were more questions than answers, questions that hammered away at him like a drum. *She lied to me about her identity! Did she also lie when she told me she loved me?* He couldn't seem to grasp his thoughts, his mind swirling with bewilderment. He just didn't understand any of it. *God, it's just not possible!*

Body quivering, mind clouded with confusion, he looked at the man who had delivered such revelations. Truth be told, he didn't know Sir Victor at all and it was quite possible the man was lying to him, too, mayhap to throw him off somehow. But why? What would be his purpose? One thing was certain, however; until he could get to the bottom of things, and until he could talk to Emllyn, she was still Emllyn to him and not the

Lady Catherine St. John as Sir Victor had suggested.

She was still his Emllyn!

Yet, as his mind reeled about Emllyn, it also reeled about Sir Trevor. Two incredulous bits of information in as many minutes. If what Sir Victor said was true, then it made perfect sense as to why Sir Trevor had rebuffed Emllyn. The man preferred men in his bed but rather than tell Emllyn outright, as he would not have so boldly announced such a thing, he had led her to believe that he simply wasn't interested in her. And Emllyn, determined, gave chase.

The entire situation was convoluted with lies and truths, things he couldn't easily discern as they rolled over and over in his brain. But one thing was increasingly clear to him; he had to get to Emllyn because he had to discover the truth and then, and only then, would he be able to settle down.

With strained composure, he turned to Sir Victor. God's Blood… he and the man had much to discuss, now more than ever.

"If you are finished grooming, then finish dressing and I will order food," he said in an oddly strained tone. "You and I have much to confer."

Sir Victor did as he was told. Very quickly, he had his clothes on although the armor had been taken from him because it was so badly rusted that there was no way he could wear it. In fact, there was a pile of mail and another smaller pile of plate armor at the corner of the kitchen yard. As he finished securing his tunic and approached Devlin once again, he pointed off to the pile of expensive protection.

"I believe that is salvageable, my lord," he said to Devlin. "I hope you aren't intending to melt it down."

Devlin, who had managed to regain most of his composure

whilst Sir Victor dressed, turned to look at the pile the man was addressing. He grunted in response.

"I am not going to melt it down," he said, leading Sir Victor over to where several long tables from the great hall had been brought outside and were now assembled near the stable yard entry. Servants were setting out all manner of food for the Englishmen who were winding down their bath and beginning to dress in clean, stiff clothing. "I am going to return it to you and your men and you will have the unhappy task of cleaning the rust from it. You're going to need it again, and fairly soon by my estimation."

Sir Victor was mildly confused by the statement. "Why is that?"

Devlin took a seat at the end of the table and indicated for Sir Victor to sit on the bench next to him. He silently indicated for Victor to partake of the bread and wine that had been laid out and Victor did eagerly. As Victor ate, Devlin spoke.

"First, I will dispense with the formality of titles," he said, his voice low. "I see no need to address you as 'sir' and surely you see no need to address me as anything other than de Bermingham."

Victor, his mouth full, nodded in agreement. "As you wish."

Devlin continued. "What I am about to tell you is the gist of the situation since Kildare's ships crashed upon my shore," he said, his gaze intense. "Much has occurred since you were locked up in the vault and I will swear you to secrecy on this. If you divulge this information to anyone I do not approve of, you will never see your wife and five daughters again. Are we clear?"

Victor wasn't intimidated but he took the threat seriously. "Of course. I will not speak a word without your approval."

Devlin eyed the man before moving on; he knew he had to

tell him of the situation involving Emllyn because he had no choice. The entire purpose of releasing the English prisoners was, in fact, to use them as a bargaining chip to regain Emllyn should Frederick have gone to Glenteige to betray Devlin. But now, there was so much more to it if, in fact, Emllyn was in reality the Lady Catherine St. John.

Devlin's head was still swirling with the possibility and it was a terrible struggle not to feel anger or betrayal or utter grief about it. So he took a deep breath and pushed on.

"As I mentioned, much has occurred since you were locked up in my vault," he said. "The most important occurrence has to do with the Lady Emllyn Fitzgerald. I am not quite sure how to address this so I will simply come out with it; a woman declaring that she was the Lady Emllyn Fitzgerald stowed away on Kildare's armada."

Victor stopped chewing and his eyes widened. "What's this you say?" he repeated, shocked. "Lady Emllyn? But… but that is impossible. The woman died last winter."

Devlin could see how astonished the man was and he understood the feeling well. "Be that as it may, a woman declaring she was the sister of Kildare was captured when the fleet foundered," he said quietly. "She was brought to me and became my property. I need not explain what that entails, do I?"

Victor pushed aside his bread, his face pale with shock and horror. "You do not," he said, his tone hoarse. "But since the Lady Emllyn is dead, I am curious as to who this woman is and why she said she was the Lady Emllyn."

Devlin sighed heavily; there was a pitcher of wine off to his right and he collected it, drinking straight from the pitcher. He found he desperately needed it.

"She said she was following her lover, a Sir Trevor, into

battle because she wanted to prove to him what a good and fearless wife she would be," he said. He took another drink before looking St. John in the eye. "Does that sound like anyone you know?"

Victor was beside himself. The calm, collected, and seasoned veteran looked to be verging on a breakdown. "Of course it does!" he finally hissed. "It sounds like Cate!"

Devlin nodded, the feelings of nausea and despair overwhelming him once more. "She is a petite woman with reddish-gold hair and beautiful green eyes," he said, his tone dull and lifeless. "She has a dusting of freckles on her nose and a darker freckle near her right ear. Does this sound like the Lady Emllyn to you?"

Victor shook his head, closing his eyes tightly against the realization. "It does not," he muttered. "You have described my daughter perfectly."

Devlin actually felt tears in his eyes. He couldn't help it. He was so utterly devastated. "Why would she tell me she was the Lady Emllyn?"

Victor was devastated, too. He was so very pale with astonishment. "I do not know," he muttered. "I am sure she was terrified to have been captured in battle. Mayhap she told you she was the Lady Emllyn because she hoped you would treat her with more respect than if she told you she was a mere knight's daughter. But you didn't treat her with respect, did you? You… you brutalized her anyway."

Devlin couldn't look at the man; he was staring at the pitcher in his hand. "She was a casualty of war," he said softly. "She became my property to do with as I pleased."

"She was an innocent young maiden!"

"An innocent young maiden who stowed away on a battle

armada to be with her lover," Devlin reiterated steadily. "Even after I claimed her as my own, she could have told me at any time that she was not the Lady Emllyn. The damage had already been done to her and pretending to be an earl's sister wasn't providing her with any safe securities."

Victor's pain-filled gaze lingered on him for several long seconds before looking away. He had to; the longer he looked at Devlin, the more grief-stricken he became. "I do not know the answer to that, either," he whispered. "As with all lies, the more time passes the more difficult it is to tell the truth. Mayhap she was fearful of your reaction should she tell you who she really was."

"Mayhap."

"For the love of God, where is she?"

Devlin hesitated. "You should know that I love her," he said, feeling the man's pain mingle with his own. "She started out as my property but she became my heart. I suppose I honestly do not care if she is Emllyn or Cate; I love her regardless."

Victor didn't think he could have possibly been more astonished, but he was. "You love her?" he asked in disbelief. "Or is she simply a possession you are fond of?"

"I love her with everything that I am."

"Then tell me where she is."

Devlin sighed heavily and took another long drink. "She is at de Cleveley's settlement to the south," he said. "I took her there myself. She is safe."

"Why did you take her there?"

Devlin considered the pitcher again, pensively, before responding. "With Kildare's attack, I was sure there was another one coming shortly," he said. "Do you recall that we asked you of missives that had been delivered to de Cleveley? You told us that the missives indeed mentioned plans to regain Black Castle, as I had suspected, so I was convinced that de Cleveley was planning an attack on the heels of Kildare's. This is where Emllyn came in; she and I had a bargain. When she first came to me, she very much wanted to see if Sir Trevor was amongst the English prisoners. I told her I would let her see the prisoners for herself if she went to de Cleveley and found out what more she could about an attack against Black Castle. Being Kildare's sister, they should easily confide in her. But our plans did not go exactly as we had hoped."

Victor was hanging on every word. "What do you mean?

Devlin thought back to those days leading up to Glenteige. "On our trip south to the settlement, we were set upon by raiders and Emllyn was injured," he said. "By the time we got to Glenteige, she was very ill and unable to speak for herself, so I had to think of a suitable story to explain my presence. I told de Noble, the commander of the settlement, that I was a farmer who had found the lady washed up on shore after the defeat of Kildare's armada. Somehow in our discussions, Black Castle came up and I told him I had been there before to sell my produce. Much as I used Trevor against Emllyn to ensure her cooperation, de Noble has used Emllyn against me to ensure mine. He believes that Black Sword is planning an attack on Glenteige and has sent me to gather information to that effect."

Victor's eyebrows lifted in surprise as he digested what he was told. "So… you are essentially spying on Black Sword?"

"Aye."

"But *you* are Black Sword."

Devlin nodded. "De Noble has assured me that I could see Emllyn upon my return to Glenteige, provided that I bring him crucial information."

"Does he believe you in love with her?"

Devlin shrugged. "I spoke of her enough and asked repeatedly to see her after we arrived," he said. "I am sure he figured it out without me saying so."

Victor fell silent; he was reeling as much as Devlin was, about all of it. It was madness, all of it, but in truth he wasn't surprised. Cate had always had a knack for inviting trouble, but this time, she'd invited more than she could possibly handle… if, in fact, Emllyn's imposter was indeed his daughter. But all signs pointed to her.

"Then why am I here?" he finally asked Devlin. He gestured to the men now heading to the table to be fed. "Why are we all here? What do you want of us?"

Devlin eyed the men approaching as well. "One of my commanders has become an untrustworthy rogue," he said, lowering his voice. "He knows of my plans with Emllyn and de Cleveley – that she is there to gather information on the English plans against Black Castle. It is my belief that he has gone to Glenteige with the purpose of betraying me and, consequently, Emllyn. If he does this, she will be in great danger. I realize we are bitter enemies, St. John, but in this case, we must forget all of that. We must help each other in order for all of us to survive. It is my intention to exchange thirty-three English prisoners for Emllyn should that now be the situation."

Victor stared at him a moment before rolling his eyes miserably. "Dear God," he breathed. "Is it truly possible?"

"It is."

"But why would he do this?"

"The man is bitter and ambitious. He tried to kill me and when he realized he was unsuccessful, he fled. There is more to it than that simple explanation, but that is the gist of it. Mayhap he will side with the English because of his in-depth knowledge of me and of Black Castle. Mayhap he hopes to destroy me once and for all with the help of de Cleveley."

Victor was studying his hands despondently. "And you are sure he has gone to de Cleveley's settlement?"

"It is as viable a possibility as any," Devlin replied. "In any case, I need Emllyn returned to me."

Victor's head came up. "What if she had not gathered sufficient information about the English plans towards you?"

"It does not matter. I simply want her back."

Victor fell silent as the English soldiers crowded up to the table, taking seats and grabbing at food and drink. They were starving and helped themselves to whatever was offered but at the end of the table where Devlin and Victor sat, it was a quiet and morose atmosphere. It was as if the two of them were in their own little world.

"If the woman you know as Emllyn is my daughter…," Victor ventured.

"If she is your daughter, then I will ask permission to marry her," Devlin cut him off. "Make no mistake; she belongs to me already. The marriage is simply a formality."

"And if I refuse?"

"I do not believe you will."

"But if I do?"

Devlin's features hardened. "Must I answer that?"

Victor met his gaze and, after a moment of seeing death and destruction in the man's dark blue eyes, he shook his head and looked away. He knew this was a battle he could not win.

"You do not," he said quietly. "But you will promise me something."

"What?"

"Be good to her," he said, his eyes welling with tears. "She is stubborn and willful, but she is also the sweetest and most glorious creature that God has ever created."

Devlin was touched by the man's obvious adoration for his daughter. Devlin leaned into him so no one else would hear.

"I vow upon my life that I will treat her only with the greatest respect," he muttered. "And I will love her more than my own life until the day I die. She will be my queen, I swear it."

"Black Sword's queen."

"Aye," he whispered with a surprising show of reverence. "Black Sword's queen."

The English slept in the great hall that night and before sunrise the next morning, they were well on their way to Glenteige.

CHAPTER SIXTEEN

Glenteige Castle

"WHO *IS THAT* old bird?" Merradoc asked. "She has been following us around for days."

Strolling through Glenteige's massive bailey, a small party consisting of Emllyn, Elyse, Merradoc, and Christopher Connaught was enjoying the rare afternoon sunshine. The ward was rather large and there were a few things to see, like a gnarled and bushy yew tree with a stone bench next to it that the ladies liked to sit upon. In fact, that was their destination as they headed from the keep.

Merradoc, however, was more concerned about Eefha following them several feet behind, muttering to herself. He was uncomfortable with the shadow of a small, obviously insane woman. As the physic asked the question of Eefha's identity, Emllyn looked over her shoulder at the old woman and grinned.

"She seems harmless," she said. "She has appointed herself my personal servant. She helps me wash, helps me dress, and other tasks. I like her."

Merradoc rolled his eyes. "She is mad, mumbling nonsensical stories. Have you heard her? Things about death and destruction and the birth of the world!"

Emllyn laughed softly. "I find her fascinating."

"Fascinating until she pulls out a dirk and slits your throat."

Emllyn frowned at him. "How horrible!" she gasped. "She will do nothing of the kind."

Merradoc made a face that plainly displayed his disagreement in her statement but he kept silent. He and Emllyn had their arms linked companionably as Elyse and Christopher, walking in front of them, were conspicuously close and giggling to their own private jokes. To anyone looking at them, they looked very much in love.

Emllyn grinned when Connaught stole a kiss, watching Elyse as she fussed about it. It was quite humorous to watch and in spite of Elyse's declaration that she wished there were other marital prospects at Glenteige, it was obvious that she was quite smitten with Connaught. It was sweet to watch.

"Those two do nasty things late at night when de Noble is asleep," Merradoc muttered in her ear. "I have been forced to make pessaries for Lady Elyse so she will not conceive a bastard child, but she assures me that it is not possible for her to conceive because whatever Connaught does, he does in her arse."

Emllyn lifted her eyebrows as she looked at him. "I hope you do not speak so frankly of me as you speak of Elyse," she said with disapproval. "Although I do not do anything nearly as exciting as she does, do you still tell people of my endless hours of embroidery and make it somehow seem thrilling and deviant?"

Merradoc snorted. "Since your farmer left, there is no such excitement in your bed chamber."

"Who says there was before?"

Merradoc wriggled his eyebrows, his gaze scanning the ward, noting the usual servants and soldiers. "You could at least be honest with me."

"And you could at least keep your lips shut."

Merradoc broke down into laughter. "Good God, girl," he said. "You pretend to be as pure as new-fallen snow. I know you have secrets. As a friend, you should tell me what they are."

Emllyn winked at him. "As a friend, you should not ask. You might not like the answer."

They had reached the yew tree and Connaught had politely helped Elyse to sit upon the stone bench beneath it. Merradoc assisted Emllyn to sit, standing politely beside her but twitching impatiently. The man never easily remained in one place for too long; he was flighty. Eefha was several feet away, now loitering near the well and muttering incoherently. Because Merradoc and Emllyn were looking curiously at the old woman, Elyse and Connaught looked over at her, too.

"Who is that old woman?" Elyse asked.

"A bloody assassin," Merradoc muttered.

Emllyn slapped him weakly on the arm to shut him up as she turned to Elyse. "A serving woman who seems to be quite attached to me," she said. "Have you not seen her before?"

Elyse shook her head. "I have seen her in passing, mostly near your chamber," she replied, her gaze lingering on Eefha for a moment longer before turning away. "I am sure she is someone's mother or aunt. As long as she is efficient with her work, I will not send her away. Speaking of efficient, my father tells me that he has arranged for minstrels to perform tonight. They have come all the way from Cork."

Emllyn forced a smile because Elyse seemed so thrilled, but

she knew it was a ploy by de Noble to somehow get into her good graces or otherwise introduce communication. The man hadn't given up since he'd declared his intentions. It had been three days and since that time at every evening meal, he'd tried to speak with her or otherwise engage her, or even ask her to dance.

He'd asked her to dance twice; once when there had been nothing but a lute player and the second time when there had only been singing by one of the servants. It was bad singing at that. Emllyn had politely declined both times but de Noble was persistent. She suspected the minstrels were part of his master plan.

"I am sure they will be lovely," she said, "but I am feeling something of an aching head coming on. Unless it goes away, I may have to take my meal in my room tonight."

Elyse's smile faded; she knew it was because of her father. In fact, it was probably the worst kept secret at Glenteige. The great and powerful Raymond de Noble was in love with the newest visitor to Glenteige, the very lovely Emllyn Fitzgerald. It was all anyone could speak of, especially Merradoc and Elyse. The gossip was flying fast and heavy.

"Please, Emllyn," she leaned over, begging softly. "I will tell my father to stay away. Please come and keep me company."

Emllyn forced a brave smile at her, patting her arm, and Elyse clutched her hand tightly. As Elyse continued to hold her hand and engaged Connaught in a conversation about the hunting he had done earlier in the day, Emllyn found her attention wandering back to Eefha.

The old woman was still over by the well, now sitting on the edge of it and fumbling with her robes as if she had lost something in the folds. The night de Noble had told her about the siege of Black Castle, Emllyn had gone hunting for the old woman but had been unable to locate her so she had returned her chamber and gone to sleep for the night. Eefha had shown up in the morning, however, to bring Emllyn her morning meal, and Emllyn had tried to talk to her about the siege and about returning to Devlin.

Eefha, however, had been fairly unresponsive. She kept muttering something about sorrow and longing, and at one point sang a song about a woman who waited for her husband to return from the sea, and Emllyn deduced that the woman was trying to tell her not to go. It was perhaps sage advice because Emllyn knew that at Glenteige, in spite of de Noble and the cast of eclectic characters, at least she was safe. Were she to flee and try to make her way to Black Castle, there was no knowing the perils she would face.

The more she thought on it, the more she realized that running off to Black Castle would be foolish. The last time she had done something foolish for a man, her entire life had changed, more than she would ever care to admit. To run off to try and save Devlin, or to find out what had become of him, was a ridiculous thought at best. Soon enough, they would know what happened to Black Castle and consequently to Devlin. Patience was not her greatest virtue but for Devlin's sake, and for her own, she would have to wait. Sooner or later, she would know.

Everything leads me to thee. She had to believe he would return for her.

Still, it was disappointing and the wait, three days after she received the news, was becoming excruciating. De Noble's well-intentioned suit didn't help matters. Emllyn found her patience was very short these days.

A soft wind lifted the hem of her surcoat, a beautiful linen garment that Elyse had loaned her. It had a bodice that was crisscross laced with a golden ribbon, giving her an exquisite figure. With her hair pulled away from her face and elaborately braided into a bun at the nape of her neck, she looked positively magnificent. As she brushed away a bit of chaff that had blown onto her skirt from the yew tree, a shadow fell over her.

"Greetings, everyone."

It was de Noble. Emllyn looked up, startled by the man's swift appearance. He was perfectly groomed, as she had come to expect from him, and his handsome features smiled timidly at her. He had greeted the group but it was evident that his attention was only on Emllyn. She smiled wanly as Elyse caught her father's attention.

"Greetings, Father," she said, trying to pull his scrutinizing gaze off of Emllyn. "I thought you said you would be busy all day. New horses, wasn't it?"

De Noble nodded, looking at his daughter. "Indeed," he said. "An entire herd was brought to me by a local chieftain. They're hairy and stocky from the winter season but I believe they will work out. Would you like to come and see them? I believe there are a couple of gentle mares you might find suitable."

Elyse tried not to look at Emllyn for her reaction before responding. "I…" she began, glancing at Christopher before continuing with some uncertainty. "I think that would be lovely. Emllyn, will you excuse us?"

Emllyn opened her mouth but de Noble interrupted. "I should like for the Lady Emllyn to choose a palfrey, also," he said, reaching down to take Emllyn's hand. "There are quite a few horses to see. She might find more than one horse for her pleasure.”

He was gently holding on to Emllyn's hand, encouraging her to stand, but Merradoc stepped in and took Emllyn's hand away from him. He practically yanked her up from the bench and began pulling her in the direction of the keep.

“Not today, my lord,” he told de Noble briskly. “The lady's head is aching. Why, before you came, we were contemplating retreating inside so that she could lie down. You would not want to make her ill by taking her into the dust and flies of a bunch of unruly horses, would you?”

De Noble wasn't pleased by Merradoc's actions. His expression reflected his displeasure intensely. “Of course I have no intention of making her ill,” he said. “But you yanking her around like that isn't doing her any favors, either. Stop acting like I want to take her into a corner and ravage her.”

“Father!” Elyse gasped. “What a terrible thing to say!”

De Noble glanced at is daughter, his temper now unleashed. That hadn't happened in a long time but he was truly frustrated by the attempts of his daughter and Merradoc to remove Emllyn from his presence every time he got near her. It had been going on for several days and he'd finally had enough. It was frustrating as well as embarrassing.

“That is enough from you,” he snapped at his daughter, pointing at her. “You act as if I have the plague every time I get near the Lady Emllyn and I will thank you to stop. I realize she is not interested in me at the moment but there is no way to convince her otherwise if you and your silly physic are constantly removing her from my presence every time I get close to her. I want it stopped, I say. Do you understand me?”

“Silly?” Merradoc repeated, grossly offended. “I am *silly*?”

Elyse shushed Merradoc loudly. “Hush!” she hissed, returning her attention to her father. "Father, must we discuss this in the open for all to hear? You are embarrassing me!"

De Noble frowned. "And *you* are embarrassing me," he said. "You should be encouraging your friend to allow my suit rather than running off with her every time you as much as hear my voice. And if anyone should be ashamed of anyone, it should be me of you. Do not think for one minute that I don't know what you and Connaught do when you think I've gone to sleep. I'm not an idiot, Elyse, but evidently you are. I thought I had raised you better than to be a common whore."

Elyse's mouth popped open in shock before bursting into tears and fleeing to the keep. Emllyn, her mouth agape at the turn of events, pulled away from Merradoc and ran after her. No one seemed to notice that Eefha, too, was headed after them. With the woman all running into the keep, Merradoc turned to de Noble.

"I hope you are proud of yourself," he said, disgust in his voice. "Even I would never say to her what you just did."

De Noble scowled at the man. "Shut up, you woman," he snapped. "You are the worst of the bunch. Are you sure there is a manhood between those legs? From the way you gossip and congregate with womenfolk, I would be sure it was a great gaping cow's vagina between those skinny limbs."

Merradoc threw up his hands in an astonished gesture. "Good God, de Noble!" he cried. "When you throw an insult, you can do it with the best of them! I would not have believed you capable of it, old man!"

He was actually giggling as he scurried after the women, leaving de Noble alone with Connaught. The young knight was looking at the ground, waiting for the inevitable blast to come his direction. In fact, he would be lucky if it was only a verbal lashing. From an enraged father, the punishment could be anything up to and including a physical bashing.

But de Noble didn't anything to him right away. He gaze lingered on Merradoc as the man disappeared into the keep. Then, as the dust settled from the verbal sparring, he turned to Connaught.

"Did you really believe I was that stupid that I did not know what was happening?" he asked the knight.

Connaught shook his head firmly. "Nay, my lord."

"What do you intend to do about it?"

"Marry your daughter, my lord."

De Noble's gaze moved over him a moment, feeling disgust and frustration coming out of every pore of his body. After a moment, he took a deep breath, struggling to calm himself. He realized that he had just said everything he'd always wanted to say to the gossipy little group and strangely felt better now that he had. Perhaps a bit of honesty was good for the soul.

"You'd better," he finally growled, his eyes fixed on the keep. "But for now, you are going to go up to see how my daughter and Lady Emllyn are faring after I unleashed my barrage of insults. I care not about the physic, but at least see how the women are. Then, after they are sufficiently calm, you are to bring the Lady Emllyn to my solar. Is that clear?"

"Aye, my lord."

"And do not tell her where you are taking her; otherwise, she will not come. Tell her that she has been summoned by another."

"Aye, my lord."

With that, de Noble headed off to the keep, leaving Connaught to wonder what next step the man was going to take in the pursuit of the Lady Emllyn.

He couldn't imagine that he was going to remain passive any longer.

CHAPTER SEVENTEEN

Kiltimon Castle
Newcastle Village, 40 miles north of Black Castle

FREDERICK HAD NEVER been to the O'Byrne stronghold before and even though he was on a mission of allegiance, it was difficult not to feel apprehension clawing at him. As he rode into Newcastle Village three days after leaving Black Castle, everything around him was dark and dull and warped. The village itself was warped, twisted little structures without much light or life. It was a depressing sight.

The Clann O'Byrne was a very large clan that had once held much of the land to the north and east of Wicklow. They had never been particularly fond of the House of de Bermingham because they were not native Irish even though they had owned a vast amount of land for hundreds of years and held an earldom. De Bermingham was more Irish than Norman, but it still didn't matter. The O'Byrnes had been their enemy for more years than anyone could remember. They hated de Bermingham in general and they had a special hatred reserved for Black Sword.

Kiltimon Castle sat atop a rise outside of Newcastle Village, a great stone keep built from field stone and a great hall with a thatched roof, all set within a massive circular wall. Just like the village, the castle seemed to be dark and foreboding too, and Frederick had spent several days in the village, living in alleyways or out in the surrounding forest, trying to gain access to the castle.

Evidently, the O'Byrne didn't trust strangers and, unlike Black Castle, Kiltimon was sealed up tight and did not permit farmers or other tradesmen to conduct business at the castle. All business was conducted in town. So, after six days of languishing, Frederick decided to announced his identity. He hoped that would at least get the interest of the castle commander.

Unfortunately, the names Black Sword and Black Castle did more than gain the man's attention; it gained his ire as well. Within seconds of Frederick standing at the front gate and announcing his name and his relations, the iron grate mandoor set within the massive gates opened and several men rushed forth.

In little time, Frederick found himself tied hand and foot, and in this state he was carried into the castle grounds and the door sealed up behind him. They took him into the great hall where they proceeded to toss him onto the floor and kick him.

This went on for hours. It wasn't enough abuse to truly damage him but it was certainly enough to make him hurt. Frederick screamed and yelled angrily as he was kicked and beaten, but he eventually fell silent, even when they kicked him in the groin and caused him horrible pain. But eventually, they did stop, and when they did, Frederick proceeded to vomit all over the dirt floor of the hall. And then he simply lay there in utter pain and silence, wondering if his intention to side with

O'Byrne had indeed been a good idea. He was coming not to think so.

He lay in front of the smoldering hearth until morning, his cheek and part of his head sticky from where he had lain in his own vomit. At some point he had slept, but sleep had been fleeting and uneasy. He awoke in the morning when servants began milling around him, lighting the hearth and preparing for the coming day. He had briefly opened his eyes to see them moving about, wary of his presence. Therefore, he kept his eyes closed until someone rolled him over onto his back.

"You," came a deep, steady voice. "Open your eyes."

Frederick did. He found himself gazing up into two serious and unkind faces. Both men had dark hair and were rather short and wiry, though one was clean-shaven and one had a mat of a beard on his face. The man with the beard spoke.

"The mention of Black Castle is not taken well around here," he said. "Tell me your name and no lies, or I will feed you to the dogs."

Frederick gazed back with dulled eyes. "Sir Frederick óg Branach," he said. "My cousin is Devlin de Bermingham."

The man with the beard gazed down at him a moment before shaking his head in disbelief. "My soldiers told me that," he said. "But I cannot believe you would be foolish enough to come here and announce it. Do you have a death wish, man?"

Frederick tried to shake his head but it was difficult to move. "I am no longer loyal to Black Sword," he said. "I have come to make a deal with you."

"What kind of deal?"

"Untie me, feed me, and I shall tell you."

The two men standing over Frederick looked at each other as if silently debating the request. There was wariness there but there was also curiosity. After a moment, the man with the beard motioned to a few other men Frederick couldn't see, men standing out of his line of sight, who then reached down and lifted him roughly off the ground.

The world rocked unsteadily as they plopped Frederick onto a bench. Someone cut the bindings off his arms while someone else bent down to cut the bindings off his ankles. Just as the leather ties around his ankle fell away, Frederick lashed out a big boot and kicked the man who had cut his legs free in the face, knocking the dirk out of his hand. Quick as a flash, he grabbed the dirk, and the man he had kicked, and held the blade to the man's throat.

"So you see fit to treat me like an animal when I come to you with information about your greatest enemy?" he hissed. "I was always told you were a bunch of brainless barbarians and I would say from my treatment, those rumors were true. Do you not even try to seek out a man's business before you beat him nearly to death?"

The two dark-haired men who seemed to be the leaders stood by patiently. No one made a move. The man with the beard finally spoke.

"My name is Daniel O'Byrne," he said, then indicated the other dark-haired man standing next to him. "This is my son, Brandon. I would know what you've come here for before I put a blade in your belly."

"Put a blade in my belly and you'll never know the secret of Black Sword."

"And what do you want in exchange for this secret?"

"Command of Black Castle when you take her."

Daniel lifted his eyebrows, half in disbelief, half in curiosity. "What makes you think we'll take her?" he asked. "We laid siege to the place for almost a week and were unable to breach her walls.”

“Tell me we have a bargain or I will not speak. I will leave here and you will never see me again.”

Daniel glanced at his son, who cast him a look of caution, before continuing. “We will come to an agreement but I am not sure Black Castle will be a part of it,” he said. “I have many fine men who I would chose to command Black Castle over a man who claims to be a kin to Black Sword.”

Frederick hardened. “You will agree to put me in command of Black Castle when you breach her because I guarantee you will breach her with information I provide.”

Daniel O’Byrne had been a warrior for almost thirty years. He had seen his share of hardship and of battle. He had also seen his share of traitors, of which this man evidently was. Traitors made him ill; he may have been a barbaric warrior, a knight of the lowest and most brutal form, but he could not tolerate treachery from men who had given their oath to others, even if that man was his worse enemy.

Already, he didn’t like this man but he wanted whatever information he had, providing it wasn’t a lie. It was quite possible that Black Sword had sent this man to trick him. He would have to proceed carefully.

“You cannot have everything your own way,” Daniel finally said. “If you want to make a bargain, then you will have to accept terms from me as well.”

Frederick didn’t like that answer and his grip on the dirk, and his captive, tightened. “I want a guarantee that I will command Black Castle after you confiscate it.”

Daniel could see he wasn’t going to get anywhere unless he promised the man what he wanted. Well, at least told him he could have it. He wasn't about to promise a traitor, and an enemy, anything and still keep his word.

"Fine," he said shortly. "If that is all you want, then that is what you shall receive. Now tell me what this information is? Are the heavens about to open up and reveal a revelation?"

Frederick didn't let go of the dirk or the man; he continued to hold them both but not as tightly as before.

"Swear it," he said.

"I don't swear," said Daniel.

"Swear it upon your mother!"

"I most certainly don't swear on my mother," Daniel said, his patience fading. "Tell me your business or I'll order my men to kill you."

Frederick tensed again, eyeing the men in the room, a group that was numbering around twenty. He knew he wouldn't make it out alive if O'Byrne ordered his men to swarm on him. So he backed up, ending up against the wall that was adjacent to the hearth. His dark eyes were nervous and edgy.

"If you want to take Black Castle, now is the time," he said. "De Bermingham is occupied with the de Cleveley settlement to the south. He fears they are planning to attack him, as Kildare did, so his focus is there. In fact, when last I spoke with him, he was planning on going to the settlement. He was leaving Black Castle."

Daniel was very interested. He knew that with Black Sword in the heart of any battle, his victory was assured. But if he had removed himself from Black Castle, then the fortress, and the men, would be without their beloved leader. And they would be vulnerable.

"I see," he said, contemplating. "Was he at the fortress when we attacked it those days ago?"

Frederick nodded. "He was," he said. "But it was his plan to leave Black Castle immediately after you retreated."

"He was going to the English settlement?"

"Aye."

"How many men was he taking with him?"

"None."

Daniel's eyebrows lifted in surprise. "None?" he repeated. "Then how does he plan to lay siege?"

Frederick shook his head. "You misunderstand," he said. "Black Sword has a spy in the settlement. He was returning to gather information. While he is gone, the fortress is not only compromised since the beating it took from your attack, but it is further vulnerable because de Bermingham is not there. Don't you see? If you really want to destroy Black Sword and take his castle, now is the time."

Daniel looked at his son, who seemed to be taking the information quite literally. When Brandon spoke, it was to his father.

"If what he says is true, then we would be foolish not to take advantage," he said, but then he looked at Frederick. "If you are close to Black Sword as you say you are, then why are you so willing to betray him?"

Frederick lost some of his confidence. He seemed to deflate, consumed with depression. "Because…," he began, then recovered and stood tall. "Because he chooses others over me. I have always been true and faithful to him, but he would reward others before me. He will not listen to my advice. It is clear he has no use for me. I am an excellent commander and deserve all recognition."

"So this is about rewards?"

"This is about getting what I deserve."

Brandon eyed his father a moment before continuing; they were starting to get into the heart of the traitor's visit. "So you feel that you deserve more than Black Sword is willing to give," he reiterated. "Does de Bermingham know this? Have you ever spoken to him about it?"

"He will not listen to me."

"So you come here to betray him and to punish him."

"Aye."

Brandon believed him. "At least you are being honest," he said. "Unlike my father, I have no reservations about placing you in command of Black Castle if we breach it. But you are going to help us accomplish this."

"How?"

Brandon crossed his arms; he was a bright young man with a cunning mind. He was about to prove it.

"You will return to Black Castle," he said. "In three days, on the rise of the full moon, you will open the gates and we will charge in. We will be hiding in the woods to the north of Black Castle and once the gate is unlocked, you will send us a signal. When we see the signal, we will come, and Black Castle shall be ours. Will you do this?"

Frederick didn't want to refuse him; he'd fled Black Castle after killing Shain and attempting to poison his cousin. He'd seen Devlin from a distance as he'd fled Black Castle, so he knew his attempt to murder him had failed. Naturally, he was reluctant to return, but if he wanted to prove his worth to O'Byrne, and if he wanted to have command of Black Castle when Devlin was deposed, then he had no choice. After a moment, he nodded faintly.

"Very well," he said. "I will return and open the gates for you. What sign would you have from me?"

Brandon considered that for a moment. "Exit the open gates with two torches," he said. "We will be able to see them from a distance. Wave them into the night and we will know the gates are open and come."

"I will have to do this without raising suspicion."

"That will be your problem. If we do not see the torches, we will not come because we will assume you have failed."

"I will not fail."

It was an acceptable plan. Frederick dropped the man he was holding and marched over to the table. As he reached it, he drew the sharp end of the dirk across his forearm, immediately drawing blood. It dripped onto the table top, rich and red. He pointed at the blood.

"I swear by my blood that I will do this," he said, his voice raspy and intense. "Mingle your blood with mine and swear you will uphold your end of the bargain. Do it now."

Brandon held the man's gaze for a moment before moving to the table, taking the dirk from Frederick's hand, and carving it into the flesh of his left forearm near the elbow. His blood dripped down his white flesh and onto the table, mingling with Frederick's. Then, he planted the dirk right in the middle of the bloody patch.

"There," he said, sounding unhappy and irritated. "Now you have your promise. You will ride to Black Castle tomorrow morning and open the gates in three days upon the full of the moon. Betray us and we will hunt you down and make you pay. Is this is any way unclear?"

Frederick smiled at him, a surprising gesture. "Betray me, and I shall do the same."

Brandon returned the smile, an odd and uncomfortable gesture. "Then we understand one another."

"We do indeed."

The next morning before sunrise, Frederick was on his way back to Black Castle, trying to figure out a way to gain access to the castle without getting killed in the process. The only logical solution was to plead forgiveness and hope Devlin was in a forgiving mood. He was sure he could placate the man and apologize, swearing he was not in his right mind when he acted in haste. He hoped it would be enough to get back into Devlin's good graces.

And then he would destroy him.

CHAPTER EIGHTEEN

Glenteige Castle

EMLLYN REALIZED TOO late that she had been summoned to de Noble's solar.

Having spent the past two hours comforting Elyse against her father's slander, truthful though it might be, Connaught had shown up at Elyse's chamber door and had asked Emllyn to accompany him. He gave her some story about something happening in the kitchens and asked if she would attend to it on Elyse's behalf. Not wanting to upset her friend further with minor tasks of the household, Emllyn had agreed.

But it had been a trap. Connaught hadn't taken her to the kitchens at all; as they were heading to the keep entry which would take them outside to the kitchens, he suddenly veered to the left and took her straightaway into de Noble's solar. Once they were inside, he promptly removed her hand from his elbow, walked out, and shut the door behind him.

Startled and instantly uneasy, Emllyn looked over to see de Noble standing behind his desk. He was predictably well-groomed, standing next to the lancet window and gazing out over the ward beyond. Emllyn's surprise was turning to anger;

she didn't like being trapped. Without a word, she turned to open the door but de Noble's voice stopped her.

"Please," he said rather loudly, causing Emllyn to pause with her hand on the latch. "Do not leave. I very much wish to apologize for my behavior earlier so I asked Connaught to bring you here. I knew you would not come if he told you I had summoned you."

Emllyn looked away from him. Her hand was still on the latch but she just stood there, looking at the floor. "And so you have apologized," she said. "Surely you should be apologizing to your daughter and not to me."

De Noble turned to look at her as he came away from the window. "I will, in time," he said. "But only for the way I spoke to her, not for the words I said. She has been making a mockery out of me for quite some time. She deserved everything I said."

Emllyn didn't know what to say. She kept her hand on the latch and her gaze averted. "Will that be all, my lord?" she asked.

De Noble made his way over to her. "Nay," he replied. "In fact, you have made somewhat of a mockery of me as well."

Emllyn's head snapped to him, her eyes ripe with fury. "For what?" she said. "For refusing your suit? If anyone has made a mockery of you, it is *you*. You do not know when to abide by a lady's wishes. You push and push, making a fool of yourself over a woman who is clearly not interested in you."

By this time, de Noble had reached her. He came to a halt, his dark eyes glittering at her. "Mayhap," he said softly. "I suppose it is my arrogance that drives me to do it. I keep telling myself that I am a patient man but the truth is that I am not. There is a beautiful and unwed woman in midst and I cannot help but succumb. May I ask a question, my lady?"

Emllyn was frustrated and impatient, but she nodded her head shortly. "If you must."

De Noble smiled faintly at her reaction. "What is it about me that you find so unappealing?"

Emllyn tried not to look at him as she spoke, although his question had been gentle. She was struggling not to feel sorry for him.

"You are not unappealing, my lord," she said. "But if your daughter has told you anything about me, which I suspect she has, then you know I lost my love in my brother's attack on Black Castle. That was a mere few weeks ago and I am still mourning his loss. I cannot even think of another man at the moment so I would appreciate it if you would give me that consideration."

De Noble nodded in understanding. "She did tell me that," he said. "But she also told me that you and that farmer who brought you here, John, were lovers."

Emllyn rolled her eyes. "John saved my life," she said flatly. "That does not mean we are lovers. He is a very kind man and he made me feel safe. What is so terrible about that?"

"Nothing."

"And even if we were lovers, that would make me the whore you accused your daughter of being, so why would you want to pursue a relationship with a whore?"

De Noble just looked at her, intently. One moment, he was standing there and in the next he was pulling Emllyn into a crushing embrace. His mouth came down on hers, brutally, but Emllyn slapped him so hard that the man lost his grip on her. As de Noble stumbled back, looking both startled and horrified, Emllyn threw open the solar door.

"Try that again and I shall ram my knee into your manhood

so hard that you'll be spitting blood for a week," she snarled. "You are nothing but an old, silly fool, de Noble. Stay away from me!"

As she marched out into the foyer beyond, leaving de Noble in stunned silence, a soldier suddenly rushed in through the big, open entry. He looked around frantically in the dim light of the foyer and, spying de Noble in the doorway to his solar, he rushed the man.

"My lord!" he said swiftly. "We have sighted an incoming party."

De Noble wiped at the corner of his mouth, slightly bloodied when Emllyn's clip drove his soft cheek into his teeth. "Who are they?" he asked. "Can you tell?"

The sentry shook his head. "We are not sure, my lord," he replied. "But they are coming from the north."

Black Castle is to the north! Emllyn paused in her haste to leave de Noble, her heart leaping into her throat. De Noble didn't even look at her as he walked past her and out into the ward beyond and Emllyn hardly cared; she was happy to have the man well away from her but more than that, she was thrilled with the prospect that Devlin might actually be returning. *Was it possible?* The mere idea swamped her until her pulse pounded and her breathing came in funny little gasps.

Knowing she would receive a much better view of the village and the subsequent outlying areas from the smaller third floor chamber that was usually kept available for visiting guests, Emllyn gathered her skirts and raced up the stairs.

Her heart was throbbing in her ears as she reached the third floor and bolted into the empty chamber with its naked bedframe and sparse furnishings. This chamber was situated so that it had a view of the north and west with a big oriel window much the same as the one Emllyn had. Eagerly, she climbed upon the windowsill as much as she dared and strained to catch a glimpse of the incoming party.

In nervous silence, she settled down to wait.

THEY COULD SEE the de Cleveley settlement in the distance, a great spattering of stone and thatched buildings and the walls that enclosed them, and right in the middle was the tall and stately keep. As Devlin and Victor, leading the pack of English prisoners, drew close enough to the settlement to see the sentries on the walls, Devlin turned to Victor.

"Now," he said, eyeing the village in the distance, "if my treacherous commander has made it here before me, then they will be waiting for me, I am sure. Since I do not wish to walk into a trap, you and your men will wait here and I will continue on to the gates where I will ask to speak with the commander. I am fairly certain at that point I will know if Frederick has made it here before me. De Noble's reaction upon seeing me will tell me much."

Victor, too, was eyeing the village in the distance. "And then what?" he said. "De Bermingham, all they need do is send out a group of men on horseback to capture you if that is the case. You cannot flee them on foot."

"Do you have a better idea?"

Victor nodded firmly. "I do," he said. "Let me go to them and find out what I can. If your man has indeed made it here and betrayed both you and my daughter… I mean, the Lady Emllyn… then I will find out. If she is in the vault, then I will tell the commander that it is your wish to exchange thirty-three English prisoners for her life. You had better let me be the emissary because if you go near them and they know who you are, then both you and the Lady Emllyn will be in serious danger. I do not know if I will be able to get you out of it."

Devlin looked rather amused. "You would try and get me out of danger?" he asked. "Why?"

Victor gave him a rather dead-pan look, although there wasn't much weight behind it. It was an expression coming from a man who knew he had little choice in the matter.

"Because when you marry my daughter, you will become the only son I have," he said, watching Devlin grin. "I cannot let my only son become fodder for de Cleveley, no matter if you *are* Black Sword."

Devlin couldn't help but chuckle. "So you have come to terms with your only son, have you?"

"I have little choice."

Devlin nodded in agreement, his humor fading. "That is true."

Victor held his gaze a moment longer before waving him off in a somewhat light and dismissive gesture. "Moreover, you showed your English prisoners mercy you did not have to display," he said quietly. "I at least owe you a measure of the same."

"Even though it was I who destroyed Kildare's fleet in the first place?"

Victor shrugged. "Such are the perils of war."

Devlin's gaze lingered on the man a moment. "Indeed they are," he said, eyeing the settlement once more. "The situation being what it is, I will agree with your plans. You will go instead of me. However, if my commander has not come here and they still believe me to be John the farmer, then you will come back after contacting de Noble and bring us all in to the settlement. I will wait here with your men. You will tell de Noble that I rescued you from Black Sword's dungeon and brought you here. That will give me much credibility in de Noble's eyes."

"Agreed."

"One more thing; you should tell your men not to give away my true identity. That, too, will reflect badly on Emllyn. They must keep the secret if there is any chance of getting us all out of this situation unscathed."

Victor nodded, glancing back at his collection of weary and worn men, including Trevor and his lover. The lover was an older man, a seasoned soldier, and along with William du Reims, whose health had suffered greatly in captivity, the three of them kept vigilant watch over the men. Victor eyed his group of weary and beaten men, now exhausted after a two day march south.

"I've not told them anything, you know," he said quietly. "I was not going to say a word until you told me to."

Devlin nodded, appreciating the trust. "Now is the time," he said. "Let them know what is to happen. I will listen to what you say."

Victor went to his men, collecting them around him, and tactfully explained the situation they were about to face. Everyone either seemed confused or apathetic about keeping Devlin's identity a secret, and Devlin watched Trevor's face in particular when Victor discussed the situation regarding Lady Emllyn or, as he suspected, his daughter, Cate. The man's eyes widened with surprise and then narrowed with confusion. After a few moments as the news sank in, he shook his head with disbelief and rolled his eyes. Devlin nearly grinned.

In truth, all of the men seemed rather concerned for her, enough so that they were willing to lie about de Bermingham's true identity. The lady's peril was enough to guarantee their compliance on the matter. With his men informed and his task complete, Victor approached Devlin.

"Everyone is in agreement now," he said. "Any further instructions?"

Devlin shook his head as he gazed at the settlement in the distance. He was hesitant to speak what was on his mind, the last few words before Victor faced an uncertain situation, but he felt he had to say something. It would weigh far too heavily upon him if he did not.

"If… if you do see Emllyn and confirm that she is your daughter," he said quietly. "Do not… that is to say, I would rather that she…"

Victor cut him off. "I will not say a word to her about assuming the Lady Emllyn's identity," he said. "But if she sees you and I together, and she knows you have freed us from your vault, then she will assume we have spoken about her and she must further assume that I told you of the Lady Emllyn's death. She is a bright girl."

Devlin nodded, his eyes averted. He wasn't exactly sure what he was feeling at the moment; he was excited to see Emllyn, so much so that his hands were sweating. He couldn't even begin to describe the longing in his heart, waiting to be quenched by the first vision of his angel in days. *Everything leads me to thee*, he thought to himself. But in the next breath, he wanted to take her over his knee so badly and spank her for lying to him that he could hardly think straight. It was an odd combination.

"I know she is," he said. "I would rather she confess her

identity to me of her own free will rather than you force it out of her."

"As you wish."

With that, Victor begged his leave and headed on foot to de Cleveley's settlement while Devlin and the other knights took the group back into the forest that bordered Glenteige from the west. They would stay out of sight until Victor made his determinations. Meanwhile, as they waited for Victor to accomplish his directive, it afforded Devlin a closer look at the knight Emllyn had risked her life for.

Trevor was very efficient, helping settle the men and making comfortable the ones who had suffered the most. He even sat du Reims down because the man was in no shape to be on his feet. He seemed very concerned for the others, a show of compassion that was surprising from an arrogant young knight. When everyone was settled and breaking out the last of the jerky and cheese, Trevor approached Devlin.

"The men are settled, my lord," he said politely. "Would you eat with us?"

Devlin inspected the man; he'd grown thinner since the first time he'd seen him in the vault. He could just picture Emllyn throwing herself at the handsome young knight and the man's utter resistance to female company. After a moment, he shook his head.

"Nay," he replied. "But take what nourishment you can. It has been a two day march and I do not know when we will be supplied with more food."

Trevor simply nodded politely and turned away. But Devlin stopped him; he found he couldn't help himself.

"I understand that the Lady Em… I mean, the Lady Catherine was somewhat of your shadow," he said.

Trevor looked a little surprised by the question. And then he looked nervous. "Did Victor tell you that?"

Devlin shook his head. "The woman who introduced herself to me as the Lady Emllyn did."

Trevor was at a loss for words. But when he spoke, there was both concern and awe in his tone. "Then… then it is true she stowed away on Kildare's armada?"

"To follow you, I was told."

"But… in God's name, why?"

Devlin shrugged. "She told me that she had followed her lover because she wanted to prove to him that she could be a good wife," he said. Then, he wriggled his eyebrows ironically. "Why did you never tell her that you were not interested in women?"

Trevor was nervous still and he hesitated before answering. He knew what Devlin meant; it was obvious in his expression, but it wasn't something he was keen on discussing with a stranger. Still, there was no point in avoiding the subject. It wasn't as if he'd been hiding it since he and Nils had been joyfully reunited after their release from Black Castle's vault. Nils had been in one cell and he had been in the other. They'd hardly been able to touch each other through the bars and crowded conditions.

"I did tell her," he finally said. "But I did not use the correct terms, I suppose. I said I had no interest in a wife, but she seemed to take it as a challenge."

"She would."

"Then you have come to know her, my lord?"

Devlin nodded. Then, he laughed softly. "Have no fear," he said. "When I see her again, I will not tell her *why* you had no interest in marriage. But take heart; I have a feeling she is no longer interested in you. I believe she has moved on to bigger prey."

Trevor's dark eyebrows lifted in surprise. "She *has*?" he asked, relief in his voice. "If that is indeed true, then I would shake that man's hand for doing me a great and important favor."

Devlin just looked at him. Then, he slowly extended his hand. Trevor looked at it with confusion.

"I do not understand, my lord."

Devlin's lips twitched with a grin. "You said you wanted to shake the hand of the man who is doing you a great and important favor."

Trevor still stared at it. And stared. Then, realization dawned; his eyes widened as he reached out to take Devlin's big, white hand.

"*You*, my lord?"

"It would seem so."

"But… but I do not understand! *How*?"

"How, indeed."

"And… and you are agreeable to this?"

"Aye."

Trevor's expression washed with one of great pleasure and he shook Devlin's hand firmly. In fact, he was nearly overjoyed to shake it.

"Then the rumors of your courage are true," he said enthusiastically. "You *are* the bravest man I have ever met!"

CHAPTER NINETEEN

"ONLY THIRTY-THREE OUT of an armada of one thousand men?" de Noble was incredulous. "That is all that survived?"

Standing in de Noble's fine solar with its faintly smoky air and hide rugs, Victor nodded seriously. "It was a disaster for Kildare," he said quietly. "Black Sword and his men were waiting for us. The weather was so bad that the ships crashed together as we tried to moor them, essentially breaking them apart. Men struggling to shore were easily picked off by de Bermingham's men."

De Noble's mind ran over that horrifying scenario, men being easy prey for Black Sword's blood thirsty troops. "But you survived?"

"Barely, my lord."

De Noble sighed heavily. "Surely Kildare must be aware of this defeat."

Victor shrugged. "I would not know," he said. "Unless Black Sword sent him word that the fleet was destroyed, I suppose the man is still waiting for word. It was a little more than three weeks ago."

De Noble's gaze lingered on Victor, trying to overcome the terrible news of the shattered fleet. "And what's this you say about a traitor knight under Black Sword's command?" he asked. "You asked me if such a man had come here from Black Castle."

"Did he?"

"Nay," de Noble shook his head. "We have not seen anyone like that. However, a little more than a week ago, a farmer brought a woman to us who declared that she was Kildare's sister."

That was exactly what Victor wanted to hear. He feigned surprise. "His sister?" he repeated. "How is it possible?"

De Noble perched himself on the edge of his great oak desk. "She said she had been on a ship to witness her brother's victory over the Irish and evidently washed up on shore when the armada was destroyed," he replied. "The farmer is the only man from Black Castle's region that we have seen here. As for the woman, from what you have told me, she is lucky to have survived."

Victor's thoughts were immediately riveted to the woman they all knew as Emllyn. "Is she still here?"

De Noble nodded. "Of course," he said. "We have been providing her with the best of everything, and she and my daughter have become very good friends."

Victor digested the information but as he did so, something de Noble had said caught his attention. "You said that she 'declared' she was Kildare's sister," he said. "Do you not believe her?"

De Noble shrugged. "She is fine and beautiful enough, so she is certainly a lady of nobility," he said. "Is she who she says she is? It is possible. Why? Do you know his sister?"

"I do indeed."

De Noble's face lit up. "Perfect!" he said, coming off his desk and heading to the solar door. He opened the panel, shouting to a servant he saw in the feasting hall beyond. "Send the Lady Emllyn to me immediately. Tell her we have a visitor who wishes to see her!"

As the servant set down the broom in her hands, de Noble returned his attention to Victor. "I suppose we shall see if she really is Kildare's sister," he said. "Meanwhile, where are the rest of your men? You said there were thirty-three. Did you alone escape Black Castle?"

Victor shook his head, thinking that very soon he would be getting to the bottom of the mystery surrounding the alleged Lady Emllyn. He could hardly stand the anticipation. But even as he pondered that thought, he was also very aware that de Bermingham's defector knight had not come to Glenteige to lay wide open Black Sword and his secrets. It was excellent news, one that he felt a great deal of relief at purely for Emllyn's sake. Or Catherine's; whomever she turned out to be. In any case, the woman would be safe. And Victor had to get his men inside the fortress.

"I did not," he said, carefully planning a portion of the lie he had only briefly touched on with Devlin. "A farmer by the name of John released us. He was somehow able to get us clear of Black Castle and brought us here. He was instrumental in releasing us and should be duly commended."

"John?" de Noble looked surprised. "A very big man with a red beard and a bald head?"

Victor thought back to Devlin, who was not so much bald any longer; his red hair was growing in. Still, he nodded.

"The same," he said.

"He is the same man who brought us Kildare's sister."

"Then he is a valuable ally, indeed."

"Did he come with you?"

Victor nodded. "He did," he replied. "He is resting with my men just outside of Glenteige's gates. I came ahead to announce our arrival and give you word of Kildare's fleet."

It was a smooth and believable story that rested in de Noble's mind, so much so that the man hardly gave it another thought. "I will send men out to bring them in," he said. "It must have been an exhausting flight."

Victor was vastly relieved that de Noble didn't question him anymore about John and their escape from Black Castle; he didn't want to give the man more information than he had to because the tighter the web of deceit, the more chance there was for them to strangle themselves in it.

"It was," he agreed. "But there is no need to send men. I will go and retrieve them. You can imagine we have several that are ill, making travel very slow and difficult."

De Noble reached for a fine pewter pitcher of wine and two small pewter cups. It was a matching set he'd had shipped from England long ago. Pouring Victor a measure of wine, he handed it to the man.

"As you wish," he said. "Meanwhile, you will enjoy my hospitality until we can arrange passage for you and your men to return to Llansteffan Castle. I am sure Kildare is anxious to have you and your men returned to him."

Victor drank the entire cup of wine in three swallows; it was rich and tart and fortifying. De Noble took it from him and poured him some more.

"Mayhap," Victor said, smacking his lips as he accepted his second cup. "It is more than likely he might wish for me to remain here to fortify your numbers. He does, in fact, want you to retake Black Castle, doesn't he?"

De Noble's expression remained neutral. "Did he tell you that?"

Victor took another long drink of wine. "I know he has been sending missives to de Cleveley and I am assuming de Cleveley is informing you of what he and Kildare have discussed. The earl wants Black Castle back."

De Noble grunted and took a drink of his own wine. "That is no great secret," he said. Then, he eyed Victor. "I will be honest when I tell you that de Cleveley is disinclined to launch against Black Castle, even to support an ally. We have our own problems with the Irish without stirring up Black Sword. He came down around us three years ago and I do not want to live through that again. The man stole my damn chair."

As Victor pondered de Noble and de Cleveley's resistance to Kildare's request, he heard quick and light footsteps approaching the solar door. By the time he turned around, a beautiful young woman in a yellow surcoat was standing in the doorway.

Victor tried to control his reaction; he really did. It was the greatest feat of self-control he had ever exhibited because in truth, his mind was reeling and it would have been very easy to display his naked reaction of astonishment.

He stared at the young woman; the young woman stared at him. Eyes widened and jaws dropped. As Victor stared at her, he could see the tears forming. Already there was about to be a scene and he hastened to prevent it. Not here, not now, in front of de Noble, who was watching the entire event very carefully. Victor had to step forward and take charge, and he did just that.

"Lady Emllyn," he said, moving to take Emllyn's hand. He

kissed it with more tenderness than he should have. "I have been hearing all about your harrowing tale, how you washed upon shore and how a farmer brought you to Glenteige. Thank God you are well and whole, my lady. Thank God indeed."

Emllyn stared at Victor as he kissed her hand. It was too much for her; tears spilled over and she clapped a hand over her mouth to keep from sobbing. Never in her life had she been so surprised, or had felt so much overwhelming astonishment. She struggled not to dissolve into gut-busting weeping as Victor held her hand and smiled warmly at her.

God's Blood, the struggle!

Swallowing hard, Emllyn forced herself to acknowledge his kind words.

"And… and you, Sir Victor," she whispered tightly. "You were on the fleet. But you are alive."

Victor was still holding her hand, his dark eyes glimmering at her. "I am indeed," he said gently. "Sir Raymond has been telling me all about your adventures in Ireland. I must say that I am surprised to see that you survived everything."

De Noble came out from behind his desk, his gaze moving between Emllyn and Victor. Emllyn seemed extremely emotional but that was to be expected, given the fact that she believed all of her brother's men had been killed. He smiled at the pair.

"So she is indeed Kildare's sister?" he asked Victor.

Victor gazed steadily at Emllyn for a long moment, silent words of understanding and comfort and acceptance passing between them. From this moment forward, Victor only saw Emllyn. For all of their sakes, and for the safety of many, it was all he could do.

"Aye," he said after a moment. "This is the Lady Emllyn."

De Noble was both thrilled and relieved in spite of the deteriorating situation between him and Emllyn over the past day. He made a point of catching the lady's attention.

"You will forgive me that I had to have St. John's confirmation," he said. "Without your brother to confirm your identity, to have one of his knights know you is the next best thing. I pray you are not offended by this."

Emllyn was still overwhelmed with it all. Victor eventually let go of her fingers and handed her his half-full cup of wine. She looked like she needed it. Gratefully, and with shaking hands, Emllyn swallowed the wine in two big gulps.

"I am not offended," she said, her voice trembling. "I suppose if I were in your situation, I would have done the same thing."

De Noble was relieved that she wasn't cross with him for his doubt; he didn't want to add fuel to the fire of their already-strained relationship.

"Sir Victor says that thirty-three of your brother's men survived the destruction of the war fleet," he said. "He also said that John, your farmer friend, helped them escape from Black Castle's dungeons."

Emllyn tore her gaze off of Victor and looked at de Noble. "John?" she repeated, trying to keep the excitement from her voice. "Has he returned?"

Victor spoke. "He is with my men, outside of the walls of Glenteige," he said. "I am going to retrieve them now."

Emllyn was moving with Victor; in fact, she nearly ran him over. "I will go, too."

Victor shook his head, forcing her to stop when she tried to push past him. "Nay, my lady," he said. "It would not be safe for you. You will remain here and we will all sup together tonight, I promise."

Emllyn was as edgy as a cat and laboring not to show it. She very much wanted to go with Victor to retrieve the English prisoners simply so she could see Devlin, but she knew they would never allow it. Already they were resisting. So she forced herself to calm.

"Of course," she said, trying to look as if she was satisfied with the thought of seeing everyone at supper. "I suppose I am simply happy to know that some of my brother's men survived. May I at least walk you to the door, Sir Victor?"

Victor smiled at her. "I would be honored," he said, turning to de Noble. "I shall return within the hour, my lord."

De Noble nodded graciously. "I will look forward to it," he said, eyeing Emllyn. He knew she wouldn't be happy if he tried to walk with them so he didn't even ask. "My lady, I will see you tonight at supper."

Emllyn barely nodded at him as she preceded Victor out of the solar door. Once out in the foyer, with its rounded walls that tended to echo, Emllyn surprisingly kept a rein on her excitement and shock. She simply took Victor's elbow as he walked to the keep entry. Once the door yawned before them, spilling white light into the dimness of the gray stoned keep, she paused and turned to him.

"I…," she began.

Victor shushed her before she could speak more than one word. "I will see you upon my return, my lady," he said, hearing his voice echo off the walls and knowing there were ears listening, more than likely de Noble's. "I look forward to hearing about your adventures since you came to Ireland."

Emllyn looked at the man, wanting to say so much more. The tears threatened to return but she fought them. She knew why he was speaking so generically; if anyone understood the gossips and big ears of this place, she did.

"And you shall," she said. "I… I would also like to see John when he arrives. I would like to see the man who… who saved my life. Did he tell you?"

"All that and more," he said, letting go of her as he headed out of the keep. "I will send him to you when we return, my lady. Be of good and noble patience that all will work out as it should."

Emllyn lingered in the doorway, watching the man descend the wide, stone steps. Her heart was so full of thanks and gratefulness that she could hardly breathe. Her mind was full of a million memories and hopes, like butterflies, all living and breathing entities inside her soul. She lifted a hand in farewell to Victor.

"Will you tell him something for me, please?" she called after him.

There was no more echo to amplify their words; in fact, it all seemed rather still outside. There wasn't anyone around that they could see. Victor paused on the steps.

"What is that, my lady?"

Emllyn swallowed hard; she was coming to suspect simply by the way he was behaving that he and Devlin had more than likely been in discussions with her as the main topic. It only seemed logical. From the moment she had seen Victor in de Noble's solar, everything about him told her that he knew what had happened. All of it. She smiled faintly as she met his gaze, lowering her voice so that he could barely hear it.

"Please… please tell him that everything leads me to thee."

Victor cocked his head slightly, considering her words, as a faint smile crossed his lips. Nodding in understanding, he turned and walked away. Emllyn watched him, blowing the man a gentle kiss when she knew he couldn't see it. She simply felt that it was the right thing to do.

He did, after all, love her, too.

VICTOR HAD RETURNED to the spot where he had left Devlin and his men. The walk from the front gates of Glenteige had been a wide-open one, as the settlement was surrounded by wide open spaces to get a better field of fire when the fortress was attacked. Things that could hide rebels like trees or bushes had long since been removed.

As he stood on the precise location where he had last seen his men and de Bermingham, he noticed the trees about a quarter of a mile to the east were moving. More than moving, they appeared to come alive and Victor realized that his men were coming through the foliage. Weary, beaten, some men helping others to walk, the entire group was emerging from the forest, including the massive bulk of de Bermingham. They had evidently seen him approach and were breaking their cover. Victor went to meet them.

Devlin was at the head of the group, moving faster than the others because he was perhaps more anxious than the others. He met Victor several feet in front of the others, nearly bowling the man over in his eagerness and haste.

"Well?" he demanded. "Did my knight make it to de Noble before we did?"

Victor shook his head. "They have not seen him," he assured him. "He is not here."

Devlin, who had let his imagination go wild for the past hour, literally had to catch his breath. The shock was so great that he actually gasped.

"Freddy has not been here?" he asked again, just to be sure.

Victor shook his head again, seeing how astonished de Bermingham was. "Nay," he repeated for good measure. "De Noble and I had a long conversation where he assured me that no one from Black Castle has come. He says that the only reference to Black Castle in the past few weeks was a lone farmer named John bearing a woman who, he said, had washed upon the shore after Kildare's armada was defeated."

That was good enough for Devlin; he was beyond the ability to measure his relief. "And Emllyn?" he fired at him. "Did you see her?"

Victor knew what he meant. *Is she your daughter?* But somehow, Victor wasn't sure he could tell him the truth. From his discussions with Devlin, and his brief encounter with Emllyn, he could already see the joy and adoration when one spoke of the other. There was a warmth there, a spring of hope everlasting, that was more powerful than anything he had ever sensed. Therefore, he wasn't sure he could spoil it with reality. Sometimes reality was best left to one's own interpretation.

"I saw her," he said. "She is healthy and whole, and she is anxious to see you. She told me to give you a message."

Devlin's big body was quivering with anticipation. "What message?"

"She says to tell you that everything leads me to thee."

Devlin stared at him. Then, he emitted something that sounded like a hiss, running his hand over his bristly head, his gaze lingering on the fortress in the distance. The longer he stared at it, the more impact the words seemed to have. He could feel tears of pure emotion sting his eyes. He blinked rapidly, chasing them away, before returning his focus to Victor.

"Is she your daughter, Victor?" he asked softly.

Victor paused before answering. "Do you really want to know?"

Devlin suspected the answer but stopped short of pressing the man. After a moment, he simply shook his head.

"I suppose it does not matter," he said. "I fell in love with Emllyn. She will always be Emllyn to me."

"As well she should be."

Victor's men were starting to gather around them so they let the subject die, never to be discussed again. Neither man saw the need. Whether she was Catherine or Emllyn, it simply didn't matter any longer. She was loved either way. Together, Victor and Devlin led the ragtag band of English soldiers into the embrace of their ally's fortress.

Once the party reached the enclosure that contained the great stone keep, de Noble sent out men and servants with blankets to assist them into the feasting hall where they would be fed and tended to. De Noble was also there to greet Devlin in the flesh. He made a point of seeking the man out as he stood next to the feasting table where the English were eating, stuffing his mouth with roast fowl. Two days without decent food had left him ravenous.

Devlin looked big and raggedy, and his hair was starting to grow in as bristly as a thistle. He was also starting to look more and more like someone de Noble had once seen, although he still couldn't place him. He came up behind Devlin and clapped him on the shoulder.

"Greetings, John," he said rather amiably. "It seems you are the English's greatest ally in Ireland. I am sure you have already been thanked profusely for rescuing these men from Black Sword's vault, but let me add my thanks as well. We are very fortunate to have you on our side."

Devlin turned to the man, swallowing the food in his mouth as he did so. He forced a smile as de Noble reached out and took his hand to shake it.

"It was my pleasure," he said. "I was glad to assist."

"But how?" de Noble wanted to know. "How did you manage to do it?"

Devlin had to think fast. He didn't dare look at Victor for fear of appearing uncertain, so he simply began speaking.

"When I arrived at Black Castle after I left Glenteige, all was quiet for the most part," he said. "Since I had no produce for delivery, I tried to get in to see the cook under the pretense of finding out what he needed so I could supply the appropriate things. I managed to get into the fortress because they knew me but shortly after I arrived, Black Castle was besieged and I was trapped inside."

It was mostly the truth, at least about being trapped inside. De Noble nodded in understanding.

"We heard that Black Castle was besieged," he said. "Did she hold?"

Devlin nodded. "She did," he replied. "Say what you will about Black Sword, but the man is a master tactician. Brilliant. In any case, once the siege was over, there was general chaos. I heard talk about killing the English prisoners because they could no longer feed them, so I managed to get into the vault and released them. We escaped through the postern gate and here we are."

It was a simplified tale, one he prayed de Noble wouldn't

demand more details to. He honestly wasn't sure how much more he could tell the man and not start tripping himself up with lies. But then, de Noble asked him a question that completely stumped him, more than any other question could have. It was very simple.

"But why?" de Noble wanted to know. "Why would you do this?"

Devlin was momentarily stumped. He did look at Victor, then, to see that the man was gazing back at him. He had heard the question, too, and was curious to see what Devlin would say. Weakly, Devlin smiled.

"I'm not sure, to be truthful," he said. "My grandmother was English and I loved her very much. Then, I found an Englishwoman on the shore and saved her life. I brought her here and met a great many English who were kind. Why did I save Black Sword's English prisoners? Because I couldn't let them die. I just couldn't. I cannot explain it any better than that, my lord. You'll just have to take my word for it."

De Noble, fortunately, did. He smiled at Devlin. "Then you are a truly noble and self-sacrificing man," he said. "We are grateful. But I *did* send you to Black Castle with a task in mind, John. Do you remember?"

Devlin knew what he meant; he had been waiting for the man to get to this line of questions. "I do," he replied.

"And?"

"And I heard or saw nothing that would interest you," he said, quite honestly. "It seems to me that Black Sword has his hands full with the O'Byrne. He's not planning anything against Glenteige."

"How can you be sure?"

"I just told you; he's consumed with the O'Byrne. The English are of little consequence right now."

That seemed to satisfy de Noble, at least initially. But it was clear his mind was working. "Very well," he said, still chewing on the information. "Finish your meal and then we shall speak more when you are finished."

Devlin was grateful for the momentary reprieve but there was something else on his mind, something he wanted very much. "And the Lady Emllyn?" he asked. "You said I could speak with her if I completed my task satisfactorily. I would hope that freeing Black Sword's English prisoners will buy me a few moments with her."

Jealousy shot up de Noble's spine; he could read the interest in Devlin's face and it cut him to the bone. How could he compete with this big, handsome man? He couldn't, of course, and he knew it. He'd suspected that the Lady Emllyn had romantic intentions towards the man even though she had denied it, and now he could hear that same amorous hope in Devlin's voice. It inflamed him. He turned away from Devlin, struggling to control himself.

"Mayhap later," he said, almost coldly. "She has not been feeling well. I will see if she is willing to receive visitors."

Devlin wasn't happy with that answer at all. He could see the man's demeanor change when he brought up Emllyn and immediately, he suspected that de Noble was deliberately denying him. He fought back his rage; he was so close he could nearly smell her. He wasn't about to let this insignificant English commander deny him his heart's desires. He was a man who was never denied anything, by anyone. His quick mind began to concoct a plan.

"Thank you," he said, although he didn't mean it. "Since I face the prospect of visiting a fine lady, I would like to wash me hands and face. Is there somewhere I could accomplish this?"

De Noble was moving for the pewter pitcher of wine on the table. He glanced at Devlin as if to see for himself that the man was dirty. Where there had once been pleasantness between them, the mention of Emllyn's name had erased all hint of that. Jealousy was in each man's mind. Now, there was tense politeness.

"Aye," he said. "There is a well outside and soaps in the knight's quarters. Ask any soldier or servant. They will assist you."

"Thank you," he said politely. "If you will excuse me, then, I'll go wash."

De Noble let him go; at the moment, he seemed more interested in speaking with Victor, who suspected where Devlin was going. He also suspected he'd better occupy de Noble for as long as he could. He certainly didn't want de Noble following Devlin or, worse, showing up at Emllyn's door and hearing things he shouldn't.

He had to keep the man busy.

CHAPTER TWENTY

"THIRTY-THREE ENGLISH PRISONERS," Merradoc said with disgust. "And I am supposed to tend them. They're in the great hall as we speak, eating all of our food and shedding their lice everywhere. The Romans would have stuck the whole lot of them in a giant bath and made them stay there until their hides were nearly boiled off of them!"

Emllyn giggled. "Again with the Romans?" she asked. "I heard they were a violent lot."

"No more so than the Irish."

Chuckling, Emllyn turned back to her embroidery loom. Seated in her cozy chamber with Merradoc, who was hiding from de Noble's command because he did not want to tend a bunch of filthy prisoners, he was creating a bit of a distraction for her. It was rather off-putting. Emllyn was so bloody excited to see Devlin that she could hardly sit still, and it was an effort to focus on her embroidery. Merradoc was just creating more chaos.

Emllyn had moved the Garden of Eden scene up from Elyse's solar and it was now the main piece she was working on because the words emblazoned upon it meant so very much to her. *Everything leads me to thee.* She had finished stitching the letters in fine green silk, as bold and bright as the sun. The garden picture was taking shape around it. When finished, it would be a magnificent piece.

But there was something more pressing on her mind at the moment other than Merradoc's tantrums or lovely embroidery; Victor had said he would send Devlin to her and she didn't want Merradoc to be in the chamber when Devlin made an appearance. She didn't want to have to restrain herself and she certainly didn't want Merradoc and his flapping lips to witness the reunion. Therefore, she had been subtly attempting to get the man out of her bower for the past half hour, at least since the prisoners arrived. But Merradoc was unwilling to go. He lay upon her bed and rolled around in the linen pillows feigning misery.

Misery that was feeding her impatience. Emllyn opened her mouth to make another go of removing Merradoc when the door to her chamber opened and Eefha entered. The old woman waddled in, puffing on her shite pipe as she brought in a tray of bread and cheese. Merradoc took one look at the woman and her stinking pipe and hurled himself off the bed.

"Good God," he said, scowling as he moved past the old woman. "Medusa appears with her shitty pipe. Did we ever figure out who this woman belongs to? Why do you allow her to serve you?"

Emllyn fought off a grin, pleased that Eefha's appearance had accomplished what she had not yet been able to; get Merradoc off her bed.

"Because she is quiet and respectful," she said. "She does not talk my ear off and she cleans up after me. Why would I not want her around?"

Merradoc turned his nose up into the air. "Very well, you ungrateful goat," he said. "I will leave you now and I shan't ever return."

"Promise?"

He looked at her as if greatly hurt. "This would please you?"

Emllyn broke down into giggles. "Of course it would not," she said. "But I would suggest you go downstairs and tend to the English prisoners. You know de Noble will come looking for you and if you lead him to my doorstep because you are hiding from him, I shall never forgive you."

Merradoc lifted his eyebrows in resignation. "I would believe that," he said. "Very well, then; I shall take my leave of you. But if I catch lice from those prisoners, I will come back and give them to you."

"You'd better not."

Merradoc snorted as he headed out of the door. "I suppose I have no choice but to go and see to the lot," he muttered sarcastically. "I would seek out Elyse to keep me company, but she is with Connaught somewhere doing something naughty because her father is occupied. Oh, the thrill of it! Next year I will be able to deliver her two-headed baby who will look just like his idiotic father."

He shuffled off, muttering to himself, leaving Emllyn far gone with laughter. The man was humor personified, even when he was being petulant and nasty. As she continued to snort, Eefha moved to the door and shut it quietly.

Emllyn's smile faded as she paused in her embroidery, looking at the closed door, wondering when Devlin would be able to visit her. She knew he was here, in the complex, and she was wrought with anxiety over the fact that he had yet to make an appearance. He should have been here the very moment he set foot in Glenteige. If he truly loved her, then he would have made all due haste.

But then… there was Victor. Darker thoughts swamped her. She knew that Victor had spent time with Devlin and she knew that words had been spoken between them about her. She had been worrying about it, terrified that Devlin would think she was a deceiver and a liar. She was terrified that perhaps he might have changed his mind about her, although Victor didn't seem to indicate that. In fact, he had seemed rather calm and resigned about the entire situation, unusual for a man who was normally very protective of those he cared about.

It had been a silly thing for her to do, of course. All of it. From the moment she stowed away on the war cog until the moment she'd met Devlin de Bermingham and he had asked her name, all of it had been wrought with foolishness. But she'd had her reasons. With a sigh, this one of sadness, she returned to her embroidery.

As Emllyn lost herself in sorrowful reflections, Eefha settled into her usual place, a chair near the window so the smoke from her pipe would have an immediate outlet. She knew that Emllyn was not fond of the smell so she was considerate about it, as least as considerate as the old woman could be.

As Emllyn stabbed at the fabric, sewing her careful little stitches and struggling not to let her apprehension overwhelm her, there was a soft knock at the door. Eefha struggled to her feet and shuffled over to the panel, quietly opening it.

Emllyn didn't look up to see who it was before making her last stab in the fabric. Finished with the stitch, she finally looked up to see Devlin standing just inside the doorway. Startled at the sight of him, Emllyn stood up from her loom so abruptly that she nearly knocked the loom over. She hastily grabbed it to steady it although her eyes never left Devlin. She was incapable of looking at anything else.

But his focus seemed to be on Eefha as the old woman pulled him into the chamber quickly and shut the door behind him. Devlin hugged his aunt, as he hadn't seen her in weeks and had no idea of her whereabouts until this very moment. He was very glad to see her alive, thrilled that she had somehow made her way into Glenteige to watch over Emllyn. When he was finished hugging the tired old bag of bones, he finally turned his attention to Emllyn. That was what he had come for, after all.

Their eyes met and bolts of excitement, of longing, and of pain hurled between them. There was tangible emotion in the air, tense with uncertainty. Emllyn's eyes were wide on Devlin and, for a moment, the words seemed to catch in her throat. She had no idea what to say to him and the fact that he wasn't rushing at her and throwing his arms around her was concerning. Her heart began to race and her stomach to twist, violently, so much so that she began to tremble. But somehow she managed to find her tongue.

"Devlin," she finally murmured, tears stinging her eyes. "They said Black Castle was besieged. Are you well?"

He was standing a few feet away, his face pale with emotion. He looked utterly drained and overcome. "I am," he assured her softly. "The castle held."

She sighed with great relief. "I am so glad," she murmured. "As long as you are whole and sound, that is all I am concerned with."

"I am."

"Then my heart is eased," she said. "I saw Victor earlier today and…"

"Emllyn," he cut her off, his voice low and gritty. "Why

didn't you tell me the truth about who you really were?"

Emllyn's eyes filled with tears. She could hear the accusation in his tone, or at least she thought she did. Her stomach bunched up in knots and she abruptly turned her back on him, plopping down on her chair. She was so ashamed and so distraught over the situation, knowing that he had more than likely come to berate her and then walk from her life forever. Already, she couldn't stand the pain.

"Because," she said, breaking down into tears. "I had foolishly stowed away on a vessel chasing a knight who clearly had no interest in me. When I was captured and brought to you, I thought that if I told you I was the earl's sister, someone with great nobility, that you would spare me your wrath. But you didn't. It made no difference to you. In fact, it seemed to feed your bloodlust at the thought of punishing Kildare's sister. And then, when it was over, what good would it have done to tell you that I was the daughter of a lesser knight? You would have thought I was lying. You might have even killed me for it. So I let you think I was the Lady Emllyn simply to keep myself alive. In Kildare's sister, you had a valuable prize. In a mere knight's daughter, you had an expendable commodity."

She was weeping so much that it was difficult to hear her, but Devlin understood much in those halting words. God, it made so much sense now. He should have known her reasons, or at least sensed them, and her pain radiated outward, grabbing at him with icy fingers. He could not avoid the pull. But it only added to the pain he was feeling himself, feeling so very barbaric and cruel. He had once thrived on his reputation; all men feared the great Black Sword and his horrific rule. But at this moment, watching Emllyn weep as if her heart was broken, all he could feel were daggers through his soul, like great shards of glass. They were shredding him. He wasn't used to emotion on this level, not by a far sight.

"But you were so clear with everything," he said hoarsely. "You told me of Emllyn's life down to the last detail. You made me believe that you were her."

She nodded, not bothering to wipe the tears that were dripping off her chin and onto her yellow surcoat. "Emllyn and I had been best friends since we were babies," she whispered. "I knew every detail of her life as she knew mine. We fostered together and knew the same people. It was not such a great stretch to tell you that I was her. Even the things about her brother I told you… he did not care for her at all. He let her die in that cold room in his cold castle. The poor woman deserved some happiness and he gave her none. I miss her every day."

Devlin could hear the pain in her voice. "Then you will answer a question and you will not lie to me," he said quietly. "When you told me you loved me… was it just to save yourself? Were you afraid I would kill you if you told me otherwise?"

She shook her head, so hard that her careful hairstyle began to come undone. "Never," she hissed. "When I told you I loved you, it was because I did. I still do. I love you more than anything in this world, Devlin. Everything leads me to thee."

Devlin felt tears sting his eyes as he watched the back of her head. This time, he didn't try and stop them; he let them come. Slowly, and very quietly, he made his way over to Emllyn as she sat on the chair and sobbed. He lowered his bulk beside the chair, on his knees before her, as he gently grasped her by the arms and turned her to face him.

"Look at me," he whispered tightly, forcing her to open her eyes. "Look at *me*, Emllyn. I am Devlin de Bermingham, a man who has had to fight and kill for everything he has ever achieved in life. You called yourself the daughter of a mere knight; the truth is that I am the bastard of a great earl, his great son whom he acknowledges but wants little to do with. I have no family. I have no one but you. I am sorry you were so terrified of me that you felt you had to lie in order to save your life; I truly am. It is true that the Lady Emllyn Fitzgerald was a great prize at first but she soon became the love of my life. I don't care if you are someone else; to me, you are my Emllyn, my love and soon to be my wife. Nothing else matters, do you hear? Nothing at all."

Emllyn gazed back at him, his words slowly dawning on her. Her tears came to an unsteady halt as she digested his meaning. "Nothing?" she repeated, surprised.

He shook his head firmly. "Nothing," he whispered. "*Everything leads me to thee.*"

When Emllyn came to realize that Devlin didn't hate her, that he still loved her as she loved him, she threw her arms around his neck and knocked him over backwards with the forced of the gesture. Devlin ended up on his bum, holding Emllyn so tightly that he heard bones in her spine crack. And still, he squeezed harder. He couldn't begin to describe the joy in his heart at the moment.

All he knew was that it was brighter than the sun.

"My sweet love," he crooned, kissing the side of her head. "All is well now, I swear it."

Emllyn was weeping steadily, but this time from sheer joy. She had never been so happy in her entire life. "Oh, Devlin," she breathed, releasing him from her embrace so that she could kiss him. Her kisses were fast and furious. "I adore you, my darling. I have missed you so very much."

He returned her kisses, his big hands on her face, feeling her soft cheek in his grasp. "You are all I have thought of, day and night," he murmured, suckling her lower lips and listening to her gasp. "You are all to me, now more than ever."

Their clothes were coming off. The heat of passion, of joy, had overwhelmed them and all they could think of was joining their bodies, of completing an act that had once meant only fear and domination between them. Now it meant adoration, fulfilling the need to touch and be touched. Emllyn had hold of his rough tunic and she unfastened the belt that hung at his hips, tossing it aside as she grabbed the tunic and yanked it off his body, nearly yanking his head off with it.

"Your son, Dev," she whispered as she ran her hands over his soft, smooth chest, rippling with muscles and covered with a soft matting of red hair. "You promised to give me your son. I will hold you to it."

Devlin wrapped her up in his massive arms with a growl, picking her up and carrying her to the bed where Merradoc had so recently lain. The pillows were everywhere because of him and Devlin kicked them aside, laying Emllyn down and covering her with his naked torso. Kisses were heated and lusty, sensual and moist. Devlin managed to yank his shoes and breeches off, tossing everything haphazardly around the room in his haste.

Emllyn already had her surcoat nearly off and Devlin finished the job by pulling it down her body. That, too, landed somewhere on the floor as Devlin's lips came to bear on a tender nipple, suckling firmly.

Emllyn gasped aloud with pure joy, writhing beneath him, daring to put her hand between their bodies and feel his erection against her thigh. His manhood was warm and soft, stiff with desire, and she shifted so her legs were parted. She could hear Devlin groan as she continued to touch him, and even as he buried himself deep into her wet and waiting flesh. The pleasure he felt went beyond words.

His weight was atop her, his maleness filling her, and Emllyn's hands moved to his buttocks, digging her nails into his flesh as she drew him into her body. Her legs, usually spread open to receive him, were now wrapped around him, holding the man fast against her. As he thrust into her, she couldn't remember when this wasn't something she hadn't loved, the sheer pleasure of their bodies becoming one. The more he thrust into her, the more incoherent with need she became.

Swiftly, Devlin stopped thrusting and grasped her around the waist, flipping her over and laying her flat on her belly as he settled in and entered her from behind. Emllyn had never experienced mating like this before and she gasped as he pushed his way into her body, sliding in with ease, and then resuming the familiar mating ritual.

His hands moved underneath her, fingers slipping in between her legs to touch her as he continued his thrusts. He seemed to hit a spot that made her entire body tremble and soon enough, she was biting off screams of release in the nearest pillow. It had been a wild and beautiful awakening. But still, Devlin continued to move, his hands now moving to her breasts, holding them fast and toying with her nipples as he made love to her.

But Devlin couldn't maintain his control much longer. As much as he adored bedding her and as much as he had waited for this moment to be reunited with her, he was greatly anticipating the moment of his ultimate release. When it came, it came hard, and he grunted as he filled her womb with his seed. He found himself praying for a healthy son from her. It would be the greatest thing he could imagine. For a man who never gave much credit to thoughts of sons or family or even wives, the past few weeks had seen his opinion of that change dramatically. Now, he could imagine a future.

Exhausted and spent, he collapsed forward, collecting her in his arms and holding her close as he lay down beside her. He gently kissed her neck, her shoulders, and her hair, reacquainting himself with the taste and smell of her. It was like a drug, one that flowed through his veins and flooded his senses. Shoving his face into the back of her now-mussed hairstyle, he closed his eyes and sighed contentedly.

"I am taking you back to Black Castle," he muttered. "We will be leaving this place tomorrow, early. I have a feeling it will be difficult to remove you, however, because I suspect that de Noble and his daughter have taken a great liking to you."

Emllyn had been snuggled up in his arms, dozing lightly, but her eyes opened when she thought of the implications his words brought forth.

"More than you think," she murmured. "De Noble has been trying to court me since nearly the day you left. I have been beating the man off at every turn and he keeps close watch on me. Removing me may be more difficult than you think."

Devlin's eyes opened as she spoke, processing her words. "I suspected as much," he said. He did not sound pleased. "When I spoke of you to him, I could see his demeanor change. The man is jealous."

"I know," she said softly. She twisted in his arms so she could look him in the face. "What will you do?"

Devlin lifted a red eyebrow, reaching down to push a stray lock of hair from her face. She was such a glorious creature and he studied her features for a moment.

"We will have to be secretive," he said. "De Noble mentioned something about an evening meal tonight, which you and I will undoubtedly attend. When we see one another, we must be polite but nothing more. I have a feeling if he believes we are attracted to each other, he will watch you far more closely than he already does."

Emllyn agreed. "Usually he tries to have me sit on his right hand," she said with some disgust. "I have refused so far. I sit on Elyse's right hand, well away from her father."

Devlin's gaze lingered on her a moment. "Has he been bold with you?"

She could hear hazard in the question but she was honest. "It started out quite sweetly, in truth," she said. "He sent me notes, anonymously. But then it escalated to inviting me to walks or sitting next to him at sup. Earlier today, he tried to kiss me. I slapped him so hard I believe I left a mark."

Devlin was fully prepared to rage at the attempted kiss until she mentioned the slap. That had him grinning. He sighed heavily, fighting down his natural jealousy. He'd never experienced the emotion in his life so it was something new, and uneasy, to deal with.

"Better you to slap him than me," he mumbled. "I would most definitely leave a mark."

Emllyn grinned at him. "And so you would protect me, my beauteous lad?"

"Upon my honor, I would do all that and more."

She reached a hand up, rubbing his bearded cheek. He kissed the palm of her hand sweetly but as he did so, he caught sight of something over by the door. He paused in his kisses, his gaze glued to whatever had his attention.

"God's Blood," he finally hissed.

Emllyn could see that something had his focus. Lifting her head so she could see over his big arm, she could see that Eefha was seated over in the corner by the door, in the shadows. She had something in her finger she seemed to be toying with, the unlit shite pipe between her lips. She was so quiet that she had blended in with the shadows, and the two lovers had utterly neglected to remember her.

"Oh… goodness," Emllyn muttered, looking at Devlin, horrified. "I completely forgotten she was here."

Devlin looked at her, giving her a resigned expression. "Hopefully she will not talk and spread rumors about what she saw."

The humor in that statement was obvious and Emllyn giggled. "She will sing out the praises of Black Sword's prowess as he bedded the English maiden," she said. Then her giggling increased. "She was here one day when de Noble came to call. Like a wraith, she came out of the shadows and snuck up behind him with a dirk in her hand and surely would have stabbed him had I not called her off. Truthfully, Dev, I've heard of protectors and guards, but I have never heard of an old woman who goes around protecting young women as Eefha does."

He grinned, glancing affectionately over at the old woman who acted as if she had no idea that anyone else was in the room. She was truly in her own world.

"She is the best protection there is," he said. "I am not surprised she chose to follow you here. When I returned to Black Castle and she was nowhere to be found, I suppose I always knew that she had come to Glenteige to be with you. It brought me some comfort to hope for that."

"She has been my protector since the beginning."

"So she has. Mayhap… mayhap she sees a bit of herself in you as she was when she was young. She was quite beautiful, I was told. Mayhap she simply wants to take care of you."

"And so she has," Emllyn said softly, arching her head up to kiss Devlin's cheek. "But so have you. Now, about tomorrow; we should make our plans now because we may not have the opportunity later."

Devlin nodded, thinking on the course that the morrow would take. "It should be simple enough," he said. "Does this complex have a postern gate? I am not yet familiar with it enough to know."

Emllyn thought on the layout of the inner wall and the keep. After a moment, she nodded "There is a small man gate near the kitchen," she said. "I have seen servants passing between it."

"It would more than likely be locked in the morning."

She shook her head. "That may be, but I know the cook," she insisted. "I am sure she will open it for me."

"Good," Devlin said, relieved that he had one less detail to worry over. "I will leave through the main gate and meet you somewhere outside. There is a well towards the center of town."

"I know it."

"You will meet me there just before sunrise."

Emllyn grinned. "I will be there."

"Swear it?"

"Of course. But if I am not, know that somehow I was detained. Wait for me, however; I may have to climb the inner walls to get out of this place, but know I will be there."

"I will wait as long as it takes for you to join me."

Emllyn knew he would. But as she thought on that, another idea struck her. "What about Eefha?" she wanted to know.

"Should I bring her with me?"

He shook his head. "Do not worry over her," he said, glancing over at the old woman. "Eefha does as Eefha wants. If she wants to come with us back to Black Castle, she will."

Emllyn smiled in agreement. She'd heard that from him many times before. Yet there was one more thing on her mind, something she was hesitant to bring up but something that had to be spoken of. It was important to them both.

"And… Victor," she finally said. "If we are to marry, then…"

"He has already given his consent."

Her eyes widened. "He *has*?"

"Aye."

"Even though he knows who you are?"

"Even though."

Emllyn was surprised. Pleased, but surprised. As she mulled over what surely must have been Victor's reaction to Black Sword's proposal of marriage, Devlin interrupted her thoughts.

"There is something more you should know," he said quietly. "Trevor le Mon is among the prisoners. I am sure he will be at the feast tonight. I did not want you to be surprised."

Emllyn's eyes widened. "Trevor?" she gasped. "He… he survived after all?"

Devlin nodded, watching her reaction. She was surprised but that was all. He saw no longing nor pleasure in her expression. Simply surprise. "Well and good for him," she said. She meant it. "But I suppose I should thank him."

"For what?"

She grinned. "For rejecting me," she said, rather exaggeratedly. "If he had not rejected me, I would have never followed him aboard ship. Had I not followed him, I would have never had the joy of knowing you. We both owe him our thanks."

Devlin grinned, thinking of the last thing le Mon said to him – *you are the bravest man I know!* He shook his head and kissed the tip of her nose.

"Indeed we do," he said. "But I will do whatever thanking needs to be done. If I see you anywhere near him, I will kill him. Remember that. You belong to me now and I will not tolerate competition of any kind."

Emllyn snorted; she wasn't entirely sure he wasn't serious so she thought it would be the safe thing to obey him. Even though her feelings for Trevor were long gone, still, she didn't want to cause the death of the man. So she giggled and threw her arms around his neck, hugging him tightly.

Devlin squeezed in return. She felt so soft and warm against him that he could feel his loins grow hard almost instantly. As he began to nibble her silky white shoulder, there was a loud knock at the door.

Emllyn and Devlin froze, staring at the panel with apprehension. Emllyn called out.

"Who comes?" she asked, hoping she didn't sound breathless.

"Sir Raymond, my lady," de Noble said, his voice muffled through the door. "May I have a word?"

Emllyn looked at Devlin with complete, utter fear. He was quite calm and nodded at her, encouraging her to respond. As he bolted off the bed in silence and went for his clothing, Emllyn sat up.

"Of course," she called in return, accepting the surcoat that Devlin handed her. "A moment, please. I was resting."

"At your leisure, my lady," de Noble replied.

She knew he didn't mean it. He wasn't a patient man in the

least. In a panic, she threw on the surcoat and had Devlin fasten her up the back. The bed was a mess and her shift was still on the floor; she'd dressed without it. As Devlin finished dressing, Emllyn pulled on her slippers and straightened her hair as she headed for the door. She eyed Devlin as the man came up behind her, to be positioned behind the door should she open it. Taking a deep breath, she struggled for calm.

"Are you alone, my lord?" she asked politely.

"I am, my lady."

"Then you know it is not proper for me to open my door to you without a chaperone or an escort to stand with me," she said firmly. "What did you wish to speak to me of?"

De Noble went from sounding polite to sounding frustrated. "I came to ask you if you would grace us with your presence at sup tonight," he said. "We are having a rather large meal in honor of our English prisoners. De Ferrer and his men went hunting this morning and killed a three point buck. I know that you usually take your meals in your room, but I am asking if you will attend us as a special favor."

Emllyn leaned up against the door, her hand on the iron bolt. She was very thankful that Eefha had locked the door once Devlin had entered the chamber.

"Aye," she said. "I would be happy to attend."

De Noble's tone went back to a pleasant cast. "Thank you, my lady," he said. "We are most honored. May… may I escort you to the meal?"

Emllyn turned to look at Devlin, who looked mightily displeased. After a moment, however, he reluctantly nodded. Emllyn looked at him with great disappointment but obeyed.

"You may," she said, making a face at Devlin as she did so. "I will be ready at the appropriate time."

"Thank you, my lady."

They could hear the man's footfalls fade away. Emllyn looked at Devlin with disgust. "I do not want to touch the man," she said petulantly. "Why did you tell me to allow him to escort me to the meal?"

Devlin was patient with her, rather amused at her tantrum. "Because it will keep his mind off of me and any thoughts of attraction between you and I," he said. "A spurned suitor is not what you want tonight. You want a man who is not suspicious and therefore will more than likely let his guard down, allowing you more freedom of movement."

She paused over by the wardrobe, fumbling with the stays on her dress. "You mean more freedom when I flee the keep tomorrow morning?"

"Exactly. Mayhap he will not be watching you so closely, making it easier for you to get away."

It made sense. Pacified, Emllyn opened up the wardrobe to a gallery of borrowed dresses from Elyse; the woman had so many clothes that to loan several to Emllyn had been no hardship at all. Consequently, she had inherited a beautiful new wardrobe.

Devlin watched her as she began to rummage through the clothing, pulling out belts and surcoats and girdles. He had all of his clothes on but not his shoes. As he finished pulling on his worn peasant boots, Emllyn turned around holding up a pink satin surcoat in front of her.

"What do you think?" she asked. "Would you like to help me dress?"

He grinned as he went over to her, putting his hands on her shoulders and kissing her on the forehead.

"If I have anything to do with touching your body, even if it is to fasten a surcoat, the garment will more than likely come off than stay on," he said, releasing her. "Surprise me with what you wear. I would have my breath taken away when I see you."

It was a sweet thing to say and Emllyn smiled dreamily at him. "Are you leaving now?"

He nodded. "It is probably for the best," he said. "I should not stay here any longer than I have. I will go find Victor and the others, and then see you at sup tonight."

Emllyn curtsied deeply for him. "I am looking forward to it, my lord."

Devlin's response was to wrap her up in a crushing embrace and kiss her until she gasped. It was such a sweet kiss, one of great longing and passion. When he finally released her, it was with a wink. Then, he quietly opened the door, checked the dim corridor outside to make sure it was clear, before silently slipping into the shadows. Eefha rose from her seat by the door and dutifully shut the door behind him.

Heart swelling with love and adoration for the massive Irish knight, Emllyn went about dressing with great eagerness. Tonight, she would have the opportunity to look beautiful for him as she never had. Up until today, the man had only seen her in dirt and rags and borrowed clothing that did not fit her. Tonight, she would change all of that. The man had already fallen in love with her beauty; now, she would show him what it was like to shine. His unconditional love had made it possible.

She would make it an evening worth remembering.

CHAPTER TWENTY-ONE

G LENTEIGE'S GREAT HALL had been made into a massive place of warmth and food and great pungent smells. As Emllyn entered the hall on de Noble's arm, her eyes were wide at the extraordinary setting.

The hall was built from the same fieldstone that the keep was constructed from, a very long room with an open fire pit in the center of it. Smoke escaped through a series of vents in the thatched roof, which had also been coated with mud to prevent the thatch from catching sparks.

Two long tables flanked either side of the fire pit, worn tables that had seen their fair share of feasting. One had a broken leg that was propped up by rocks. Even now, both tables were burdened with food, more food that Emllyn had seen in a very long time. Both tables held huge flanks of the buck that de Ferrer had killed and men helped themselves to the meat. The room was a busy, noisy place filled with the hungry and the drunk.

Dressed in a pale green silk surcoat with a beautiful white shift underneath that fit her figure to perfection, Emllyn had taken great care with her appearance. Her hair had been carefully brushed and braided, knotted into an intricate bun at the nape of her neck and anchored with big iron pins, and Elyse had even shared some of her cosmetics with her. She wore a dusting of ocher on her cheeks and beeswax mixed with the same ocher on her lips, giving her a lush and rosy glow. To finish off the look, Elyse's maid had dusted her neck and shoulders with a fine powder mixed with gold dust. Literally, the woman was shining.

It was an effort that was not missed by de Noble when he came to collect her for the meal. He'd never seen anything so lovely, and it was a proud man who entered the hall with Emllyn on his arm. She was glorious. He took her around the feasting English and scavenging dogs to deposit her at one of the tables. The moment Emllyn sat, servants appeared with a trencher and drink. She didn't even have to say a word as food was instantly being heaped onto her trencher.

Elyse was there with Connaught, both of them sitting conspicuously close in conversation until Emllyn sat down. Then, Elyse's focus shifted to her friend.

"You look so beautiful!" Elyse gasped, visually inspecting her. "That dress never looked so good on me."

Emllyn smiled as she collected her pewter cup of wine. "I am sure that is not true, but it is kind of you to say so," she said, sipping her wine. "You look stunning, darling. Yellow becomes you."

Elyse smiled demurely. "It is a gift from Christopher."

Emllyn wasn't surprised because the neckline of the garment was rather low and daring. "It is perfect," she said. "He has wonderful taste."

As Christopher dipped his head in thanks, Elyse grasped Emllyn's hand and began perusing the room. Together, the women looked curiously at the crowd of diners.

"Where is Merradoc?" Emllyn asked. "Have you seen him?"

Elyse made a face. "Not since this afternoon," she said, evidently displeased. "He made some comment about a two-headed baby so I chased him away. I am sure he will be here later."

Emllyn fought off a grin at the physic's comment and changed the subject. "It feels like a party, doesn't it?"

Elyse nodded fervently as she surveyed the room. "So many unfamiliar faces," she said. "These are your brother's men; do you know many of them?"

Emllyn looked at the men congregated around the tables, eating and drinking, and throwing scraps to the hungry dogs. After a moment, she nodded.

"A few," she said, suddenly spying Victor seated at the end of the other table. It took her a moment to realize that Trevor was seated across from him; she recognized the back of his head. Even though Devlin had told her he had survived, she still felt a jolt of surprise to see him. "I… I know the knights. There are at least two that I see."

Elyse was trying to see what she was seeing. "Which ones?"

Emllyn pointed to the end of the opposite table. "Over there," she said. "The bald man. That is Sir Victor St. John."

Elyse's focus settled on Victor. "Him?" she said as she pointed. When Emllyn nodded, she smiled. "Oh, he is handsome, is he not? But what of the dark –haired man sitting across from him? He does not look like a mere soldier. Is he a knight, also?"

She meant Trevor; the man was very handsome and well-formed, and he certainly didn't look like a common man. Emllyn nodded. "He is indeed a knight."

Elyse leaned in close to her, whispering in her ear. "Your friend John is here also," she said. "He left the room a few minutes ago, probably to use the privy. I should have followed him to see how big his member was."

Emllyn looked at her in shock before breaking down into a grin. "Elyse," she hissed. "Christopher is sitting next to you and still you speak of other men?"

Elyse giggled. "Have you ever seen horses mate?" she asked. "Have you see how long their male members become?"

Emllyn shook her head reproachfully. "This is hardly appetizing dinner conversation."

Elyse laughed. "That is what I tell Christopher he looks like," she murmured. "He believes me. The truth is that it is not nearly so long and hard, unfortunately. I wonder if the farmer's is?"

Emllyn laughed softly as she took a bite of bread, listening to Elyse prattle on about men and their manhoods. She had just reached for her wine cup again when she caught sight of Devlin entering the room.

Her heart leapt at the sight of him coming in through the main entry. Surprisingly, he looked quite different from the way she had seen him lately; he was dressed very simply in clean linen breeches, the worn peasant boots, and a clean tunic that was not torn or shabby. It was obviously borrowed because it strained against his broad chest, revealing his magnificent physique, as he headed to the table where Victor was sitting. He sat down beside the man and reached for a cup, leaning over as Victor said something to him. As the man spoke, Devlin's eyes moved with great speed to the other table where Emllyn was sitting. *She's here, Devlin!*

His gaze found her in a room filled with dozens of noisy,

feasting people. There were several feet between them, smoke and servants and dogs, but he looked at her as if she were the only thing in that entire room. Their eyes locked and Emllyn smiled faintly at him. Through the haze and crowd, he smiled back.

"Excuse me for a moment," Emllyn said softly.

She stood up just as de Noble was sitting down. He looked at her with curiosity and concern, but she waved him off politely. In her pale green gown that made her look like a goddess, she made her way over to the table where Victor and Trevor and Devlin sat. She smiled as she came upon them and, noticing that she was approaching, the three men rose to their feet politely.

"Greetings, good men," Emllyn said, speaking to the group even though her gaze was on Devlin. "Is the feast to your liking?"

Devlin literally could not take his eyes from her; she looked like an angel. "It is, my lady," he said as evenly as he could. "Everything is quite delicious."

Emllyn's smile broadened. "I am pleased that you are enjoying it," she tore her gaze away from Devlin to look at Victor and finally Trevor. For a moment, she simply looked at Trevor, wondering what she ever saw in the man. It was an odd realization that there wasn't as much as a skipped beat of her heart when she looked at him. "Are you well, Sir Trevor? I am pleased to see that you survived the destruction of my brother's armada."

Trevor knew the story of the mysterious Lady Emllyn; they all did. Victor had drilled it into the group. In truth, he had been a bit wary to see the woman now known as Emllyn Fitzgerald but her manner was quite different than it had been before. No longer did she look at him with adoring eyes; the woman before him seemed completely different from the one he had come to know and he was both thankful and pleased. He'd had visions of fighting her off again in spite of what Devlin and Victor had told him. Relieved, he nodded to her question.

"I am well, my lady," he replied. "Thank you for asking."

Emllyn smiled politely at him before she returned her focus to Victor. "I hope you enjoy your evening," she said. "What are your plans after tonight? Is de Noble sending you home?"

Victor shook his head. "Not right away, my lady," he said. "We will stay here until Kildare has been contacted and decides where he wants us to be. He may ask us to remain here to reinforce de Noble's ranks or he may recall us home."

"I see," Emllyn said. She wasn't concerned in the least that Kildare had been contacted, no longer fearful of his reaction to be told that his dead sister was now in Ireland. After tonight, she would go with Devlin back to Black Castle and that would be the end of everything. There was such relief in that knowledge. "I wish you all good fortune, then, in whatever path you take."

Victor and Trevor nodded and Emllyn was about to say something more when there was some commotion behind her and she turned to see three men carrying instruments enter the hall. One man carried a *clairseach,* or Irish harp, while the second man carried a two-headed hide-covered drum, and the last man carried what looked like a wooden flute. Victor politely pulled Emllyn aside as the three musicians made their way to a corner of the room where they began to set up. Emllyn watched the group with delight.

"Musicians!" she exclaimed happily. "I do love music."

"Have you ever danced a proper Irish jig, my lady?" Devlin asked.

She turned to look at him, perhaps a bit coyly. "And strain myself so?" she asked with feigned shock. "I should say not."

The men grinned, including Devlin. "Then you must allow me to show you how to dance one without straining yourself."

It was Emllyn's turn to grin. "*You* know how to dance?"

"Very well."

She couldn't quite picture it and giggled when she tried. "Very well, then," she said. "You may show me how you do it. But do not be disappointed if I do not join you."

The banter flowed, all quite proper in front of Victor and Trevor. In fact, Trevor moved aside and cleared a space for Emllyn to sit, and the four of them continued their witty conversation for quite some time, much to de Noble's displeasure. The group talked, de Noble fumed, and the musicians struck up a beautiful folk ballad.

It was all quite normal and lovely, hardly belying the chaos the course of the evening was about to take. When Emllyn finally excused herself because she needed to utilize the privy, she couldn't have imagined what lay in wait for her.

It would be the last pleasant moments any of them would remember for a very long time.

SHE HAD BEEN running for days.

Nessa had fled Black Castle at Shain's request, running into the night and heading south to de Cleveley's settlement. She wasn't sure exactly where it was but Shain told her if she remained near the coast, eventually, she would find it. It was of dire importance that she find it. The pale little servant, Enda's timid daughter, was on a mission to find Black Sword. She was the only one left to do it.

She had to locate him.

So she pushed on through the intermittent rain, running and then walking when she became too tired to run, straining to reach the settlement of Glenteige where the feared and hated English lived. Only today, it was different. She wasn't afraid of them. At the moment, she saw them as salvation.

It had been near sunset on the third day that she had finally located Glenteige. Fortunately, the gates were open as peasants spilled from the settlement to return home before the complex was sealed up for the night and she was able to slip in without any notice. There had been English soldiers at the gate but they hadn't paid any attention to a small, lone female.

Once inside the settlement of Glenteige, Nessa was nervous and in tears. The sun was setting and she had no idea where to find Black Sword, so she wandered fearfully into the heart of the town, near the well, and got chased by a pair of dogs.

Scurrying away in terror, she ran down a narrow avenue and ended up at another big wall that was less guarded. She could see the top of a big keep on the other side and she clung to the perimeter of the wall fearfully, knowing that the commander of the settlement was surely inside the walls. She reasoned that if Black Sword was anywhere within this settlement, it would not be in obscurity. Surely he was near the heart of the place.

There was a single big gate that constituted the main entry to the inner compound and it was open as men and servants passed through it. This deep into the village, they would be less concerned about the people passing in and out. Security was not as tight as it was for the exterior walls. Nessa huddled in the shadows, waiting and watching for the opportunity to present itself for her to enter. She certainly didn't want to ask anyone if they had seen a big man with red hair and a red beard because Shain had told her that de Bermingham was in disguise. She didn't get the entire story but she knew that Devlin was on a great mission here amongst the English. She didn't want to give the man away.

Still, she was desperate to find him. He had to know what was happening at Black Castle. When she saw a man leading two shaggy horses in through the gate, she crept up behind the horse that was farthest away from the sentries and slipped into the inner complex in the shadow of the big horse's arse. Once inside, she bolted off and hid behind a big cart that was laden with thatching material. Here, she vowed to stay until the sun set completely. She reckoned it would be easier to search for the man once people settled in for the night and went to sleep. Less chance of someone see a suspicious woman lurking about.

So she remained, hidden behind the cart, watching with some interest as the great hall went ablaze with lights and people. There seemed to be a celebration of sorts happening. Exhausted, she must have fallen asleep because when she awoke, the hall was full of music and there were people milling outside in the small ward, talking and drinking. There was also a steady stream of men moving to the privy, which was built into the only corner tower of the wall. She knew that because she could smell the strong stench of urine radiating from it.

Huddled against the wheel of the wagon, she remained crouched in the darkness, watching all of the activity. Here in the heart of the English settlement, there was gaiety that was foreign to her. There was no such gaiety at Black Castle. At one point, a woman in a beautiful pale green gown quit the hall, the light from the fire illuminating her dress as she stepped out into the darkness. On her heel came a massive man clad in a simple tunic, evidently escorting the woman, and as they drew close Nessa immediately recognized Devlin and his English captive, the Lady Emllyn. Heart in her throat and a prayer of thanks upon her lips, Nessa moved out of the shadows and approached them as they passed by the wagon.

"My lord!" she hissed. "My lord, *please!*"

Emllyn came to a halt and Devlin nearly ran into the back of her because he didn't make it a habit of responding to voices hissing from the darkness. But Emllyn had – she recognized Nessa in an instant and, in disbelief, pointed her out to Devlin.

"Look!" she whispered. "It's Nessa!"

Devlin turned to see Nessa coming out of the darkness. She was wrapped in an old shawl and smelled of smoke and dampness. She was pale and trembling, and his brow furrowed intensely at the sight of her. Immediately, he charged forward and grabbed the woman by the arms, forcing her back behind the shadowed wagon. Emllyn scurried after them as all three of them faded into the darkness.

Devlin went to his knees behind the wagon, taking Nessa with him. He realized that he was quite panicked at the moment; there was no earthly reason the woman should be here, and that concerned him greatly.

"What is it?" he demanded. "Why are you here?"

Nessa was in tears. "My lord, ye must come," she wept. "Sir Shain has sent me. He sent me to tell ye that Black Castle has fallen."

Devlin wasn't sure he heard correctly. He stared at her and

his eyes narrowed in disbelief. "It *what*?" he said, staggered. "My castle has fallen?"

Nessa started to weep more heavily now. "Sir Shain sent me to tell ye," she sobbed. "Sir Frederick came back. He came back with the O'Byrne and let them in! They killed many people and they killed yer bird and ate it! Oh, please, my lord, ye must come and help us!"

Devlin just stared at her. He could feel a sense of grief and rage sweeping over him, filling his veins until every part of his body was hot with fury. The fingers grasping Nessa tightened on her arm to the point of causing her pain. She shrieked softly and tried to pull away.

Emllyn had been listening with horror. She could hardly believe what she was hearing and when Nessa winced because Devlin was hurting her, she pried the man's hands off of the serving wench. She grasped the woman, giving her a gentle shake and forcing her to look at her.

"Nessa," she said, trying to keep an even tone because she could see how affected Nessa and Devlin were. "Tell us what happened from the beginning; you said that Sir Frederick returned? Returned from where?"

"He tried to kill me," Devlin told her, his voice faint and dull. "When I returned to Black Castle after leaving you at Glenteige, Freddy poisoned my wine but Iver drank it instead. He also tried to kill Shain but failed. When Freddy fled Black Castle, we feared he had come here to Glenteige because he knew of my plan to spy on the English. We thought he had come here to betray me and, consequently, put you in great danger. That is why Victor has only known you as Emllyn and why his men have only called you Emllyn. They did not want to put you in any danger in the eyes of your host."

Emllyn listened with seriousness in her expression. "But Sir Frederick did not come to Glenteige," she said, confused. "If not here, then where did he go?"

Devlin sighed heavily; it was all becoming very clear to him now what had happened. He and Shain had discussed two options; Frederick would either go to Glenteige to betray Devlin or he would go to an enemy and side with them against Black Sword. It would seem that even though Frederick hadn't gone to Glenteige, he'd clearly created issues elsewhere. The man simply hadn't faded away.

Devlin was overwhelmed with the realization of Frederick's actions but he fought it; a muddled mind would do him, or his people, little good. What mattered now was what to do about it. Struggling for composure, he faced the weeping servant.

"What happened when Freddy returned?" he asked her quietly.

Because Devlin was calming, Nessa calmed, too. "He came back after ye had left," she said, sniffling. "He begged for Shain's forgiveness. He wept and called him brother. Shain believed him and feasted with him but that night, after everyone had gone to sleep, Sir Frederick murdered the gate guards and opened up the gates. The O'Byrne came in and killed everyone they could, including my mother. I escaped with Sir Shain and we fled. Shain sent me to find ye because most of yer soldiers are dead or have scattered."

More than rage, Devlin felt utter and complete devastation at the thought of Neart. "And my falcon?"

Nessa sniffled sadly. "They took him first when they came into the keep," she said. "A man cut his head off and they roasted him."

Tears popped to Devlin's eyes for his falcon, his friend and companion, who had suffered at the hands of his hated enemy. Devlin would make them pay; with God as his host and witness, he would make those bloody bastards pay.

There was a spark of revenge burning in his chest, growing by leaps and bounds. The fire filled his veins, causing his hands to shake and his heart to pound. It was revenge against the O'Byrnes, to be sure, but more than that it was revenge directed against Frederick. He'd always defended the man against others, refusing to think ill of him even when his maliciousness was obvious. But this was where every last scrap of good will towards Frederick ended and now, he became Devlin's most deadly enemy.

He would find Frederick and the man would pay with blood and anguish a thousand times over. Now, Devlin's vengeance was unleashed. Somehow, his anger helped him think clearer. He knew what he had to do.

"Emllyn," he turned to her as she held Nessa's hand. "Go inside and bring Victor to me. Bring him here, please, love."

Emllyn nodded obediently and left them behind the wagon as she went into the hall. Meanwhile, Devlin turned to Nessa.

"Where is Shain and the remnants of my people?" he asked, his voice oddly calm now that his initial shock and fury had faded. Devlin was, if nothing else, able to maintain a level control in the face of madness. It was one of Black Sword's greatest attributes.

"At Dungans Castle," Nessa said.

Devlin's gaze glimmered with recognition, and also with some concern. "Did he take the tunnel?"

Nessa nodded firmly. "That was his intention," she said. "I heard Sir Shain order men to collapse it so that the O'Byrne couldn't follow them."

There had been a tunnel linking Black Castle and Dungans Castle since the two castles had been built and shared by the same clann. That had been decades ago, however, and both castles had changed hands many time since then. Now, Dungans belonged to a sect of Hospitallers, men who were hermits and most fearful. In fact, Devlin had never had any dealings with them, mostly because it was common knowledge to stay away from them. Rumors abound through the Wicklow countryside that the Hospitallers were really worshippers of Satan and that they drank human blood. Devlin wasn't sure if he believed that, but he had stayed clear of them nonetheless.

"The castle must have been greatly compromised if Shain chose to take the survivors through the tunnel to Dungans," he muttered. "That is a feared place."

Nessa nodded. "I am glad I did not go with them," she admitted. "Sir Shain lowered me over the wall as the castle was overtaken. I just started running and never looked back."

"Then you do not know if they actually made the trip to Dungans?"

"Nay, my lord."

Devlin sighed heavily as he pondered the information. "It's very possible they never made it," he muttered. "Those tunnels are very old. They could have been blocked any number of ways. It's very possible that they are still at Black Castle, all of them, and if that is the case, then I must go directly to Black Castle."

Now that her information was delivered and the highs and lows of her emotion were even for the moment, Nessa was showing signs of real exhaustion. She slumped back against the wagon wheel, sitting in partial mud and not even realizing it.

"There weren't many, my lord," she said. "I heard Sir Shain

say there were no more than a few dozen men left."

With that, she fell silent. Devlin sat next to her, his mind whirling with the revelations that had come this night. He knew he had to return and reclaim his castle; there was no doubt in his mind. But he needed men in order to accomplish that. He didn't have any men at his disposal; but de Noble did.

De Noble did.

As he sat there and pondered that possibility, Emllyn returned with Victor. When Victor saw Devlin and a distraught serving woman hiding behind the wagon, he peered at Devlin with great curiosity.

"My lord?" he asked with concern. "You have need of me?"

Devlin did. He had need of an Englishman. In fact, he had need of many Englishmen. With a heavy sigh, he rose to his feet.

"Aye," he said, his voice low and quiet. "I have just received word that Black Castle has been overrun by the O'Byrne clan."

Victor's eyes widened with surprise. "O'Byrne?" he repeated. "By God, if those aren't the most warring men we've ever come across. They've overrun most of northern Wicklow and have destroyed several Kildare estates. Once we reclaimed Black Castle, Kildare intended to use Black Castle as a base to recover lands held by O'Byrne."

Devlin smiled weakly as the man revealed some of Kildare's most secretive plans. "They are a scourge," he agreed. "They have ever been our enemies just as they have been yours."

"They are everyone's enemies, English or Irish," Victor said with conviction. "I know de Cleveley has had problems with them as well."

"Anyone in Wicklow has. What they have just done to me, they can do to Kildare and de Cleveley alike."

"What will you do?"

Devlin sighed sharply, his mind working quickly. As he looked at Victor, he could only think of one thing.

My enemy's enemy is my friend.

"You and I are soon to be related," he said softly. "You said yourself that I am therefore your son. As your kin, I am to assume I have your support in all things."

Victor's gaze lingered on the man for a moment before shaking his head in resignation. "Black Sword," he hissed. "She had to marry Black Sword, didn't she? Why not a good, clean English knight who lives piously and is kind to his mother?"

"I am kind to my mother."

"You are?"

"I would be if she was still alive."

Victor tried to look disgusted by the comment but ended up laughing. His gaze moved to Emllyn, standing next to Devlin and gazing back at Victor with so much hope in her eyes. It was the hope of the young and foolishly in love. But Victor could not deny her.

"Aye," he finally said. "I will support you above all others, including Kildare should it come to it. But you and he had better make peace very soon or you will put me in a very bad position."

"Agreed," Devlin said. "But for now, I need you to stand with me. Will you do it?"

"I will."

"Then come with me. I have something to say to de Noble."

Victor suspected what it was. Dreading that particular conversation, he followed Devlin and Emllyn back into the warm and glowing great hall.

CHAPTER TWENTY-TWO

D E NOBLE WAS in conversation with de Ferrer when Devlin, Emllyn, and Victor entered the great hall. Thrilled to see Emllyn return, he rose from his seat and headed in her direction but Devlin waved him off. It was then that he noticed that Emllyn had been holding on to Devlin's hand, very tightly. When de Noble cast them both a quizzical glance, Devlin kissed Emllyn's hand and turned her over to Victor.

Standing near the open hearth with its great pile of blazing wood, Devlin faced an increasingly puzzled and frustrated de Noble. He was braced for the conversation.

"My lord," he said politely. "I have a matter of great importance I wish to discuss with you. Something critical has happened that will affect us all."

De Noble wasn't in the mood for a farmer's sermon. His eyes narrowed. "I have no idea what could be so important," he growled. "But your behavior towards the Lady Emllyn is both astonishing and distasteful. By what right do you kiss her hand?"

"By mine," Emllyn said firmly. She wasn't going to let de Noble bully Devlin. "I have given him permission. In fact, we are to be wed."

De Noble's eyebrow rose in shock. "Wed?" he repeated, incredulous. "What's this you say?"

Devlin garnered the man's attention once more. "You will hear me and hear me well," he said in a tone that de Noble had never heard from him before. "I have just received word that the O'Byrne have overrun Black Castle. They killed many men and are now in control of the fortress. If you know the O'Byrne as I suspect you do, then you know they are wicked and barbaric. If they are on a rampage, the next fortress they overrun could be yours. They will kill you, rape and murder your daughter, and destroy everything you have worked to establish here. Do you understand me?"

De Noble was pale with shock and outrage. "How would you know this about Black Castle?" he demanded. "Who has told you this?"

"A servant who lived at Black Castle," Devlin told him. "She escaped the carnage and has informed me of the status of the fortress. Unless we regain Black Castle and move to stop the O'Byrne, I fear this is just the beginning. You have served in Ireland a long time, de Noble; you know what I am saying is true."

De Noble was confused and agitated. He eyed Devlin with exasperation. "Of course I know it to be true," he said. "But I fail to see why any of this is your concern? You are a mere farmer!"

Devlin shook his head slowly, his eyes glimmering in the weak firelight. "I have never touched a plow in my life," he said lowly. "But I have touched a sword, many times. My name is Devlin de Bermingham. I am the Lord of Black Castle, the knight they call Black Sword."

A collective gasp went up in the room. Elyse even shrieked. By now, everyone was listening to the conversation between Devlin and de Noble, and several of de Noble's men went for their weapons. Seeing this, Victor emitted a piercing whistle to his men seated at the nearest table and they all leapt up, rushing to Victor as the man indicated for them to encircle Devlin. They did, without question, including Trevor. In fact, Trevor picked up a burning log, flaming madly at one end, and swiped it at the nearest de Cleveley man who tried to charge forward.

It was a protective circle they had placed around Devlin and de Noble both, keeping out the element that would seize Black Sword as a prize. It was English against English as the skirmish lines were established. As the men surged and a fight was imminent, Victor leapt upon to the nearest table and emitted a whistle so shrill that even the dogs cried. Men froze where they stood, all gazing up at the English knight who had commandeered their attention with his piercing sounds.

"Enough!" Victor roared. "Touch de Bermingham and you will have to deal with me. You, de Noble; you will listen to him. If you do not, you risk your life, your daughter's life, and the safety of your fortress. If anyone moves against de Bermingham, my men have orders to kill."

The room was crackling with uncertainty as men eyed each other with hostility. There was inbred hatred against Black Sword but there was also a sense of self protection and curiosity. Great curiosity, oddly enough. Something bold and epic was unfolding before their eyes and unless de Noble himself told his men to charge, they were going to hold their actions. Things were happening, historic things.

The only man in the room that hadn't moved during the entire shuffle was Devlin. He simply stood there, gazing at de

Noble as if there was no one else in the room. He had a great deal to say to the man and wanted to make sure he was clearly understood.

"The O'Byrnes threaten us all," he said steadily. "Right now, it is me. They have killed my men and confiscated my castle, but tomorrow, it could be you. It could be any of the English settlements in Wicklow. We must rid Wicklow of the O'Byrnes once and for all or, at the very least, subdue them. But I cannot do it alone; none of us can. If we band together, however, I believe we can accomplish this and make Wicklow a peaceful place once again."

De Noble was taut with rage. It was very difficult for him to control himself. "What peace?" he snarled. "Black Sword has ensured that there has been no peace for years. You are the worst rebel of the lot of them, the Irish revolutionary that has moved Ireland's resistance against the English by leaps and bounds. If I had a sword I would kill you or if I had a rope I would hang you, but I only have my hands at the moment and you are bigger and stronger than I am. You would kill me first."

Devlin could see the fury in the man's face. "Would you rather kill me and face the O'Byrne's alone?" he asked. "You cannot win against them. They will destroy you as they have tried to destroy me."

"In God's name, what do you want from me?"

Devlin's eyes flashed. "I hold no great love for the English," he said, showing some emotion for the first time. "They have moved across Ireland like a disease, killing and looting and taking lands to satisfy their greedy hearts. You are an invader in my land, de Noble. Never forget that. Yet I am willing to overlook that in order to save us both. Are you going to be so stubborn and arrogant that you would rather die than join forces with the Irish?"

De Noble was trembling with rage, with shock, but he forcibly calmed himself. Taking a deep breath, he raked his fingers through his graying hair. He glanced over his shoulder at de Ferrer and Connaught, who were looking rather stricken about the entire thing. Elyse was in tears. Drawing in another heavy breath, he faced Victor, still standing on the table top.

"You," he said to Victor. "How, in the name of all that is holy, can you support Black Sword? The man destroyed Kildare's fleet and held you prisoner. You accompanied him here and swore he was your ally. You lied."

Victor shook his head. "You sully my honor, de Noble," he said with threat in his voice. "It is true that Black Sword defeated Kildare's armada, but let us be honest about it; we are warriors and defeat is part of that vocation. We were moving in to attack Black Castle, to reclaim her for Kildare, and de Bermingham did what he had to do in order to hold her. Would you do any less if someone was trying to take Glenteige away?"

De Noble didn't like the man's response. "No one is taking Glenteige away," he growled. "No one can."

Victor scowled. "Do not be so ridiculous, man," he said. "Glenteige was an Irish holding before de Cleveley's ancestors confiscated it and anyone can take it away from you if their army is powerful enough. We have all had our share of give and take, of property won and lost. Did Black Sword hold me and my men prisoner? He did indeed. But when the heat from battle had passed and in an act of mercy rarely seen, he released us, cleaned us, and fed us. And here we are. In spite of his reputation as a rebel and a barbarian, Black Sword is also a man capable of mercy. It is for that fact that I stand with him now. He tended my men when he did not have to, and now he needs our help. He is trying to help *all* of us. Is your hatred for the man so great that you cannot see he is trying to do good for us all?"

De Noble saw he had no ally in Victor and it frustrated him. It frustrated him more that Victor made some sense. Was it really true? Was Black Sword trying to band all of them together to fight, and destroy, a common enemy? He was having a great deal of difficulty entertaining the fact that it just might be possible. The truth was that he feared the O'Byrnes; they all did. If Black Castle fell, which was a shock in and of itself, then there was no knowing if the O'Byrnes would set their sights on Glenteige.

"This is madness," he finally hissed. "It is madness to ally with Black Sword!"

"Would you rather be with him or against him?" Victor asked.

Victor looked disgusted, mostly because he knew what the logical answer was. *With him*, he thought. *I would rather be with him if I have a choice in all of this.* But he still wasn't completely sold. With exasperation, he looked at Devlin.

"Why?" he finally asked. "Why are you suggesting an alliance with the English? Surely you have Irish allies who would do just as well."

Devlin was honest. "There is an old proverb that says my enemy's enemy is also my friend," he said. "O'Byrne is an enemy to all of us. Of course I have other Irish allies to turn to, but none of them with the risk that you and I face daily against that savage clann. Moreover, my Irish allies would not fight off O'Byrne from Glenteige. They would let you burn. That is why I have come to you; this is something very important to all of us that face this threat. Help me against the O'Byrne and I will help you, too. Should you ever need my support, all you need do is summon me and I will come."

It made complete and utter sense and de Noble, as resistant and uncertain as he was, could no longer deny it. De Bermingham was correct in every way. Turning to look at de Ferrer and Connaught, he could imagine them in a fight against the O'Byrnes. Then he could see his lovely Elyse in the clutches of the barbarian clann, being tortured and raped. It was just too much to bear. He had to release his pride. He had to take a stand for the common good.

Pushing aside the last of his resistance, de Noble focused on Devlin. "Very well, then," he said. "Let us say, for argument's sake, that the O'Byrnes are on a rampage. Now they have Black Castle. What will we do?"

Devlin was feeling some hope at the man's reaction; at least he was willing to discuss it. "You and I will ride with your army north to Black Castle and reclaim it," he said. "I will summon more de Bermingham men from my father as well as O'Connor men. I can have an army of five thousand men within a week. At that point, we ride north to Kiltimon Castle and destroy it. We will burn it and everything that reeks of O'Byrne. With Kiltimon destroyed, attacks in south Wicklow will ease considerably. We will also march upon Balleyhorsey and Ashford. Once those smaller castles are taken, I will turn them over for Kildare and de Cleveley to administer. You can station English armies there."

De Noble hated to admit it but he liked very much what he was hearing. But there was one thing left he wasn't clear on. "What about Black Castle?"

Devlin's gaze was deadly. "That remains my holding. I will not give it up."

At least he was honest with his intentions. De Noble looked up at Victor. "What say you about that?" he asked. "It is Kildare's property, after all."

Victor considered the question. "I am sure the earl will relinquish it to Black Sword if he gains new properties instead," he replied. "Kildare will receive Ashford and Kiltimon."

"Then de Cleveley will receive Balleyhorsey."

Attention returned to Devlin. Deals were being made and they wanted his reaction. He had, after all, started the entire thing. De Noble, much calmer than he had been minutes earlier, cocked his head.

"It would seem we have made a deal with the devil, de Bermingham," he said. "I hope I do not live to regret it."

"Nor do I," he said honestly. "Look at it from my perspective; I just promised three Irish castles to English lairds. I have spent years trying to force the English out of Ireland but in this case, if it will save my castle, my people, and wreak havoc with the O'Byrne, I am willing to compromise. If anyone is making a deal with the devil, it is me."

De Noble's gaze lingered on him. There were many things on his mind at the moment but one thought in particular; strange it would occur to him now.

"Several years ago, I saw you with your father when I visited Dublin," he said. "It was a meeting between Irish chieftains and English lords. You had flaming red hair and were as big as a bull. Now that your hair is growing in, I can see you haven't changed much. When you walked into my keep those weeks ago, I knew I had seen you somewhere but I simply couldn't place you."

Devlin was feeling a huge amount of relief now that the conversation was becoming one of understanding. It could have gone so badly in so many ways. He finally took his eyes off of de Noble to see that there was still a ring of Englishmen surrounding him, protecting him from a roomful of hostile men. He found it rather ironic.

"And now you have," he said. "I would presume that I need not fear for my life within the walls of Glenteige now."

De Noble looked around at his men and motioned them to lower their weapons. "Nay," he said, a hint of defeat in his voice. "Although it would have made a mighty prize to capture Black Sword."

"I will make a better ally than a prize."

De Noble's expression took on a hard cast; even though they'd made the deal, trust in an innate enemy was still hard to come by. "I sincerely hope so," he said. "And by the way; I have one request to make of you."

"What is that?"

"Three years ago, if you recall, you looted Glenteige."

"I recall."

De Noble's brow furrowed and he frowned most terribly. "You took something that belonged to me," he said. "I want my damn chair back!"

DEVLIN, DE NOBLE, Victor, de Ferrer, and Connaught had stayed up most of the night discussing strategies and plans, and the English got their first real look into the brain of a brilliant rebel, a man who mapped out tactics and strategies better than they had ever seen. He was precise, deliberate, and covert. After the first few minutes of strategizing, de Noble shut his mouth and let Devlin do the rest. He knew genius when he saw it. No wonder Black Sword had never been beat. His respect for the man grew.

Devlin's basic strategy was two-fold; the majority of de Noble's eight hundred man army would approach Black Castle from the front and divert attention while they went through battle preparations, while seventy hand-selected men would approach from the sea side. The cliffs were sheer and difficult to pass, but there was a very narrow and secretive staircase carved into the side of the cliff just below the keep that could be used to breach the castle. It had been used long ago by supply ships approaching from the sea but they had given up using it because it was so treacherous. Devlin seemed to think that it was the perfect opportunity to sneak into the keep and take the fortress from within, and those around him were forced to agree.

So after much planning and wine, the die was cast and those who could grabbed a few hours of sleep before sunrise. De Noble had offered Devlin a bed in his solar where Victor, Trevor, and William du Reims were sleeping, and Devlin accepted his offer only to sneak up to Emllyn's chamber after everyone had gone to sleep. He had to see her before he left. There was so much pain and longing in his heart for her already that he was sure it would kill him. He was desperate to hold her one last time.

Not surprisingly, she was awake and waiting for him. While Eefha snored in the corner, Devlin came into her room and swept her into his massive embrace, feeling her life and warmth against him. He continued to hold her, very tightly, for quite some time. Emllyn finally had to force him to release her because she couldn't breathe. With a grin, he complied.

"Come and lay with me," Emllyn took him by the hand and led him over to her bed. "Tell me what is happening."

She climbed onto the bed and he lumbered up after her. Together, they snuggled in the folds of her linens. It was simply enough to hold one another at the moment; no wild lust, no fevered passion… this was more than that. It was emotion, in its purest form, the need to hold and be held, to love and be loved.

Devlin buried his face into the back of her hair, thinking how much he had changed since he had first met her. In the first few days of their acquaintance, all he could think of was bedding her. It was purely a physical need, something that required satisfaction. But now, being with Emllyn went beyond the physical. His heart was so full of emotion for her that to feel her alive and well in his arms was the most wonderful thing he could imagine.

"Well?" she prompted him.

He grinned; he hadn't realized he'd lost himself in his reflections. "We leave before dawn," he murmured. "We hope to reach Black Castle in two days whereupon we will commence with a strategy to remove the O'Byrne from my fortress."

Emllyn waited for more of an answer but none was forthcoming. "That's all?" she asked. "No great revelations or plans?"

He kissed the back of her head. "None that would interest you," he said. "It will be a great comfort to me knowing you are here, safe with Eefha to watch over you."

Emllyn gazed off into the darkness, her soft hands caressing the arms that were around her. "I will not pretend that I am not concerned for you," she said softly. "This is a great and terrible undertaking."

"It is."

She turned in his arms to look at him. "I was very proud of

you tonight and what you said," she whispered. "Mayhap… mayhap Black Sword's legacy will no longer be one of war and rebellion. Mayhap it will become one of peace."

He was very close to her face, rubbing his nose against hers. "Mayhap," he agreed softly. "It has occurred to me that I do not want to be constantly warring and placing my family in danger. I have you to think about now. I do not like the idea of you at a castle that is constantly at war. And what of our sons? Although I wish for them to be great knights, I do not like the thought of them always in danger."

Emllyn smiled, her eyes glimmering at him. "Do you know what I think?"

"What?"

"I think that Black Sword has evolved as both a warrior and as a man," she said softly. "You would not have spoken this way on the day we met."

"Nay, I would not have," he said. "But I have heard that men's priorities change as they marry and have children. I just never thought it would happen to me."

Emllyn's smile faded as she brought a hand up to stroke his stubbled cheek. "When will we marry, Dev?"

"As soon as I have regained Black Castle."

She didn't like that answer. "But why wait?" she pressed. "Why not before you go?"

He sighed. "Because it is better this way," he said. "If you marry me now and I perish in battle, you will forever be known as Black Sword's widow. That will make it difficult for you to remarry. This way, if I perish in the attempt to reclaim my castle, no one will ever know that you and I were lovers. It will make it much easier on you to marry a man of standing."

Emllyn wasn't happy about that at all. She abruptly sat up,

smacking him in the chin as she moved. Devlin grunted, putting a hand to his jaw, as Emllyn climbed off the bed.

"Listen to me and listen well," she said angrily, pointing a finger at him. "I do not care about remarriage. You will be my husband and you will be the only one I have, and I will shout to the heavens how proud I am to be Lady de Bermingham. Don't you dare say that you will perish in this battle, do you hear? I'll not listen to you."

He put up a placating hand in the face of an angry lady. "As you say," he said, meek and submissive. "I did not intend to upset you. I am simply trying to think of you."

"You make what we have between us sound cheap!"

He sat up, genuinely trying to soothe her. "I would never do that," he insisted. "I was simply trying to… God's blood, I don't know what I was trying to do. Get into bed with me this instant and stop your scolding. I'll not have our last few hours together be filled with anger."

Emllyn cooled. She didn't want any anger between them, either. But she pretended to be stubborn. "I will not get back into bed until you tell me you love me."

"I love you with all that I am."

"Swear it."

"I do, a thousand times over."

"Swear you will return to me."

He paused, gazing at her with warmth and adoration. Reaching out, he grabbed her wrist and pulled her onto the bed beside him. Emllyn wrapped her arms around his neck and together, they fell back onto the bed. Gone was the scolding, now replaced by a warm and fluid tenderness.

As Devlin kissed her neck gently, peeling back the top of her shift in his hunt for more delicious fruits, she wrapped herself around him and gave herself over to completely. Devlin buried himself in her softness.

"If I have control over my own fate, know that I will do everything in my power to return to you," he murmured. "But if I don't…."

"Do not say that!"

"If I don't," he said, louder, "then it is my wish that you marry a man who will be good to you. I want to know you are well taken care of and treated with the greatest of respect."

Emllyn's eyes filled with tears at the thought of Devlin not returning. "Please," she whispered tightly. "Do not say such things. I cannot bear it."

He stopped kissing her and grasped her chin gently between his thumb and forefinger, forcing her to look at him. Tears streamed down her temples and he tenderly kissed them away.

"Such is the life of a wife of a knight," he murmured. "There is always the possibility that I will not return and it something you must live with. But know this; you have shown me more about joy and love in the few short weeks that I've known you than I've ever been shown in my entire life. If I die tomorrow, I die a contented man and it is you who have made it so. But if I return, it will be to live every day with you by my side, a better man than I have ever been."

There were still tears in Emllyn's eyes but there was great happiness there as well. She put her hands on his face, feeling the warmth against her skin.

"Please, Dev," she murmured. "Can we please be married before you go?"

He sighed heavily. Of course, he want to marry her immediately, this very moment, but he was honest with her when he said he thought it would be easier for her to marry well were she not the widow of a hated Irish rebel. Still, it would be his fondest desire to call her wife before he headed off to battle. He wanted it as badly as she did.

"I am not entirely sure we can find a priest at this hour," he said.

Emllyn nodded eagerly. "We can," she said. "De Noble has a priest who gives mass every Sunday. There is a chapel to the east of the keep."

"Outside of the walls?"

"Aye."

He could see how excited she was. He didn't have the heart to deny her. Therefore, he pushed himself off the bed and headed for the chamber door.

"Then I shall return for you," he said. "Make sure you are dressed and waiting. I will seek out de Noble and have him send for the priest."

Emllyn was thrilled beyond measure; it was almost enough to make her forget her fear of the impending battle. "Do you think he will?" she teased. "After all, you will be marrying the woman he wants for himself."

Devlin gave her a wry expression. "I will twist his arm if he doesn't help me," he said. "I might even kick him."

Emllyn giggled as he winked at her and quit the chamber. Quickly, she dressed in the pale green silk she had worn to the feast. Then, she ran to wake up Elyse. Surely the woman would want to attend a wedding.

Together, the women waited for Devlin to return and he did, nearly two hours later. There was very little time for the ceremony before the knights had to dress for the impending battle march, so before Victor, de Noble, Elyse, Connaught, and Trevor, Emllyn wed Devlin in a ceremony that took place in de

Noble's solar. Having no ring to give her new husband, Emllyn gave him the incomplete embroidery she had made instead. It was all she had to give and it said everything she wanted to say.

Everything leads me to thee.

When Devlin rode from the gates just before sunrise, it was with that piece of half-finished sewing next to his heart.

CHAPTER TWENTY-THREE

Eleven days later

MEN HAD BEEN trickling back for two days now. Beaten, bloodied, the men of de Noble's command returned to Glenteige telling stories of horror. At first, Emllyn had posted herself at the gates of the settlement, watching every single soldier who passed by and asking them of the battle. She particularly wanted to know of Devlin and Victor, but so far, no one could seem to tell her much of anything. The stories were much the same, however; the O'Byrnes would not go quietly. It had been a blood bath.

But Emllyn would not give up her vigil. She had been at the gatehouse of Glenteige for two straight days, even sleeping inside the small sentry room that was just inside of the great gates. The soldiers had given the woman their cot. On the morning of the third day of her lonely and apprehensive vigil, Emllyn was awoken from a restless sleep by Merradoc.

She could barely see the old physic in the light of the early morning as he quietly roused her. Somewhat startled to see him, she sat up on the creaking cot, rubbing her eyes sleepily.

"Merradoc?" she said. "What is amiss?"

Merradoc shushed her quietly, draping a cloak over her shoulders in the cool temperatures. "Nothing is amiss," he said. "I came to see how you were faring. Elyse is concerned."

Emllyn yawned as she pulled the cloak more tightly around her shoulders. "I am well," she said. "How is Elyse?"

Merradoc sat next to her on the cot. "She cries constantly," he said. "But she remains in her solar, trying to keep busy."

"I asked her to come and wait with me."

Merradoc gave her a wry grin. "She will not leave the comfort of her rooms, you know that," he said. "Moreover, she will not let Connaught see that she has been waiting for him. She is very prideful."

Emllyn laughed softly. "Never let it be said that Elyse has waited for any man."

"Precisely."

Emllyn yawned again and looped her arm affectionately through Merradoc's, leaning her head against his shoulder. "Seventeen men returned last night," she said softly.

"I know."

"None of them could tell me anything about Devlin, although one man said he saw him fighting near Black Castle's keep several days ago," she murmured. "At least now I know he made it inside."

Merradoc patted her hand comfortingly. "Truly, girl," he said. "You must learn to be braver if you are to be the wife of a great warrior. If you worry like this every time de Bermingham goes off to fight, then you are going to drive yourself into an early grave."

She eyed him. "What would the Romans do?"

"Throw a lavish party to wait it out."

Emllyn grinned. "I hope to get better with practice," she

said. "This is my first battle with him. Do take that into consideration."

Merradoc patted her hand again, noticing that the sentries outside were preparing to open the gates for the day to come. It was usual for them to crank open the great wood and iron panels before daybreak so the farmers could enter the city and conduct business. Emllyn yawned again and he gave her a tug.

"Come back to the keep with me," he said. "Let's get a good meal into you and mayhap a bath. Then you can return to your lonely vigil of watching men return from battle."

Emllyn almost refused but on second thought, she rather wanted a bath. Two days of sleeping on a dirty cot in a cold room with a dirt floor was wearing on her. Perhaps she should allow herself a bit of comfort. With a reluctant nod, she stood up next to the man and allowed him to lead her from the room.

It was cold and dark in the gatehouse as they turned for the village, which was just now coming alive. People were out, preparing for the day, as the great gates slowly opened behind them. Emllyn was exhausted, holding on to Merradoc's arm as they moved away from the gatehouse, thinking of sleeping in her own bed for a few hours before returning to her vigil. They hadn't gone too far when they heard the sentries take up the cry.

More returning soldiers were sighted.

Emllyn paused, turning to the gates as the sentries moved about urgently. Merradoc saw the look on her face, knowing he could never remove her now, so he sighed heavily and turned her back around for the house. Slowly, they made their way in that direction. By the time they reached the gates, they caught sight of three soldiers stumbling towards them. It took Emllyn a moment to realize that one of them was a badly wounded

Trevor.

She gasped at the sight of him, being dragged by two other men, and she broke out in a run. Merradoc was right behind her, as were several soldiers, and they took Trevor from the two exhausted men who had been trying to carry him. Very carefully, they lowered him to the ground.

"Blankets!" Emllyn snapped at the nearest soldier. "In the guard room; get the blankets from the bed!"

The man went on the run as Emllyn returned her attention to Trevor. He was on the ground now with Merradoc leaning over him, and Emllyn sat down by his head, cradling it so it would not be on the cold, moist grass. She could hardly look at what Merradoc was doing, inspecting the rather gaping wound in the man's torso that was hastily wrapped. It was a horrific sight and tears sprang to her eyes.

"Oh… Trevor," she breathed. "Do not worry; Merradoc will fix you as good as new."

As she said it, Merradoc cast her a long glance and grimly shook his head. Emllyn bit off her sobs, feeling Trevor's loss already as she stroked the man's clammy head.

"All will be well," she assured him tightly. "Trevor, what happened? Is the battle over?"

Trevor was as white as snow and his lips were an odd shade of gray. He squeezed his eyes shut and tears streamed down his temples. It was indicative of his pain and sorrow. Emllyn began to openly sob, reaching down to hold the man's hand tightly. He knew he was dying.

They both did.

"Have no fear," she wept, squeezing his hand. "I am here. You are not alone."

Trevor's entire body was trembling as he opened his eyes

again and looked at her. "Forgive me," he whispered. "I should have told you…"

Emllyn gazed into his pale face, thinking that perhaps she already knew what he meant. "There is nothing to forgive," she assured him, stroking his head. "You had no interest in me. I am not angry with you in the least, truly."

Trevor looked up at her, his eyes muddled and red. His mouth worked as if he wanted to say something more but he ended up sighing heavily and closing his eyes. It was just too difficult for him to speak. Still, there were things Emllyn had to know. He'd spent three days trying to make his way back to Glenteige; he had to tell her what he had seen. She had to know.

"De Noble and his men went to the castle gates to create a diversion," he muttered, grunting when Merradoc did something to his wound that Emllyn refused to see. "I went… went with Sir Victor and de Bermingham. While de Noble held the attention of the O'Byrne army, we climbed the old sea steps that took us into the rear of the keep. There were men in the bottom of the keep, de Bermingham's men that the O'Byrne had captured, and they helped us take the keep."

He faded off and Emllyn shook him gently. She was hanging on every word. *Don't stop now!*

"Trevor," she pleaded softly. "Where is Devlin? Where is Victor?"

Trevor coughed, bringing up gobs of black blood. Emllyn flinched but she didn't become ill at the sight, as horrible as it was. Using her cloak, she wiped the blood from around his mouth and neck. Trevor spoke with a red tongue and red teeth.

"We… we held the keep as de Bermingham and Victor and de Noble charged into the ward to regain the rest of the fortress," he mumbled. His voice was becoming weaker. "We could see the fighting from the keep; de Bermingham fought his way through swarms of O'Byrnes as he tried to get to the gates. He was able to make it and the gates partially opened, and de Noble's men poured into the gap. It was truly a sight to see, Emllyn… it was a sea of men and swords. When the swords fell, they used their hands. Clothes were torn, flesh was damaged. It was terrible."

Emllyn was nearly mad with concern. "*Where* is Devlin?" she demanded. "What happened to my husband?"

Trevor's eyes opened and he gazed at her; she could see the life fading. His eyes were dulling rapidly. "I… I could see that the battle was very bad indeed," he whispered. "Connaught held the keep while de Ferrer and I went out to help. It was complete chaos. Those who were not fighting were fleeing. Men were running from Black Castle with horses and their arms laden with goods. It was clear that Devlin and de Noble were gaining the advantage because the O'Byrne were running for their lives. Then, towards sunset, I saw de Bermingham in a mortal battle with a big Irish warrior. He seemed to know him. He called him Freddy."

Emllyn's emotions took another hit with that stunning news. "Frederick," she breathed. "That was the man who betrayed him. He was the one who let the O'Byrne take Black Castle."

"De Bermingham killed him," Trevor muttered. "I saw it myself. He cut his head off and then threw the head and the man's body into the sea."

Emllyn closed her eyes tightly to that horrible scene, swallowing away the nausea she felt. But her eyes opened once again and focused on Trevor. "Was Devlin well after that?" she asked. "Was he wounded in his battle with Frederick?"

Trevor's eyes closed again. "He did not seem to be," he whispered. "But de Ferrer did not survive... I saw him fall. After that... the battle lasted all night and the next day, too. Those who did not flee were killed. There were bodies of the dead everywhere. I did not see de Bermingham or Victor or de Noble again once the battle waned. But I found this."

Clumsily, he reached into his torn and bloodied vest and pulled forth a piece of material. He held it up to Emllyn and she immediately recognized it; *Everything leads me to thee.* It was the embroidery she had given Devlin on their wedding day.

Emllyn stared at it; it was muddied and torn, as if had been stepped on and buried in the dirt. As she stared at it, she could feel Merradoc's hand on her arm. He was pulling gently at her, trying to force her to stand up, but she couldn't hear him. She was in a fog, a fog that swathed her in memories and reflections, something that prevented her from screaming out as she saw the symbol of her love for Devlin crumpled in her hand. It was a fog of self-protection, a pain too deep for tears. In one swift motion, her heart was ripped out and she hadn't even felt it.

She was hollow.

"Emllyn," Trevor was grasping at her. "I do not know where your husband may be. When O'Byrne fled, I know that several men went after them. De Bermingham might have been among those who gave chase. I simply do not know. I was chasing the last of the O'Byrne out when I was gored. I... I knew I had to make it back here to tell you what I saw."

Emllyn was still staring at the fabric but she heard Trevor's words. In her haze of sorrow, it was all she heard.

"Thank you," she murmured. She realized she was still holding onto his hand and she squeezed it tightly. "If... if you did not see his body, then he must be somewhere else. He is not dead."

"Nay… he is not," Trevor said, although he wasn't entirely sure that was true. He simply said it for Emllyn's sake. "It was so chaotic in the battle that it was possible your favor fell and he didn't even realize it. You… you will tell him something when next you see him."

"What would you have me tell him?"

Trevor was so weak that he could no longer hold on to her. He couldn't even keep his eyes open. "You will tell him… tell him that it was a privilege to serve under Black Sword."

Emllyn watched him take two more breaths and then he was gone. Clutching Devlin's wedding embroidery against her chest, she wept deep and painful tears for the man who had brought her and Devlin together.

THEY BURIED TREVOR in Glenteige's small cemetery, placing him in a lovely spot near an oak tree that had been there for hundreds of years. It was peaceful and serene. After the burial, Emllyn sat next to the grave for the rest of the day, pondering Trevor's short life and wondering if she would soon be sitting next to Devlin's grave as well. The embroidery Trevor had returned to her had become a permanent part of her body, as much as a finger or an ear. It was clasped in her left hand, never to leave it. When she held it, she felt very close to Devlin.

Merradoc and Elyse had sat with her next to the grave. Elyse had sobbed the entire time, having been told the story that Trevor had relayed to Emllyn. She had seen the embroidery in Emllyn's hand and she wept over the missing men, including her beloved Connaught. Having heard of Black Castle's complete destruction, she was terrified for the man and also for her father. Holding Emllyn's free hand, she had wept deeply of her fear.

Towards sunset, Merradoc managed to coerce Emllyn back into the keep and Elyse followed. He took both women into Elyse's fine solar where he ordered warmed wine and food for them. Elyse picked at the food but didn't actually eat much; she was too distraught. Emllyn was a shell of her former self, sitting like a stone and staring off into nothingness. Merradoc managed to coax her into drinking some wine and she did. By the third cup, Merradoc put a sleeping potion into the drink when she wasn't looking and by the time she was finished with the fourth and final cup, she could hardly keep her eyes open. Merradoc did the same thing for Elyse and soon, he had two unconscious women on his hands. He breathed sigh of relief.

It was very late by the time he made it down to de Noble's solar for some solitude of his own. He'd spent so much time healing the injured, burying the dead, and tending emotional women that he was quite exhausted himself. He had no idea what had become of de Noble and de Bermingham and Connaught, but he hoped they would know the truth soon. He doubted that Lady de Bermingham could take much more waiting and he knew that Elyse was doubly upset with the unknown whereabouts of both her father and lover. As he sat in de Noble's solar and drank the man's fine brandywine, he found himself praying for a miracle.

But prayer and brandywine didn't mix because he drank far too much of it and ended up passing out, his head lying on de Noble's desk. He had no idea how long he'd been asleep when he felt someone shake him.

"Merradoc?" came a familiar male voice. "God's Bones, Merradoc, get up. Stop drooling like a drunkard all over my vellum."

Merradoc sat up with a start, blinking rapidly to clear the sleep from his eyes. The room was very dark but he could see bodies moving around in the darkness. Grabbing for the flint next to the taper near his right hand, he struck it so hard that he nearly broke it but the sparks were enough to light the taper. As the flame took hold in the darkness of the room, he could see three men standing before him.

De Noble, Connaught, and Victor St. John.

"De Noble!" Merradoc shot up from his seat, his eyes wide with shock. "You have returned!"

De Noble was filthy and bloodied, but he was in one piece. He scowled at the physic. "Indeed I have," he scolded. "I have returned to find that you have taken over my solar. Get out of that seat, you whelp. This is *my* desk and *my* seat."

Mouth hanging agape, Merradoc did as he was told. He thought he actually might be dreaming until de Noble gave him a shove because he wasn't moving fast enough. It was enough of a jolt to make him realize that he wasn't, in fact, dreaming. He was very much awake, and de Noble and his men were returned. Excitement filled him.

"Connaught!" he gasped at the young knight who looked disheveled but very alive. "And St. John! You are all returned!"

Victor had several day's growth on his face and a big bandage on his left hand. "Indeed we are," he said tiredly. "Were is Emllyn?"

Merradoc pointed to the floor above. "She and the Lady Elyse are in Lady Elyse's solar," he said. "I had to give them a sleeping draught. They have been so overwrought with worry that I had to make them sleep."

Connaught smiled wearily. "So Elyse was worried over me, was she?"

Merradoc nodded sincerely. "Very much so," he said. "And if she tells you otherwise, she's a liar and you can tell her I said so. She was mad with worry over you."

"And what about me?" A voice came from the doorway. "Was no one mad with worry over me?"

Everyone turned to see Devlin entering the room. He was carrying a massive chair with a leather cushion on it. It was a chair confiscated in Black Sword's raid three years before, and the back of the chair that had once been beautifully carved with the de Cleveley crest was now all hacked up. Merradoc recognized the chair once stolen from de Noble as Devlin set it down.

"De Bermingham," he gasped in disbelief. "You are alive!"

Devlin grinned weakly at the man. "Indeed I am," he said. "Where is my wife?"

Again, Merradoc pointed to the floor above. "Sleeping in Lady Elyse's solar," he said, flabbergasted at the turn of events. He didn't know what to say next, what to ask about, or what to comment on. His mind was whirling with surprise. He finally pointed at the chair. "Where did you find that?"

Beaten, worn, and thoroughly exhausted, Devlin gave the chair a good kick. "De Noble wanted his chair back, but the O'Byrne had run off with it, and many more items of value from Black Castle," he said. "We spent two days chasing them before we finally caught up to them and were able to get my possessions back. De Noble saw his chair among the booty and demanded its return. As a generous man, I have graciously complied."

Merradoc's astonished gaze moved between de Noble and Devlin. "Your *chair*?" he asked. "In all of this battle, in the midst of death and destruction, all you could think of was a *chair*?"

De Noble frowned petulantly. "It's *my* damn chair," he declared. "De Bermingham took it three years ago. I wanted it back!"

Merradoc could hardly believe his ears. He started to laugh, joyfully and full of relief. The pain and uncertainty of the past twelve days was about to see a release; men had returned from battle, whole and sound, and there would be laughter once again at Glenteige. Happiness had come back.

"But what of Black Castle?" he wanted to know. "What has become of it?"

Devlin's expression changed; his eyes lost their glimmer. "My commander, Shain, is once again in command until I return," he said. "The O'Byrne had him, and about a hundred more of my men, shoved into the basement of the keep. They had tried to escape through an old tunnel but it turned out the tunnel was blocked off and it thwarted their escape, so O'Byrne was able to capture them. Right now, what is left of my army and about four hundred de Noble men are holding the castle secure. I've sent word to the O'Conner and expect another eight hundred men by late tomorrow. I've only come back to Glenteige to return de Noble's chair and retrieve my wife. We will be returning to Black Castle immediately on the morrow."

Merradoc was both surprised and thrilled to hear that the horrible battle Trevor had described had gone in de Bermingham's favor. "And the O'Byrne?" he wanted to know. "Where are they?"

"Running," de Noble said; he was pouring what was left of

the brandywine into a cup. "They are scattered and on the run. Once we secure Black Castle and strengthen her, we're going after them. We have plans to see this through until the end, and that includes the obliteration of the O'Byrne once and for all. I will not see Wicklow suffer in fear any longer. It is time to end this."

It was as good an answer as any he had heard. Merradoc, accepting that the battle had ended for the moment and that good men had returned, scratched his head. "Very well, then," he said. "But do not continue this battle before you see Elyse and Emllyn. You'd better go wake them up and tell them the joyful news. They'll never forgive you if you do not."

Connaught was already out the door, heading up the narrow spiral stairs to the second floor. Devlin pushed de Noble's chair out of the way before following Connaught's path. When Merradoc went to follow, Victor stopped him.

"Nay, man," he said. "Let the women see their lovers first. Give them that time alone. We shall follow shortly."

"After we've had our well-deserved drink," de Noble put in. Then he swirled the remaining liquid in the decanter as he peered at it. "It seems that someone has been into my brandywine."

Merradoc was standing in the doorway of the solar. "It was the women," he lied. "Terrible drunkards, both of them."

As de Noble lifted his eyebrow dubiously, they could all hear a faint cry as Elyse and Connaught came together on the floor above. A few moments later, they could distinctly hear a much louder shriek as Emllyn caught sight of Devlin. They could even hear Devlin's low laughter.

It was a good sound. Merradoc turned back for the solar, accepting a cup of brandywine from de Noble, who had also given one to Victor. Raymond lifted his cup to the two of them in a toast.

"To love," he murmured.

Victor grinned as he lifted his cup as well. "To the future."

Merradoc lifted his cup last. "To me!" He downed the drink in one gulp.

All was right in the world again.

CHAPTER TWENTY-FOUR

1328 A.D.
Black Castle

H E KNEW HE was in trouble. God's Blood, they were *all* in trouble.

Devlin was carrying his second son towards the keep of Black Castle and the child was screaming loudly in his ear, having just been clobbered in a mock fight by his older brother. Flynn, Devlin's eldest son, was scurrying after his father.

"Daven and I were only playing, Papa," Flynn was trying to explain. "He wanted to fight me, truly. My sword slipped."

Devlin glanced over his shoulder at the blond five-year-old on his heels. "I know," he said with tension in his tone. "I was there."

"Will Mam be angry with us?"

Devlin sighed heavily, trying to comfort Daven and hold his hand over the puncture wound on the child's forearm at the same time.

"I am afraid she will," he said with resignation. "She has told us she does not like us fighting with swords, hasn't she? She does not know that you and Daven have swords. I did not tell her I gave them to you."

Flynn thought on that a moment. "Then she will be angry with *you*, Papa."

"Thanks for the confidence, lad," Devlin grunted. "I will be fortunate if her fury is the only thing I receive."

As they neared the keep, they could see old Eefha emerging from the entry. Her pipe was smoking away as she crossed the footbridge, heading towards them. Flynn, seeing the old woman, ran over to her.

"Daven has been wounded," he told her urgently. "You must fix his arm."

Eefha patted the boy on the head as Devlin came to a halt in front of her, his son howling unhappily. Eefha pulled away the piece of linen on the child's soft white arm to reveal a little nick. It was hardly anything to grow so upset over, but Daven screamed as if he'd been mortally wounded.

"Will you take him and clean the wound?" Devlin asked the old woman as he handed her the child. "I fear that Emllyn will hear him crying. She hears everything, you know. She will…."

He was cut off by the sight of his wife emerging from the keep. *Too late*, he thought. Dressed in flowing dark green garment with her beautiful hair braided and wound into a bun at the nape of her neck. Emllyn had a toddler in her arms as she crossed the footbridge towards them, her skirt whipping about in the sea breeze. Devlin did the only thing he could do – he went right to her to try and block her vision of Daven's injury. He hoped that Eefha would immediately take the child away but the old woman stood there, smoking on that damnable pipe and setting Daven to his feet so she could use both hands to inspect the injury. She was only making the matter more obvious now.

Emllyn was looking at Devlin and her older boy with curiosity and concern. Devlin met her just as she crossed the bridge, putting his arms around her and kissing her. The baby in her arms, however, didn't take too kindly to his father kissing his mother and put his baby hand on Devlin's bearded mouth to prevent him from going any further. Devlin laughed softly at his two-year-old son, Corey.

"You cannot have her all to yourself, lad," he said. "She belongs to me."

Corey didn't like that response and started slapping at his father as Devlin continued to laugh, kissing the fat baby hand. Emllyn, meanwhile, would not be distracted. Daven was crying over something and she would know what it was.

"What is the matter with Daven?" she asked. "I could hear him crying from the keep."

Devlin was trying to avoid the question. "He and Flynn were playing and he has a small cut on his arm," he said casually, reaching out to take Corey from her arms. "Eefha will tend him. It is nothing to worry over."

Flynn, seeing his mother and having no idea that his father had not told her what had truly happened, ran over to her. He was a very big boy for his age, and husky like his father, nearly coming up to his mother's chest in height as he stood next to her.

"We were playing, Mam," he said eagerly. "I poked Daven but I did not mean to."

Emllyn's brow furrowed. "What do you mean that you poked him?" she asked. "Poked him with what?"

Devlin rolled his eyes as Flynn looked at his father fearfully when he realized that his mother had no idea what had happened. Devlin took pity on the child; as the father and the instigator, it was his duty to take the blame.

"With his toy sword," he said with the greatest reluctance. "They were mock fighting with Shain and Daven was accidentally poked with the dull tip of Flynn's sword."

Emllyn's eyebrows shot up in surprise. "What toy sword is this?" she demanded.

Corey decided that now would be a good time to pat his father in the face and as Devlin tried to explain, he had to suffer through the two-year-old's displays of affection.

"The one I had made for them," he said honestly as Corey smacked him in the mouth. "Love, I realize you don't like the boys playing with anything that has the potential to harm them, but they are growing older now and must be made comfortable around weapons. It is important to their growth as warriors that they learn how to handle a sword. I know that I should have told you I had swords made for them, but it's often difficult to discuss things with you once your mind is set. You can be very stubborn."

Emllyn looked at him with an increasingly threatening scowl. Without a word, she went over to Daven to inspect his injury. The young lad was being tended to by Eefha but when he saw his mother, he lifted his arms to her, sniffling. Emllyn took a quick look at the boy's arm and, seeing that it wasn't a terrible wound, lifted him up and began to carry him back towards the keep.

She didn't say a word as she walked past Devlin and Flynn and Corey. They all watched her walk across the footbridge, carrying Daven with his feet dangling, and disappear into the keep. When she was gone, Devlin looked at Flynn and, with a resigned wriggle of the eyebrows, followed his wife into the keep. Flynn skipped after him.

The keep was dark and cool in the entry, leading into the

feasting hall with its big tables and pack of dogs. Flynn went to play with a litter of puppies near the hearth as Devlin carried Corey up the narrow spiral stairs. By the time he reached the big chamber at the top of the keep, Emllyn had Daven stripped from the waist up. She was washing his little torso with cool rosewater and as Devlin came up behind her and set Corey to his feet, Emllyn began cleansing Daven's wound with witchhazel.

Devlin sat silent on the chair near the wall, watching Corey as the baby wandered over to the three little beds near the window where the boys slept. It was a messy spot. The big chamber, which had once been Devlin's lair, was now home to five people. Devlin and Emllyn's big bed was still where it always was, now with a big wooden screen blocking it off from the rest of the chamber, and then the boys had their beds near the tall lancet window that overlooked the sea.

Devlin's eyes perused the big chamber, thinking that it was the place most in the world where he derived comfort. He had his entire family here with him, his three boys and his wife, who was newly pregnant with their fourth child. Perhaps that was why he was so afraid to upset her. Early pregnancy tended to make Emllyn quite emotional.

"Are you ever going to speak to me again?" he asked softly.

As he feared, she was cross with him. "You hid your covert deeds from me and then you accuse *me* of being stubborn," she said, wiping at Daven's arm and then pulling the cloth away to wave at Devlin to emphasize her point. "I do not want them to have swords because they are too young to properly handle them. This time, it was only Daven's arm that was injured. What if it is an eye next time?"

He was properly contrite, his gaze soft on her. "I was watching them the entire time," he said quietly. "They were doing quite well and listening to my instruction."

That wasn't a good enough answer for Emllyn. In fact, it was no answer at all. "They are just babies, Dev," she scolded. "I realize they are Black Sword's sons and there is a certain legacy attached to that, but they are my sons, too, and it is my job to keep them safe."

"You do an excellent job," he said. "I have never seen a better mother."

Emllyn removed a strip of boiled linen from the basket of items she kept in their chamber, items meant to clean and tend three active little boys. She began to wrap the strip carefully around Daven's small arm.

"If that is true, then why do you give them swords when I ask you not to?" she asked.

Devlin was coming to feel like a terrible man. "I only gave them the swords today," he said. "I had the metalsmith make them and I was going to keep them until the boys were a little older, but I just couldn't help myself. It was a proud moment to see my boys hold a sword for the first time."

Now Emllyn was starting to feel like an ogre for scolding the man. He was only doing what was natural to him. As she finished wrapping Daven's arm, she sighed heavily, a gesture of defeat, and glanced at her husband.

"You know I cannot become angry when you put it that way," she said softly. "But I think the boys are far too young to play with swords, even as a toy. They see you and Shain and even Connaught with weapons and they naturally want to be like the knights. Thank the Lord that Elyse only has girls or I am sure her children would be the same way. As it is, we are the only ones with lively little boys who want to do everything the knights do and sometimes it is very frustrating when I do not get any cooperation from you."

Devlin tried not to feel guilty. "I am sorry," he said. "I will take the swords away from them for now. But next year, we will have this conversation again. The boys must start learning to handle weapons at some point, love. It's the way of our world. The sooner they become used to them, the sooner they will become adept at not putting eyes out or stabbing their brother."

Emllyn knew that but she didn't want to admit it. She didn't want to admit her boys were growing older. She stood up and went over to the big chest where she kept the boys' clothing and pulled out a clean tunic that wasn't torn or dirty. Silently, she went back to Daven and pulled it over his head. Resilient as children were, his tears were forgotten as he went to see what Corey was playing with. The toddler had little wooden cart and the two began fussing with it. Emllyn watched her two younger children as they tussled over the toy.

"I got something else from the metalsmith today," Devlin said, hoping to break her out of her morose mood. She looked like she was about to dissolve into tears at the thought of her boys growing up. "Come to me and I will show you."

She wandered over to him and he reached out, grasping her hand and pulling her down onto his lap. She relented fully as his big arms went around her and he buried his face in her neck. It was enough to douse her irritation as she felt the man against her. As Flynn barreled into the room with two fat puppies, Devlin kissed her cheek.

"Do you want to see it?" he said.

Emllyn cocked an eyebrow. "What is it?" she said. "A sword?"

He grinned, displaying his big white teeth. "Nay," he said,

"because you would more than likely use it on me in moments like this."

Emllyn broke down into soft laughter. "I would consider it."

The boys began squealing because Flynn wasn't sharing his puppies. Emllyn went over to break up their argument before returning to her husband. Just as she resumed her seat on his lap, he held up something in his fingers. Clutched between his thumb and forefinger was a small piece of metal; upon closer inspection, Emllyn could see it was a ring. She plucked it out of his grip and inspected it.

"When we were married, I never gave you a token of our union," he said softly as he watched her study the ring. "Although you have never asked for one, I have been thinking more and more on it as of late. I am sorry it has taken me so long."

Emllyn had never been concerned at the lack of a wedding ring; her life had been so full and her marriage so wonderful that it never really crossed her mind. But as she held the smooth, gold ring in her hand, she was genuinely touched by his gesture.

"It's gold," she said appreciatively. "I have never seen that metalsmith do anything other than steel or pewter."

Devlin nodded. "I know," he said. "But I asked him if he could do a gold ring for you and he said that he could. I paid him well and he bought the gold in Dublin. It's a simple ring, without stones. I hope you don't mind."

Emllyn shook her head firmly. "I love that it is without adornment," she said. "It is something very solid and beautiful. Like you."

He smiled at her, reaching out to turn the ring over so she could see the inside of it. "I had him inscribe words," he said.

"Can you see them?"

Emllyn had to strain to see what he was talking about but when the message dawned on her, tears sprang to her eyes. "Everything leads me to thee," she murmured.

Devlin kissed her cheek and took the ring from her, sliding it down over the third finger on her left hand. It was a bit large but it fit nonetheless. Emllyn admired it greatly.

"Thank you," she said, giving him a sweet kiss. "It is the most wonderful ring I have ever received."

Devlin was pleased with her delight. "I'm glad you think so."

Emllyn admired it a few more moments before wrapping her arms around his neck and hugging him tightly. It was a sweet and tender moment as their boys played a few feet away, the sons Devlin had threatened her with those years ago, only now it was not a threat. It was a reality, and one she had embraced completely. A new generation of sons, a legacy to their great and noble father. Emllyn was proud to be part of it, proud to bear the sons of the man she loved with all her heart. Letting go his neck, she kissed his cheek and resumed admiring her ring.

"Dev?" she asked.

He was enjoying watching her expression as she loved up her ring. "Aye, love?"

Her attention came off the ring and her expression washed with reluctance. "I… I suppose it would be well enough for the boys to have toy swords," she said. "But only if you are with them. They are never to use them alone."

Devlin's grin broadened. "Are you sure?"

"I am."

"I didn't give you the ring so you would agree to the

swords."

"I know. But you are correct; it is their legacy, after all. They must learn."

Devlin wasn't too enthusiastic in his response because he wanted Emllyn to feel as I she had final say in the matter. Were he too happy about it, she might have second thoughts because she would think he was happy that he had his way in all things.

"I promise we won't run out and start any wars with them," he said, but shrugged as if reconsidering. "At least, not this week. Mayhap next week. Mayhap we'll ride down to Glentiege and challenge Connaught and de Noble to a battle."

Emllyn laughed softly. "You would, wouldn't you? And Connaught would lay down and pretend to die while de Noble tried to explain to them the finer art of swordplay."

Devlin wriggled his eyebrows in agreement, glancing over at his three boys, healthy and intelligent children that he was extraordinarily proud of. They were, after all, his legacy, as his wife had said. They were born of this land.

"I will do the teaching," Devlin said. "I told you once we would breed fine Irish sons to wreak havoc on the English. Mayhap it's not so much havoc now as it is now an understanding."

"What understanding is that?"

Devlin looked at her. "That sometimes peace and family is the far better path to take," he said, reaching out to stroke her cheek. "And that no matter what, you cannot put a price on true happiness."

Emllyn smiled faintly. "Is this what you hope to teach them?"

He nodded, watching Flynn and Daven chase a puppy under the bed. "God, what glorious days lie ahead for us," he said, squeezing her gently. "And no matter what happens, no matter where I go or what I do, know that everything leads me to thee."

She did.

EPILOGUE

Present day
National Museum of Ireland
Dublin

T UESDAY MORNING AND he could already hear the school-children yelling in the foyer. As a docent for the archaeological department of the National Museum of Ireland, he always seemed to get the school children who, at times, acted more like wild animals than human offspring. He wished for ladies' clubs but those always went to the female docents who couldn't be heard over the shouting of excited kids.

As he approached the foyer, listening to the yelling of the wild scallywags reverberate off the one-hundred-year-old walls of the museum, he braced himself. It was going to be a long day.

The children were primary school-aged, dressed in their Catholic school uniforms. But there were Catholic schools all over Dublin so one uniform didn't look too different from another. As he approached the group, he headed for the woman who seemed to be the zookeeper. She was up to her ears in wild beasts. When he caught her attention, he forced a smile.

"Hello," he said, extending his hand. "I'm Peter Ward. I'm

to be your guide today."

The woman took his hand and shook it. "Hello," she responded. "Helen Walker. Thank you so much."

Peter continued to smile weakly, watching the children who were thumping each other and generally playing loudly. He eyed Ms. Walker. "May I?"

She nodded wearily. "Be my guest."

Peter's smile vanished and he suddenly emitted a piercing whistle from between his teeth. The kids shrieked but immediately stilled. Some of them even put their hands over their ears. The entire group of thirty-three of them turned to the bald, middle-aged man with the shrill whistle. When Peter saw he had their attention, he smiled thinly.

"Greetings, ladies and gentlemen," he said formally. "My name is Peter Ward and I will be your guide today. How many of you have been with us before?"

A few hands lifted and Peter acknowledged them. "Good," he said, his manner growing clipped. "Then you know that this is a place of culture and learning, not a schoolyard. Keep your voices down and your hands to yourself, or you can go back and sit on the school bus until we are finished. Is that clear?"

The kids nodded with uncertainty as Peter waved then onward. "Excellent," he said. "Now, we can get started. Our very first stop will be the Medieval exhibits. Can anyone tell me what Medieval means?"

The children followed Peter as he led them across the cavernous foyer towards the first floor Medieval exhibit section. One or two raised their hands to his question. Peter, walking backwards, pointed to a serious young man with a crown of reddish-blond hair.

"It means Medieval times," the boy said. "It means Middle

Ages."

Peter nodded his head, impressed. "It does indeed," he said. "It means the High Middle Ages, or at least the section we will be attending does. This was a very important time in Ireland's history. Can anyone tell me why?"

No one seemed to know. They were entering another room now, a big exhibit room that had a variety of displays. Peter drew the children into the center of the room and had them gather around him as he continued.

"The High Middle Ages was a very important time in Ireland's history because it was the time beginning with the Norman conquest of England," he said. "The Normans were very greedy people from France; once they began to spread all over England, they came to Ireland as well and claimed lands."

"Didn't the Irish fight them off?" a boy from the crowd yelled.

Peter grinned and pointed over to an exhibit near the south side of the room. He began to move in the direction of a series of cases and a large, imposing display sign over them that said "BLACK SWORD".

"Take a look at this over here and that will help answer your question," Peter said. "This is an exhibit of an Irish rebel known as Black Sword. He was also known as the Lord of Black Castle, which was a strategic castle at the time. Black Sword was one of the great freedom fighters in the fourteenth century against English rule. Now, if you take a look at the first exhibit, it shows a map of Black Sword's family territory. He came from the de Bermingham family which was, interestingly enough, Norman. The family married into the Irish nobility over the centuries so much that they were essentially Irish. By the time Black Sword was born, he was so Irish that he bled green."

The kids giggled as many of them, mostly boys, began to crowd around a display that had things like an old dagger and other warfare implements. Peter pointed to the display.

"This display holds items that were dug up in an archaeological dig around the turn of the last century," he said. "Devlin de Bermingham lived at Black Castle in Wicklow, just south of here. It was his castle from around 1320 A.D. to 1351 A.D. as far as we can tell. There aren't a lot of records to tell us what happened during these years but we do have records from the English settlements to the south that recorded a peace treaty with Black Sword. We know that Black Sword was a great man because rather than use mostly warfare to gain his ends, he was very good at negotiating treaties with the English that kept them from grabbing more Irish land in the Wicklow area."

A boy with dark hair and freckles raised his hand. "Did he really have a black sword?"

Some of the kids giggled. Peter smiled. "Well, we never found one, if that's what you mean," he said. "Who knows why he was called that? People back then earned nicknames and reputations for reasons that have become lost to history. We do know, however, that he married an English bride and that they had eleven children, ten of whom lived into adulthood, and out of that group, nine of them were boys. Can you imagine having all those brothers?"

The kids giggled and joked with each other. Before it got out of control, Peter lifted a hand to quiet them.

"It was important back then to have a lot of children to help with the household or with the fighting," he said. "In Black Sword's case, he had nine sons to help him with his fight against the English. Several of those boys grew up to be great warlords in their own right, and two of them, as far as we know, went to

England and actually served in the court of Edward III and Richard II. Like their father, they were said to be great knights."

The children were growing increasingly excited about Black Sword, which is how Peter had planned it. He usually took children's groups to the Black Sword exhibit first because the thought of a great Irish knight usually got their attention. But it was time to move on because there was much more to see, so he began to move slowly past the rest of the exhibit, pointing to the last case as they moved out.

"Here you can see some other things that we found during our excavations of Black Castle, but I want you to notice this one item in particular," he said as he paused by the case and pointed to a small scrap of material, very old and stained, but with faded green stitching on it. "Do you all see this piece of fabric?"

The kids were climbing all over each other to see it. They started shouting in the affirmative so Peter continued.

"This piece of fabric actually has a very interesting history, much richer than Black Sword's short history," he said. "Black Sword's wife evidently gave this to him on their wedding day and it's a very special piece; it's said that whoever possesses it will have luck in love. It was passed down through Black Sword's family, from father to son for generations, until it ended up in the possession of Marie Antoinette. The legend says that one of Black Sword's descendants was Marie's one true love and gave it to her. She kept it until she was executed and the piece somehow became lost in the French revolution before reappearing, centuries later, with Wallis Simpson. Does anyone know who she is?"

The kids shook their heads even though the teacher nodded. In fact, the teacher seemed more interested in the piece than her students did.

"She was the wife of a former king of England," Peter said. "In fact, she gave this piece to her husband, the former Edward VIII, who actually gave up the throne in order to marry Mrs. Simpson. I would say they had great luck in love, indeed."

"But how did it get here?" one of the children asked.

Peter gazed at the faded piece of cloth. "The British royal family donated it to the National Museum of Ireland because we asked for it," he said. "We knew what it was and the significance of it. It belonged to one of the greatest Irish figures in history and we wanted it back, so they were gracious enough to comply."

The children gazed at the cloth for a few seconds longer before their short attention spans had them looking elsewhere. Peter took it as his cue to move on.

"Let's come over here, ladies and gentlemen," he called out to the crowd. "There are some swords over here we will take a look at."

The children followed him in a group, surging forward towards the weapon display, but one young man hung back. He had bright red hair and a dusting of freckles across his nose, a big boy for his age. He was still looking at the piece intently. The teacher, seeing that she had a straggler, went to retrieve him.

"Come along, David," she said.

Young David looked up from the case. "That thing is very old," he said.

The teacher nodded, her gaze falling on the faded piece of embroidery and feeling a romantic tug to her heart. "It is indeed."

"It has words on it."

The teacher bent over to see what he was seeing. "It does," she said. "But it's hard to see what they are."

David stared at the piece. "It says 'everything leads me to thee'."

The teacher looked at him with surprise. "How can you tell?"

"I just can."

By this time, Peter saw the dawdlers and was waving them over, but the teacher motioned to him instead. Leaving the wild animals lingering by the sword case, Peter scurried over.

"Yes, ma'am?" he asked quickly. "Did you have a question?"

The teacher pointed at the case. "He says that there are words on that piece of fabric."

Peter nodded. "There are, indeed."

"Do you know what it says?"

"It says 'everything leads me to thee'."

The teacher looked at young David with shock. "That's what he said," she exclaimed softly. "David, how did you know that?"

David gazed up at the teacher and the docent with his dark blue eyes and shrugged. "I just do," he replied. "He carried it with him all the time, didn't he?"

Peter was impressed with the young man's apparent knowledge of the Irish rebel. "He did," he confirmed. "Do you know much about Devlin de Bermingham?"

David shook his head as he looked at the cases with all of the items that seemed oddly familiar to him. He had no idea why and, being nine years old, didn't give it much thought. But he had an odd sense of déjà vu. Still, it wasn't particularly concerning. He wanted to go see the Medieval weapons.

The boy wandered off, leaving the teacher and docent standing at the case, looking rather perplexed. Peter wriggled his eyebrows.

"How on earth could he see what that cloth says?" he wondered. "You can't tell that just by looking at it. It's very faded and torn."

The teacher shook her head, a lingering gaze on the case. "Who knows?" she said. "He's always been a bit of an odd duck. He's had violent outbreaks at times and when we've met with the mother to discuss them, she says he has violent dreams as well. Battle, death, destruction, and a particular hatred for England."

Peter shrugged and they began heading back over to the Medieval weapons case. "Perhaps he's just a good Irish rebel," he said.

The teacher grinned as they came upon the children, who were very excited by the Medieval swords and weaponry. "I suppose that's true," she said. "Maybe there's a little Black Sword in every Irish boy."

ଔ THE END ଓ

Children of Devlin and Emllyn
Flynn
Daven
Corey
Conor
Bryant
Kiandra
Bowie
Lorcan
Gwendolyn
Niall
Ryan

Kathryn Le Veque Novels

Medieval Romance:

De Wolfe Pack Series:
Warwolfe
The Wolfe
Nighthawk
ShadowWolfe
DarkWolfe
A Joyous de Wolfe Christmas
BlackWolfe
Serpent
A Wolfe Among Dragons
Scorpion
StormWolfe
Dark Destroyer
The Lion of the North
Walls of Babylon
The Best Is Yet To Be
BattleWolfe
Castle of Bones

De Wolfe Pack Generations:
WolfeHeart
WolfeStrike
WolfeSword
WolfeBlade
WolfeLord
WolfeShield
Nevermore
WolfeAx
WolfeBorn

The Executioner Knights:

By the Unholy Hand
The Mountain Dark
Starless
A Time of End
Winter of Solace
Lord of the Sky
The Splendid Hour
The Whispering Night
Netherworld
Lord of the Shadows
Of Mortal Fury
'Twas the Executioner Knight Before Christmas
Crimson Shield

The de Russe Legacy:
The Falls of Erith
Lord of War: Black Angel
The Iron Knight
Beast
The Dark One: Dark Knight
The White Lord of Wellesbourne
Dark Moon
Dark Steel
A de Russe Christmas Miracle
Dark Warrior

The de Lohr Dynasty:
While Angels Slept
Rise of the Defender
Steelheart
Shadowmoor
Silversword
Spectre of the Sword
Unending Love
Archangel
A Blessed de Lohr Christmas
Lion of Twilight

The Brothers de Lohr:
The Earl in Winter

Lords of East Anglia:
While Angels Slept
Godspeed
Age of Gods and Mortals

Great Lords of le Bec:
Great Protector

House of de Royans:
Lord of Winter
To the Lady Born
The Centurion

Lords of Eire:
Echoes of Ancient Dreams
Lord of Black Castle
The Darkland

Ancient Kings of Anglecynn:
The Whispering Night
Netherworld

Battle Lords of de Velt:
The Dark Lord
Devil's Dominion
Bay of Fear
The Dark Lord's First Christmas
The Dark Spawn
The Dark Conqueror
The Dark Angel

Reign of the House of de Winter:
Lespada
Swords and Shields

De Reyne Domination:
Guardian of Darkness
The Black Storm
A Cold Wynter's Knight
With Dreams
Master of the Dawn

House of d'Vant:
Tender is the Knight (House of d'Vant)
The Red Fury (House of d'Vant)

The Dragonblade Series:
Fragments of Grace
Dragonblade
Island of Glass
The Savage Curtain
The Fallen One
The Phantom Bride

Great Marcher Lords of de Lara
Dragonblade

House of St. Hever
Fragments of Grace
Island of Glass
Queen of Lost Stars

Lords of Pembury:
The Savage Curtain

Lords of Thunder: The de Shera Brotherhood Trilogy
The Thunder Lord
The Thunder Warrior
The Thunder Knight

The Great Knights of de Moray:
Shield of Kronos
The Gorgon

The House of De Nerra:
The Promise
The Falls of Erith
Vestiges of Valor
Realm of Angels

Highland Warriors of Munro:
The Red Lion
Deep Into Darkness

The House of de Garr:
Lord of Light
Realm of Angels

Saxon Lords of Hage:
The Crusader
Kingdom Come

High Warriors of Rohan:
High Warrior
High King

The House of Ashbourne:
Upon a Midnight Dream

The House of D'Aurilliac:
Valiant Chaos

The House of De Dere:
Of Love and Legend

St. John and de Gare Clans:
The Warrior Poet

The House of de Bretagne:
The Questing

The House of Summerlin:
The Legend

The Kingdom of Hendocia:
Kingdom by the Sea

The BlackChurch Guild: Shadow Knights:
The Leviathan

Regency Historical Romance:
Sin Like Flynn: A Regency Historical Romance Duet
The Sin Commandments
Georgina and the Red Charger

Gothic Regency Romance:

Emma

Contemporary Romance:

Kathlyn Trent/Marcus Burton Series:
Valley of the Shadow
The Eden Factor
Canyon of the Sphinx

The American Heroes Anthology Series:
The Lucius Robe
Fires of Autumn
Evenshade
Sea of Dreams
Purgatory

Other non-connected Contemporary Romance:
Lady of Heaven
Darkling, I Listen
In the Dreaming Hour
River's End
The Fountain

Sons of Poseidon:
The Immortal Sea

Pirates of Britannia Series (with Eliza Knight):
Savage of the Sea by Eliza Knight
Leader of Titans by Kathryn Le Veque
The Sea Devil by Eliza Knight
Sea Wolfe by Kathryn Le Veque

Note: All Kathryn's novels are designed to be read as stand-alones, although many have cross-over characters or cross-over family groups. Novels that are grouped together have related characters or family groups. You will notice that some series have the same books; that is because they are cross-overs. A hero in one book may be the secondary character in another.

There is NO reading order except by chronology, but even in that case, you can still read the books as stand-alones. No novel is connected to another by a cliff hanger, and every book has an HEA.

Series are clearly marked. All series contain the same characters or family groups except the American Heroes Series, which is an anthology with unrelated characters.

For more information, find it in **A Reader's Guide to the Medieval World of Le Veque**.

About Kathryn Le Veque

Bringing the Medieval to Romance

KATHRYN LE VEQUE is a critically acclaimed, multiple USA TODAY Bestselling author, an Indie Reader bestseller, a charter Amazon All-Star author, and a #1 bestselling, award-winning, multi-published author in Medieval Historical Romance with over 100 published novels.

Kathryn is a multiple award nominee and winner, including the winner of Uncaged Book Reviews Magazine 2017 and 2018 "Raven Award" for Favorite Medieval Romance. Kathryn is also a multiple RONE nominee (InD'Tale Magazine), holding a record for the number of nominations. In 2018, her novel WARWOLFE was the winner in the Romance category of the Book Excellence Award and in 2019, her novel A WOLFE AMONG DRAGONS won the prestigious RONE award for best pre-16th century romance.

Kathryn is considered one of the top Indie authors in the world with over 2M copies in circulation, and her novels have been translated into several languages. Kathryn recently signed with Sourcebooks Casablanca for a Medieval Fight Club series, first published in 2020.

In addition to her own published works, Kathryn is also the President/CEO of Dragonblade Publishing, a boutique publishing house specializing in Historical Romance. Dragonblade's success has seen it rise in the ranks to become Amazon's #1 e-book publisher of Historical Romance (K-Lytics report July 2020).

Kathryn loves to hear from her readers. Please find Kathryn on Facebook at Kathryn Le Veque, Author, or join her on Twitter @kathrynleveque. Sign up for Kathryn's blog at www.kathrynleveque.com for the latest news and sales.